The Quiet Life

The Quiet Life

Cover design and book layout
www.mmw-design.com

www.adrianmillar.ie
Twitter @AdrianMillar

ISBN-13: 978-1514121030
ISBN-10: 1514121034

The Quiet Life

Adrian Millar

In memory of
Patrick Crawford
the boy who didn't make it through.

Once upon a time, on long summers' evenings, three school girls used to stage plays in their neighbour's garage in Cork.

The first became my 'reader' as I wrote *The Quiet Life*. The second became my wife, and the third told me that I had it in spades as a writer.

The first is Eileen McSwiney, my neighbour and friend; the second is Mary Deasy, and the third is Marian Keyes.

I am grateful to all three of them for believing in me as a writer. *The Quiet Life* is dedicated to my wife, who couldn't put it down.

Chapter 1

Marlene perched her chin on her arched shoulder, then taunted her sister with words that rose and fell like swallows at play, "But how did you just know?"

"The air!" Kathleen shouted, glaring at her as if to say anyone with an ounce of wit would have known the answer.

From the moment Kathleen had caught George's scent in Belfast Central Library, she had just known that they were destined for each other. Her sense of smell had been the ground of her existence ever since the odour of meconium had assailed her nostrils, obliterating the trauma of the birth canal and the midwife's slap. Soon, she was grabbing unsuspecting feet for a sniff, even those of perfect strangers, as her mother discovered to her disdain on a trip to the Falls Baths. The simplest of rubs was enough to keep her going for days, her hands cupped at her nose as she inhaled her bouquet. No, whether Marlene liked it or not, she could tell: everything in her life had brought her to the Astronomy section on that spring Saturday morning for her encounter with her husband-to-be.

Marlene rolled her eyes up to heaven.

Infuriated by her martyr act, Kathleen yelled, "How did you think I'd know? The parting in his hair?"

Marlene protruded her lower lip and nodded repeatedly, intimating that in her professorial opinion the parting in George's hair was, on balance, a more persuasive explanation for love at first sight than the air. Kathleen saw red.

"It was in the air! I could smell it! I could smell it!" she blurted, retreating to her original position.

The words had no sooner left Kathleen's mouth than she realised that she had given her sister more ammunition with which to attack her, and Marlene didn't lose a second. "Uh!" she tooted as if to awaken the Gods, "Dear Lord, what next?" she implored, now shaking her head heavenwards in despair, her hands joined for added effect.

While Kathleen had expected more of the same, it did little to protect her from harm. Like a high-rise in an earthquake, her face concertinaed, her jaw sliding crossways to reveal smoke-damaged teeth. Quickly assessing the situation, she pulled herself together and broke into exaggerated applause, lavishing her sister with damning praise, "Yeah, definitely, dad's right, Marlene! You should be on the stage! You missed your vocation alright!" To her delight, Marlene pouted on cue and banged her teacup down on the table with panache, boosting Kathleen's morale. "See, told you, you're a natural!" Kathleen lauded her, refusing to let up.

Marlene's eyes disappeared, amoeba-like, as the compliment wound its way to its intended target. Upon impact, she flung her cup and saucer aside, lowered her head and began sniffing the table like a tracker dog. Pretending not to be paying any heed, Kathleen opened 'Weddings of the Century', which George had earlier helped her lift off the library shelf, and fingered the bridal wear in the illustrations in the hope that her delicate movements would not be lost on her sister. Marlene was too busy straining her neck to notice. Frustrated by Kathleen's apparent lack of reaction to her canine mime, Marlene now added sound. "So it was in the air, was it? Did he fart or what?" she squeaked, holding her snout.

Incensed by Marlene's crudity, Kathleen got back in the ring and let fly.

"Look, you! Aren't you the one's always going on about you being born a Catholic, aren't you? 'Catholics are just born Catholics, not like Protestants. It's not drummed into us, like'. Well, love's like that. It's just one of those things. It just happens. You just know! Uh! Not that you'd know much about that though!"

Experience had taught Kathleen that what Marlene had in theatrical prowess was no match for her powers of logical argument, and from the look of fear in Marlene's eyes she could now see that it was only a matter of time till her sister bowed out. She could literally smell victory as Marlene broke into a sweat in response to a tension in the pit of her stomach that she tried in vain to ignore. *She's right, she's right, you silly wee shite, she's right as right can be!* The words throbbed in Marlene's head, but left a sick taste in her mouth that made speech impossible. Chances were love would never be on the cards for her, Marlene thought. Even when it had stared her in the face, she had failed to recognise it—like the boy who had regularly come to sit on the wall of the schoolyard and watch her play handball. She hadn't even been aware of him until her friends teased her about him, and by the time she had worked up the courage to say hello, he was gone.

Marlene fed her hair through her moist hands like rope as she attempted to steady her nerves, and the fortuitous sight of Kathleen unselfconsciously knotting the end of the tablecloth gave her the burst of vitality she needed. She would give Kathleen a taste of her own medicine. Detesting logical arguments, she topped up on air with a sharp in-take of breath, which brought a pink hue to her cheeks, then spat out the words, terrified she would choke on them.

"Catch yourself on, will you, Kathleen? You mean to say falling in love is like being born a Catholic? Sure, then, Protestants would never fall in love, would they, like? Did you not say Georgie boy kicked with his left?"

The horror on Kathleen's face demonstrated that whatever it was she had said must have made sense but instead of relief, Marlene once more felt fear: Kathleen wouldn't take it lying down.

Kathleen banged her book shut and knitted her brow. "Oh, give over! You have to have an answer for everything, don't you? The fact is you're just jealous! That's all that ails you!" she thundered, her voice rattling the Venetian blinds.

Marlene hid a smile with her hand in Geisha fashion. Rising to the provocation, Kathleen made up her mind to finish her off, even if she had to go down with her in Kamikaze style. "That's what's up your arse! You'll never get anybody because you wouldn't part with a fart, you're that mean!" she exploded, then cringed. She hated stooping to Marlene's level of insult; victory always felt like defeat. However, her shame at having let herself down was short-lived. As Marlene jumped up from the table screaming, Kathleen already had herself convinced that she had had no choice; Marlene had driven her into a corner and shooting her down was all she could do to prevent her from robbing her of her future.

Marlene scurried like a monkey into the scullery, her limbs knocking off the couch, mantle-piece, bookshelf and door handle on the way. "You leave me alone, you! I'm telling mummy on you when she comes home!" she screeched from the safety of her den.

It came as no surprise to Kathleen to hear Marlene invoke her mother, and she ignored her threat confident that her mother, Benny, was no match for her father, Frank, on whom she regularly relied in arguments. Besides, she finally had Marlene on the run.

"Destiny," Kathleen whispered under her breath. "It's a matter of destiny, not that you'd understand that!" she called out to Marlene who was now scouring the pantry for comfort food. The sudden recollection that somewhere there were crisps that her mother had bought the day before gave Marlene a second wind.

"Oh, so it's your des-ti-nee, now, is it?" she shouted back into Kathleen, drawing out 'destiny' as if to draw blood from her opponent.

"Yep! Now you're talking!" Kathleen declared triumphantly, turning a blind eye to her sarcasm.

Marlene poked her head through the beads hanging at the entrance to the scullery, lifted her hand to her ear, bent it at the wrist and shook it. "Oh, so, it's wedding bells, then, is it?" she enquired, expecting, indeed half hoping, that her assumption would be rejected.

"Well, you didn't think we were going to live in sin now, did you?" Kathleen shot back.

Marlene's jaw dropped.

"And what are you gaping at?" Kathleen chided her in an effort to dislodge her from the vicinity of the lintel. She was too close for comfort.

Marlene closed her mouth and turned away, more to please herself than to please Kathleen. She tied her hair in a pony-tail with a tea-towel, donned an apron and set about washing the dishes to put some badly needed order on her world. She scrubbed and scrubbed and scrubbed in the hope of erasing the thought from her mind that her sister was set on marriage to someone she had chanced upon that morning in the public library when she could just as easily have been at home getting ready for Confessions.

Kathleen was glad that Marlene hadn't bothered to respond. She could at last savour her dream in peace and quiet. Gazing out at the flowers in the garden, she pictured herself walking up the aisle clutching her father's arm, the church redolent with the fragrance of lilies and chrysanthemums, the man from the Astronomy section awaiting her at the altar—embalmed. *Embalmed*? As she frantically plucked the pungent smell of death off her clothes like confetti, her knees trembled and the table shook. She laid her cheek on the cover of her book to iron out her thoughts, but the truth, namely that she was born a widow, remained the furthest thing from her mind in spite of the fact that it had always been clear to those around her that she was drawn to the drama of death from an early age. When her mother had scolded her "Kitty-Coo" for leaving the toilet seat wet, Kathleen would invariably burst into tears and cry out "I miss my granda!"—even though her paternal grandfather had passed away while she was still in her mother's womb. And it was her Uncle Damien who was the first to observe that whenever she played with Snow White the latter inevitably failed to wake up when the handsome prince plonked his kiss on her lips. Kathleen would proceed to bury her in a wooden pencil-case to the lament of the seven dwarfs, each of whom she played individually, then go into mourning bereft of her appetite for whatever sweets Damien had brought her.

It was her penchant for widowhood, indeed, that explained her adoration of her grandmother who periodically boasted "I buried my man in '52", denoting her shameless pride in her endurance as a widow, though some of those who remembered him viewed it, rather, as an expression of her pride in having put up with him for so long. It was from around the time Kathleen was old enough to realise that her grandmother had never held a shovel in her hand, and the latter consequently fell from grace, that Jackie Bouvier-Kennedy conveniently came into the frame and graced her life with her tragic beauty and beautiful tragedy. This period also coincided with Kathleen's tendency to miss the school bus, leaving her late for class, significantly only on bright mornings (an important detail that was not picked up by the school authorities.) Consequently, she would often find herself obliged to process alongside a bereaved wife as a cortege crawled caterpillar-like to the cemetery beside her school. Then, more often than not, unable to extricate herself without appearing disrespectful, she accompanied the inconsolable widow to the graveside where, fighting back tears, she bid the deceased adieu and discreetly slipped through the railings into the recreation yard, resolving yet again not to wear her heavy coat in fine weather because it slowed her down and left her late for the bus. However, the most obvious indication of Kathleen's soulful predisposition was that in her married life there was no shortage of times when she wished George dead well before his time. Guilt-ridden, she would typically brush off her outburst with some comment about her short fuse and an assurance that she never meant a word of what she had said, and George, for his own reasons, opted to take her at her word.

George had to be Kathleen's first and last love so much so that even when she discovered that she had confused astrology with astronomy, and that ignorance had brought her to the wrong bookshelf, this simply confirmed her gut instinct: she and George were meant to be together "till death us do part". She would have her day of passion in a candlelit church, and the congregation would see her in her finest hour (albeit attired in black). Learning of her designs on George, her brother Johnny commented, "That's them there lucky stars for you again!" and Kathleen beamed at him deaf to his mordant sarcasm, confirmed in her belief that the God of All Things had brought them together. The only thing she found odd was that Johnny, who hadn't a romantic bone in his body, should have recognised this. Maybe, just maybe, he too had a poker in the fire, she thought, but she dismissed the idea as quickly as it had appeared. It was too fanciful.

Kathleen prised her moist face from the now smudged bride and groom on the book cover. Her panic had to be a result of all the pressure Marlene was putting her under. She smelled George's scent—a mixture of talc and sweat—emanating from her gloves that lay on the couch by the fireplace and she relaxed again. One sniff of him and she had swooned. His hand had reached out to support her and she had let herself go in his embrace. In that moment George saw his life pass before him and all his heretofore, pat answers were thrown into question as he sensed with every fibre in his body that every step he had ever taken had led *her* to this spot. (This conviction was later confirmed for him by her candid revelation that it was his scent that had drawn her to him.) He carried the damsel to a nearby alcove where he stroked her cheek until she regained consciousness some five minutes later. (He had considered a chivalrous slap, but, he later told her, he had not wanted to alarm her.) He later claimed that when she had opened her eyes he had seen a lost soul which he resolved to rescue like a knight in shining armour. According to Kathleen, true to his nature as a man, he had failed to grasp things correctly. He had seen his own reflection. George yawned at her drivel.

Molly leapt onto the table and gave Kathleen a start. She felt afraid again: it wouldn't do if her mother found out about George and her just yet. She flung the cat on the floor, got up from the table and went into the scullery where Marlene stood with her head in the air, holding the bag of crisps over her nose and mouth like an oxygen mask. She needed to knock her out. Molly fled under the sideboard.

"If you open your beak to mum, I swear to God I'll get you with the gullet knife in your sleep!" she threatened her.

Marlene choked and coughed hysterically as Molly shrieked in her stead.

That evening Marlene protested to her mother that what had shocked her about Kathleen's resolve was not at all the fact that George was a Protestant but the fact that Kathleen was going to marry a man, whom she had only just met, because he smelled nice. "When will you ever learn to turn a deaf ear and a blind eye?" her mother dismissed her protestation. Marlene shrugged her hips at her mother's complacency, unaware that Benny had her eye on the bigger picture and the possibility of ridding herself of a problem daughter with a problem past.

As darkness fell, Marlene crept into bed and pulled the blankets tight up around her neck. She knew Kathleen well enough to take no chances.

* * *

It was their first date, and Kathleen's aunt Maura, who had always been like a mother to her, had offered her the use of her front parlour. "There's no point in doing it up against an alley wall or on the back of a lorry," she had frequently counselled her niece. "If you're gonna do it, you have to do it in style." "Ambience", she confided in Kathleen, "was crucial", blushing as she let slip that it was "everything". 'Ambience' sounded French, and that was a good enough reason for Kathleen to accept her aunt's offer.

Sandwiched on the settee, Kathleen was aware of her heart thumping with fear as George's belt pressed into her groin and their bodies kissed to the tinkle of cardigan buttons rubbing together. She struggled to release an arm from under him to dim the gas lamp purposefully left on the table for the occasion. Stretching backwards, she placed her hand on the switch, whereupon a halo, which could just have easily have been the effect of the lampshade, caught her attention on the ceiling and the Blessed Virgin appeared in her full regalia. It was the first apparition outside the privacy of Kathleen's bathroom, where she was a regular visitor, and Kathleen immediately felt guilty because she had failed to mention George to her on her last visit.

"Casleen, my schild, You are going to regret," the Virgin murmured in her heavy Lourdes accent as she fiddled anxiously with the rosary beads that hung from her royal blue girdle. Her divination, which would prove eerily correct, had come too late to save Kathleen from temptation—her fingers turned the switch full circle and Our Lady was assumed heavenwards.

Kathleen fell into a bewitching darkness. Her thighs tightened as a wave of excitement washed in around her bay area where his thing nested. She groped for his head, and scrambled to find his lips to kill the desire that now possessed her. George's body jerked at the hips and he emitted a deep sigh; she had stuck her finger in his left eye. Instinctively, she quickly covered his mouth for fear that her mother, two streets away, would hear him, then kissed his turnip gasp. Writhing, he tried to get her in focus, as his left hand fumbled with his zip. From the moment the light had gone out, he was conscious that he was in with a chance. He longed to lie it on her flesh. That would be enough for the first night. As he searched for her tummy, he was suddenly overcome with regret that he hadn't come across this lucky break sooner. It should have been love at first sight, glorious like first light which he had witnessed once over Belfast Lough on the Twelfth after a night of binge-drinking, but it was not that. Love at first sight had passed him by over and over again on his way to Sunday service in the form of Kathleen making her way back from Mass only a few feet away. His thoughts had been elsewhere. "Show your father a bit of respect!" "Do as you're told!" "You'll never know how much we've loved you." As he finally touched down on her soft belly, his regret turned to anger at his parents for depriving him of the pleasure that now charged his body. He would shake off his parents and his past as he had shaken off his depression in order to be there for Kathleen. With that thought in mind he climaxed. By the time he had buttoned up his cardigan he was already planning their next date.

Kathleen was no stranger to love at first sight, if indirectly. Her father would periodically gather his children—Kathleen, Marlene, Nicholas and Johnny in descending order—on the settee for the story of his first date with their mother after he had spotted her the previous week on the dance-floor and fallen in love with his "Armagh apple". Having gone to meet her by the main gates of the Royal Victoria Hospital, she was not to be seen. Crestfallen, he had just got back on a bus to return home when he spied her standing by the side-entrance of the hospital. There had been a mix-up. He jumped off the bus again, and without bothering to ask for his money back, ran across the road to her. "How different my life would have been had I not got back off that bus and met your mother!" he would excitedly regale his audience. As Kathleen prepared herself for the punch-line, she would inevitably feel butter-flies in her tummy. "For one thing," he would always say, stating the obvious to the now weary faces, "none of you would be here now." The obvious confused her. Was he excited because he had met the woman of his dreams or was it because he imagined a life where none of them existed? The very thought that he might wish she never existed frightened her all the more given that Marlene constantly narked at her about how he worshipped the ground she walked on. The day it struck her that he himself probably didn't know the cause of his excitement, her fear vanished only to turn up in the form of a suitcase that she hid under her bed in case of an emergency. It was shortly after that that she decided there was only one way of getting on top of her anxiety—she would get out from under him. George was the perfect ticket.

As she watched George button up, Kathleen determined to ask her aunt if they could borrow her parlour another evening the following week. He was too good to be true. She couldn't let him slip through her fingers, though she was not about to let him slip in. He would have to wait before she let him go the whole way. She got up off the settee and brushed herself down. Her aunt had told her to knock on the kitchen door when she was through and she would get some Milo ready for them, but Kathleen now had other plans. She felt an inexplicable urge to have him walk her home and kiss her goodnight up against McGovern's gable wall just within sight of her home. She stood George in the porch and returned to the kitchen to inform her aunt that they had to be off because it was getting dark and George had to be careful going through the predominantly Catholic streets. Aunt Maura pulled a long face, but it was the smell of Milo emanating from the kitchen that forced Kathleen to recognise what she already knew—Aunt Maura had eagerly been awaiting an account of the 'action' in the parlour to brighten up a life strong on atmosphere but weak on concretes. Only Kathleen's promise to report back the following week softened the blow for Maura and eased Kathleen's conscience.

However smitten Kathleen was, she explained to George on their second date that he would have to do all the running. It was a woman's prerogative to be chased, and she didn't want to give him the wrong message. His pride getting the better of him, George decided that his younger brother Fred, who was in George's street book-club, would do some of the running for him, delivering messages between them. Kathleen accepted the arrangement.

Three weeks later, and six dates under their belts, she sat George down by the back of the *Orchid* dance hall and brought him up to speed: an engagement ring and a further six months trial would do the trick in her book. The big news knocked him for six—he had not been thinking beyond *Fanny and Zoe*, the reading material for that coming Sunday—but delighted Fred who already had had his fill of acting as conduit. Noticing George turn pale, Kathleen assured him that she would be there for him if he made the effort. George wondered had he missed something—it had all happened so fast. He never suspected that she was in a hurry because she was afraid that she might lose interest. Indeed, she did not suspect as much herself.

George slept on it and still woke up in two minds regarding Kathleen's ultimatum. He swung like a pendulum, and got the jitters with the result that everything he ate passed through him like water. To complicate matters, however much he wished otherwise, his appetite would not desert him. In the end, the decision was taken out of his hands: circumstances dictated that he jump for the simple reason that there was no other way to stem the flow. Having jumped, he never strayed, remaining faithful to his initial belief that he was and was not going to go through with it, with the result that he was forever leaving her and not leaving her from one day to the next. His confusion formed the bedrock of his commitment. It got him up in the morning and knocked him out, jaded, at night, for the most part in his prison cell. The only change was that in due course his stomach cramps became as regular as her period and were particularly bad during her pregnancies.

When George jumped, Kathleen caught hold of him by the hand and presented him with a bottle of Kaolin & Morphine for 'the runs' before leading him off to the jeweller's to choose the engagement ring. He requested more time to get the money together but she saw through his ploy and lent him a tenner that her mother had given her for unexpected eventualities. Like a lamb to the slaughter, he stepped up into the shop in one of his 'I'm not going to go through with it' moments. Her future sparkling before her eyes, Kathleen took up the rear by the door. Down through the years, he would cast up to her about how as she stood there she had said that a double diamond would "do the trick." She denied the allegation time and again, adding that it hardly mattered as it was only a figure of speech. For George, her denial simply served to prove his point, namely that he had been tricked all along. He fancied her and all of that, he later told his drinking mates, but she had pulled every trick in the book to get him to the altar.

In time it became evident that Kathleen was infected by her father's doubt. Within a few months of buying the ring, she began to labour over how she had let herself be taken in by that first kiss with George when she had sensed such a lack of commitment in him. But she would go through with it. Soon, the memory of how his lips had caressed hers that first night evaporated like hot water off dishes. A mere five years later, all she could recall was that he had turned up because he had a bet on with his mates in the book-club that he would go through with a date with "a wee Catholic from Clonard." Anyway, she sometimes pondered, alone in her bed, whether this was a trick of memory or not, it was obvious that his heart had never been in it all along. Bar the passion she had felt for him in the library, their relationship had always lacked an initial spark, and it was all his fault. Over the years, of course she never revealed this to her children, Rosy and Jack, because, she told herself, that would only turn them against him, and George already had enough on his plate with a life sentence for "crashing the lights". However, the reality was that the children knew everything, even the real reason why their father was doing time. It was never what Kathleen said, so much as what she didn't say, which gave her away, though George was often the last to know.

* * *

It was Kathleen's big day. With the exception of the best man, Fred, George's family boycotted the proceedings on religious grounds, unhappy about him marrying into "the Church of the anti-Christ". Nonetheless, convinced that Kathleen's family would put their absence down to Protestant bigotry rather than to conscientious objection, George's father, Alistair Lackey, offered to put the Lackey-Dunne wedding over. The Dunnes wouldn't hear of it. They knew exactly what the Lackeys were at; they were out to embarrass them with an offer that was, Frank had to admit, hard to refuse. Friends and relatives rallied around, pouring into the Dunnes' home on a daily basis to commiserate with the latest victims of Protestant sectarianism, which was on the rise in the wake of Catholics' calls for civil rights for British citizens. The Lackeys were showing their true colours. However, Benny, with largesse to boot, defended her future in-laws, "That's just the way they're brought up. There's no point in gloating," she told her sympathisers. Her magnanimity was the talk of the road, although there were those in the know who had a suspicion that

Benny was being big about it because she was relieved at being able to marry off a daughter with a history. The world and their mother knew that the one person who wouldn't be invited to the wedding would be Padraig Corr from the lower estate. And anybody could tell you that Protestants were less likely to kick up a fuss about 'damaged goods' because they didn't know what sin was, unlike Catholics. They were also in no doubt that Benny was secretly pleased that there would be virtually no Lackeys at the wedding because it was less likely that Kathleen's story would get out to them. The irony that Benny trusted her own even less than she trusted Protestants was totally lost on them, as was the irony of their admission that Catholics knew all about sin. As for Frank, the gossip was that he was delighted to save on the guests, an added pleasure being that they were "the other sort".

When Kathleen broke down in tears a month before the wedding because her father had hinted that being a man of few words he would rather give the wedding speech a miss, this gave Benny the opportunity to inform Kathleen that she would completely understand if she decided not to go through with it as George was moving too fast, and Kathleen patently needed time to think. Pretending that her mother had hit the nail on the head, Kathleen threw her arms around her and assured her that she was fine—it was just that all the organising was getting in on top of her. Benny could never have imagined that what had prompted Kathleen's tears was her fear of having sex on her wedding night.

The wedding ceremony passed off peacefully, but not without incident. Frank put the "boo-boos" down to a case of wedding nerves, but it confirmed for Benny what she wanted to believe—the whole mixed marriage thing was too much for Kathleen. She even believed the rumours about how forgiving she was in relation to her future in-laws, while she berated Frank for the obvious pleasure he took in not having to fork out money for Protestants. She argued that her people were from close to the Border so the whole Protestant thing had never been an issue, unlike the way it was for the ones from Belfast. Besides, her parents had been supporters of the Northern Ireland Labour Party, so there was none of the republican thing in her blood with the result that they had nothing against Protestants. Frank found it hard to disagree with her analysis; Belfast had indeed a history of Protestant pogroms against Catholics that had left its mark, but he did argue in his defence that he had bent over backwards to please them, even offering to have the Lackeys collected and brought to the church at his expense.

The wedding incident occurred at the exchange of marriage vows.

"Please say after me, 'I, Kathleen, take you, George, to be my lawful wedded husband," Fr. Cunningham instructed Kathleen.

"I, George, take you…, uh, I, I, I," Kathleen stuttered.

The congregation, until then half asleep, cocked their ears. George giggled nervously but Kathleen's mistake sent a shudder down Fred's back. He could hear his mother bellow, "See, I told you so! They want to take us over!" His parents were right—Kathleen wore the trousers and she would make George into one of their own. Fred had to do something to calm the voice in his head that beat like a Lambeg drum, but before he had a chance to do anything, Fr. Cunningham smiled, and repeated the words as if enunciating them for the first time. Fred looked at Kathleen who waited as long as she could before speaking in the full knowledge that she still wasn't ready.

"I, Kathleen, take you,…." She blanked. *His name—what's his name? Jesus, somebody…*"I, I…," the words trickled to a stop.

The congregation shuffled their feet, George went the colour of Kathleen's dress, and Benny took a fit of coughing, setting off a wave of spluttering and nose-blowing the length and breadth of St. Paul's. Fred stepped in.

"Em, reverend, cud ye, take it one word at a time, cud ye?" he asked as politely as he could make it.

"No, it's alright. I'll be alright. Just give me a second!" Kathleen said, cutting across the priest who had opened his mouth to speak. She clasped her hands together and shook them like a child with a dice, as if the outcome she needed could be guaranteed by the intensity of her movement. The words rolled off her tongue, tumbling out so fast as to be almost indecipherable to the congregation. Benny bit her lip, not knowing whether to laugh or cry, and pulled the net on her hat further down over her eyes. It was all down to George now.

"Please repeat after me, 'I, George, take you, Kathleen, to be my lawful wedded wife'," the priest proceeded, easing each neatly formed word out like bubbles so as to avoid any further glitches.

"I, George, take you Kathleen to be my loyal wedded wife."

The congregation chuckled. Their suspicions had been confirmed—George had only one goal and that was to make of Kathleen a *loyal subject*. Unable to look George in the eye, Fr. Cunningham now read the words off the page. Wondering what the commotion behind him was all about, and why the priest was making him repeat himself, George obliged, this time without a hitch.

The celebrant, who until the Consecration hadn't put a foot wrong, finally came a cropper himself, probably, Benny surmised, as a result of all the pressure. Raising the host high above his head to recite 'Behold the Lamb of God!' he faltered. "Behold the leg of lamb!" he intoned. While those who were awake fought back their desire to giggle, Benny didn't bat an eyelid, satisfied that no matter what went wrong now, it was too late; Kathleen was well and truly off her hands.

Before the ceremony had ended, rumour had it in parts of North Belfast that a Catholic woman had led an innocent, God-fearing Protestant up the garden path into the arms of the Pope, and that the best man had sold his brother down the river.

Having an aversion to covering her head ever since she was little, Kathleen was delighted to reach the bridal suite that night if only in order to remove her veil. As she unpinned it a smoky smell caught her nostrils. The veil was singed. She realised that she must have almost gone up in flames as she signed the register on the altar. She tossed it aside, raised her head and shook her ringlets free, her train taking up the rhythm in turn, lending the appearance of a swan shaking off water. For those few seconds she had forgotten about her fear of doing it with George who hovered behind her.

* * *

Kathleen wolfed down the nerve tablets she had pinched from her mother's private cache, which Benny kept hidden out of Frank's sight in her packet of Dr. Whyte's, and bared her all in the light that shone in from the corridor. She gripped George for dire life where it mattered and he felt appropriately embarrassed. She had hoped that he might settle for that, but he touched and tickled her, then found her entry point. She felt again the pain down under which had haunted her since the day Benny had revealed to Mrs. Carlin from across the street how excruciating it was when 'himself' lay on top of her of a Sunday night. As intended, Benny's dispatch had lodged like a bullet in Kathleen's groin as she sat between them on the floor reading the Four Marys.

As the tablets took effect, Kathleen's pain subsided and George played himself out until he fell flat on his face, by which time Kathleen had already sunken into a deep sleep where she dreamed of missing the train back to Belfast. The bear that got the honey, George disappeared without a trace into the great beyond where they failed to find him till first light when he had to be smoked out, the smell of sausages and bacon from the kitchen below their room bringing him slowly to his feet.

When Kathleen awoke, she made her way to the dining-room, leaving George to shower before he came down. In the reception area, she smelled the chlorine from the pool off to her right and felt, it seemed to her for no good reason, agitated. Although she had allowed herself plenty of time, her pace gathered speed in spite of herself. She sat down to breakfast with thoughts of getting home to Belfast on her mind, for the idea of six more nights of sex put the fear of God into her.

On day three, as if an answer to prayer, the threat of a rail strike persuaded George to cut the honeymoon short and they made their way to the bus. He returned to Belfast with left over condoms for his mates, which he duly distributed from a brown paper bag he hid on top of the wardrobe, for a price. He acknowledged to his friends that he had enjoyed himself on his honeymoon, but his enjoyment had left Kathleen feeling he had married her for lust, not love.

The lustful George signed on the dole within days of returning to Belfast from his honeymoon. He would never work another day in his life. "What kind of a maaan are you?" Kathleen frequently mocked him. George complained to her that she was like her mother—she had married for security, a need that blinded her to all the other ways he was there for her. Her "high security marriage", as he liked to refer to it, annoyed him more than anything else in the world, even more than Rangers losing to Celtic, although in the case of the latter he was known to conceal his anger better to keep in with his Republican buddies. Kathleen hemmed him in on all sides. In time, he was forced to do the weekly shop with her, and was only allowed to leave the house after one o'clock on weekdays, for that way the neighbours might take him for a bin-man back from his collection rather than the good-for-nothing layabout that he was. "Marriage isn't a free ride," she hollered on occasion. "It's about goals, and God knows you ought to know enough about them, for you're never done watching that football on that bloody box!" "I'll have my day in Court," she once screamed at him with all the self-pity she could muster. George replied that she might have it sooner than she thought if she kept on at him, but he didn't mean it. When she continued to moan at him, he told her that he would never recognise the court, and anyway she would probably drive him to his grave first and succeed where his loyalist brethren had failed.

The only 'positive' for George in their deteriorating relationship was that Kathleen's preoccupation with her 'high security marriage' gave him something to moan about, thus keeping their lines of communication open and leaving him with what he described to his friends, whenever he was permitted to meet them, as a warm feeling for Kathleen. Meanwhile, Kathleen, in her wisdom, felt appreciated because of all his complaining on her account. Arguing was therapeutic and, as a result, they argued for hours, and, later, for years on end. It kept themselves, their neighbours, and more rarely the prison wardens entertained. It was, however, 'book-keeping' that really did it for Kathleen. Before their first anniversary, she was already making entries in her ledger in red biro, listing all her woes. She wrote at it feverishly, never happier in her early married life than at such moments. *He got out of the wrong side of the bed today. Sitting in there grouching! The lazy bastard left his monks on the floor. Bouncing, they were. And used up the last of the milk for his Cornflakes and didn't even bother his ass to go down to the shop for more. Hasn't washed himself for a week. What he needs is a good kick up the arse! You'd think his mother would have given him one long ago, but sure they're as bad. What did I ever see in him? As long as he gets his oats.* Try as he might, George could never find where she hid it. Once, in a fit of rage, she threatened to have it read out at her funeral Mass, and George, who never attended church, offered to serve as a reader at the "celebration".

Shortly after their second anniversary Kathleen expanded her astrology portfolio and took a shine to reading tea. She longed for a child to replace the one that she had lost before her marriage. (Kevin was born premature, and her grandmother, who had taken him home to rear him, returned Benny's cabinet drawer which had served as his cot.) It wasn't long until Kathleen discovered children in foetal positions on the inside of her cup, though sometimes she swallowed an arm or a leg. They were always girls. Her consumption of tea had the added effect of a badly needed caffeine kick six times a day, which, crossing her heart the Platex way, she regularly denied to George was her objective.

At night she relied on her dreams for solace. Her bed was her cinema—whatever she could conjure up on the white sheet. She directed, produced, and played all the parts. Once she flew over houses, each breath carrying her ever higher over the snow-covered countryside. She was freed. She felt the air flow through her body, and then a sudden surge of pee that startled her out of her sleep. Trance-like she leapt out of bed and made a dash for the bathroom, holding her head as she strove to make the feeling of freedom last on the loo. She had to know her destiny. Eyes still closed, she wiped herself and managed to bundle herself into bed where, now half-awake, she wrapped the sheet tight around her flesh in an attempt to re-ignite her future. She took off momentarily again only to come down to earth with a bang as the odour of sour pee drifted into the exam hall and an invigilator brushed up against her. George turned over. She put her hand on his penis, but it was lifeless: male hormonal shutdown. The child would have to wait.

Another night, she saw her father coming towards her, his open nightshirt revealing his hairy chest. He lifted her up in his arms and she had just begun to count his hairs like sheep when Aunt Maura appeared out of nowhere to announce that Frank had just sailed out into the deep blue sea on a "sheep". Kathleen burst out laughing for she had always found Maura that wee bit grand and gaily ran over to the water's edge to see her father off, but his ship sank in the high winds from the vent above her bed, and she woke up in a sweat face to face with George who was scowling at her. Her laughter had woken him up. She rolled over on her sodden pillow. Was it grief, or was it fear that had exuded through her pores, she wondered? In an effort to find out, she rubbed her face with her finger and daubed it like a dealer on the tip of her tongue. It tasted of spice, some foreign land, unchartered territory. It was fear.

"Fra!" she cried out one night in bed.

"And who is Fra?" George asked, raising himself up on his elbows.

"The boiler man," she answered in her sleep.

Next morning at breakfast, feigning jealousy, George asked who Fra the boiler man was.

"Who? What? Boiler man? What boiler man?" she replied.

"The one you were sleeping with," said George, half joking.

"I don't know any boiler man! What boiler do I have to get checked anyway?"

George regretted his question, realising from the heaviness in his chest that his jealousy was for real. Was there something she hadn't told him? Kathleen, who normally would have stood her ground to the point of arguing that a black crow was white, threw her breakfast bowl in the sink and nipped offside. It was exactly the conclusive proof he needed, but he watched her go. He didn't want to know who Fra was.

Chapter 2

"And what are you going to be when you grow up?" uncle Alexander asked him. George was too busy being a spinning-top to answer. He tipped over on to the card-table which collapsed with him on to the floor.

"Oops! Careful!" Alexander exhorted after the fact in the hope of minimising the expected wailing.

"I meant it! I meant it!" exclaimed George, hiding his sense of failure from himself.

"You wanna watch it but!" Alexander admonished him with a gentle tap on the crown of his head.

George elbowed Alexander's leg and marched off to the opposite side of the room.

"Well, wee man, what'll you be?" Alexander persisted as George took off again and again on a long, narrow stretch of mat that served as a runway. "Thunderbirds! Thunderbirds!" George sang over and over as the planes departed. Alexander gave up waiting on an answer, picked up a pack of playing cards and began placing them in clock formation on the table.

"I wanna be a fireman. No, no, a soldier," said George, realising that he was about to lose Alexander's attention.

"A soldier?"

"No, I wanna be a B-Special actually."

"Hello, hello, hello! And what do we have here then?" said Alexander bringing his arms behind his back like a British bobby. "Fenians at it again, are they, young sir?"

"Actually, could I be a pop star, uncle Alex?"

Alexander burst out laughing. "Oh, a pop star, ac-chi-ly," he enunciated, mocking his nephew. "You know what? You'll never end up in Purdysburn Mental Hospital, that's for sure, for you never stop changing your mind, now, do you?"

Alexander's reference was lost on George, but he blushed none-theless.

"Ach, but, sure, you can be whatever you want, son, so you can," Alexander added, noticing the child's embarrassment.

George dropped to his knees and picked up a Batman car. He hated the way adults always said one thing but meant another. He could tell that Alexander was just trying to be nice. He lifted the batmobile into the air and glided it by to the sound of an engine which he dragged out in order to prevent Alexander from lying any further. Alexander returned to his card game.

"I'm Batman!" George said defiantly as the car swooped onto the carpet and slowed to a stand-still. "Uncle Alexander, can you get me a cowboy outfit for when I'm twelve?" he asked, annoyed at Uncle Alexander's short span of attention.

"Whatever you want, son," Alexander fobbed him off, the sight of the wild horse now galloping past him exhausting him.

George had always believed that he could be anything he wanted. He was already a businessman at weekends when he went from door to door selling firewood. At Christmas it was the holly branches, and the ones with the berries were an extra two pennies. His parents were enthralled by his sense of initiative and expected he would go far. He was their little dreamer. On weekdays, though, their dreamer would come to in class to the tittering of the "eejits" that shared the better part of his day with him. There was nobody at home, the lights were out, that's how the teacher put it as he called him up for another whack of the strap. George was in a world of his own. It was safer there where he could be whatever he wanted because he had already sensed that he could never fill his father's shoes and love his mother.

"Uncle Alexander, are you going now?" George piped up as Alexander sneaked off-side.

"No," Alexander lied. "Why? Do you want rid of me or something?" he added to throw him off his tracks.

George blushed. Alexander had meant his question as a joke, but George's red face suggested he had hit upon the truth.

That was another thing George didn't like about adults—they knew what he was thinking even before he did.

"Oh, here, granny told me to give you this," said Alexander, taking a lucky bag from his pocket.

George snatched it from him as if his life depended on it. He could always count on his granny, whatever about his parents. He tore it open, and its contents went flying across the floor. A Tom and Jerry card landed at Alexander's feet and Alexander sighed as he picked it up and handed it back.

"Here, she said to give you this as well because she won't see you on Saturday because she and uncle Barney are off on a bus-run to Antrim."

Alexander slipped him two bob, then turned on his heels, relieved to be leaving the chaos of George's world behind.

* * *

Another thing George came to hate along with the way adults lied and read minds was the way they used big words, like "Catholics" and "bastards". He awoke one morning to find his parents at the front door, neighbours milling around, a smell of smoke, and talk of "Taigs". His mother was centre stage.

"Sure them Cath'lics get more here than they'd ever get in the South in a month of Sundays—and they want civil rights?! The cheek of them! And they breed like rabbits, into the bargain."

The rabbits must have been in the cabbage patch again, he thought. *Cath'lics—are they the ones with the long, floppy ears*, he wondered?

"Aye, tell us about it!" said a woman with a black and white scarf on her head. Her man stood beside her with peeked cap and a patch over his left eye. George had never seen them before but recognised them immediately; Captain Pugwash and his second-in-command.

"You go out of your way to please them," George's mother continued, waving in the direction of the Falls Road, "and then this is what they do to ye, running amok in our streets and putting law-abiding citizens out of their homes in the middle of the night. Sure, we're givin' them jobs in all them there big factories," she waved her hand over her left shoulder as if she were thumbing a lift in the direction of the Springfield, "and now what do they want? One Man One Vote! Did you ever hear the likes in all your life? Like, do you see our ones out marching? And they've every bit as right! No, I'm telling yous, there's no call for yon!"

"What time do you make it there, big lad?" George's father asked, spotting George behind them on the stairs.

George rubbed his eyes and squinted as he studied his watch. His father had got it for him at the start of the summer holidays on a day-trip to Bangor. It was different from all the others he had bought him which he kept on a shelf in the wardrobe—it had 'waterproof' stamped on the back of it and it had made bath-time something to look forward to.

"Ten twenty," said George, pleased as punch.

"And what in the name of God are you doing sitting there in your pyjamas at this hour of the day? Get away up them stairs and get dressed before I skin you alive!" his mother scolded him. His father winked, and George took this as a signal that he could bide his time.

"There's no way they'll ever get us out of here," she continued, turning her back on George. "No, not a chance! There's just no bloody way we'll give up our home for a pack of wee bastards who can't see the trees for the woods."

"Mummy, what's a bastard?"

"A Ca'h'lic," came her unequivocal reply.

He found himself wondering if he could become one when he left home; he liked the idea of hanging out in the woods near Napoleon's Nose. The one thing he didn't want to be when he grew up was an adult.

* * *

As Belfast burned, George was a regular at his grandmother's. He was often warmed in her two up, two down of a summer's evening, wringing the light out of the stretch in the day, darkness taking its time, and hers, as she slowly faded before him. Over a wee sup of tea she piled her love high for him upon a tea-plate that she filled up with biscuits and fresh cream cake whenever she could. "You're in your granny's!" she would say to him, laughing at herself. The man of the house, George felt at home. Not even the rioting in the streets could keep him from her door.

One afternoon the smoke was still rising from the neighbouring burnt out streets when he had made his way around to her. "See them'uns! See them'uns!" she began. The mention of 'them'uns' meant he was in for the long haul and he settled back into the armchair. "We're Prodasins—for God and Ulster, son. But them'uns, them Taigs over the way, they're layabouts," she proclaimed. When she said 'Protestants' her upper lip curled up and for a split second it would appear to George that it was Protestants she hated, though he knew nothing could be further from the truth. Thanks to her, he knew he came from good loyalist stock; it was not that she ever said much about loyalists themselves but it was what she had to say about 'them'uns' that convinced him of this.

"There's no pleasing Catholics. They're never happy. And what have they got to complain about? Sure look at me in a two up, two down, and an outside toilet. Do you hear the likes of me complaining? No, you must be joking! And, you know, if it wasn't for them two wee lodgers of mine going to that Stranmillis college, I wouldn't be able to pay for the coal to keep a bit o' hate in this place. Sure, I'd freeze in this place only for them two."

She lifted her feet off the ground and gently rocked herself in her chair. When her feet touched down again she nibbled the pig's foot in her hand then coughed out her insight. "No, they'll never be happy till they get their United Ireland over our heads, them'uns. Well, wait till I tell you, son, we Prodasins didn't come up the Lagan in a bubble, and we won't go down it on a canoe either."

It was one of her favourite expressions, and she would always stop her tirade long enough to laugh in its wake, and now was no exception.

"That's the problem with this country of ours," she continued, now screening her false-teeth in her hands, "you give the other side an inch, and they take a mile."

George watched the piano keys on her upper lip depress as he folded his arms on his chest to hold back a laugh at her garbled speech.

"That Prime Minister O'Neill fella has them that way with all his talk of 'our dear wee neighbours'. Well, the Captain doesn't have to live with them'uns, does he? It's not his fancy house they're takin' over, is it?"

George imagined the Captain taking the first fence in the one o'clock which had just started on the television and which by far had his rapt attention. Leaning on the arms of his chair, he pushed himself up and down as he took the jumps.

"Move that cushion from under you there. Is it bothering you?"

George did as he was told. It was always easier that way, for he knew granny had a temper, just like his father. It could flare up in an instant, like the time she had hit out at him for using her first name. He had simply wanted to hear how Pip felt on his lips, but she called him a "cheeky wee article" and that was the end of that.

He waited for her to get her flow going again before glancing at the television. She wouldn't notice that he wasn't listening for she always talked to her reflection in the side-table mirror, running her hand through her hair as if to gather her thoughts.

"Catholics want everything their own way and they're forever looking hand-outs. They'd hardly work a day in their life, so they wudn't. Cud you see your da not working, cud ye?"

George turned to look at her just before she caught him in her sights. It was a close call; he was engrossed in the race.

"Uh, no!" he said, chancing his arm.

Satisfied that he was listening, she returned to her reflection.

"Them'uns want us out of our homes—that's what they want— and the sooner the better. Well, I 'clare to God, the Prodasin people won't stand for it. This is our wee country, son, and if they don't like it, they can lump it or hump it!"

She reached for her tin of snuff. It was the signal that the monologue was over. George knew he had to pay attention now. She stuffed some up her nose and wiped away whatever she dropped on her pink, chequered house-coat.

"Here, son, away in there and make us a wee cup o' tae, aye, and there's a wee bit o' barnbrack in there for you that I got the other day 'cause I thought you'd be coming alright. You never forget your poor wee granny, do you now?"

It was time for the weekly interval. George cantered into the scullery, jumping over the newborn kittens. The fact that she hadn't drowned them in the bucket in the back yard like all the others was a good sign, he thought. She was in good form; he could probably expect a little bit extra from her this week.

The scullery looked like a bomb had hit it. Mrs. Rooney must be blind, he thought, as he picked his way through the delph to find a cup that was semi-clean and set about making the tea. It was something his mother would never let him do at home, though he hated picking out the dried sugar from the bottom of granny's tea-stained cups. He lifted the tea-towel that covered the butter from the flies, fetched the bread board from the bath, and bore his way through the barnbrack. He would eat it because it was worth it, convinced that granny knew that he loved her then, for she always rewarded him generously. Any of the rest of the grandkids would have balked at week-old, seconds from Kennedy's bakery.

"Granny, how many sugars do you want?" he shouted in his father's voice. She was deaf in one ear, having worked all her days in the mill. He knew how many sugars she took but he asked just to give her the illusion of being looked after. It always paid in the end.

"Six!" she called out, followed by her predictable nasal laugh which he had reckoned to his dismay he had inherited from her. She frequently laughed at her self, even over the fact that her Christian name could be spelt backwards. As he strode into the sitting-room with the tea—he had put three sugars in it in the knowledge that his father always did likewise and she could never tell the difference—she was still laughing. She flung her head back, then came up again for breath, reaching up her sleeve to quell her tears of joy with a handkerchief. Pressing her perm down on her Noh mask of rouge, she found her way back to him. She placed her cup beside her on the floor and got up to get some cake for him from a tin she kept under her bed.

"Granny what's them for?" he asked, pointing to some bottles under the bed by the cake tin. It was too late; he should never have posed the question, he realised. It never paid to be too inquisitive, for once when he had asked her about her first husband she had snapped at him like a dog.

"Oh, them's for the lemonade man, son, when he comes round of a Saturday," she commented. The nervous tremor in her voice got him thinking; why had he never seen any lemonade in the house? And how come he'd never seen the lemonade man when he was visiting on a Saturday?

After tea their quiet was disturbed when George was in the outside toilet. Two RUC officers came charging into the yard chasing a man who had just run in through the house, and out the back door. George dropped his Hotspur on the ground and savoured the moment. Through the crack in the wooden door he saw the man scale the wall. He knew him to see but never asked his name afterwards because he didn't want to take away from the excitement of the moment. He pulled up his trousers and came out to support his granny. The older of the two officers apologised for the intrusion, and she quickly showed them out.

"Them boys," she exclaimed as she closed the door behind the police, "what do they expect our ones to do? To lie down and take it, is that what they want, is it but? The likes of your man is only doing us a good turn in the long run, like. Who's going to be there for us when the other persuasion make their way up onto our streets? The RUC won't be able to save us then, will they? It'll be too late for that then."

"The bastards!" said George, even sounding like his mother.

"What? What's that you said?"

"Uh, nothing. Eh, the brats!" Thank God for her hearing, he thought. "Aye, right enough, you'd think they'd have better things to be doing, granny, with the antics of the other side."

Proud of her wee man's good sense, she lifted her purse down off the mantelpiece to reward him. George felt affirmed. He was every inch a loyal Protestant. Her purse in hand, she moved to close the curtains as George eyed the stale barnbrack which he had yet to tackle. He took a bite; it wouldn't be lost on her.

"You'd better get up the road, son, before the dark."

She would always see him right, which is why he came to see her every week, but he was certain she never cottoned on to his motives. His only gripe was that she would never part with his shilling before an hour was up, for once or twice he had to leave early to catch a blue bus, and the dough had not been forthcoming. He knew time was almost up when she started to clear her conscience with talk of Mrs. Rooney from over Leeson Street, her poor wee Catholic home-help. It was always a variation on a theme.

"The poor wee crature," she began, her purse lying open on her lap, cheese in a mousetrap. "Sure, your heart wud go out to her with all them kids pulling out of her. Ach, but she's quare and good like, for she'd always bring me a wee bap, for her man has one of them good jobs in the bakery. Aye, like, they aren't all bad."

"Aye, I know, granny," he chipped in at what he thought was an appropriate moment but the truth was he was confused. Were they like a rotten apple, with good bits here and there? Or were they like a barrel of apples, some good and some bad?

"Ach, between you, me and thon wall, son, you can be sure he knocks it off, the same man, but, sure, you wudn't say anything to her, like, for the poor wee crature has it hard like. She has a bit of a want in her when all is said and done."

A bit of a want, alright, thought George, the state she leaves them cups in.

"Some of them can behave like Prodasins when they want to, if you treat them nice. I mean I wudn't let her lave without offerin' her a wee cup in the hand."

Her conscience clear, she took a two-shilling piece out of her purse.

"Ach, granny, that's too much!" lied George, checking his winnings. If Uncle Alexander could lie, so could he, he thought.

"Sure, what would I be keeping it for? I haven't far to be going now and there's no pockets in a shroud! But what," and at this point George would say it in to himself before she could get the words out, "will the good Lord say when I get to the Gate and my two husbands are fighting over me?"

"Look, sure, you can just tell them they'll have to take turns," said George, for that was his father's response, though George was still not clear why it always made her laugh. She and George brayed together, but to her relief, she could see in his boyish looks that he didn't know what he was laughing at.

"Here, take it! Say nathing to the rest of them'uns! What they don't know will never hurt them. Sure, there's not a one of them that'd make you a cup o' tae."

She had a soft spot for him. She had given him an extra shilling for tackling the barnbrack. The previous week she had been so busy complaining about the other side that he was half way out the door when he had to give her a reminder. "Um, granny, do you need any messages before I go?" he had prompted her memory. "Oh, Lord bless us and save us!" she had said as she got up to press the shilling that was still in her hand into his. He had felt guilty but it was a feeling that didn't last the length of the corner shop.

Chapter 3

George cleared the hedge and pulled his mask down over his face. How do I keep the heat in? he thought. Granny was right, he heard himself say. Protestants kept the 'hate' in. He grimaced, keeping an eye out for straying police patrols with their British army back-up. The cheek of your man on the television saying that people had not come out to riot because the weather was too wet, and that other eejit saying how if they had the weather they have in Spain, they wouldn't be out fighting on the streets; they'd all be too busy sunning themselves. People talk through their arses, he thought, but Granny was right: a bit of heat wouldn't go amiss. He clasped his hands together and blew between them to warm them up. If she could only see me now, waiting on the next foot patrol, he thought. Bad enough and all as it was me marrying a Fenian, she'd have died if she thought I'd have been out doing jobs for the IRA some day. Mind you, she wasn't exactly enamoured with the Peelers herself, was she, so she couldn't harp on that much.

'HARP', he thought. He smirked, for it hadn't been until some years later that he discovered that the lemonade bottles under his granny's bed were in fact bottles of HARP. She had a 'wee weakness', as his father called it. She was a bit of a tippler of a Saturday night, and only for the age of her, and the fact that the Ulster Volunteer Force could lie low in her house, she would certainly have fallen foul of 'the boyos'. He wiggled his toes now to keep them warm. Her behaviour would be called anti-social behaviour nowadays, he thought, if at the lower end of the scale, but back then it was just plain, old, one too many. Them were the days!

George had learned of her drinking habits when his father, Alistair, had got a call from the local Ulster Defence Association commander to go down to her house. Word had it that she had 'created a riot' in Harriet Street. Alistair knew that the UDA had no time for his mother because the young fellows from the UVF had her around their little fingers, and he guessed that the UDA commander was simply stirring things up, but he decided to check up on her just the same. When they arrived on the scene—he took George with him for security—granny Lackey was sprawled out on the scullery floor with an open tin of Kitty Kat in one hand and a fork in the other.

"Mummy, for God's sake look at the state of you!" Alistair growled as he dragged her towards the settee. She was out for the count. "Jesus, ma, you should be ashamed of yourself!" He was just beginning to feel the better of letting his anger out while the coast was clear when Pip briefly came to her senses.

"My ma used to say Queen Victoria was lying in state the night I was born, son, but that she was lying in a worse state herself!'" she slurred her words.

Alistair got a fright and hoped that even if she had heard what he had said she would have forgotten it by the morning. George didn't know where to be looking as his father lifted granny Lackey up off the floor and her stained bloomers showed. It was about half an hour later however, after Alistair had settled her down, propping her up with cushions in case she choked on her vomit, that George got the biggest shock of his life. He had gone outside to use the toilet when he discovered Uncle Barney sitting on the pot, trousers around his ankles, his head on his knees, and the place smelling like Mrs. Monaghan's house after the wee one threw up her milk.

Hearing George yell with fright, Alistair rushed out. There was no keeping things from him now: granny and Barney were drinking mates whenever Barney's money ran out. He could always count on her old age pension. From away back, granny had always enjoyed a wee tipple with her second husband. She could always depend on Alistair to put the happy couple to bed, and to stoke up the fire. When his step-father died, Barney had stepped into his step-father's shoes.

The Saturday after Alistair and George had found her on the kitchen floor, George went to see her again and was pleased to find that she had no recollection of him being there the night they had found her on the floor and her bloomers showed. When she reached for the cake tin she cursed the lemonade man for not getting round the previous week to get the bottles from under the bed. George recognised her guilt.

"And you would think he would've come and collected them, like. After all, I only keep them for the money back on them to help the Mission Fund. There is black babies dying all over Africa of the thirst. The Good Lord forgive and pardon him for leaving them poor wee childer to die!"

George knew where the rent money from the lodgers was going, and it wasn't going to Africa. That was the first of many summer binges. Whether it was the Twelfth of July celebrations ringing in her ears, or the fact that the lodgers were away till the end of September, George got used to things heating up in the school holidays.

A light went on in the kitchen of the house behind him, and George ducked for cover behind a coal-shed wall. He had lost his concentration. A woman hurried over to the shed in her slippers and dug out some coal. He watched her return inside, then, with no more ado followed her in. He sauntered through the kitchen and into the living-room, passing behind the man of the house who was dozing with his feet up against the hearth. Mrs. Murphy jumped back from the fire as George flitted like a ghost to the front door. He stepped outside.

Kathleen appeared into view with Jack in the pram. She fiddled with the baby's blankets, removed a rifle and handed it to him. He fired three shots in quick succession, threw the rifle back in to the pram, and within seconds Kathleen was away one way, and he was gone the other. By the time she dropped the rifle off in O Hare's garden, and came in the backdoor of her house, George was in front of the television, thinking his granny would have been proud of him, for when all was said and done, she always had a thing about people getting a raw deal, like Mrs. Rooney. The Brits deserved what they got for sitting on people's backs.

Without a word to George, Kathleen left the pram in the living-room and ran outside. He turned up the television to drown out Jack who was crying hysterically. Mrs. Diamond from next door was out to check out what had happened.

"Ach, Mrs. Diamond, are you there? What's all the commotion?" Kathleen strained to hide her pleasure.

"Ach, did you not hear? The Brits fired at a group of young lads playing hand-ball on Cummmings' gable wall. Would you credit that, would you, like? It's despert, Mrs. Lackey. How could anyone put up with that? You know, by right, them boys should have a hand-ball alley. Somebody told me the other day that they have one up on the South Circular. Oh, aye, them Protestants look after their own."

Kathleen took up her refrain, "Oh, aye, they look after their own ones alright. There's no two ways about it. Sure, you've come to expect that like. It wouldn't take much for the Council to put a hand-ball alley up, and keep them out of trouble, sure it wouldn't. But do you think Belfast Shitty Council'd bother their arses? No way! Sure they are as black as your boot!"

"And how's your wee Jack doing, God bless him? Like it's not fair on the kids like. And he's not the two years yet, sure he's not?" Jack was still screeching in the pram.

"No, he won't be two till another three weeks. And he's not able for it. Them Brits have his nerves wrecked. And, like, he's not a bad child. Do you know, I've a right mind to tell them Brits where to put their literature, only I wouldn't stoop to their level. Did you get one of those leaflets through the door last night too? They woke up my Jack, they did, and I'd only just managed to get him down."

"Aye. Like, the Brits really got IRA bombing materials up in Rossnareen! What bombing materials?" Mrs. Diamond began. "Did you see anything laid out on the television? You couldn't believe that BBC anyway. British Broadcasting Corporation! Aye, British alright! British propaganda! Don't tell the truth at all. Don't even tell half the truth! I swear to God, manys a night I feel like kicking that TV. Is it any wonder we don't pay our licence? I'd say them Brits put them bombing materials there themselves. Did you ever read the like of it, like? And *'if it wasn't for the vigilance of the British Army, lives would have been lost, and widespread carnage caused.'* If it wasn't for the British Army being here in the first place, lives would have been saved in this country by the dozen! Do you think they would put that in a leaflet and put it through the doors? But sure they wouldn't know their arse from their elbow. Sure the half of them's, they're, em, they can't, they can't read or frigging write, em, whatdoyemecallit, you know, they're...?"

"Illiterate?"

'Aye! Li...literate, em. I'm telling you, Liverpool lads with nothing else to do but come over here and harass poor Paddies, and sure they're half Irish themselves, the same boyos. They cudn't get a job in their own country, that's what's wrong with them'uns. Haven't a brain between the lot of them! Did I tell you that one of them stopped my Charles bringing one of the sons to the airport on Wednesday and he asked who the boy in the back seat was, and my Charles, as nice as nine-pence, just tol' him, 'That's my son', and he wrote SUN down in the book. Now, would you credit that, Mrs. Lackey? S, U, N. That's what we're up against. Did you ever hear the like? And they're over here to sort us out! God help us, that's all this country needs, a few more lunatics."

Kathleen nodded. She was too excited about the fact that Mrs. Diamond hadn't a clue that George and she were involved in the IRA, to be bothered about her analysis of the Irish war, even if in large part it confirmed her view.

"Aye. I better get this man's dinner on. He's just in," said Kathleen.

"God be good to him, and him in there now looking after the child!"

"Aye," said Kathleen. There was no point in disappointing her.

"My Charles just tol' the Brits as nice as nine-pence that's my son!" Kathleen began as she shut her door.

George looked up.

"Is that bloody woman at it again? And they wouldn't put their light on for the internment night commemoration when the rest of us would be out there half the night banging bin-lids! She puts my head away that one! She's more faces than the Albert clock!"

Kathleen followed his lead.

"Two-fucking-faced! I tell you what, I'll fucking put her windies in next year if she doesn't put that fucking light on!"

Though secretly flattered that her neighbour felt the need to keep in with her by saying the right things, Kathleen detested Mrs. Diamond's hypocrisy.

"Kathleen, is the dinner near ready, is it?" he interrupted her.

"Jesus, Mary and St. Joseph, will you wait a minute? This child has my head turned!" She headed to the kitchen to pre-pare George's dinner with Jack crying in her arms. George saw her off with a roll of his eyes. They had come a long way since the days when they used to pass each other unawares on the corner of St. Cecilia Street. Funny how people meet and the mountains never meet, he thought. Shortly after Kathleen and he had got married, they were told to leave their flat or be burned out. The local UDA had made it clear to George that while they had nothing against Catholics, they could not take a chance having a member of a nationalist family living in their midst. In his anger, George wanted to stay, but Benny told him that Kathleen could not sleep a wink at night from when they got the threat. George buried his shame at being put out of his home by his own people and moved out of respect for Benny who never failed to bend over backwards for him since the day and hour he had tied the knot with Kathleen, though he could never figure out why.

Kathleen jumped at the chance of a brand new house up in Andersonstown, although they would both be strangers to the area. She imagined a house like the ones she studied each morning on the back of the Cornflakes box: a dream house with a garden and an indoor toilet and bathroom. In the early days after their move she had missed the Falls area, and for some months she had felt worried about how her new neighbours viewed the fact that George was not a Catholic; they were asking questions because he didn't attend Mass on Sunday. Consequently, Kathleen and George kept to themselves initially, but gradually they relaxed their guard, in time becoming active in the community, graduating from leaving their lights on in the house on the anniversary of internment, to rapping their bid-lids when the Brits came to raid, and from that to putting out petrol and bottles for petrol bombers, and then doing a bit of rioting themselves. George took to 'vigilantying' and even got friendly with the local parish priest on whom he would call in on occasion to help mediate with the Brits. From that point onwards, George was just another nationalist.

George would have been happy to have left his community involvement at that but for the fact that he was coming up the road one day when the Brits got him out of a black taxi and threw him up against the wall to search him, thinking, he supposed, that they had Catholic scum in their hands. He knew if he had been wearing a suit, they would not have laid a hand on him, and this only added to his rage. The Brit who held him by the scruff of the neck sensed George's indignation and went out of his way to goad him on.

"And what's this we have here then, mate?" he asked as he took chewing-gum out of the breast-pocket of George's Wrangler jacket.

"Would you care for some?" the Brit teased him as he helped himself.

George felt his shoulders tighten. The soldier pulled George's books out of his hand.

"An intellectual Paddy, eh?" he mocked him as he leafed his books. "You won't be needing these where you are going, mate," he continued, throwing them on the ground.

The instant George's City and Guilds books fell on the wet ground, he knew there was no going back. Kathleen could like it or lump it, but there was definitely no going back. Besides, he had only taken on the study to appease her.

"Right, lads, let's go!" shouted an officer from the back of an armoured personnel carrier. In a matter of seconds the soldiers were gone.

The passengers climbed back into the taxi and George shook the rainwater from his books. A woman—she appeared to be in her sixties at least—sitting opposite him went into a rage.

"A bloody disgrace! Having an old widow like me out on the road a night like this, and it teaming. A load of fucking cunts!"

She tugged her skirt down over her knees, lady-like. George could feel his face blush; she was too old for that sort of language. The taxi started up again.

"They wouldn't get away with it if my man was alive, God rest his soul. The God's honest truth, I'm telling you, love, is that the IRA's the only ones that have got the balls to take the likes of them bastards on. It takes balls and brains, and the Provies have plenty of that. My husband, may he rest in peace, used to say, 'Ann, dear, Ireland was a child when England was a pup, and Ireland'll be grown up when England's buggered up!' And you know what, son, he was right."

George nodded.

"Would you rap the windie there for me son, like a good lad?"

He rapped the window and the taxi began to slow.

"And I'll tell you another thing. They go on about all the damage the IRA's doing to Belfast with their bombs.. But anyone with a bit of sense can see that Belfast is booming. Sure, if it wasn't for the Provies, you wouldn't have all those spanking new buildings. And, sure, the Council has saved a fortune, 'cause the half of them buildings were dilapidated anyway and were due for redevelopment. How much have I got there, love? Is that a fifty?" she asked, sorting through her coins. "I'll never get used to this new money."

George sat forward to sort out her money.

"There you have it. You have it there now," he said.

"Thanks, love. It takes a man! My man, RIP, used to say that he wouldn't mind it if they burned the buses on the other side of town, but they burn our own, so they do. What's the sense in that, like, I ask you? Have we not suffered enough? And them'uns on the other side, sure they're just laughing all the way to the fair and saying 'Hell slap it up them, for they deserve all they get!' And that annoys me no end!"

The taxi drew to a stop, and George held her arm as she got out with her bags. A few minutes later he rapped the window himself.

"It's alright, mate." The taxi-driver winked at George as George stretched the fare in across the front of the cab. It was the driver's way of making up for the hassle they had got from the Brits. George thanked him. He loved that about the Catholic community: they stuck together.

Kathleen called into him from the kitchen. Jack had just gone over to sleep in the Moses basket at her feet. "Your bloody dinner's ready now. Do you want gravy made up?"

"No!" She always asked him the same question, and he always resented it. He turned up the television to hear the News. Something must have happened because the place had been swarming with British soldiers when he had been out doing his bit with Kathleen earlier.

"Ssshh! Listen! Wehh! Well, that's another fucking one less to worry about anyway! Jesus Christ, the IRA have balls but, don't they? Fucking ace! Did you hear that, Kathleen?" he shouted, leaping up from his seat.

"Ach, now, just a wee minute, George! Do you think I've ears in the back of my head?" she asked, racing in from the kitchen.

"A Brit's been shot dead in Edenmore," he continued, ignoring her bickering.

"Jesus, I never heard a thing either! What time about?"

"Must have been just before we went out on our job. That's you and that hair dryer! You can't hear a thing with that thing!"

Kathleen threw up her head and returned to the stove.

The IRA had balls—it was this that had convinced George to do his bit. It also got him away from Jack's incessant crying. It was easier to be a republican than to be a father, though he was also firm in the belief that he was, in a roundabout way, doing it for his baby son.

One evening he had been making his way downstairs when Kathleen had noticed his shirt hanging out at the back. "What the fuck is that?" It was his IRA uniform. Although Kathleen shared her father's republican views, she had no desire to see George join up. He sat her down on the stairs.

"Listen, love, it's like this. I'm not prepared to sit back and watch young fellas doing nobody a bit of harm have the shit kicked out of them. You know yourself, sure you saw them Brits the other day kicking the fuck out of Da McKearney. There's no call for that like."

"Yeah, but George, there's more to this now than just you and me. There's the child to think about." Kathleen had seen the effect on her own family since her dad had got involved in Prisoners' Support. Benny had been left carrying the can. They had taken him in for interrogation in Goff barracks. He came home in a boiler suit, all because they had found a toothbrush in the back of his van. The police claimed the toothbrush was for cleaning guns. Kathleen would never forget it because of her mother's reaction.

"The next thing they'll be taking you in for having a Jimmy, and they'll be saying you use it with a lethal weapon," she had said.

Kathleen had never thought her mother knew what a condom was, never mind a 'lethal weapon', and had felt appalled.

George felt defensive. He hated the way Kathleen had developed a habit of guilt-tripping him about baby Jack. He turned the tables on her.

"Exactly" he replied. "I'm doing this for the child. It's for his future," he said and left for his meeting.

At first, all he had to do was keep at eye out, let people know there was a job going down, and signal to the lads as a British army personnel carrier approached. It was Hotspur stuff, and he had never been short on enterprise. Next, they wanted him to hijack vehicles to block the roads to keep the Brits out. George would not be found wanting. He took springs, beds, chocolates, televisions, whatever happened to be going to the airport, off the back of lorries, as distraught drivers ran for cover and a phone to the sound of petrol tanks exploding. He handled the situation well, and no one noticed that he had got a colour television for free. He was soon promoted to following a guy who was passing on information to the RUC. George spotted him asking an RUC man for a light by the cemetery wall, and a couple of Volunteers subsequently gave him a beating and put him out of the area for six months.

George had a sense then that he was making a difference. He soon got sworn in to the IRA, and was asked to turn out in a colour party. Once, leaving the cemetery after the funeral of an IRA man who had blown himself up in his own bomb, he was stopped by the Brits and taken in for questioning. Fortunately he had just slipped his dark glasses and beret to Frank. Gradually he was brought in on bigger jobs and soon he found himself holed up in other peoples' homes for cover. If it was not for the Brits, he had thought, he would be out there leading a normal life with Kathleen. His resentment grew.

George could smell the bacon and cabbage now. They had come a long way in the past year alone, he thought. Kathleen had rowed in behind him and had started going out on 'jobs' with him of late. He assumed that it was a case of 'if you can't beat them, join them', though it crossed his mind that maybe it was also a break for her from looking after Jack.

He leaped up from his chair. Three British Army saracens whizzed past and stopped at a house further down the street.

"Will you hurry up with my dinner, Kitty, they're raiding McArdles?"

Kathleen hurried in with the dinner and ran to the window.

"Holy fuck! Here, George, I'm away over with the bin-lid. Will you keep an eye on the child?" She handed him his plate and a towel for his lap.

* * *

It was after ten by the time Kathleen finally got Jack to sleep, having nursed him in her arms for the best part of an hour. The Chinese take-away, her first since she had started breast-feeding Jack almost two years earlier, had obviously affected her breast-milk and he had got cramps. She laid him down on the settee, removed his bib, tucked him in with a coat, then, exhausted, turned to close the living-room window to keep the draught off him. As she reached her hand through the blinds she heard laughter. She flicked up a leaf of the blind and peeked out. A soldier was squatting behind the hedge. Strange that she hadn't heard any dogs barking, she thought, for that was normally the first sign that the Brits were on patrol. She closed the window and made her way into the kitchen to rinse out the milk bottles. She hooked the cleaned bottles on her fingers and carried them to the front step for collection the next morning.

As she stooped on the doorstep, the thought that with the soldiers out so late, it'd be unlikely that the bottles would see the light of day amused her. The Army presence was sure to bring out the rioters before the night was out and they would be certain to make good use of the bottles as missiles. The soldier spoke into a walkie-talkie. Are you still there, thought Kathleen? And who do you think you are, anyway, holding us to ransom in our own homes? And us hardly able to walk the length of their own path without being accosted!

A loud crack shattered her idle ranting. She ducked and swore under her breath. It was a single shot. Like a safety-blanket her father's words consoled her almost immediately, 'If you hear the bullet, it didn't have your name on it'. She was okay. She was uninjured. She stood up only to find that her legs were barely able to hold her weight, and as she stared into the distance her heart jumped at the sight of a gunman with a face she wished she hadn't recognised running across the light of an open door, his rifle still in the firing position.

The thud. There had been a thud. Something had fallen in the garden. Her eyes scanned the bottom of the hedge. "Oh, my God!" He was face down. Next, she was kneeling, turning a body over, her hand slipping under a head, a smell of blood oozing along a sleeve and onto a tartan skirt. A watchstrap flopped into her hand—her favourite colour—which matched dark green eyes that writhed in agony. Her mouth at an ear, and then the sound of a familiar prayer that ricocheted the length of her windpipe, "Bless him Father for he has sinned. Have mercy on him a sinner. Hail Mary, full of grace..."

"Mary, Mary," the soldier groaned.

Perturbed by his interruption, she tried to silence him.

"You'll be alright, love. You'll be alright."

"Mary," he defied her.

She stroked a forehead, smooth, cold, bloody—words which shunted her from shock to fear, and then to questions; why doesn't somebody do something? Is there nobody there? Can somebody help? The sound of dogs whimpering brought her to her senses. *She* had to do something.

She rushed inside the house and whipped Jack's pillow from under him with its medal of Our Lady pinned to it to protect him from an untimely death, and ran back out again. The grass was now black with blood. She lifted the soldier's head and placed the pillow under it.

"You're going to be okay," she knowingly lied as she took his heavy, limp hand in hers. He gasped. "The ambulance is coming," she added, smothering in tears.

A squaddy who had been taking shelter nearby muscled in and shoved her back on the lawn.

"Leave him fucking alone!" he bellowed. From the quake in his voice she realised that he would shoot her without a second thought, and, cowering, she crawled on all fours towards the house.

"Mick! Mick! For Chrissake, mate!" the squaddy pleaded, gripping his comrade against his chest.

Kathleen got up off her knees and held onto the window-sill with one hand to steady her nerves.

When the Red Cross ambulance arrived along with military reinforcements, they lifted the corpse into the back of the ambulance without bothering with a stretcher. Standing in the hall with her back against the front door, Kathleen listened for the bang of saracen doors, and the hiss of wheels, that would usher in the loneliness.

Jack had slept through it all. She stroked his forehead, peeled off her soaked clothes and burned them in the fireplace, then carried him upstairs, lying him down in her bed. George could let himself in.

He found her lying on her back with one hand behind her head in a sexy pose. He relished the idea of getting into bed beside her but his desire was derailed when he caught sight of Jack under the blankets.

"Jesus Christ! What's that on his face?"

Startled, Kathleen woke up, squinting.

"What? What? What's up?" she asked.

"What the fuck is that on his face?"

She pulled the blankets back.

"I must have forgot to clean him up. I'll clean him now."

"Clean him? But what is it, for Chrissake?"

"The blood. He died. You, you…"

Fuck, I got him in one, he thought! It was George's first Brit, and the excitement throbbed in his veins.

The searchlight from a British Army helicopter filled the street and then the room, and for a few short moments it seemed to offer Kathleen clarity. She knew what she had to do.

Chapter 4

L ong Kesh had been hell for Nicholas. The furthest he had got
was the exercise yard, and the only people he ever saw were
the same old prison wardens and block mates, his mother, Benny,
up on a visit, and the priest of a Sunday. Once in a blue, George
would cross his path at Mass, but even the sight of his brother-
in-law had done little for him. He was tired of them all. Still, he
kept them sweet, telling himself that it just wasn't in his nature
to be unkind. He kept Benny sweet by saving his weekly visit for
her. He kept the wardens sweet by empathising with them about
their long shifts, the dangerous nature of their jobs, and, more
rarely, sympathising with them when one of theirs got killed off-
duty. The priest could rely on him to serve Mass, the mates could
depend on him to dish out the meals everyday, twice a day, and
a nod and a wink in his brother-in-law's direction kept George
happy for he knew then that Nicholas wouldn't let slip to Fr.
Murphy that he was a Protestant. "Keep it sweet! Keep it sweet!"
The words went around his head all day like a mantra till his
head hit the pillow and he was out for the count. Nothing would
disturb him—except his conscience.

From the moment the judge had sentenced him to six years,
Nicholas regretted his actions: he had done it alright; he was the
guilty party. There was no turning his back on the court, no fingers
to the judge, no salute from the dock to a forlorn Benny and inconsolable Kathleen—a double whammy for Kathleen as she watched
Nicholas go down to join George who had still over a third of his
life sentence left to serve. Innocent as the day he was born, Nicholas
believed himself guilty. It was the only way he would get his time
done. He was returned to his cell in due course, but not before
he had first thanked the judge profusely for her good counsel.
Unbeknownst to him, she had miscarried, and not for the first time.

Nicholas spent the next three and a half years sifting through the evidence for his guilt. If only he were not such a hateful person and had not gone that morning to the funeral of a local IRA member to spite his mother who had warned him to let the dead bury the dead. If only he had minded his own business and had not got involved in the melée that ensued there. If only he had not been such a coward, and had left the frenzied crowd when things appeared to be getting out of hand. If only he hadn't been so naïve as to believe the police that if he signed the confession that they had fabricated he would be back at home that night. He was guilty because he was hateful, nosey, a coward and stupid. He was every inch the cold, calculated IRA man that the judge had described, a fact that was confirmed for him whenever he looked in the mirror in his prison cell and his cold, blue, angel eyes stared back at him. It was his bad character that had him behind bars.

He had been standing watching the funeral go by when two men reversed their car into the cortege. Thinking it was a loyalist attack, some of the mourners pushed in on the car, wrenched the occupants from the vehicle and carried them into a nearby park. Nicholas followed them inside. His nerves were at him. Things were quickly getting out of hand; a group of men were stripping their two captives. The park gate opened briefly to let a priest and a woman with a buggy out. He pushed forward, muttered something about being the father of the child and exited with his hands in his pockets, nursing his testicles.

Later, under interrogation, a terrified Nicholas admitted to the police that he had partially stripped the two men, kicked them and planned their eventual deaths, but he knew he was telling lies; it was Sunday; and he had wanted home to get ready for Mass.

Nicholas' religious fervour was not unusual in republican circles. Like many of his fellow republicans he had kept the faith in the face of unwarranted provocation on the part of the Catholic bishops who had forbidden military trappings at the funerals of IRA Volunteers and were forever condemning IRA violence. As if that wasn't enough, they were also against integrated education, which galled Nicholas who could say with his hand on his heart that he hadn't a sectarian bone in his body, espousing as he did the republican vision of a United Ireland for Catholic, Protestant and Dissenter. The bishops' politics had also sorely tested him: they supported the Social Democratic and Labour Party—if the Catholic people changed their attitudes to the security forces, and kept their heads down, things would sort themselves out in the long run—a sure guarantee that the status quo would, Nicholas reckoned, continue for some time to come, and consequently that more people would needlessly lose their lives, an outcome too horrific for him to contemplate. Nicholas and co. looked to the past, to republican tradition and the wounds the country had endured at the hands of the British, not least of which was Partition for which the only solution was to get the Brits out of Ireland.

Ironically, though there again, perhaps not, the more obstacles Mother Church put in Nicholas' way, the more he clung to her, keeping his Sinn Féin politics a private matter and doggedly queuing up with his nationalist brothers and sisters for Communion. When more extremist (though, he was clear, by no means more radical) elements threw his eagerness to attend church in his face, he gave them short shrift, quoting liberation theology which, conveniently, was the vogue at the time: the Church was the people, not its institutions, and republicans (unlike the extremist Irish National Liberation Army) had the people's best interests at heart. He omitted to mention his mother who was also a part of his motivation: he went to Mass to keep her off his back. And yet he knew there was no shame in this—Padraig Pearse, he discovered in literature smuggled into the jail, had a thing about his own mother, as did St. Augustine, though he only learned of this in novitiate later. But one reason for going to church that he was especially loath to admit to his foe, not to mention to his friends, was his bourgeoning desire to be a priest.

Nicholas' niggling vocation offered him security: the bishops would always come out the winners—for in the long run they were as likely to lunch with the Queen as with the President of Ireland—though he didn't exactly shout this from the rooftops in West Belfast. Instead, from the quiet of his prison cell, he petitioned Our Lady of Perpetual Succour for early release and promised her that if his prayers were answered he would complete a Novena in Clonard Monastery in an effort to discern his priestly calling. She came up trumps; on the first day of the Novena, in the fourth year of his sentence, he was back where he belonged, in the front row. The Novena had always done it for him: the drone of the Aves, the newfangled priest up on the old-fashioned podium, the people of God turning out in their thousands, reminiscent of the glorious Hunger Strike marches. At the heart of the communion of believers filing out of church through thousands of penitents arriving in for the next Mass, Nicholas had felt, well, special. Surrounded by people who epitomised the suffering of the wider Catholic community, he was swept up in a sea of quiet grief, and he loved it. He was part of a simple people with a simple faith—an awareness heightened by the close proximity of the myriad Protestant churches just across the Peace line behind the church, so close but, conveniently, so far. The memory of these moments had never failed to buoy him up when his prayer-life was at a low ebb in prison.

On the way home from his second Mass of the day, Nicholas observed that the women seated around him in the 'black taxi' seemed, as in years gone by, more at peace after the uplifting eucharistic celebration. This was evident in their silence, their blank faces, and the way they read each others' minds, rapping the window before being asked so that their kindred pilgrims could alight. He sensed that their peace came from the conviction that they were all involved in something greater than the violence that surrounded them and which determined so much of their lives. The Novena was something that relativised their suffering for one week in the year. They had all suffered. Mrs. McCafferty, a case in hand, sat opposite him, her red and black headscarf draped around her shoulders. She had lost a daughter in the Troubles. The sight of Mrs. McCafferty brought back memories of his own pain to him. The IRA had nearly killed him one night as a Volunteer took a pot-shot at the Brits in a jeep that was passing right beside him. An inch to the left and they would have killed him by mistake. The bullets had raced by his ear.

"Ach, I didn't recognise you there for a minute. You're out, thank God!" Mrs. McCafferty interrupted Nicholas' morbid thoughts.

"Ach, Mrs. McCafferty, what about ye? Aye, just in time for the Novena."

"It's an answer to prayer, son. How's your poor mother keeping this while?"

"Same as ever. You know her, as long as she's busy!" replied Nicholas, feeling guilty about the fact that his mother would not be seen dead at the Novena, even though she was known for eating the altar rails at the local parish church.

Mrs. McCafferty's saintly smile seemed to light up the taxi as she returned to her calm. He glanced at the reflection of her eyes in the window. They were tired. He had frequently come across her in Milltown cemetery at her daughter's grave before he was imprisoned. Loyalists had picked her daughter up as she was coming out of choir practice and dumped her hacked body on the other side of town. How, he had wondered, could she have forgiven Michelle's killers on the TV the way she did? "I forgive them. I don't want this to happen to anyone else's child. Protestant tears are the same as Catholic tears," she had said. Mr. McCafferty had sat silent at his wife's side throughout, his hands joined on his lap, his head bowed.

As Nicholas looked through her eyes at the orange street lighting, his thoughts strayed.

It made great television but. Aye. Nowadays but, they're all in on it. "I don't want anyone to suffer what we have suffered. There's to be no retaliations." I don't know how you done it, he thought. It would have brought tears out of a statue—though, mind you, not from them fuckers up in the Northern Ireland Office! *"It's the Mr. and Mrs. McCaffertys of this world that always have to suffer—decent, law-abiding, hard-working folk, who are being held to ransom by a few sectarian thugs on either side."* Aye, they always have their answers ready! Uh, but I tell you one thing, I'm sure they whooped with glee every time one of us called on the paramilitaries to stop. It was just the type of propaganda they needed. *"People have to understand that the problem in Northern Ireland, if indeed you could call it that, is that Catholics chose to study the Arts and there weren't enough jobs for them whereas Protestants chose sciences and found employment, thus creating an imbalance. And if Catholics had have had property, they'd have been as entitled to vote as the next, regardless of religious affiliation."*

Oh, aye, pull the other one! And you, Mrs. McCafferty, sat there with your husband telling us that Protestant tears are the same as Catholic tears! My arse! Nothing could be further from the truth!

His gaze returned to Mrs. McCafferty's face in the window as they passed the dark expanse of the Falls Park.

Have you seen any angelic pictures of your Michelle doing the rounds lately? No, not a chance in hell! But she was a prettier picture than that Gordon Wilson's daughter who died in that bomb in Enniskillen. Aye, and there was never a fucking chance this side of death that your husband would be appointed to Seanad Eireannn either on the back of Michelle, unlike that Gordon Wilson, for she was only a poor wee Catholic. Two a penny, one a penny, hot fucking cross buns! Not that I for a moment doubt the sincerity of Gordon Wilson. Oh, no, don't for a minute get me wrong like. "We don't want anyone else to go through what we've had to go through"? Here, wait till we roll over, and give us another good hiding when we're down. It's not like your Michelle was the first innocent Catholic to die for her faith, aye, nor will she be the last.

Nicholas smiled for the cameras. It was his maiden speech in the House. Mrs. McCafferty smiled back. Embarrassed, Nicholas uncrossed his legs, and Mrs. McCafferty moved her bags to make room for his feet. Her thoughtfulness irritated him.

With all the nice, understanding people in Northern Ireland, you'd be forgiven for thinking that there was a tea-party going on in this beautiful wee province of ours, dear Honourable Members. Not that we want conflict or anything, no. Indeed, Honourable Members, wasn't I one of the first to march with the Peace Women in the Seventies? And I didn't exactly enjoy hardly being able to go for a pee without thinking the whole fucking roof of the house was going to come in on top of me! No, and there's no gain in having to tell the rest of the world how we wouldn't bat an eye-lid when we heard gunfire. No, I never wanted people to suffer.

"Could you rap that windie for me, Nick, son? Mrs. McCafferty's words disturbed his thoughts like a poker in a fire. He tapped the window and the taxi stopped.

"Good night, Mrs. McCafferty," said Nicholas.

"Tell your mother I was asking for her," she replied.

"Surely! God Bless!" He watched her pay her fare, and waved her off.

By the time he stepped out of the taxi, he was certain that his meeting with Mrs. McCafferty was a case of serendipity. No matter how much he had previously resisted, it was clear to him now that God was calling him to the priesthood to work for the Mrs. McCaffertys of this world so that the day would come when they would not have to get up on television and tell people that they forgave their children's murderers. The fact that he'd have no children himself would be an expression of his solidarity with them in their grief; he would share their loss. Besides, he hated television, and, in particular, had an aversion to the News that Benny had passed on to him, both of which characteristics were appropriate, he felt, for religious life. He was also non-materialistic; prison had knocked all self-conceit out of him: he had not been in a clothes shop in years, and had never felt the need to have money in his pocket all the time he was in Long Kesh. Novitiate would be a dawdle.

As the roof of his home came into view the fear that his old ways might come back to haunt him suddenly gripped his throat.

He had spent many a Sunday morning hung over in the converted attic of his home before the prison years, sometimes his finery covered in vomit. Aunt Maura's face flashed before him. Way back he had heard that she was closing her Littlewoods catalogue account and had decided to get in a few last orders. He sent away for over 200 pounds of corduroy trousers and matching polo neck jumpers, and a winter coat, paid the first instalment of 10 pounds and then conveniently forgot about the remainder. Several threatening letters later, the Littlewoods man had arrived at his door.

"Good day! Can I speak to Mr. Nicholas Dunne?"

"Nicholas Dunne?" Nicholas replied, thinking on his feet.

"Yes, it's in connection with payments to Littlewoods," said the salesman.

"Nicholas? I'm telling you now, mister. My mother's dying up those stairs. She's fucking heartbroke. Do you hear me? That Nicholas fella has his mother's heart fucking broke, I'm telling you! Every fucking salesman under the sun has been to this door this past month looking for him. Now, listen, mister Littlewoods, I'm telling you now, if you find that alco of a brother of mine before I do, will you tell him from me that I'm looking for him too, and if I ever lay my hands on him I'll ring his fucking neck for him, for he has my mother crucified! I'll kill the fucking bastard!"

Professional to the last, the stunned salesman repressed his very real urge to flee, which attacked his bowels.

"Eh, I'm awfully sorry for troubling you. You'll hear no more from us. I'll, I do hope your poor mother will recover," he acquitted himself, then fidgeting with the lock on his satchel, he beat a path to his car, appalled by the f-word.

Everybody had a past, and, if they lived long enough, a redemption story, Nicholas told himself, as he fumbled now with the keys to the house. Prison had been his road to Damascus experience. He was only out of Long Kesh a week, but, no, he was right to believe that his old ways were mended. Hadn't he refused a welcome home party because of all the alcohol they'd wheel out and he'd be forced to drink and the new clothes he would have to buy to look right? No, he had been successfully rehabilitated. He grimaced—'rehabilitated' was not in the Republican dictionary. They didn't need rehabilitation for they weren't Ordinary Decent Criminals, but political prisoners. He was different, though, he reminded himself: he had been innocent all along. His breath frosting the glass door, he snorted with incredulity at his propensity for self-doubt. His innocence had only sunk in the day the governor had told him he was a free man. At least, he now mused, one good thing had come out of the lies he had told himself; he had got an education inside to pay back society for his crime. He now had three A Levels, in accountancy, social studies and religious education: he would manage the parish finances as efficiently as some prisoners had managed IRA racketeering, organise the local community into militant cells, and pass on the Good News of the parousia with the zeal of a terrorist convert (though he used the term 'terrorist' tongue in cheek.).

It was the parallels with Jesus, however, that had most convinced him of his calling. He had edged towards this conviction in religious education class in jail, helped along by his teacher who was a Presbyterian, and thus had a sharp eye for Scripture unlike her Roman Catholic counterpart who hadn't handled a bible in her life. Unlike his comrades on the wings who were guilty to the core, he now accepted that like Jesus he was innocent but had paid the price—JOHN 18:39. He did not raise his voice or cry out—ISAIAH 42:2—there was no way you would catch him parading his grief on television. He had seen the misery of his people—EXODUS 3:7—and would free them from (British and Unionist) oppression—EXODUS 3:9-10. He was a man devoid of beauty and familiar with suffering—ISAIAH 53:2-3—'beauty' in the sense of glamour, not in the sense of good looks, (he clarified the etymology in the Hebrew with the aid of his teacher, though he kept his motivation to himself for fear she would ridicule his calling to the Church of Rome.) On a more practical level, he had experience of male community life in Long Kesh, for the most part celibate, which would undoubtedly stand to his benefit. When all was said and done he would—like Jesus—bring a wealth of experience to religious life.

He stood at the front door, still fumbling with the keys as the biblical citations raced through his mind. It helped that he was good with figures, he thought. He never forgot the reference for a good citation. "As long as they don't give me the Keys of the Kingdom!" he said aloud. He bit on his tongue to stifle his mirth; if there was one thing he had had no experience of in the past three years or more, it was keys.

"Ma, I'm back. Is the dinner in the oven?" he shouted as he finally shut the front door behind him. He could smell his favourite dinner from the kitchen.

Yum-yum! Lamb stew, he thought. It isn't something I cooked up out of nowhere. No, it's a vocation. And all them years serving as altar-boy at mass in the Kesh! Of course, I could refuse, he thought, but a calling is a calling, whatever about all the religious trappings. I know the Hunger Strikers in prison fought to wear their own clothes, but I'll wear the garb for you, Lord. Everybody has a Cross to carry, and I won't be found wanting, will I?

Benny came downstairs to serve him his dinner. Now that she had him home where he belonged, she was intent on spoiling him. She adored her son, and he was only too happy to make up for lost time by indulging her, however strange it still felt to have someone serve him, and not the other way around.

"Ma, I've decided to join up." It burst out of him as Benny placed the dinner in front of him.

"Jesus, Mary and St. Joseph!" she said, practically tipping the dinner off the plate with alarm. "Well, I'm telling you now, you won't be living here under this roof! What planet are you on at all? Haven't you put me through enough all these years, and me and your father not getting any younger? You can't sneeze but the Brits are on to you."

"Ma! I'm joining the priests!" he explained before she did any more harm.

"Ach, son, the Fathers!' she cooed, up-righting the dinner plate. "I don't know what made me think you were joining the IRA!" She laughed now as much to persuade herself as him that her misunderstanding was funny. Nicholas frowned.

"Are you sure that's what you want?" she continued in a further effort to cover her tracks. "I don't want you thinking that that's what we'd want for you. I mean, I don't want you think…"

Nicholas interrupted her to stem her confusion and deaden his pain.

"Ma, I'm as sure as I'll ever be! I just know it's right. I've been mulling it over for years. Sure, Aunt Sally saw it coming, and tonight it all just seemed so right."

Benny had never been strong on affirmation. After he had been sentenced and led to his cell in the Crumlin Road jail, all she had seemed concerned about later that day was that he did his six years with the Ordinary Decent Criminals in Maghaberry Prison and not with the Republicans in Long Kesh. "You have to choose one way or the other!" she had cautioned him. There had been no tears, not even a hug. Now, she forced herself to say the right thing.

"That's all them prayers I've been saying to Our Lady for you. It's an answer to prayer, son. I knew it! I knew it'd happen some day. I knew I could bank on it ever since Auntie Sally brought you back that rosary from Medjugorje. Wait till your da hears this."

As Benny set about lighting a candle on the windowsill she mumbled, "I'd be a long time waiting for that Johnny fella to make us proud like..."

The smell of sulphur caught Nicholas' nose.

"But, ma, I'll be moving to Dublin," he said, deliberately cutting her short. He had heard enough.

"It's not that your brother Johnny doesn't listen to us, but you know, yourself what he's like," she continued.

Nicholas tried to ignore the thought that she seemed to believe that he was entering the priests to make her proud, though it also crossed his mind that if her pride in him repulsed him so much then he shouldn't be making such a big deal of it.

"They train all their people there at first, Ma, but I can move back up here to Belfast after the first two years," he said, attempting to lessen the blow of his imminent departure. Surely, she wouldn't take that so easily.

"Look, son, I've done without you these past four years nearly, so I'll get by. Don't you worry about little old me!" She laughed at her Texan accent and proceeded to pinch his cheek. "And to think I thought you were going to join the Provies! My head must be cut! I'm losing my marbles altogether!"

Nicholas couldn't reconcile her Texan persona with the fact that she had been the epitome of the bereft mother while he was in prison. The lads inside were forever teasing him about how when their mothers met her at the shops, they could never get away from her because she was always going on so much about her Nicholas and the fact that he was a poor wee innocent whose only crime was to have been in the wrong place at the wrong time. Embarrassed by their ribbing, he had been secretly consoled by her affections.

He lowered his head to hide his disappointment at the speed with which she had now cut her ties with him, and tucked into his dinner. 'Fuck you, anyway!' he thought. She could sink or swim for all he cared.

Chapter 5

Kathleen's heart was in her mouth as she entered C Block. How was she going to tell George that the IRA wanted their Jack out of the area by Sunday night? No, better say nothing; no point in breaking the habit of a lifetime.

Under the scrutiny of a group of prison wardens by the coffee vending machine, she took her seat in cubicle 12b and waited for George to come down off the wing.

What the fuck...? Where the fuck have I gone wrong? Jesus Christ, I'm losing it here! Fuck, I'm going to crack up! I made choices. I mean, I had to, for Chrissake. You fucking loyalist bastards put me out of a home!

Her eyes gazed up at the ceiling.

You fucking blue noses upstairs! It's yous fucking loyalists that have me here. That was the start of it! What was I to do, like? Stand back and take it? Yous loyalists had it too good for too long! "Catholics need not apply!" Uh, terms and conditions fucking apply now! Not that that makes a blind bit of difference to you, George. It's not you who's paying the bills, is it? "Tabhair dom a few of them there sausage rolls, le do thoil." Lifted and laid in here!

Her arms quivered as one of the wardens banged on the vending machine. *Looters!* She uncrossed her legs and felt a draught creep in around her thighs. The door slammed shut behind two prisoners who poked fun at each other as they strutted on stage, a comedy duet.

What is it about this place that has everybody smiling? Who's fooling who?

She brought her knees together, and was reminded of her period. *Here, tell me, do I smell, Kate? You'll do!* She blew through her nostrils to expel the memory of mornings when she swept George's body with her nose like a guard with a detector at a city centre security gate.

What the fuck is keeping you, George? God, but you've got it easy. Aye, and...I had to make a stand. Sure, somebody had to. I mean, I'm not a bigot or anything, even all the things yous loyalists done on us, but, like, I couldn't just lie down and take it, and yous'uns trampling all over us.

"Ach, hi ye, Bubbles!" Her eyes had locked on his by accident and demanded her to speak.

"Not so bad, love. How are the wee'uns?" Bubbles asked, about to take a seat on the other side of the partition that divided the room.

"Ah, sure you know yourself! Not so wee any more, and as bold as fucking brass!" Her words felt like a recording of an original; they were someone else's.

Bubbles smirked as if to say he knew the story, and sank from view.

Fuck, what is it about you Bubbles that you never wipe that smile off your face? Must be the food in here. And what would you know about life outside anyway, stuck in here?

She folded her hands on her lap and addressed her knuckles, her words flooding her head like rain down a gutter.

Brass fucking neck, he has. Have you no fucking wit to be fucking around with the Mob, have you, Jack? You should have known better than to be giving the Provies a run for their money, But what was I supposed to do, like, on my own with the two of you children? A fucking father figure is right! Aye, a fucking father figure alright! One of them fucking figures of an aul' lad on the mantelpiece would have done a better job than you fucking ever did, George! Aye, and it's all my fault, like? Don't you come that crap with me! Am I the one ended up in jail?

The sound of laughter from the direction of the vending machine: she looked over at the culprits.

Punch and Judy wouldn't be in it! More fucking English bastards over here making a fortune off our backs!

Some fucking catch I got, I'm telling you, George! You soon wiped the smile off my face, didn't you? And I never missed a family photograph up here once, and sure the whole prison was able to tell me how well the two kids were turned out, and you sitting up here in your cosy cocoon. When did you ever have to worry about whether you'd have enough at the end of the week for the coal, never mind the messages? No, I'm not...I'm not to blame. I did my best, and sure, God knows, I may as well have reared you as well, leaving you in birthday cards from you to the kids, and sticking a few pound in along with them for your tobacco. Aye, and the Christmas parcels! Oh, aye, a few pound was never good enough for you. You had to have sweets, a jumper, and even fucking underwear. Were you soiling it or fucking what? And it wasn't like I could depend on your da or anything for anything either. It didn't take him long to wash his hands of you once his son was a republican prisoner.

What the fuck is keeping you, George? Do I have to go in and take you out by the hand, is that it?

George was a bit like having an extra child. Even when phones were installed in the prison and she thought things would get easier, it had only got harder because she had to send him in the money for the phone cards. There was no one she could turn to. Her own family was a dead loss. Within the first few months of George's incarceration they had pulled back entirely. She could never understand that. They 'bummed and blew' up and down the road about their brother-in-law who was doing time for the IRA for killing a Brit at his own door, but they were never prepared to put their hand in their pocket for him, with the exception of her mother at Christmas.

She had no choice but to take on extra hours at the local pub, but that brought troubles of its own. For one thing, she was unable to be around the house to keep an eye on Jack as much as she would have wanted. For another, she had to pay a baby-sitter to mind Rosy, the surprise daughter whom she had had seven months after George had been locked up, and the apple of her Daddy's eye. Worst of all, though, was the pressure she felt on the job. She had to keep her slate clean, and the pub was not exactly the best place for a grass widow to avoid scandal. There was no way she wanted a bad word against her getting back to George—that would be her cards marked forever. It wasn't like she had any interest in that kind of thing, anyway, but people talked. On New Year's Eve she had gone out with her brother, Nicholas, and a guy she worked with came over to her while Nicholas was in the toilet.

"Fuck, you'd wanna be careful Kathleen, for you never know who's watching," he advised. "Is everything alright with you and George?"

She held back her tears till she was in the Ladies.

"Fucking SSRUC wouldn't ask you the like!" she yelled at herself as she dried the tears from her cheeks in front of the mirror.

Kathleen stopped slipping on and off her wedding ring; she didn't want to give the prison officers the wrong idea. Their smooth tanned faces and manicured moustaches were veiled in steam from their hot drinks now as they maximised on their luck—the machine had jammed and the drinks were free. *Thugs!* She tried to focus on the window on the wall high above her head to still her mind.

The local Sinn Féin councillor she had known from her days in the Cumann na mBan had been over to her door the night before to let her know that he was aware of the situation with Jack, and that he would be there for her, but that justice had to follow its own course. The IRA could not let it be said that there was one set of rules for republicans and another for everyone else. She understood. She had to face the music. Jack would have to take what was coming to him.

The jangle of the prison officer's keys brought her to herself again. George bounced in, clean-shaven, smelling of Old Spice, in his best jeans, and wearing the blue pullover she had left in for him with security on the last visit. She took him all in. She had always loved the look of him.

"Hello, love!" he said, kissing her before he sat down. "Ach, hi ye, Bubbles!"

He had caught sight of his prison mate out of the corner of his eye.

"Ach, whataboutye, George? Fuck, you're looking brilliant today!"

"It's the food in here, you know yourself!" said George. "Any word yet on the other?" he added.

"Nah! Not a whistle! Sure you know them solicitor fuckers—they drag it out as long as they can. More money in the bank! And me a fucking innocent man and all!"

"Aye, sure, we're all fucking innocent! If it wasn't for the war, none of us would be in here in the first place! You know yourself! Listen, sure, I'll catch ye again!" said George, giving him the thumbs up for his court appeal.

It was Kathleen's turn now.

"Well, what about ye?" she asked, disgruntled.

George didn't bat an eyelid. He had expected her to be annoyed because she was always the same when anyone interrupted her 'date'. She would doll herself up for her visit, looking the part with her matching earrings, thick lipstick and flaky eye-shadow. All the women were at it. He and the boys joked about how the visitors' waiting-room was like a brothel. Someone had said the women were like vestal virgins out for the day. "Vestal? None of them could hold a fucking match to my wife! She's not out burning the candle at both ends!" George had jested.

George ignored her mood and her question. "Have you the money there for a cup of coffee?" he asked.

"It's a free for all up there. Them English fuckers jammed it! Fucking picketing that machine by the looks of things! So much for visitor access!" she moaned. George rubbed his hands together with glee and returned a few moments later with four cups of free coffee.

"Well, so, what about you?" she asked again, her voice still angry.

"Ach, sure, you know yourself, there's fuck all to report from in here. The same fucking four walls! Yourself? What's up?" he enquired, putting her on the defensive.

"Nothing. We're alright."

What's up? What's fucking up? The whole shebang is up.

George could read her thoughts from the way she moved her head like a cockerel looking all around, her widow's peak tilting from side to side.

Once George was imprisoned Kathleen had always made it a policy not to bother him with her troubles on the outside. She reckoned that he had enough worries of his own without hers, though she never knew what exactly it was that she was convinced he had enough to be worrying about. This thought had always enabled her to keep George at arm's length and, coincidentally, anaesthetised her from the pain of living alone: preoccupied with "poor George", she didn't have time to be concerned about her own predicament. George respected her decision; she had a lot on her plate and there was no point in her dragging him into it because there was nothing he could do from inside. He also kept his woes to himself. It was odd, but once he picked up his transparent polythene bag from the tuck shop with a Mars bar and Cheese & Onion crisps and passed it through security for the visit, he automatically slipped into hospital visitation mode; Kathleen was the patient and he would go easy on her. The rare times that he had forgotten their goodies, his depression had slipped out and Kathleen was loaded down with guilt for the rest of the week.

George ripped open the polythene bag and broke the chocolate bar in two. Kathleen knew there was trouble in store; it was a Crunchie and he knew she didn't like them.

"Is Jack giving you grief again? I'll fucking break his legs, if I get a hol' o' him! Is he up to his old antics again?" He had already got wind of Jack's behaviour from the Officer Commanding before he left his cell for the visit. Kathleen picked up her half of the Crunchie. There was no point in holding back now; George was in the know.

"Jack's in a bit…Look, em, Tommy B. was over last night. Jack has got into a bit of troub…bother. They threw the heap at him."

"The wee bastard! I fucking knew it! I'll fucking kill him, I will! What to fuck has he done now, the wee cunt?"

George crushed the plastic cup in his hand. Kathleen jumped back as the coffee splashed into the air and onto the table.

"For fucksake!" she roared.

"Shit!" he exclaimed.

"They, they gave him a warning about a month ago," she whispered in an effort to sweeten the pill, "but you'd enough on your plate without me adding to it."

She began wiping the table with some tissues, glad of the fact that she didn't have to look him in the eye as she spoke.

"Anyway," she said, "Jack said then that was the end of it. There'd be no more robbing."

"Robbing? What the fuck is he robbing for? He fucking wants for nothing!" George banged the table thrice with exasperation.

Judge, jury and executioner, thought Kathleen. "Keep your voice down, will ye?" she pleaded. "Otherwise the whole fucking town'll know before I get to the fucking gates. He's not on trial!"

"Keep my voice down? The fucking wee bastard! Wait till I get my fucking hands on him! What to fuck is he robbing anyway?"

"Ca..ca...cars. I told him he should know better than to be out stealing cars, and them Brits dying for an excuse to shoot a few youngsters. He should have known fucking better. Jesus Christ, stealing fucking cars! Where did I go wrong, George? Tell me! What the frig did I do wrong?"

"The wee bastard! Robbing our happiness, that's what he's doing! Dickhead!" George clamoured.

Kathleen rushed to Jack's defence. She hated the way he knocked him. "I mean, alright, he didn't steal them in our area. At least he had the good sense to go over to the Malone Road and steal them. God knows they can spare a cAAr or two."

"Here, have you brandy balls in your mouth, or what?"

There was no point in ripping the arse out of it, she decided. Bad enough having Jack pulling against her, without George as well. She'd give him some ground.

"That's not the point, but, is it?" she continued.

"No, it's not the point, is it? The point is he shouldn't be stealing in the first place, should he? That's the point!" George shot back.

Kathleen was smarting. It mattered little to George what Jack did so long as it didn't reflect on his reputation, and being a Protestant simply put him under more pressure to prove his bona fides to the other Volunteers. She would give him a taste of her mind.

"Fuck, listen to yourself! It isn't as if you were ever a fucking saint! Many a Friday you pished the buroo up against the wall of the Whiteford Inn, and me sitting at home waiting on the money to pay the rent-man. And I'd have been bloody lucky if I'd have had the money for the messages on the Saturday, and you'd be looking money back off me on Monday for a pint."

George had ducked to get out of the line of fire but in spite of his precautions, she had hit bull's eye.

"Ah, for fucksake, Kathleen, that was a long time ago. Fucking give it a rest, will you? I'm a changed man now! I've had plenty of time to think things over in here. Communicating's the name of the game."

"Communifuckingcating? You men don't talk, George, yous, yous, yous sing."

"What the fuck are you on about?"

Kathleen blinked as if to deflect his question. She had no idea what she had meant but scrambled now to explain herself.

"They, they…" she stammered. "They, sure, they're never done singing to themselves."

George's eyebrows tipped like scales in disbelief at her mumbo-jumbo but he refused to elaborate.

"And do you know what he said when he came in last night and I confronted him?" she continued, getting back on solid ground again.

"Fuck me, love, was I hanging out of the rafters, like? Was that me in the corner?"

His jealousy about Jack hurt but she ignored it.

"'For fucksake, ma, ge' me head pace! It's not like yous didn't steal cars in your day!'" She stopped long enough to let George get his hackles up, but not to get the first word out. "And I told him that we didn't steal cars," she continued, taking the wind out of George's sails. "We never robbed cars. We might have hijacked car…, I mean, lorries and vans and the like, but we weren't doing it for ourselves, like. The whole community was behind you. We had to do something to protect our area. How else were we to defend ourselves?"

She knew he'd like the bit about self-defence. It didn't pay to keep him on her back for long.

George spoke as if preaching to the converted. "Them was different times then. Everyone was in on it. Sure, there was even people that would give you their cars to burn. That was the way of it. It was a community thing, like."

She placed the wet tissues in her cup and moved on to the practical issues now that she had calmed him down.

"But it's like this here now," she began. "He has to go, love. He has to go over the Border. He has a week to get out. Fair enough, like. He has to take his medicine just like the rest of them. What's good for the goose is good for the gander, no matter what way you look at it. Anyway, it's better than a beating. They took a wee nipper out the other day and beat him with sewer rods. Can you imagine? His ma had him drugged to the eyeballs, like. At least he had that good fortune. Nicholas can find him a place. The priests have any amount of houses down there. I mean, alright, I'm left thinking there's been much worse done by some of their cronies and nothing's ever said about it, but he'll take it on the chin. I wouldn't have them talk about us."

George softened, though it was too little too late for Kathleen.

"Look, love, never mind, look, send the wee shite up to me, and I'll have a wee word with him. Jesus, it was bad enough the trouble he got into last year with the Brothers."

Jack had been caught doing drugs in school, news that had also filtered through to the jail. That was the sort of him. If somebody was going to get caught, it had to be Jack, Kathleen had thought. He was suspended from school for two weeks.

Kathleen imagined Jack's reaction when she'd tell him his father wanted to see him. She hadn't had the nerve to explain to George that Jack hadn't been up to the prison since the annual family photograph almost ten months earlier because he had seen through his father's bluster. When she had threatened him with his father over the drugs incident at school Jack had turned on her, "What the fuck does he know about anything, locked up twenty-four hours a day? And what the fuck does he care about me, anyway, with his three square meals a day, and all the cigarettes and poitin you could wish for?"

The prison warden placed Kathleen's visitor pass on the table between them, and she acted as if she hadn't noticed it, not wanting to upset George any further.

"Jesus! Is it time already? What time do you make it?" George asked.

"Twenty past."

"Twenty? I make it ten. Are you sure?"

Kathleen nodded.

"This fucking watch is a dead loss getting! I'm fucking doing enough time in here without this fucking thing adding to it!"

"The definition of an English gentleman is someone who never adjusts his watch in public, or so I heard the other day on the radio," she said as he began to set his watch. Her indirect criticism of his manners was the best she could do to vent her annoyance at the ribbing he had given Jack.

"Aye, and an Irish gentleman is someone who never adjusts his crotch in public," George laughed, saying the first thing that came into his mind. Then, with a flick of his head, he signalled to her to come round to his side of the table to snuggle up. Her disapproval hadn't registered.

She stood up and yawned and he returned the compliment.

There were days when Kathleen would spend so much time getting through security that they were lucky if they had time to say hello by the time they got to meet each other. This had been one of those days, though neither of them was regretful. She settled down in his arms and kissed him on the lips. No use in making things any more difficult than they were.

"Don't be worrying!" he said. "We'll get through this. I'll talk to the OC. I'll get something organised." Kathleen feigned belief. She knew how to handle George's great ideas. Jack would have to go to Nicholas in Dublin.

"So, do you want Jack to take my visit next week?" she asked, ignoring the issue of the Officer Commanding.

"Aye, but tell him I have a 'comm' for Head Office for him to take out. I don't want him saying I never warned him."

"Aye, okay. Listen, I'd better be going, George. By the time I get Rosy's dinner on, it'll be near time for work."

"OK, love. Right, sure I'll give you a wee bell Friday night." Her kiss had sweetened him.

He had slipped her a message, a 'comm', into her mouth when he kissed her, his regular love letter, but she didn't foresee any hassle with the prison wardens on the way out. It was more usual to get searched on the way in. She had also slipped one into his mouth, and was more worried about him getting through security because she had noticed that the warden at George's end of the room was the one the IRA had attempted to shoot while he was off-duty the previous Easter.

They blew farewell kisses to each other as they went through the doors at opposite ends of the room.

George got through security no problem. He knew the warden had learned his lesson. It was a matter of 'you scratch my back, and I'll scratch yours' now. Both the IRA and the wardens had agreed to back off. He climbed into the van that would bring him back to C Block.

"Bubbles, twice in the one day! Jesus, it never rains but it pours!" said George.

"Back to the holiday camp!' said Bubbles. "Is everything all right, Georgie boy?" He had heard Kathleen and him raising their voices.

"Aye, her aul' ma's not doing the best this weather. You know yourself," replied George.

"Sorry to hear that, George." Bubbles was long enough in the tooth to know lies when he heard them having done ten years inside; he would leave well alone.

George stared at the floor, lost in thought.

You've always been far too hard on him. If only you had have give him room to breathe instead of molly-coddling him. Honest to God, you'd wanna wise up, Kathleen. That's what has him hanging out with a pack of hoods! I'll fucking give him a good hiding when I get out of this hole! I'll kick the shite out of him. How the fuck will I get the dogs off of you now, not that you'd bother your arse to thank me for it? No, you always did things your own way. Any other wee lad would have pulled his weight, with me inside and everything, but, no, not you! Too fucking busy collecting British stamps!

As soon as he got back to his cell, George grabbed his gear for the gym. He would have just enough time to squeeze in a hundred press-ups and do ten kilometres before lunch.

Kathleen popped into the loo to freshen herself up before entering the waiting-room. She threw on a bit more lipstick and shook her hair into position, patting it a little at the front to take the unkempt look out of it. She must have been running her hands through her hair without realising it as she spoke to George, she thought. She ripped a toggle in her poncho as she straightened it. In the waiting room she stepped over the crossed feet that were there just to make life difficult for her.

Have people no wit? What sort of a rearing did yous get? Did no one ever set yous down and tell yous to keep your fucking feet in? How the fuck am I supposed to get by, like? Yous were fucking dragged up, the lot of yous. I have a home to get to this day.

She took a seat directly opposite the television which was perched high in the corner of the room like a sentry box.

Jesus, not that fucking Diana Princess of Wales thing again! If you'd have fucking put your money into us instead of throwing it away on them flowers! And have you lot nothing better to be doing than watching that bloody Sky News all day? It's well knowing what fucking foot they kick with in that security box. That's to keep their ones happy no doubt.

From across the corridor the wardens were peering in at the television.

"Lackey, Maginnis, Kelly, Ross, Timmons, Stone." Her name penetrated her consciousness as if someone had slapped her with a leather. 'Anseo' surfaced on her lips; the school roll. She shut her mouth like a door caught in a gust of wind, got up from her place and snatched her screened pass from the warden. Her first taste of welcome sunlight lasted but a moment, for she had barely taken two steps before she was in the prison van with the other visitors. Another warden carried out a head-count, locked the doors and got into the front.

Dying for a smoke, she searched the window opposite in vain for a scratch in the protective tape to get a glimpse of the outside world and take her mind off cigarettes, then took everyone in the length of the bus, bar the man smelling of vinegar squeezed up against her to her left. She could tell what they were; it was full of Orangies today. A voice found form near the door.

"How can somebody be shot down in the most secure jail in…, and fucking screws everywhere? I'm telling yous now, the British government is up to their eyes in this for he was a fucking thorn in the side of the Irish peace process!"

Kathleen stretched her feet out.

What about shutting your aul' trap and respecting the rights of the rest of us? Have you never heard of parity of esteem or what? Aye, like, loyalists never collude with the security forces when it comes to knocking off nationalists, but now the Brits are guilty of killing one of your own under the eyes of these fucking lazy screws that are growing fat on over-time. And the fucking language of yous, and kids and all here in this van! A good mouthwash wouldn't go awry. You'd let yourselves down a bucket like. Our ones would never let you down. They might think it, but they wouldn't let you down, not like yous.

The woman who had been extolling her viewpoint that British undercover was up to its tonsils in the killing of Billy Wright in the prison caught Kathleen's eye and stared at her as if she could read her mind. Kathleen looked straight through her.

Who are you looking at? Okay, I'm married to a Lundy but who gives a fuck? Just goes to show that some of yous has brains—my George had enough sense to abandon ship before yous went down. Yous learned all yous know from us, and if you had an ounce yous'd be signing up to the fucking peace process because it's your only hope, love. We have yous on the run!

Kathleen heaved an unintended sigh. She was in bits, no matter how her hair looked, and would have to hold it all in until she got to the car. It wouldn't do if her own ones saw her in this state in the car-park either.

She glanced at the woman directly opposite her.

Aye, and the state of you up to see thon bastard. I go to all this trouble to get ready and then I'm forced to share a van with a loyalist trollop like yourself, tripping in gold, that the world and his mother knows is fucking him in jail, and fucking all around you outside, aye, and all because he stiffed a couple of Taigs.

The van jolted to a stop, sparing her victim any more of her venom. The prison warden jumped out of the van and floated like a spectre on the other side of the shaded window. He opened the doors and carried out another head count. Kathleen got into gear again.

And what do you think this fucking is, like, fucking Shawshank Redemption? Do you see any hole in the side of this bus, mister, or am I fucking blind?

The warden smiled at her and once more locked the door. Moments later, the last set of security gates opened, the van drove through and stopped. Still gasping for a puff, she begged the electric gates to close quickly behind them. The van doors swung open and, refusing the pleasure of physical contact to the warden who helped the ladies alight, she smiled at him just to let him know she wasn't bigoted and held onto the side of the van to let herself down the step.

I wouldn't take your fucking hand if I were drowning, except to pull you in with me. One fucking less screw to worry about! You stand there fucking all day only to cut down on the amount of claims that people are making for falls. You don't give a fiddler's fuck about me personally. It's not your son they're putting out of the country, now, is it? And you lot should know all about falls, for isn't it your ones making all the claims for compo. Fucking Prime Minister Faulkner fell off a horse! If only fucking Ian Paisley'd fall off a horse, he'd be doing us all a favour!

From the hatch where their personal effects were kept until the visit was over she collected her car keys and envelope with her couple of pounds in it, and a wooden harp that George had made for her from matchsticks. The turnstile rattled like machinegun fire and she was out. She could hear it in her sleep. It was worse than the British Army helicopters with their searchlights keeping them awake all night. She managed a final smile for a few familiar faces piling into cars in the car-park along side ghosts from 'the other side' doing likewise, whom she looked straight through. There was only one thing for it—the Quakers' café for a pee and a smoke and a look at the Derry 'wans'. She needed it. She took a seat by the door.

And here they come now, the Fountain boys, big, beautiful, a nod and a wink to their own from Belfast. Two eggs and chips, well done, beans to beat the band, tomatoes, rashers and sausages. Tea, please. She could have placed their order for them. Then the bit she really liked: them finding their way to their table as if braving a battleground, avoiding burning buses, dodging bullets, taking refuge behind unsuspecting Catholics, escorting women and children out of the line of fire as they manoeuvred their way around them. They take their seats, careful that elbows and clod-hoppers don't touch. Kathleen studied their shaven necks from the corner of her eye, felt their hands on her shoulders, their lips at her neck, soft, wet, strong, then caught herself on. *This'll have to stop. I can't keep coming in here like this.* She tucked her skirt under her legs and stood up.

Thank Christ I don't have to get on the bus with all of yous next, she thought as she headed for the toilets and caught sight of some of her own ones by the crèche area. *How in the name of God will I ever get through this? I never reared fucking Jack for this!*

She took care not to slam the car door, and held back her tears until she joined commuters on the M1. A car upturned in a ditch like a beetle got her thinking. If only we could drop our kids in ditches, she thought. Like them'uns from wherever they are—Japan?—that bring their grannies up into the woods on their backs and abandon them when times are hard. One less mouth to feed, one less person to worry about.

When she reached home, she heard steps behind her on the garden path and, holding her keys as if ready to jab someone, turned to find Tommy Brannigan. It had to be bad.

"Kathleen, please, I have to do this. It isn't personal. Don't get me wrong! I'm just the messenger here. Look, they got Jack at Hennessy's house and they got carried away a bit. It wasn't orders, believe you me."

"Oh, Christ!" screamed Kathleen, raising her hands to her forehead to form a coronet. "No! No! Ach, no! Not my Jack! My Jack! He never done anyone a bit a harm around here!"

Tommy made to put his arm around her.

"No, Tommy, piss off! Where is he?" she hollered at him.

"The Royal."

"Oh, Blessed Lady this day! What have they done to him? Rosy, Rosy, come on!" she called out to her in the house.

"Do you want me to drive you down?" Tommy asked as they tore past him.

"Like fuck I do!"

She expected the worst. Thoughts of Uncle Damien came flooding back to her as she fought with the gate at the bottom of the path. Jack had only been a nipper then. She had been finishing boiling Jack's nappies in a bucket when the knock had come to the door. Benny looked sufficiently shaken for Kathleen to invite her in. They had not been on speaking terms since Benny had complained two weeks earlier about the noise of Jack and Rosy when she was trying to watch the Bruce Forsythe Show. If there was one thing that upset Kathleen it was people complaining about her kids, while for Benny it was anyone coming between her and Bruce, other than Anthea, who swung into him at the end of the show to prove to Benny that all was well with the world.

Benny's complaint had been the second in just over a week. A stranger in a café near their home had come up to Kathleen to complain about the racket of the kids.

"Can I just tell you something?" the woman had begun, her hands joined school-marmish at her waist, "In all my life I have never seen two such unruly children! You should have taken them out and let the rest of us have our lunch in peace!"

"Get a life, lady!" Kathleen had spluttered, bits of her sandwich landing on Rosy. It was a line from some American film.

The woman vamoosed, leaving Kathleen with all the guilt and anger. She wanted to throttle the kids, but restrained herself in front of the customers. She paid her bill and fled the shop. For close on a week, she was constantly on the children's back. She had felt such shame. When Benny shouted at the kids to be quiet that following Saturday, Kathleen had walked out of her mother's home and hadn't laid eyes on her since.

"What brings you here?" Kathleen asked, refusing to let down her guard as her mother followed her through into the kitchen.

"Uncle Damien's dead."

"What?"

"Uncle Damien's dead, dear."

"Dead? What? What do you mean he's dead? What? How? De…Dead? Good God!"

"He's been shot, Kathleen. He, the IRA has issued a statement saying he was acting as a tout for the RUC."

"What? Jesus Christ!" exclaimed Kathleen. Jack screeched at the sound of his mother's voice. "Uncle Damien passing on information to the police? Sure, he wouldn't know what he was doing!" she said, pulling Jack back from the scalding bucket of nappies.

"I'm going over to the hospital now," said Benny. "Do you want to come over with me? Mr. Sloane'll drive us down."

"What? What? I...? Where's my handbag? But what about the kids?"

"Mr. Sloane'll mind them in the car."

Two days later she walked on the footpath arm in arm with Marlene as the hearse pulled away from Damien's house. The next day, Johnny made it his business to talk to the top IRA man in the area about his death. They met in the Prisoners' Defence club. The story was that Damien's information to the police had resulted in two bombs being intercepted and a couple of good men being arrested and charged. When Johnny got back home he put the rest of the family in the picture and Kathleen had no quibble with him, but she blamed the RUC, and not the IRA, for his death. Everyone knew that he was "a bit slow." He was easy fodder for the police. Sure, one day lining up for Communion he had drank all the wine in the chalice, and the priest had to send out to the sacristy for more. However, her distress over Damien's death was still evident at his Month's Mind Mass. Damien had always had a soft spot for her. Once when she had felt faint at Mass and had gotten up to leave, he had followed her out. Some of the parishioners brought a chair out to her on the steps of the church and, like a guardian angel, Damien had held her forehead until she was able to stand up again. Another time, she had run in to his house to escape some Protestant kids who were taunting her. He had sat her down like royalty, given her a big bowl of Sugar Puffs and told her that he would keep an eye out for her in future. In the porch of the church, she had cornered Nicholas and voiced her fear that Damien had suffered. He tried his best to console her.

"I don't know whether the IRA beat them or not," he vacillated. "I hope not. I don't know. You know the way the families of some touts say their loved one was badly marked. Well, I wonder. I wonder if they're just saying that he was black and blue because the family is all annoyed, or whether maybe he got injured trying to get away from them, in the struggle, like. I just don't know, Kathleen. But, look, he's gone now. There's no point in torturing yourself, Kathleen."

It wasn't enough. Kathleen continued.

"But, look, Nicholas, see that taking them away for days and leaving him lying naked at the side of the road, like. How do they do it, like? It's beyond me! Jesus, if the police threw you out of Castlereagh Holding Centre naked, there'd be an outcry!"

"Look," Nicholas began again, "we're not talking about the Orangies here. Those butchers'd cut your tongue out and slit your throat. They've no conscience. They don't know sins. Our ones know si…know what a sin is. You can be sure Damien didn't suffer."

"Ach, Nicky, son, are you not a priest yet?" a voice called out.

"Ach, Aunt Sally, what about you?"

Sally had always teased Nicholas about being the priest in the family, hoping that he would study for the priesthood after he left school.

Kathleen turned away and stepped out into the bright morning sunshine. In her imagination she was a child again, back with Damien just a few feet from where she now stood, his hand to her forehead. Tears welled up in her eyes. Jack looked up at her.

"Mummy, don't cry!" he said.

"It's okay!" she said. "The world won't fall apart, not just yet, anyhow!"

The Royal Hospital came into view. It was an age since she had rushed there with Benny and Mr. Sloane to see Uncle Damien, but she hadn't forgot what the IRA was capable of, and she feared the worst. She drove her car up on to the footpath and, clinging to Rosy, ran across the four lanes of traffic. She yanked the hospital door open—the strong wind making it more difficult, she noticed, than that other time—and headed for the escalator.

"No, mummy! No! I don't want to go down here!" pleaded Rosy.

Kathleen could barely make out the floor numbers in the lift. She blinked, evacuating the tears from her eyes, and pressed LG.

"My son has just been admitted. Jack Lackey," she explained to the duty-nurse downstairs.

"Oh, yes, dear. Follow around to the left and it's first on your right."

Kathleen moved quickly but carefully in and out between patients and visitors.

"Jack Lackey?" she enquired of the first person in uniform in Accident and Emergency. It was all her breath would allow her to get out.

"Are you Jack's mother?"

"Yes" Kathleen replied, sensing in her heart she would never answer thus again.

"Come this way, Mrs. Lackey. I'm afraid the news is bad."

Chapter 6

After prison life, novitiate life was a relative dawdle for Nicholas. Once a week he was granted permission by the novice master to go for a cycle into town on a Saturday. Having pinched a pound from the community kitty, which he put through the books as extra postage stamps for his fellow novices, he would observe the hedonistic world in the crowded ILAC Centre, on which he had turned his back, a cup of tea and a cigar in hand, minor indulgences which he was careful not to divulge to the novice master in confession. It never paid to be too honest. Besides, God was already in the know for He had knit Nicholas together in his mother's womb and had counted every hair on his head, so it wasn't as if he was hiding anything from anyone when all was said and done. But it amazed him just the same that he never felt the slightest bit of guilt until it dawned on him that guilt was something he had left behind for good in prison: he had no use for it now. Fear, on the other hand, had replaced it such that he puffed furiously on his cigar certain that at any moment the novice master would come around the corner and catch him flagrante delicto.

It was already dark when he arrived at Busáras to meet Jack who had been given a further week by the IRA to leave Belfast after his discharge from hospital. After almost two years of life in Dublin, Nicholas still felt as if he were on the run himself, and the drab winter night did little to alleviate this feeling, even though it constituted his second trip into town that day, having already been to the ILAC centre for his weekly clandestine smoke. He had never settled down in the South, and was itching to get back to the North. What the North needed was someone with experience of the conflict and a bit of spirituality to get peace off the ground. He was the man for the mission: his prison experience and training for the priesthood made him the ideal candidate. He would save Northern Ireland single-handedly. It was not, of course, a prospect he relished, given its high risk of failure, but following in the footsteps of St. Ignatius, the founder of his religious order, he would pray for the gift of the Third Class of Humiliations, and, if necessary, take failure on the chin, if that were God's will for him. The only problem was that his superiors in the order would not consider this option at present. For Nicholas, then, Jack would bring him some badly needed Northern sparkle that would brighten up his quarantine down South.

He abandoned the community car on a double yellow line, hid his mobile phone and Bach CD in the glove compartment—you could never trust the Dubs—and charged into the station through the pouring rain. He was safe; the station was a sanctuary in a foreign country. From here, the Border and home were only a short hop away on the bus.

He scanned the Departures and Arrivals screen—he had to get those glasses soon: age was catching up—then looked for platform 12 only to discover that the Cork bus had just pulled in there. He spotted the Belfast bus parked outside the station—no doubt shoved out of sight so as not to offend the sensitivity of Southerners for whom Northerners were like a red rag to a bull, he concluded. On the verge of going over to the information desk to complain about anti-Northern discrimination, a figure waved a crutch at him from inside the bus. Nicholas drew closer. God, could that be Jack? Janeymac, he hasn't half grown, he thought.

"What about ye, Jack? It's great to see you!" Nicholas called out as Jack approached the front of the bus steps. Nicholas had always been fond of him because, quite simply, he had always been close to Kathleen growing up. Barely a year older, she was a light for Nicholas in the darkness that was the macho world of West Belfast. She taught him to knit and crochet, she coloured and plaited his long hair, gave him a love for cats, and taught him to swing his hips. He had forgotten none of these, though he had given them all up to follow the Lord.

"Hi ye, uncle Nicholas!"

Jack's eyes immediately honed in on Nicholas' clerical collar. Although he hadn't the full Roman garb on, the collar was more than enough to make Jack feel awkward in the presence of his fellow passengers. Nicholas grabbed Jack's crutch and rested it up against the side of the bus, then put his arm under him to help him down the steps. From the feel of his biceps it was clear that

Jack was much stronger than him and he found himself struggling both to take his weight and to hide his embarrassment. "Welcome to the Republic of Ireland, seat of the Holy Roman Empire!" Nicholas joked in a mock Paisleyite voice to compensate for his feelings of inadequacy. A man—his excessive weight and checked green shirt sticking out from under the cuffs of a white Aran jumper suggested an American tourist—turned to examine the man in the dog-collar, and Nicholas all but took a bow.

"Should I kiss the Holy Ground?" asked Jack.

Nicholas' cheeks flushed. He was back in the previous day's class on the rules of celibacy where the novice master had instructed the novices never to kiss a woman, not even on the cheek, for fear of misunderstanding. Under fire from the recent homesick arrivals, he conceded that kissing ones mother was in a different league, well, genus, actually, in the Aristotelian sense, for no one could possibly read anything, you know, sexual into that, and, sure, Jesus himself was known to have…to have kissed his Blessed Mother on occasion. It was as if Nicholas could hear him speak, and he was shocked at how much he had retained.

Seeing Nicholas blush, Jack regretted his sacrilege and fixed his gaze on the holy ground. Meanwhile Nicholas pulled himself together in time to see his American admirer off on the Killarney bus with a smile. It was nice to be nice, to show how friendly Northerners were.

Nicholas stretched out his hand to Jack who took it as if it were marked FRAGILE. Nicholas was a Dunne—he would keel over if you blew on him.

"Have you a bag in the hold?" asked Nicholas as he tried in vain to get Jack's hand to move in his.

"Aye."

"What colour is it?"

"A big black one."

"Perfect for where we'll be going!" Nicholas quipped.

Jack chuckled, taking care not to squeeze Nicholas' hand in the process and Nicholas skipped to the rear of the bus, chuffed that Jack had found him funny.

As the bag knocked off the calf of Nicholas' leg it struck him that there was no way he could ask Jack for help. Jack's hands were better suited to heavy loads than his own but in Jack's present state it would be effort enough for him to walk to the car.

"Right, em, the car is 'round the back. It won't take us long to get to the castle where I live. Did I tell you the novice master has assigned you the gardener's cottage at the back of the grounds?"

"A cottage?"

"Yep. That way it'll be more private for you."

He could skip the real reason: visitors were not welcome in the novitiate itself because the novices could get distracted from their pursuit of the Lord. It was the same with chocolate biscuits, sweets and soft drinks—they wouldn't be tolerated on the premises except on Haustus, in-house speak for feast-days. Nicholas now found himself hoping that Jack hadn't a sweet tooth.

Soon, they drew up at a set of traffic lights. Nicholas hummed and tapped a beat out on the steering-wheel as he waited for the lights to go green. "The lights must be broke," he finally said.

Jack felt relieved that he had spoken; he couldn't take any more of his humming. Why don't you just go, he thought? Sure, the whole thing about George being in prison for going through a red light was just another one of Kathleen's yarns which she spun to delude herself.

"The state of the roads down here is something shocking," Nicholas continued, filling in the silence. Life in a religious community had given him an edge for table talk and mention of the roads got him going again. "When I came here to Dublin two years ago I really felt as if I was coming home. Do you know what I mean, like?"

Jack pursed his lips and nodded, but he hadn't the faintest idea what Nicholas was on about.

"It was in my blood. It's in your mother's blood too. Our roots are here. This is the capital city we have been denied. This is where Pearse and Connolly hail from."

"And Roger Casement," Jack chipped in in part to affect interest, and in part to quell his mounting anxiety: how much longer was Nicholas going to sit there while the cars behind him passed him out?

"No, was he not English?" said Nicholas uneasy about the interruption. He had just been finding his flow.

"What? Who?" asked Jack who had lost the train of his thoughts.

"Casement."

"Oh, was he? I thought he was from here."

Nicholas was happy that Jack had as good as conceded he was wrong. He had the floor again.

"It was like a dream come true, being down here. No Protestants breathing down my neck! This was one place I wouldn't run into Brits on the streets either. And it was great to get away from all the trouble up North."

That much Jack couldn't agree more with: sick to death of harassment from all quarters, he had felt a weight lift off his chest upon crossing the Border earlier.

"I mean, at least down here, I felt we were all Irish men. But, do you know something? I couldn't have been more wrong about anything. The people here are more British than the Protestants in the North. Down here what you have is another British statelet."

Jack listened politely; politics bored him. Nicholas conveniently mistook his silence for attentiveness.

"Now, they'll tell you that we Northerners are English and they're Irish, but, Jack, we are more Irish than they are because we've stuck to our guns. These'uns down here, they've sold out. By the way, Jack, while I'm at it, can I just warn you, don't start calling them 'Free Staters', or even 'Southerners'! They hate that. 'Dis isn't a Free State, tiz a Republic'," he said, putting on a Dublin accent.

As if looking for enemy aircraft, Nicholas checked the skies then edged forward, breaking the lights. His knuckles knocked off Jack's knee as he changed gear and he apologised. Novitiate life had left him on edge about physical contact as well, outside of the sign of peace at daily Mass. Jack's head twitched: Nicholas' apology had caught him just as he was about to doze off.

"Is your leg okay? Do you want to put the seat back and stretch your legs out? Go on, lie back there if you want."

Feeling obligated, Jack adapted the seat and stretched his legs out. Nicholas couldn't help noticing how he filled out the space beside him. How time flies! Only yesterday he was a scrawny young schoolboy, he thought. And now look at him!

"Did you do Irish in school? Whether or which, you should definitely take some Irish lessons the first chance you get down here. Southerners hate it when Northerners can speak their language and they can't. They hardly have a word between them. I've brushed up on mine. The only words they know down here are 'Slán abhaile!' They're everywhere. 'Safe Home!' And they tell you this is the land of 100,000 welcomes! My arse! They're glad to see the back of people, especially us lot. When I came here the only words I had were bainne and prátaí and whatever you're having yourself from serving out the prison food in the Kesh."

"I have some Irish," said Jack. "I learned it off a fella in the Cluann Ard."

"That's great! It's good to keep Southerners on their toes! Do you know something…?" Nicholas began again. Jack wondered what Nicholas was going to say next. He looked at him, pouting his lips and lifting his shoulders to appear interested.

"What really brought things to a head for me, though," Nicholas continued, "was the way the people down here lined up to sign the book of condolences for them two kids who died in Warrington. That bomb went off prematurely. Anybody'd tell you that. Sure, there was no gain in the IRA blowing up two children in England, was there? So how could the Brits argue that it was deliberate? And, do you know what? They lined up in their droves down here. Uh! They seemed to forget that dozens of kids were killed in the North by the Brits, and not a word about it. Did anyone queue up for them? No, the truth of the matter is the South abandoned us in 1921 and never spared us a second thought after that."

"Is that when they got their Republic?" enquired Jack. He had to say something after all that.

"Aye, em, yep, em, I, I think that was it. Em, to be honest, I'm not exactly, uh, they called it the Free State. Free of what? We certainly weren't free, were we? A nation once again? That's a geg! What nation, like? That's what really gets on my wick about down here. 'Do you know their 'national' news for them is the 26 counties. We don't get a look in. And do you know what's even worse?"

"Uh, uh."

"The poor people of Donegal! They don't exist, and they're from down here. Do you know, there's people down here that wouldn't dream of crossing the Border to go through the North in order to get to Donegal. They're so afraid of us in the Black North that they'd rather drive another two hours around the Border to get to Letterkenny. Did you ever hear the likes of it? Oh, but they tip the cap to the poor Northern Catholics who have to hold up the dam wall; after all, 'they're the ones have to put up with them Protestants'. That much they get right, but in the next breath they'd be bending over backwards to please the Unionists."

The car turned into the castle grounds. Jack sighed with boredom.

"Are you alright? You must be really cramped sitting there. You've just got so big all of a sudden," said Nicholas misinterpreting his sigh.

"Yeah, I'm a bit sore alright, but, sure, we're there now, aren't we?" asked Jack, immediately regretting his question which he felt too easily belied his relief at being at his destination.

Nicholas drove past the castle to the end of the garden and stopped in front of the cottage by the white-washed grotto of the Blessed Virgin.

"It's not much, as you can see," Nicholas explained as he lugged Jack's bag into the hallway of the cottage for him. "But you can stay as long as you want. In fact, the longer, the better." He was delighted to have Jack's company; he was such a good listener, and there was no one he could bounce ideas off on the North in the novitiate. No one wanted to know.

"No one has used this place in a long while. You may open the windies and let some air in," suggested Nicholas. He hadn't realised the cottage was so dank. Paint was peeling off the walls.

"The gardener used to live here. Now, the novices do the gardening. And as you can see for yourself, there's no kitchen so you have to have your meals up in the community house with the rest of us. It's also warmer up there!"

Nicholas rubbed his ears to create heat while Jack took in the devastation.

"And you're a big boy now, Jack, so you can eat as much as you want, whenever you want, up at the house."

"Thanks!" said Jack. At least the food would keep him warm, he thought.

"You won't go hungry here," said Nicholas, giving him a slap on the back. It felt natural—he was family for goodness sake. It didn't count. No need to report it to the novice master, he thought, smiling at his scruples. "Listen, I'll leave you for a while and let you get settled in. There's hot water there, if you want to get a bath. Dinner's at six, so, what if I called for you about ten to and brought you up to the community house?"

"Ace! Thanks, uncle Nicholas."

"See you so!" said Nicholas, heading out with Jack's bag.

"Oh, uncle Nicholas, my bag!" Jack shouted.

"Oh, God, sorry! What was I thinking?" asked Nicholas.

Jack smiled, not knowing what to say.

Over at the novitiate, Nicholas put on a wash, made a few pastoral phone-calls and had a quick shower. All the while thoughts came to him of Jack. He felt excited about him being around, but he was also anxious. Where would Jack do his washing? He also had no phone or, come to think of it, shower, and young people preferred showers.

He called for him as arranged, gave a gentle knock on the door, waited a moment, and walked in, as was the custom in the novitiate.

"Oh, my God, oh, my God!" he declared.

Jack instinctively dropped his towel to cover his crotch, though sufficiently slowly to make it appear that he was doing it more for Nicholas than for himself.

"Oh, my God, oh, my God!" Nicholas said again, transfixed.

"I, I.." Jack searched for something to say.

"My God, Jack, what have they done to you? Jesus Christ! The bastards!"

"I know, uncle Nicholas. They beat the crap out of me but it looks worse than it is. It's nowhere near as sore as it was either."

"God Almighty! How could anyone do that on another person?"

"They just slayed me. They mauled me like fucking lions. There was nothing I could do, and I'm a big fella, like. One of them held my head, while the others beat the tripe out of me with hurley bats."

"Jesus! Look at your legs. The animals!"

"I know. Look, this bruise here was done by a nail." Jack pointed to his thigh in the hope that his attempt at openness would conceal his awkwardness at being naked. "They drove it into me with a hammer."

"A nail? Jesus Christ, Jack! God, it still looks so raw. It must be so raw."

"No, you can touch it yourself. There's a hole. See!" said Jack, touching it with his finger.

Nicholas stretched out his hand. "Are you sure?" he asked.

"Yep. No probs. Go ahead. Feel it! The doctors said it'll never go away."

The tip of Nicholas' finger disappeared into Jack's flesh.

"God Almighty!" exclaimed Nicholas.

"It's not all that sore now. You should have seen it in the early days."

Nicholas withdrew his finger.

"You know, mummy said that uncle Damien got it even worse. They tortured him."

"The bastards!" said Nicholas.

Jack felt a sudden urge to put his arms around his uncle; it was always worse on relatives. He had felt the same way for Kathleen.

"Oh, I'm sorry," said Nicholas, pointing to the door. "In the novitiate there are no bathrooms or toilets in our rooms. They're all shared. I'm really sorry! I'm so frigging institutionalised got."

"No, that's okay. It's, it's my fault. I didn't hear you at the door. No, it's cool. I mean, I don't know what happened. I had oodles of time to get ready but…. I didn't see the time going. Are we, are we late?" he asked, now pulling the towel around his waist.

"No, no, we're not. Never mind. Take, take all the time you need. It's my fault for holding you. Jesus, I'd no idea you'd been through all that. It must be hell even to lie down."

"Aye, uncle Nicholas. My back really wrecks me at night. Listen, I'll only be a minute."

"Oh, right you are," said Nicholas, feeling in the way. "I'll just use the loo, if that's alright."

"Yep, it's in there." Jack pointed out the obvious and lifted his clothes off the bed. "I'll only be a minute," he added.

"Can I give you a hand with that?" Nicholas asked on his return from the toilet, seeing him struggle with his tee-shirt.

He had managed to put on his boxer shorts and trousers, but even that had been a strain as he endeavoured to manoeuvre his limbs.

"Aye, uncle Nicholas. That'd be dead on. I didn't really like to ask. I'm enough trouble as it is. I can't really bend my head down. That's the problem."

Nicholas went behind Jack and slowly brought the tee-shirt over his head.

"It's well knowing you're young and don't feel the cold," said Nicholas as he pulled it down over Jack's bare back.

Jack laughed for politeness sake. "Can you help with the shoes as well?" he asked. "Otherwise we'll be here all night."

Nicholas lifted up a pair of Doc Marten's. "Are these them?"

"Yep. It near killed me taking them off."

"No probs!"

"I hope this doesn't leave us late for dinner," said Jack.

"Don't worry, we've all the time in the world! We can even raid the pantry later, if needs be. It wouldn't be a first!"

That night, as was his routine, Nicholas knelt down in the oratory to meditate on the word of the Lord. He soon found John 20:27-28 and over and over again read the lines aloud: 'Put you finger here; look, here are my hands. Give me your hand: put it into my side. Do not be unbelieving any more but believe.' He closed the bible and began to meditate. He saw Jack's wounds again: first his lacerated back and chest, then his badly bruised abdomen, next his buttocks which were black and blue, and finally the hole in his right thigh. Placing his hand on Jack's thigh he put his finger into the wound there.

"How could you let Jack suffer so?" he cried out to Jesus.

"Look at me!" Jesus replied.

He tried to see Jesus' wounds, but he could only picture Jack's.

"Lord, is it okay if I stick with Jack's body?" His trepidation was audible.

"That's fine!" said Jesus, in a voice redolent with compassion. "Here, place your finger here!"

Nicholas felt Jesus' wound as he had earlier felt Jack's. The thought that this was Jesus in Jack's body struck him as odd and distracted him momentarily. Soon, however, tears formed in his eyes; they had beaten Jesus as they had beaten Jack, and Jesus had borne his suffering for Nicholas' sins.

"How could anyone love me so much?" he asked. There was no answer.

Continuing to contemplate Jack's body, Nicholas prayed "My Lord and my God" in mantra form, following the rhythm of his breath, which he noticed was slightly fast. When the pains in his knees became unbearable, he was forced to draw his meditation to a close. He bowed down and thanked God for bringing Jack to him then turned to the tabernacle with the icon of Jesus on it, "Lord, help me to be your servant to those in need in the North. Help me to relieve the suffering of my people," he prayed. He rose to his feet, bowed once more, and said goodnight.

Tucked into bed he noted in his prayer journal that his prayer had borne fruit. The Lord had confirmed his vocation through the way in which he had called him to tend to Jack, a victim of 'the Troubles' like himself. (He tended to keep politics and prayer apart, and so spared Jesus references to the 'war'.)

Later, in never-never land, Nicholas dreamed he was in his prison cell lost in prayer. The Angel of the Lord appeared to him and blew the cell door open with a blinding flash.

"Do not be afraid! The Lord is with you!" the angel announced in a cloud of smoke that smelled distinctly of Semtex.

Nicholas ran out into the corridor naked but for a towel he held around his waist. This was his big chance; if he could get over the wall before the keys clanked and the lads awoke, he would be home and dry. Something dripped from his body. He looked down; it was blood. He was bleeding from the wounds in his feet. The angel spoke again, now with a distinct South Belfast accent.

"Permit me to take your crutch for you!"

Without more ado, he reached forward and grabbed Nicholas' crotch just as he straddled the perimeter wall. His hand slithered along his penis and Nicholas felt himself go hard.

"Place your hand here, look!" the angel continued, pulling back his flowing gown to reveal himself.

Nicholas strained his eye but couldn't make anything out.

"Look, I want to see, I want to believe," Nicholas cried out, his voice carrying across the bedroom.

He stretched out his hand and felt his arm go cold above the blankets.

"I need a night-shirt."

"Who told you that you were naked?" asked the angel, pulling a vest over Nicholas' head.

"He gave me fruit from the tree," explained Nicholas.

"Oh, shit!" he heard himself say. He pushed himself up in the bed. His hand was wet.

Nicholas was no stranger to excitement. In the Fourth Week of his 30-day silent retreat the previous year he had felt the presence of the Holy Spirit who revealed to him in meditation that the Lord had risen. Nicholas had set out to tell the people of Belfast that all would be well, for the Lord had risen, allelulia, allelulia! As he watched himself run along the narrow streets that were familiar to him as a child, he was filled with joy, and the Holy Spirit entered him. His penis went hard. He was in a state of utter sexual ecstasy, without having a single sexual thought. The Holy Spirit had locked into him, arousing and exciting him, as he placed his hand on his sinewy soul. He had discovered his sexual self. *The God under my skin. The Holy Spirit's resting place. Life at its most creative, warmest, natural, affirming. Resurrection. ERECTION!*

He carefully rested his hand on the duvet. God was very close to him just as he had been on retreat. In his dream the Angel of the Lord had led him into a deeper freedom symbolised in the way he had brought him out of the darkness into the light. But what was that freedom? He hadn't the foggiest. He pulled back the blankets to inspect the damage. The thought that moments like these made celibacy bearable crossed his mind but he quickly banished it from his head.

Shortly before one o'clock the next day, Nicholas made his way to the end of the garden to fetch Jack for lunch. This time he knocked and waited.

"Are you right, Jack?" he called in to him from the doorstep.

"Yes, come in just a wee sec!" said Jack, opening the door.

"Well, did you sleep okay? Is that bed okay?" asked Nicholas relieved that Jack was dressed.

"Thanks. Yep, but it's not the bed that's the problem, uncle Jack, it's me back."

"Oh, yes, now when I think of it. I found this in my bathroom this morning," he said, taking a bottle of aromatherapy oil from his pocket. "A sister I give spiritual direction to gave me this ages ago but I never got around to using it. She says it's brilliant for relaxing the body. I'm not sure why she gave it to me. It's not like I'd have any use for it myself. But, anyway, I was thinking this morning you might like it," explained Nicholas.

"What do you do with it?" asked Jack.

"You rub it on your back apparently. If you like I can put some on for you, if you want, like, if you thought it might help, like," said Nicholas.

"Aye, no probs. Lash some on now will you for me? It's killing me."

Nicholas checked his watch. They still had a few minutes to spare before grace before meals began. "Lie down there, will, and I'll see."

Jack lay down on the bed, pulling his shirt up at the back.

"Em, maybe you should take the shirt off altogether, Jack. It'd be easier to apply, and it'll only get messy anyhow, son."

"Oh, right. Well, can you help me get it off?"

"Yeah, let me see."

Nicholas carefully pulled his tee-shirt up over his head from behind. Jack drew a sharp breath as it rubbed up against his neck where they had stubbed cigarettes.

"Oh, sorry! Did I hurt you?" asked Nicholas.

"This better be worth it!" replied Jack, putting on a brave face.

His shirt off, Jack lay down flat on the top of the sheets.

"It's the least I can do for you Belfast ones," said Nicholas as he poured some oil onto his left hand. He rubbed his hands together and placed them on Jack's upper back, spreading the oil around in two circles on either shoulder blade. "How does that feel?" he asked him.

"Aye, that's lovely. It's really soo...soothing."

Encouraged, Nicholas slowly moved his hands down towards his lower back. "My own back is killing me," said Nicholas. "Must be the angle." He was stretching across the bed to Jack's right side as he stood up.

"Wait a minute!" he said. He knelt down on the floor, taking care not to touch the duvet with his oily hands. "There, that's better. I've never done this before. How am I doing?"

"Cracker! Are you sure you are alright there, uncle Nicholas?"

"Yeh. No, well, actually, maybe I should kneel on the bed, to be honest. This is doing my back in big time."

"Okey, dokey. Whatever you want. I'm happy," Jack consented.

Nicholas took off his shoes and knelt beside Jack on the bed. He reached over him to get the bottle of oil from the bedside table, prepared his hands and began applying the oil again to his upper back. As the rhythm of Jack's breathing got slower, Nicholas moved his hands along his bare arms then back towards the nape of his neck where he rubbed his shaven hairline. Jack sighed with pleasure and Nicholas' hands slid further upwards along the back of his head. Jack sighed with gratitude. In response, Nicholas glided his hands along his spine to his trouser line and massaged him there. Jack moved his lower body in and out at the hips and almost without thinking Nicholas slipped his fingers beneath the trouser line. He felt the rise of Jack's buttocks and heard a voice, "How, how does that feel?" "Mmmmh," Jack purred. Allowing Nicholas no time to think, he pulled him down towards his pillow.

"For Belfast," said Jack, moving Nicholas' hand towards his hard, and kissing him on the upper lip.

Nicholas felt his lips respond in spite of himself, kissing Jack slowly at first, then with increasing speed as Jack pressed his body against his. He felt Jack's tongue on his and experienced an excitement that he had hitherto only known in prayer. He sat up. Frightened, Jack opened his eyes; it was okay—Nicholas was only undressing. He lay down again, pressing his body fully against Jack's, resting his lips on his mouth as he unzipped him. With difficulty, Jack lifted his leg over Nicholas' hip and Nicholas pulled at his boxers while Jack in turn tugged at Nicholas' Y fronts, searching for the python within. It was already wet. His hand slid along him, and Nicholas remembered his dream and wept. "My Lord and my God!" he cried out repeatedly as his candle fired, then flickered.

"Will you do it for me now?" asked Jack.

On release, Jack wept with delight, his tears falling on Nicholas' fingers which caressed his cheeks. He observed his foot move along Nicholas' side and left buttock, hip and then thigh. Nicholas moved closer still.

"Now, I know why she gave you that oil. I think maybe you've found your vocation," Jack hypothesised.

They giggled like children.

Nicholas bathed and dressed Jack. Things were different between them now. There was no embarrassment. Nicholas sensed from the way Jack had held him and the manner in which he was now so free with him that Jack knew Nicholas cared deeply about him. He was glad he had gone with what Jack had wanted and needed, a conviction that was strengthened when moments later Jack fell fast asleep at his side.

That night when Nicholas carried out his examination of conscience in his room, he faithfully, if with some trepidation, brought his encounter with his nephew to the Lord. Dispensing with the formalities of quietening himself down, he got straight to the point.

"Listen, Lord, Jack is lonely. He's my nephew. You know he's been through a hard time. He needs love and support. I could hardly refuse it, could I? Is that what you would have wanted of me? 'When I was sick, you visited me, when I was naked, you clothed me', isn't that what you said? How could I not have kissed his broken body, as Mary Magdalene kissed yours? I bathed his wounds like Veronica bathed yours. I clothed him. Isn't that love? Isn't that what you would have wanted? There was nothing in it for me. I'll look after him until he finds his feet. I'll hug him and hold him and be there for him. He needs me. I don't have a heart of stone. Would you want that? I know you understand me. He has been through hell in Belfast. I could hardly stand idly by, refusing him the first bit of warmth that he has had since them thugs beat the living daylights out of him. No, I acted in good faith. Sure, Jack himself said "For Belfast!" I've done my, my bit for the Catholic community. You know my rising and my sitting, my waking and my sleeping. You knit me together in my mother's womb. You know everything about me. You know that I love you, Lord."

"Feed my sheep!" said the Lord.

"Yes, Lord. I will. I will look after Jack till he feels better."

A smile traced itself on Nicholas' lips as Jack's body came into focus. His thoughts turned to the crucified Christ once more.

"It's you that I want. I want to follow you, Lord Jesus," Nicholas prayed.

At breakfast in the community house, Jack was anxious to establish that Nicholas was still there for him.

"Nicholas, are you okay about...?"

"Ssshh! Come over this way!" Nicholas said, directing him out of earshot of the other community members. "About, about yesterday, you mean?" he asked, as he helped himself to milk from the fridge.

Jack nodded.

"Yep, I'm on board, Jack. I told you you could count on me for as long as you need me."

"Yes, but what will the others think?" Jack asked as Nicholas poured milk into Jack's teacup.

"The others? The community, you mean? They don't need to know," Nicholas whispered, taking a seat at a nearby table.

"I know, but like where does it leave you like?" Jack persisted. As he sat down he lost his balance before touching down on the chair. He had expected it to be higher and the extra few inches had left him in free-fall. Nicholas seemed not to notice his distress.

"What do you mean? We haven't done anything wrong, Jack. You are needy at the minute, I'm your uncle, and I care about you. I haven't done anything wrong. It's not like I've committed a sin or anything, if that's what you mean." Nicholas proceeded to put two sugars in Jack's tea as Jack tried to put words on his fears.

"Yeah, but what about your, what do you call it, promises?"

"Vows!" Nicholas corrected him. "What about them? Did I win the lotto or something, or refuse orders? And to be frank, Jack, I'm celibate still, technically speaking like. Like, we didn't do you know what, if you see what I mean. It's not like having sex with a woman," he said, stirring Jack's tea.

"Exactly, that's my point, Nicholas. Surely, that's even worse in their book?"

Nicholas stopped stirring and held the spoon in Jack's cup. "Look, I, we did nothing…nothing illegal. Didn't you say you are seventeen in a couple of days?"

"Oh, it's 17 down here, is it?" he asked, taking the cup in his hands. "In the North it's 18. You could face imprisonment in the Sex Counties, Nicholas."

"Well, thank God for the Border for once!" said Nicholas, glad that Jack was finally making light of things.

"Anyway, Jack, we aren't homosexuals, and we didn't do anything anyway, even if we were," Nicholas added.

"So, does that mean we can meet again tonight?" asked Jack, bringing the cup to his lips, forcing Nicholas to withdraw the spoon.

"Yes, and tomorrow night too, Jack, if you need me," said Nicholas as he began toying with the silver ring around his cloth napkin.

Jack visibly relaxed. It seemed Nicholas didn't have any problems with what had gone on between them, and he would still be there for him.

Over the following weeks life changed very little for Nicholas. Admittedly he bathed more than he used to, smelled of Jack's anti-perspirant, dressed a little differently, cooked the account books a bit more than before, and, tellingly, drank more alcohol than usual (stealing it form the sacristy), but he was convinced that no one in the community noticed, though now and then he thought he caught that look in the novice master's eye that said,

'There's something going on here!' At such times, Nicholas would ask him how his sick mother was. On that topic, Fr. Tim was easy to distract.

One night, about to sneak out to the pub for a drink with Jack, Nicholas found himself looking for a twenty pound note that his dad had sent him and which he had stashed away in a bag of clothes containing some things he had worn when he had first come to the novitiate with the prescribed single suitcase of belongings. As he rummaged for the money, he came across his old pair of jeans, and decided to wear them. The novice master didn't forbid jeans, but Nicholas had bagged them because everyone else wore slacks of one kind or another and he had wanted to fit in. He looked cool in them, he thought, as he zipped them up, and pressed his gusset into position. As he strutted down the avenue to meet Jack at the gate, he recalled the scene a fellow novice had created wearing red shorts to lunch. The novice master had called the offender to his room straight after the meal and told him to remove the shorts at once because his.... was too.... (he left the offences undeclared), and that was not appropriate given that the sisters sometimes joined them for meals.

"Snap!" said Jack, snapping Nicholas out of his day-dream.

"What? What are you on about?" asked Nicholas.

"Your jeans. They're the double of mine!"

"Oh, right," said Nicholas. Each day he had become more like Jack in one way or another.

Nicholas' visits to Jack became more frequent with the long summer evenings. Each of his visits was an opportunity to say a decade of the Rosary by the grotto of the Blessed Virgin for Jack's speedy recovery and, of course, for peace in Ireland—so much so that he soon confused the urge for sex with the urge to pray, a device which eased his fear of being found out. These were difficult days for the Peace Process: the IRA cease-fire was under pressure, and the impending Twelfth made things worse. Jack proposed spending the Twelfth on Dollymount Strand. It would do Nicholas good, for the North had taken up more and more of his air-time when they were in bed together.

"Seeing as I'm half Protestant anyway, you can hold my hand for the parade!" Jack quipped.

Nicholas laughed. He would 'celebrate' the Twelfth with him only on the condition that Jack wore red, white and blue, the "national colours".

* * *

"Jesus, isn't this sunshine just glorious? And aren't we dressed for it?" said Jack as he sprawled out alongside Nicholas on the sand.

"Yeah, I like the red cap and blue jeans. So, is it the Y-fronts that are white for the day that's in it?" said Nicholas.

"You're going to have to wait to find that out!" Jack teased him.

"Here! I hope to frig it's pissing out of the heavens up in Belfast. Nothing like a good downpour to dampen Orange spirits on the Twelfth! Speaking of which, what about a wee dip? Are you able and willing?" asked Nicholas.

"Aye, sure, why not? In for a penny, in for a pound," replied Jack.

They stripped off and ran into the sea in their underwear, splashing and kicking spume at each other and screaming as their warm bodies soaked up the cold sea. They swam out until Jack, exhausted, found support on a rock a little below the water-line. Nicholas came back to him, and together they leapt on and off the rock, swimming under water, like two seals, their squealing carrying across to the beach where the crowds were growing.

"White," remarked Nicholas, looking at Jack's underwear as he rested on the rocks. "So, more surprises later, I hope."

"Don't count your chickens before they're hatched," parried Jack.

"You know, there is something about water," continued Nicholas, his tone suddenly serious. "It's like, it's just so freeing, do you know what I mean, like? It's, it's erotic. It's what the Holy Spirit's like. The Spirit isn't fire, it's water."

"Yeah, right! What to fuck are you firing on, Father?"

"No, honestly," said Nicholas. "You'll understand some day—when you grow up!"

"Listen, Nick, if we don't get back soon, we'll be needing the Holy Spirit! Our things are about to be washed away. Look!" Jack was tired of spiritual conversation and the fact that the tide was coming in fast was convenient. "All good things have to come to an end, I suppose," he added before plunging into the water, briefly leaving Nicholas behind.

Back at the cottage they threw themselves down on the bed for a snooze but Jack couldn't settle. Afraid—though he couldn't fathom why—to ask him what was on his mind, Nicholas took to politics. It would kill the silence.

"So it looks like it's back to war, then, doesn't it? What did I tell you? The ceasefire won't last."

"Yeah, republicans can't wait to get back to doing the only thing they're good at—beating the crap out of people," said Jack leaping out of bed.

"What? What are you on about? Wait a while, Jack! Republicans don't want conflict. They don't want military conflict. They don't want dead bodies, towns bombed. They never have. They were forced into a military campaign in 1970 and now their hand's being forced all over again."

Jack opened the front door and peered up at the few streaks in an otherwise perfect panoply. "Yeah, right!" he commented standing with his back to Nicholas. A bee caught on the breeze swooshed upwards like a wingless embryo. *Beam me up, Scottie!* he thought.

"Look, Jack, you're too young to remember, but if it wasn't for the IRA, we'd have been slaughtered. No, the IRA has put the nationalist community back on the map. Wherever you go, you're recognised. 'Here come the Paddies'—that day's definitely gone. We have them running scared. We could grid-lock the whole of London, but that's not their style. A few good targets and we're home and dry. The only thing the Brits understand is brute force. The olde short, sharp shock! They invented it."

"So, tell me this, then, what is this peace-loving organisation doing beating the hell out of people like me for anyway? Explain that one to me!" Jack asked, flinging his bathing towel on the bathroom floor.

Drama queen, thought Nicholas. "I know they get it wrong sometimes. They're not saints, but...," he began.

"Oh, so that's it! 'Wrong sometimes'," Jack cut him short as he lay down on the bed again. "So in my case they got it wrong. And that makes it right, doesn't it? That's what you're saying, Nicholas!"

"No, Jack, I didn't say that! You're putting words in my mouth! They go over the top sometimes. There was no call for what they did on you. But, but you know as well as I do, Jack, the community is all for cracking down on anti-social behaviour. If the RUC aren't willing to do it—that lazy bunch of bastards—then somebody has to. I'm not saying they get it right all the time, but like what are people supposed to do? Put up with being tortured by hoods? Sure, joyriders fucking killed a child in West Belfast there a while back, and the very next week there was another gang of them out and they run over a young fella coming home after a hard day's work. There's no other way, Jack. You have to come down hard. The only thing that'll stop those boyos is the IRA. And the same goes for the druggies. I'm telling you, if you cut off their nuts and sent them in the post to a few of the ringleaders, they'd soon stop dealing, so they would."

Jack flinched. "That's a load of shit, Nicholas, and you know it. It's the IRA has the young people the way they are. They're the ones who are wheeling and dealing in plastic and drugs. Nothing gets done without their ones getting a cut. You can be sure of that. And what do their ones get? Beatings? Oh no, they get a week in the Canaries with the da and the ma, while the likes of me is put out of the country."

"Look, your da is a republican. Is he getting a cut, is he?"

"My da's an eejit, a fucking eejit. For one thing, he got caught. For another, he's a Protestant. How he ever ended up in the RA, I'll never know.

"Listen! Whether you like it or not, the IRA is non-sectarian."

"Give me a bucket!" said Jack, sticking two fingers into his mouth.

"I'm telling you, Jack, whether you accept it or not, the republican thing has never been sectarian. I mean, there may be individuals who have sectarian values, but that's another thing entirely. The IRA's approach has never been sectarian. Whoever wants to join up, can join. Your da's proof of that."

"Oh, so it's non-sectarian, is it? Well how come it stiffs so many Protestants?"

"Pardon me, Jack, but I don't know where you get that idea from. The IRA doesn't kill Protestants. It never has done—soldiers, police, UVF men, UDA men, aye. The fact that they are Protestant is neither here nor there. They could be Catholics and it wouldn't matter a damn. It's a political struggle, not a sectarian conflict. You've been watching too much BBC. All those funerals, 'He was just an ordinary Protestant going about his business', that's a load of crap, if there ever was. They are UVF men, Jack, and the families keep quiet about it. They keep the military trappings out of the picture because they're looking a claim."

"Ah, give my fucking head peace, Nicholas! I've heard it all now!"

"Right, so, we'll call it a day!" said Nicholas, slipping on his shoes. "Maybe I'll head back over to my place and give you some space. Seems like you've been wanting that all afternoon anyway."

"What do you mean?"

"Well, you couldn't wait to get away from me on the beach for one thing."

"What? Did I not say 'All good things have to come to an end', or what?" retorted Jack.

"Look, I know what you were thinking. Let's split for tonight. The rest will do us both good," said Nicholas.

"Nah, leave it. It's cool." Jack couldn't face being alone. "Sex, politics and religion. The three no nos! We have it all here in this very bed! Is it any wonder we end up arguing! You've probably had enough of me! It's my mixed background!"

"Stop that malarkey!" said Nicholas as Jack wrapped his legs around his to detain him in the bed. "You know," he continued, "I'll always be here for you as long as you need me. Until you get over all you've been through. After that, you can move on when it suits. You'll have to find a job, somewhere to live, and learn to cook, but I'm sure you'll manage."

Jack's smile died and Nicholas felt half sorry that he had mentioned the future—but only half. The thought that he could be there for him in his dark night of the soul consoled him. He kissed him.

"You've taken a terrible hammering and it'll be a while before you're back to yourself," said Nicholas, holding Jack's hand as he offered his damning prognosis.

Jack closed his eyes. Nicholas was right—things would be difficult. He had come to rely on him for so much, not just for accommodation and food, but for sex and, above all else, love. He had opened a whole new world to him. It would be hard to move on. How could he ever do it?

Chapter 7

Dara was a bolt out of the blue. Jack first set eyes on him on a choral youth project in Ballymun that, ironically, Nicholas had brought Jack to work on. His brown eyes, red hair, and scrawny frame were everything that Jack was not, and the attraction was immediate. While Nicholas was busy grooming the choristers in the church balcony, Jack was busy doing it with Dara in the vestry, the sacristy, and the chapel of repose. He was soul-searching, and Dara was fast becoming his soul mate. Jack soon discovered that he had a penchant for holy places which he had inherited from his grandfather, and his mother's predilection for smells—he burned incense while at it in the vestry. He was on the pig's back until that nostalgic knock at the door one day and the all too familiar incantation, "Oh, my God, oh, my God!" as Nicholas swept into the sacristy to fetch music sheets and found them at it. Without more ado, Nicholas retired to the balcony and had the boys sing 'Nearer my God to Thee', making them go over the words of the last line to the point of exhaustion, 'Sweet shall my weeping be, grief surely leading me nearer my God to thee, nearer to thee'.

Jack meanwhile assured a traumatised Dara that he was glad he wouldn't have to hide it from Nicholas anymore. Feeling exposed, Dara argued that doing it under Nicholas' nose was asking for trouble in the first place: it was like Jack wanted Nicholas to know or even that Nicholas' presence did it for him, which only proved that Jack hadn't left him behind. Jack pilloried his "psychobabble" and told him to cut the crap: Dara's nose was plainly out of joint because he had got a kick out of doing it in a Church that had ostracised gay men, and he would now have to find another venue.

Nicholas deemed that if Jack were well enough to fuck in church, he was well enough to fuck off, though he didn't quite say as much, that being too unchristian. Instead, on his way home from choir practice, he painfully compressed his feelings into manageable amounts. "Jack, maybe, maybe, maybe, you see, maybe what you need more than, I mean, more than anything else is to be with young people, I mean, somewhere where there's a bit more life, like. I mean, I've been thinking about this for some time now. I mean, the thing is, it's only natural that the thing, the cottage should get to you, I mean, with all the retreatants and everything walking around all day in silence. What do you think yourself? I mean, I think I've done as much as I can for you to be honest. What do you think?"

Jack knew jealousy when he saw it—even if Nicholas was oblivious to it—and he was glad to be going. His sixth sense told him—and Nicholas could deny it if he wanted—that Nicholas wanted rid of him. His going on about how great the IRA was was meant to drive a wedge between them. There was no point in reacting now though. He would mirror Nicholas' insincerity.

"Wee buns! I think you're right. You've been so good to me, so, so generous. I mean, it would be wrong of me to stay when you've done so much for me already," said Jack, rubbing his nose as if striking a match.

Dara could offer him a bed. A job would be easy enough to find.

That night, sensing the end was nigh, Jack, in his penury, took advantage of the novitiate abundance, packed away some fruit from the refectory, took some soap and shampoos from the pantry, helped himself to fifty pound from the community float, writing it down as expenses for stamps, and made one last free phone-call to his mother in Belfast.

"Ma, it's me, Jack."

"It's you, Jack. God, do you know what? I was only just thinking of you a moment ago when I was pouring myself out a cup of Earl Grey your grandad bought for me when he was away in Lourdes that time, and I was saying to myself, I must give Jack a wee ring."

"Isn't that funny, now?" said Jack. His mother was always just about to phone him, and Jack was always willing to flatter her illusion.

"Yes. Do you know? I was just saying to your father yesterday up on the visit that I hadn't heard from you since that time you were at the beach with uncle Nicholas. Wasn't that really good of him to bring you, wasn't it?"

"Yep. You know uncle Nicholas, he can never do enough for you."

"He was always the same. Sure, you were a child and probably don't remember but you know when uncle Damien died, Nicholas looked after you like a sore thumb while granny and me looked after the funeral arrangements, but, sure, you wouldn't remember that."

"I must ask him about that. Ma…"

"Yeah, I'm telling you."

"Ma, em, you know, Nichol…"

"Son, do you know who's after dying? I knew I had something to tell you. That's what it was. That's what I wanted to ring you about. You know the MacHendersons from the back road?"

"Who?"

"Mrs. MacHenderson. She flitted up to Andytown in 1970. You know who I mean. You know, remember the old lady that used to work in Gilmartin's of a Saturday, the one who always had her hair up in a bun. You know who I'm talking about, Jack, she was a quare fine looking woman, lovely features, and she had the wee boy that was lifted that time the Army raided Maguires and the old grandfather had a heart attack. You know who I'm talking about, she lived beside old da Murray who used to work in the school?"

"What school?" asked Jack, snared.

"St. Mary's."

"Oh, Mr. Murray, the teacher?"

"No, no, not him—his da. You know, the aul' fellow that used to run after yous with the brush when you and Mitchell were playing soccer. Do you mind soccer wasn't allowed in the school? Mind you, that's all gone now. You know, you can play whatever you like. Sure, haven't they got an RUC Gaelic football team now, with all that bloody Good Friday Agreement stuff? Next thing you know they'll be handing us back the GAA football pitch in Crossmaglen."

"Don't you know!"

"Aye, anyway, Jack, what was I saying?"

"You were saying about…"

"God, do you know, son, I must be losing it? Your da laughs at me sometimes. Did I tell you I was up to see him yesterday and they're talking of an amnesty. Like, not tomorrow, like, but just the same! God only knows where I'll put him, though, when he gets out! How are you managing, Jack? Have you enough to do you? If you're short, will you ask uncle Nicholas to see you right till the end of the week till I get my social security. I'll post it down to you. It's worth more down there."

"No, ma, I'm okay for the moment. I want for nothing. But, ma, there is something…"

"Anyway, what was I saying? Oh, aye, poor Mrs. MacHenderson. And do you know what happened her eldest fella too? Did I not tell you? You know, her son from her first marriage—the wee fellow who broke his collar-bone that time doing the Grand National over the back hedges and ended up in hospital for five days. Do you 'member? Had to get stitches out of his arm too but couldn't get down to the Royal that morning because that was the time they let them two British soldiers out of prison early, and the rioters did six million pounds of damage. You remember, don't you? That whole carry on! They shot that wee girl Reilly. You should have seen the state of that Andytown Road last week. It's a bloody disgrace! Honest to God, it would get you down!"

"Ma, one of the Fathers wants to use the phone," he lied. There was no point in trying any more. He hadn't wanted to tell her everything at the one go. But at least she could have done with knowing that he was leaving the novitiate.

"Oh, right, son. It must be something important. God, I'm glad you rang now, son. I was worried about you, you know. I was wondering how you were getting on. The things you hear about Dublin. You'd take your life in your hands just to go to the shop for a bottle of milk down there. And they think we're bad up here! There's more murders down there than you'd ever get up here in a month of Sundays. It's shocking like. What's the world coming to? But still and all, you're as well out of it up here, son."

"Ma, I'd better go."

"Oh, yes, son. God, you're awful good to phone your aul' ma. Sure, maybe I'll give you a wee tinkle this weekend to see how you're doing. But I hate giving those priests the run around. I have to try out my new mobile phone. Will you tell uncle Nicholas I was asking for him? I hope he's over the cold he had the other day. There's a terrible dose doing the rounds. Your father's dying with it. The doctor gave him…."

"Ma, I'd better go now!"

"Oh, right, son. Mind yourself now. And love to Nicholas."

"Bye, Ma."

"Bye, bye, bye, bye, bye. God bless. And thanks for ringing, son. Oh, and granddad sends his love."

"Thanks, Ma. Bye." Jack put down the receiver. She was like a broken record, forever going on about the same old things. He would have to tell her about Nicholas and him another time, if he could ever get a word in edgeways. She had her life down to a fine art, sorted—that was the problem.

* * *

Jack left the cottage while Nicholas was at community Mass. As he nipped by the chapel window, he could hear Nicholas pray.

"I just want to thank you Lord for Jack's speedy recovery, and I ask you to keep him close to you over the next while. Lord hear us!"

"Lord graciously hear us!" prayed the fellow novices.

Jack's pace quickened as he saw the gate come into view. It would not be long now until he could put the episode with Nicholas behind him: he had made a mistake. He had really thought it could last, even if it had to be on the QT, but he had come to realise that for Nicholas, God came first, and he—Jack— wanted more. Dara had more to offer.

After Mass, Nicholas ostensibly went out to sweep the first of the autumn leaves off the grass, but his real intention was to see if there was any movement about Jack's place. He hadn't shown for breakfast. After sweeping for a few minutes in the vicinity, he made his way closer to the criss-cross windows of the old cottage and ventured a peek. He was nowhere to be seen. He knocked on the door and walked in. The bed was stripped, and Jack's things were gone. The very towels had been taken. Nicholas stood rooted to the ground, his chin on the back of his hands resting on the brush. This was the day he had been working towards, but now he could scarcely take it in.

He must have stood there five minutes before finding his feet. He sat down outside on the rusted bench under the windowsill. Everything moves on, he thought, as he looked at the autumnal scene before him. He had had a life before Jack, and there was life after Jack too. He had things to do: leaves to sweep, a prayer diary to write, a choir to get into shape. He had seen tougher times through. Things would never be the same again, but, sure, things were always never the same again. Each day brought new challenges, new worries, and he wasn't alone. The Lord walked with him. He had been called to do great things, and he would do them if his superiors saw fit to send him back to the North to work with the Jacks and Mrs. McCaffertys of Belfast. He had to go on. The Lord was doing something new (Isaiah 43:19). "Can't you see it?" a voice asked as he dragged his feet to the cottage door for one last look into the abyss of his past.

The novice master had seen a thing or two. Nicholas had taken to tight jeans and loose shirts, and Jack's foraging in the kitchen and the pantry the night before had not gone unnoticed, not to mention the wash he had put on after ten in the evening when lights were meant to be out. Something was up.

"Nicholas, is there anything you would care to talk about? Is something troubling you?" the novice master asked at lunch.

Nicholas couldn't hold back. "Actually, I meant to say, but Ja…, Jack has left. He had a chance of a job on the Northside, and the gaffer asked him to start right away. He said to say thanks to the community for all your help, and to tell you he'd call in again to see you as soon as the job settled down."

"Oh, oh, my goodness, that was rather sudden. Are you certain he will be fine?"

"Yeah, he'll be okay."

"May the road rise before him! And how are you in yourself? You will miss him, I imagine. Please God, this time next week, it'll all be behind you. Why not take the afternoon off and maybe take a jaunt into the city? You could take the bus fare from the kitty, and take a few bob extra for a coffee."

Novices were scarce, and he was not about to run Nicholas out of town because of his demeanour. That panting down by Our Lady's grotto must have been the Brent geese back in from Canada for the winter, he thought. Early, this year.

* * *

Kathleen had been grinding her teeth in her sleep ever since the fateful call from Nicholas on her birthday two months earlier when he had announced that Jack had decided it was time to move on and had left without a forwarding address. Then—could it have been a week later?—Nicholas rang to say he had jacked in—those were his very words—religious life. One look and the dentist decided that Kathleen needed a big job done. Crossing and uncrossing her feet, she groaned, trying to keep her mouth open for him as he waved the needle in his hand like a conductor's wand, humming along to 'O, Mio Babbino Caro' on the radio. Irritated by her fidgeting, he briefly interrupted his performance. "I'm almost there," he said through his gauze mask, the strain of having to communicate with his patient written like sheet music on his forehead.

Well, you certainly aren't here—the Albert Hall more likely, thought Kathleen. And by the looks of things the concert's far from over the way you're pulling on that dickey bow now.

She switched to tapping her feet, whereupon the dentist pulled his gauze down, forming a hammock for his chin, and following the rhythm of the music as good as sang,

> Do you know what, Mrs. Lackey?
> Never in all my life
> have I seen such a small jaw!
> Open up now a bit more
> till I see what is going on.
> Open up wide now
> as you can!

On the last bar, a pain shot along Kathleen's jawbone into her neck and her body lifted off the chair. He pushed her backwards to prevent her head from hitting the overhead lamp, but she leaped up again. This time he was ready for her and pinned her down in a manner reminiscent of his rugby days.

"Did I, did I do...„? Eh, did I hit a nerve?" he spluttered, bringing the gauze up over his head as his assistant ducked to avoid being gouged.

"Papa, pietà, pietà! Don't go away now, folks! We'll be back with more delights after this short break," the DJ reassured his listeners.

"No, yea.., I, my, the buns, it's, they'll, they'll, it's in the, the, they're in the oven. Christ! The house!" Kathleen stammered, her voice muffled by the anaesthetic. She flung her protective shades at the dental assistant, who once more ducked, then extracted herself from the chair and scarpered downstairs. She would save her home, all her bits and pieces, no matter what. At the No. 87 bus-stop she soon found herself dismissing the fact that the transfer to the No.12 in the city centre would add close on fifty minutes to her journey. The walk at the other end would be shorter, even if the 73A was more direct. And sure, the Union Jack flying from the Ulster Hospital was cause for hope: there was barely any wind— the house would hardly go up like straw. The dental assistant caught up with her just as she was about to board the bus and draped her coat over her arm.

She continued to regain her calm nicely on the upper deck of the No. 87 until the neon shop signs suddenly became unhinged and their kaleidoscopic inferno licked at the windows. Holding on to her seat she shut her eyes to quench the flames. When she finally opened them she didn't dare look up. Forcing her eyes to avoid the black cigarette burns and pink bubble gum on the floor, she sucked in its deep green then, flapping her hands, directed its rubbery incense all over her as if cleansing herself with smoke from a temple fire, begging cactuses, palm trees and rainforests to stay with her till the bus reached the terminus.

On the No. 12, everything, including her vision, became clear. Her life was written large on almost every shop front, every street corner. All her days it had stared her in the face but she had been blind to it: Melady's GROSSeries, *what did he do on me?* St. Damnknicks, *leave them on me, please, this time!* menSWEAR, *could you just keep your bloody voice down?* GIVE WAY, *what the fuck did I do?* BeechMOUNT, *he, he rode* meeee, STALKman's Lane, *let me go*, Tyres and Exhausts, *Oh, God, why me?* I scream 99's, *please, please, oouch!! IN, OUT,* SINclair's, *but it wasn't my fault, it wasn't, sure it wasn't,* 'bacon FRANK'S SAUSAGE', *for fucksake! The Busy B.* She fled the bus, trying to ignore the feel of her thighs rubbing against each other, but rushing past the Hunting Lodge, her past struck her with a vengeance: *he hunted me and fucking lodged! Buns in the fucking oven? Fucking me, he was!*

She shouldered the back door of her home and bolted towards the oven which she switched on, adjusting the dial—seven, four, five, six, eight, nine—registering the lost years of her childhood. She fetched her favourite mug—the one with the heart with the arrow through it—from the shelf above the sink, kicked off her stilettos to let her feet breathe, drew up a chair and let the oven door down like a drawbridge. The gas transported her on an Atlantic breeze. She was back on Croagh Patrick on pilgrimage.

'This is fucking stupid! Should have left this coat behind. I'm boiling here! Breathe in, breathe out.' And then her mother's voice enveloped her like mist. "I'm going to stick my head in the oven this day and be rid of the lot of yous, for yous never give me a moment's peace morning, noon and night!" "'Here, somebody give her another shilling there for the gas-box, will ye?'" Frank's voice came in off the sea.

The smell of gas irritated Kathleen's nose and mouth, but she soon forgot about her coat and the voices in her head as she drifted in and out of consciousness. The back door whined.

"Yo ho! Are you there? Did the milkman come to you today, Mrs. Lackey?" It was Mrs. Diamond. She was forever "borrowing" alimentation in amounts that could never be returned—"a spoonful of sugar to make the medicine go down", "a half a tomato till the pension", "the heel of the loaf till the shop opens."

"Jesus bless us! Kathleen!" she screamed.

Mrs. Diamond was never the same again: in the twenty years she had been living next door to Kathleen she had never called her anything other than 'Mrs. Lackey', and her breach of neighbourly contract shook her to the core. Thinking on her feet—*you may as well be hung for a lamb as a sheep*—she called Kathleen's name again to make it appear that using it hadn't taken a feather out of her, and Kathleen's head flopped back and to the side as if she were hitching a lift to anywhere but here. (In the event, it was this second utterance that Mrs. Diamond subsequently regretted the more. The irony, of course, was that Kathleen took neither of them in.) Mrs. Diamond drew up alongside her, blaring, "Jesus, Mrs. Lackey, those friggers from the Northern Ireland Gasworks didn't leave you in that state, did they? Jesus Christ, Mrs. Lackey, you'd wanna get back on to them'uns! Thon's a bloody scandal!" Thus, twice emboldened, with a degree of discretion befitting her station as a long-time neighbour, she determined the shape of Mrs. Lackey's future with a discreet flick of the oven switch that, to Kathleen's naked—bleary—eye seemed accidental.

"Mrs. Lackey," Mrs. Diamond croaked through her fingers, "I hate to ask you, but could I borrow a wee sup of milk till the milkman comes in the morning? Do you 'member I was telling you Dr. Magee was on to me about the Complan to build myself up? There's no need for a whole bottle now. A wee drop'll do the job. It's not the same when you make it with water, you know yourself."

Kathleen gasped, mildly aware that she was being spoken to.

"A wee drop of milk," Mrs. Diamond repeated, swallowing her shame, which always left her mouth dry. She licked her lips.

"Wait, wait a wee minute till I see!" said Kathleen, finding her feet like a newborn foal.

At the sight of her rummaging around in the fridge for her out of breath, Mrs. Diamond couldn't help getting personal. "Mrs. Lackey, I know it's none of my business, but honest to God, would you not be better giving them fags up altogether?"

"What? Aye! They're a bloody curse! Will this be enough to do you?" she asked, shaking a half-empty bottle at eye level like a chemist running a test.

"Ach, you've far too much there. Half of that again'll do!" insisted Mrs. Diamond.

"No, honestly. Sure, look, here, take it for goodness sake. There's nothing as bad as Complan made with water."

"Are you sure?" Mrs. Diamond protested for the sake of form. "I'll get it back to you first thing."

Mission accomplished, Mrs. Diamond withdrew to the other side of the garden fence. She would stick some sugar in her Complan. She needed it.

* * *

No matter how much Nicholas had prayed in the days following Jack's disappearance, he had been unable to get it together. Then, when the novice master informed him that the Provincial felt that he would be better spending the next two years teaching in one of the order's private schools in Dublin, he felt the ground give way beneath him. He had joined to bring peace to the North, not to educate the spawn of the rich south of the Border. The chances of the wealthy looking after the poor (as his superiors held) were as improbable as British withdrawal from the occupied Six Counties. He had to leave. It was a matter of conscience. He was not leaving for Jack. The evening before he scrambled over the novitiate wall, he got down on his knees in the oratory for the last time. The solemn tone of his voice surprised him as he began to pray and however much he coughed, it refused to shift.

"Lord, I am not a homosexual." He stopped. Someone was at the door. No, he had gone into the sacristy. "I only offered to massage his back," he continued, whispering now. "It was just the way it happened. If he hadn't have pulled me down on to the pillow, I would never have kissed him. Not on your Nelly! Kiss a man! Are you mad? I could live celibacy any day, Lord. That's not the issue. I lived it for you in prison, didn't I? And I'm not leaving for a relationship either. I didn't join up for sex, and I'm not leaving for sex. I could have had all the sex I wanted before coming in here. You know that. You know me better than I know myself. No, I am leaving to follow you in the North, not for someone to hold me down below. No, I could never leave to love someone, when I am called to love everyone. I'll leave on my road to Jerusalem when the time is right. I know St. Ignatius taught us to make a decision in consolation, not in desolation. I will wait. I'll, I'll ask for time out. Time out."

By the time he reached the privacy of his room, he was already chewing on the inside of his cheeks and having serious doubts about having been so candid with the Lord. No, he would stay, no matter what the cost. Religious life wasn't that bad. Maybe it wasn't the ideal place for intimacy, but things weren't as off the wall as they had once been. It was no longer the world of 'no particular friendships', where novices could never meet in twos but were, instead, obliged to walk in fours, two facing two, two going backwards while the other two moved forwards. True, the men it churned out were first and foremost strangers to themselves but the theory on intimacy had changed, and anyway how much intimacy did someone need? And *he* had changed. At least now he knew what he was giving up, and that could only stand him in good stead. Jesus, too, had faced temptation in the desert. And, sure, the apostolate to Jack had been a once-off affair. It made no odds if the brethren in community could never understand his Christ-centred love for him. They didn't have to know. He had jumped the gun a bit, rushed in a little too fast maybe, but Jesus would understand because he had almost succumbed to temptation that time in the desert himself.

And so Nicholas was as shocked as the next one when he found himself that same night making a run for it. His legs impelled him to go for it. Discernment of the spirits was not an option. They would read about him some day in The Irish Times, when he had sorted the Northern problem out, or himself, whichever proved the easier. He put his right hand up on the top of the wall, straight into the tar that lined it. Jack had joked once after jumping it on his return from a late night out on the town that the tar was there to keep people in, not to keep people out. He had laughed then, but now cursed his forgetfulness and burst into tears.

Nicholas needed respite, and found it in a house in Dublin's Northside looking after the house of a lady whose son was in the choir in Ballymun. While the landlady was abroad, he fended off potential robbers for free, kept himself to himself, and kept himself intact. It was essential to purify himself for his return to the North. When she landed home her loyal tenant gave her an update on all the phone-calls there had been for her in her absence.

"Oh, and there was a call from someone called Peter. He said he used to live here before and he said to tell you he was thinking of moving back in," Nicholas explained as he peered up at her on the landing.

Little did he realise that his days were numbered, and he only trying to be helpful.

"Oh, Peter. He was so good to Max when he was here. Max was before your time. You know, the night Max died, I called Peter on the mobile and he came flying over. Max had cancer. The night he died, he could hardly make it up to the toilet. Actually, he peed right there where you're standing. And then, he only got as far as the bedroom. He got in to bed beside me and before I knew what was happening, he died of a massive heart attack."

"Poor thing!" said Nicholas. It was the best he could do, the notion of someone dying in the house unnerving him.

"Peter buried him in the garden. That's why the roses there bloom twice a year," she added.

"Uh, what?" Nicholas' jaw dropped. "You buried him in the garden? God, uh, why didn't you say? Uh, I could have…"

And just as Nicholas was about to offer to look after the grave, he collapsed laughing on the floor to the landlady's horror.

"What? Don't you know some people are very good to their dogs?" she asked.

By the time Nicholas found his voice again, it was too late.

"You, you thought that I was sleeping with some man! Nicholas Dunne! What kind of a woman do you think I am? How dare you!" she cried out with all the Catholic indignation she could muster in the back of her throat.

"Look!" Nicholas began his defence, "If you had have said 'Blackie' or 'Rex', it would never have entered my mind that you…" He stopped short of committing the offence again. "Look, I know you're not that type of person, no more than myself," he remonstrated.

"Listen, Nicholas, to be fair, that's where you're wrong. I don't know how to say this but from what I hear, we aren't in the same category at all," she said, stomping off to leave him to minister to his wounds.

It was like a dagger. Dara had been talking, that much was clear. He sped off to his room, crawled into bed and soon rewarded himself. He longed for Jack.

Precisely forty-eight hours later, still raw from her encounter with Nicholas, the landlady reappeared to announce from on high that Peter was moving back in and that Nicholas had to go by the end of the week. Nicholas packed up that night, and hit the road again, having helped himself to a bottle of whiskey and a bottle of vodka from her drinks cabinet, and whatever loose change he could find around the house. He moved about Dublin over the next few months, overstaying his welcome with churchy friends.

One night in early December he had taken out his journal and made an entry for the first time since Jack had left him:

I know that I did the right thing. It wasn't failure. It just didn't work out. It wasn't a mistake to enter, and it wasn't a mistake to leave. I had what it took, but they wouldn't make use of it. I was priest material. The Lord called me out to be faithful to his vision for me. Life is even tougher now. Now I live real poverty. No more silverware for me, no dinners on the table, no castle to come home to. No, I made the right decision. It wasn't easy leaving, but it was right. I didn't fail. I can still make a difference in the North.

It was the season of goodwill, and he had wanted to be upbeat.

* * *

Kathleen turned the key on the latch and let herself in, safe in the knowledge that Frank would be at the pub for his Thursday binge.

"Mummy, are you there?" she called out, tip-toeing on the newspapers which Benny had laid out over the wet linoleum.

"Mummy?" she called again, bereft. There was no reply but she continued, the sound of her voice bringing life to the house and tempering the self-hatred that had overwhelmed her since Mrs. Diamond had earlier left with milk for the supper.

Upstairs, Kathleen trampled the carpet on the landing, thread-bare from Benny's invocations before the statue of Our Lady of Perpetual Succour. 'You flirted with him, led him on, you must have done something to deserve it, it takes two to tango, you asked for it!' The violence of the imaginary voice startled her. 'Kids don't know any better!' a child's voice reverberated in her defence. The knot in her throat told her that this one was hers. 'It takes one to know one!' Benny's voice shot back. A shadow emanated from the box-room and she scuttled back downstairs. It was as if he were coming for her now all over again.

The smell of furniture polish, detergent from the kitchen, and Brasso from the fireplace blended together and appeased her scat-tered senses. Benny had always been freaky about cleanliness. Kathleen had complained to her once about her obsession. That was the only time her father had hit her. He punched her on the face so hard that she fell to the ground. Benny had stood there by the Super Ser watching her pick herself up. "Don't you ever speak to your mother like that again," Frank screamed at her.

The phone rang; she let it ring out. She would wait for Benny's return. Rotating her bracelet she rehearsed her confrontation with Benny. "Mummy, you must have known what he was doing to me. You must have known. He abused me under your nose. You knew, didn't you?' And then the memories struck her like hail.

He smoothed her hair with the palm of his wet hand, followed the line of her nose with his thumb, then pulled her against him on the steps of the pool.

"Go on, give me one of your koala-bear hugs!" he said.

She put her arms around his neck, and legs around his torso and squeezed him.

"You're so special, so special to me," he whispered in her ear.

Placing her hands on his mouth, she resisted his kisses as she had done so many times before in fun.

"And what's going on down there?" he joked, feeling himself get big.

She jerked. He held her tight for fear she would fall, tugged at his togs and released his penis. She giggled. He took it as a sign to press ahead. Gently lifting her up on to it he kissed her again, as a father might tenderly kiss his daughter, her cheeks now those of a clown. He slipped it away, neatly fixed her bathing costume into place again, wrapped her in her big, pink bath-towel that lay at the edge of the pool, and carried his princess to the grassy bank.

Another scene: Benny had gone next door to borrow a hot water bottle. When she returned she opened her bedroom door to find her on the bed red-faced and breathless, and Frank bouncing up and down beside her. They were "trampolining," he explained.

"Look at the state of my bed!" Benny complained.

Another night, Kathleen had heard her mother and father trampolining in their bedroom and had gone into them complaining of a toothache. A sore tooth, my hat, Benny shouted at her! There was damn all wrong with the wee cat according to Benny. She was to get back into bed. Frank took a different view. He knew that what ailed her was jealousy and he called her over and showered her with kisses. Benny stormed out of bed. She was a spoiled wee bitch.

Another memory: this time she vomited. Seeing her pallor, Benny laughed at the sight of her, and plucked her cheeks to bring her back to life.

"If I had known you were bad, I wouldn't have set foot in the bingo hall! Say 'Ahhh.' Open up wide now as you can!"

Kathleen stuck out her tongue.

"God, but you're all red! You must be coming down with something."

"It's been on her for days," said Frank, appearing downstairs with a box of Maltesers he had bought for Marlene and which he handed to Kathleen.

"That's for being such a good girl," he said, patting her on the head. Kathleen's eyes lit up at the thought of Marlene's disappointment. "And what did you do to deserve those?" her mother asked.

Open up wide now as you can! She had been unable to get the words out of her head since her visit to the dentist's. They were the key to her Pandora's box.

Benny ambled by the window. She had her head-scarf on, and the sight of it caused Kathleen to gag.

"Oh, you're there!" remarked Benny. It was an expression of surprise, devoid of surprise, as good as it got. "I caught the six o'clock. Wee Fr. Donovan. It's great: he has you in and out of Mass in no time. But it's terrible the way them McCanns from over the way always come in late and them'uns only live a stone's throw away. But sure that always seems to be the way, isn't it? The closer people are to the chapel, the more late they are."

Kathleen had never considered her mother warm. Her friends had always found Benny odd in that respect, but Kathleen told them it was just her mother's way. It didn't mean that her mother didn't love her. She had other ways of letting you know you mattered. She would dress you like a doll with clothes she had knitted, right down to their pyjamas. And she had even done the very same for Rosy and Jack. Then, when George had been arrested, she would think nothing of handing Kathleen a hundred pounds at Christmas. She would bring the money up to Kathleen's house on Christmas Eve when Frank was busy getting the turkey ready at home. She would lie to Frank, pretending that she was just away up to help Kathleen get the kiddies' stockings ready for Santa. He would not have approved of her generosity. It was Benny's way of telling Kathleen that she loved her as much as, if not more than, Frank did. Benny would count the money out like a payroll mistress, and although fiercely independent, Kathleen would take it—Christmas without a man about the house was tough. Besides, Benny's gift brought her the added pleasure of being able to do without a hamper from the Society of St. Vincent de Paul which helped her out the rest of the year.

Benny slipped her prayer-book under the television, then tilting her head in the mirror removed her head-scarf which she folded and placed in the empty fruit bowl on top of the china-cabinet. Returning to the mirror, she cupped her hands and pushed her perm up from behind. Though her face was deeply wrinkled, nothing could take away from its fine Bambi structure that she now admired.

Kathleen could take no more of her preening.

"Mu...mummy, I need to talk to you. Will you sit down?"

Benny switched on the television and stood with her hands crossed at her waist, her tongue resting on her bottom lip as if about to receive communion. She hated being told what to do in her own house, and resisted her desire for a seat.

"Ma!"

"Let me get my coat off first. I'm only in across the door, like. Is it George again? Is it the Christmas visit?" she asked without waiting for a reply as she moseyed into the hall to hang up her coat.

Kathleen took her brief absence as an opportunity to speak without having to look her in the eye.

"Ma, it's da. Da, Da, he, he did it." She pushed back in the seat to steady herself.

"What? What are you on about? Your father did what?" Benny entered the room easing the fingers of her gloves off one at a time as if tuning an instrument.

"Da did it to me, ma. Da a...abused me."

Benny picked up the remote control. "What, what sort of bloody nonsense are you on about now, Kathleen?" she asked, flicking through the channels. "Jesus and all the saints preserve us this day!"

Taking two, Kathleen cast her eyes at the television. Her mother's words had sounded like a voice-over, but it was Benny alright, Benny with the whole world in her hands, Benny dispensing words of wisdom. Kathleen knew then what was coming.

"Your father never laid a hand on any of you. Maybe the odd clip around the ear sometimes, but...And me only out of Mass and here you have me taking the Lord's name in vain. I swear to God, if it's not one thing with you, it's another, Kate. You were always the same. In under of God, we're getting a bit too old for this. Go on! Go on!" she continued, now shouting at the television, "Marry him for Godsake! You won't be lonely, and if he dies you won't cry!" It was Coronation Street.

"Will you turn that bloody thing off?" screamed Kathleen. It *had* happened, she realised, as her voice rose to a pitch. It must have, because no one would ever have dared tell Benny or Frank to turn off the television. It was their first and last line of defence. It was always there in the corner to distract them from the real world, and their control over it had been symbolic of their control over the family.

"Don't you use that language in here! This is my home! You can use that sort of language in your own house, but this is no bloody jail-house. Just as well your father isn't here to hear the language of you! It was far from that we were rared!"

"Don't you do this on me! Don't go telling me he didn't! You must have seen him!" Kathleen continued, hoping even now that her mother would deny it and end her nightmare. Benny turned up the volume on the television to drown her out but Kathleen had got her attention now and was determined not to squander it.

"Ma, will you listen to me? He did it!"

Benny ignored her until Kathleen darted towards the door. Benny had to stop her.

"You're bloody lucky you didn't have a father like mine!" Benny cried out.

"I wish I had a father like yours! At least he didn't have sex with you!" Kathleen yelled back at her, sick of her mother's self-pity that had held her to ransom.

Benny scowled, the way she had always done at the mention of sex, took a deep breath, as if sucking words from the air, then spoke.

"Oh, God, my head this day! What sort of talk is that, Kathleen? I'm not able for this! I'm just not able for this any more!" She began to sob. "Let me tell you something now, Kathleen. You're never happy! You'll never be happy till you put me in the grave. As God's my judge, you'll be the death of me! Is that what you want? This can't go on, Kathleen! Haven't you brought enough trouble upon us! As God's my judge, your father loves each and every one of you, and he loved you all the same. He never loved any of yous differently."

"You, you must have seen him! You must have known what he did to me!" Kathleen continued, undeterred.

"I didn't see anything Kathleen. It's all in your head!"

"'I didn't see anything, Kathleen!'" Kathleen parroted her mother. "You never seen anything? You were meant to look after me! You *had* me! I never asked to be born, did I?" Kathleen hollered.

Benny dished it out as good as she got. "And I didn't ask to have you!"

Kathleen lifted her hand to her mouth as if dragging the words out. "Aye, and he didn't ask to have me either!"

Benny spun on her heel then waltzed off. Kathleen marched to the door. It was choreography at its best.

"You, you, you didn't see anything because you didn't want to!" Kathleen trumpeted then slammed the door behind her for acoustic effect and went out.

As far as Benny was concerned, theirs was the veritable 'happy home'. She never raised her voice unduly, or beat the kids, and things never got as far as an argument because she brought them up to believe that they would be the death of her if they raised their voices above the din of the television, or, when they were very small, that she would have them taken away if they got up to mischief. Even if there was any truth in the rumours that occasionally reached her that there was dissension in the ranks, she was determined to go to the grave a happy woman—they could sort themselves out after she'd gone. The most she would concede was that she was perhaps on the overprotective side, which explained why she had had them cooped up like chickens in the back garden till each of them turned thirteen.

Kathleen cried openly as she wandered home. Her mother had threatened the four of them with the NSPCC as they huddled together on the fireplace but even now the irony of that menace evaded her as she waded through the memory of that day: the NSPCC would have acted in their interests had they known what she knew now. All of them had a place in Benny's scheme of things—including Frank whose pay-back was the quiet life he so desired.

Flurries of breath rose in the cold air as Kathleen fumed with anger at the thought that Benny was full of contradictions. She ruled the roost at home but fell apart as soon as she crossed the door—*if only it had have been the opposite,* she thought. In the city of bombs and scares, Benny slipped another Valium, worried about holding in her 'water' the length of Royal Avenue of a Friday morning. In an interview with the Guardian's features' editor on the 10th anniversary of the IRA hunger strike, Benny had mentioned from the floor of the parish hall—churchgoers were always a safe, if skewed, source of data—that she hated going into the city centre because "it rattled her nerves something shacking [sic]". While hearts were moved for her throughout the mainland that following Tuesday—her sad tale was even taken up in the News at One (it was, tellingly, the start of the 'silly season' in London)—Benny squirmed, dropped Nicholas' copy of the Guardian on the floor and ran upstairs to the loo. It was her fear of open spaces that made her want to 'go' in spite of her best efforts. Bombs never took a feather out of her, sure, she had enough to be worrying about with her wee problem.

"Oh, yeah, it all makes perfect sense! Jesus died on the Cross so that we could have fresh fish of a Friday, and of course if you got killed into the bargain, sure, it'd all be in a good cause!" Johnny shouted up to her upon finishing the article.

Unaccustomed to mutiny in the ranks, Benny was unsure what way to take him: was he knocking her love of a good bargain or was it her religious fervour he was denigrating? (The fact that Johnny wished her dead went over her head.) Whichever it was, it was a case of the kettle calling the pot black, she thought, as she held on tight to the toilet seat. He could never have guessed how things got twisted along the way—no matter how long he stood at the toilet as a child, it never flowed—but she held her tongue for fear a word said in anger would give her agoraphobia away. Bad enough Kathleen knowing!

Whichever way you looked at it, Benny was full of shit. Kathleen's anger abated with this judgement, only to flare up again at the realisation that Benny would not have sacrificed her had it been one of her sons. At her wedding Benny had run around in a flap looking for Nicholas and Johnny for a photo. "I want a picture with my sons," she declared shamelessly and hysterically as she manhandled the photographer. Similarly, Benny had phoned her a few days previous to let her know she was going into hospital to have her kidneys checked, and mentioned how she was "well used to people hoking and poking at me in hospital since I had two, eh, the four of you." Her two sons were all that mattered, however much Johnny complained about his lot.

Her mother had sacrificed her, but Frank had singled her out. She would sooner rather than later have to face him herself.

* * *

Frank had had two winners and could count on Kathleen to celebrate his luck over a wee fry that she always put up to him when she smelled the drink. She had always understood him. Unlike Benny, she forgave him his weaknesses, and he needed no more proof of this than her silence in respect of his greatest weakness of all.

Mrs. Diamond waved to him from her front window then came out to chat to him at her front door.

"Mr. Dunne, what about you? It's got awful cold, hasn't it? You'd be glad for the wee bit of coal. I won't keep you a minute, so I won't. It's Mrs. Lackey. I think she's not feeling the best. You know, I found her in the kitchen earlier on, and between you and me, she didn't look herself one bit." Mrs. Diamond's voice had all but disappeared and Frank strained to hear her, but as he did so she raised it again, "Aye, and the stink of gas would've knocked you out. I don't know how it didn't kill her, honest to God. But that's them bloody gasmen for you!" Frank went white. "It's probably only Christmas. You know yourself, it gets in on everybody. I told her to get on to them anyway. God knows, it's a hard time of the year all over. She seemed, you know, low."

Frank nodded sympathetically but his mind was elsewhere. Mrs. Diamond took full advantage.

"Ach, it's never been the same. No, it'll never be the same again since my man...." She blessed herself to signify her loss. "You'd be sitting in there watching the hours till bedtime manys a night and I'm telling you truthfully ne'er a one would think of callin' in to see how you're doing. No. And, sure, you know yourself, the television's a dead loss at the best of times, Christmas or no Christmas. I had it on there earlier just for the wee bit o' noise about the house. You know, there's times you'd be thankful for a wee bit of commotion on the streets, God forgive me for saying it! At least you know you're not alone with the sound of them British Army helicopters up there with their searchlights on. God only knows what they think they're going to see. Santa maybe?"

She laughed, her folded arms vibrating on her chest. When she opened her eyes again she took his blank countenance as further sympathy for her plight. She had an audience and the whole evening to fill ahead of her.

"I was just going to put meself on a cup o' tea there a moment ago. Mrs. Lackey was good enough to lend me some milk earlier. Would you like a wee cup yourself?"

"What? Eh, no, thanks!" said Frank, unaware of what her question had been. "I had better check on the daughter."

"Right so, Mr. Dunne, but don't breathe a word, sure you won't. You know how Mrs. Lackey is. Sure, she wouldn't give much away, the same woman."

"What, oh, no, right you are, Mrs...!" He had forgotten her name.

"Do you know? Mr. Dunne, there's not another man like her da! The sun shines out of his..." she stopped herself in the nick of time.

Frank managed a smile. "Happy Christmas, Mrs...!"

"And many Happy Returns!" said Mrs. Diamond. She watched him make his way back down the path, clinging to the hope that he might take a fall so that she could get him in across the door.

He rang Kathleen's doorbell and peeked through the living room window but there was no sign of life. He let himself in by the back door and telephoned Benny. Her phone rang out. He would go home. He had to get to Kathleen before she got to her mother.

* * *

Benny was knitting under the light of the standard lamp when Frank made his appearance.

"So, it's on the market?" he asked.

"What?"

"The house, it's up for sale, isn't it?"

"What are you on about now?"

"The coffee! The aroma. Have you someone coming to see the house? A buyer? Who's moving out, tell me?"

She always found his jokes irresistible, often pouting flirtatiously as if against her will, and Frank realised now from the way she now threw up her head that Kathleen had already been and gone.

"Can you pour me out a wee cup?" he entreated.

"Ach, now, hol' your horses a wee minute, Frank! It's not Angeloni's café! I wasn't born with two sets of hands, like!" Benny reproved him. Frank twiddled his thumbs behind his back as he stood in front of the fire. All he had to do was to bide his time, then, when she was doing his beck and call he could get the truth out of her.

"Tch! Now, look, what you made me go and do!" tutted Benny. She had dropped a stitch.

"It's alright, it's alright, I'll get the coffee myself. I was only asking."

A few minutes later, he came back, placed a mug on the arm of the chair and sat in the light of the streetlamp.

"I called in to see Kathleen today but there was no sign of her," he began probing. "Was she up at the Kesh or what, I wonder?"

"No, indeed she was not! She was around at this door today, her usual canapscious self."

Benny took a place mat from a drawer in the leaf-table by the window and placed it under his mug. There was no use in telling him to lift one out himself from the drawer which was right beside him—she might as well be talking to the wall.

"Oh." George tensed slightly, his head twitching.

"A-ha! Not that she hung around long either. You know the way she is when you're not here—she can't sit apeace for two minutes. To tell you the God's honest truth, I was glad when she left, even though she's my own daughter. She'd put you blooming crazy sometimes. I'm not joking you, she sat there like a statue where you're sitting and didn't say a word. Made herself a cup of tea, and away she went. She's getting worse, the older she gets. As odd as a bottle of chips! Gets it from your side but!"

Benny kept her eyes on a moth that fluttered under the shade of the standard lamp as she spoke. She didn't have to look at Frank to know that he was on edge—she could tell from the sound of the mug as he placed it on the coaster.

"Are there any biscuits in the house?" he asked in an effort to appear calm.

"Do you ever let up?" asked Benny as she got up once again, stuffing the knitting between the cushions.

She spread a napkin on his lap. "He did it," she muttered as she deposited a plate with two ginger nut biscuits on top of it.

"What? What are you on about now? Do you ever start a sentence and finish it?"

"She sat there where you are, saying 'he did it'. That's all I know."

"He did it? He did what? Who did what?"

"Now, what do I know? How would I know anything? Sure nobody tells me anything around here! You may ask her yourself, Frank. Maybe you'd get more out of her. You always had more of a way with her."

"Oh, I did, did I? What 's that supposed to mean?"

"Look, I don't know what you're getting het up about. She was your shadow. Anyone could see that. There was no one like you. No, no one else got a look in, but you can't see that, can you?"

"Listen till I tell you something! I can't be blamed for that. If she asked me for anything, I'd just drop my things for her. You saw that when Kevin was born. You'd have been rid of him before he saw the light of day only for me. I was all she had."

"All she had? Uh! That's a bit thick coming from you! Who was the one buried her baby? I didn't see you nursing her through her grief either. No, you took yourself off fishing for a week."

"If you'd have had your way, she'd have had an abortion!" he snapped back.

"Is it any wonder?" Benny roared. She covered her face with her hands to hide her tears. "You did it! You did it. You did it, didn't you?" she cried, couching her head in her hands.

"I did what? I did nothing! I did nothing of the sort! What, what are you on about? I didn't do any such thing. I'd give my life for her, and you know it! So, don't you go telling me otherwise!"

"She sat there where you are now and she said it herself. You did it on her, Frank!"

"I didn't do anything on anybody, and I won't tolerate being told anything else in my own home. Do you hear me? I'll put you through that bloody window, Benny, I swear to God. Is it a crime to love your daughter?" He stood up and bore his fist at her.

Benny looked up at him. "Big bloody man! Some man you are!" she taunted him, waving her knitting needle. He walloped her and raced off.

Benny sat there holding her bruised cheek, rocking herself back and forth. When the pain subsided she pulled the blinds closed and examined herself in the mirror. Her left cheek was swollen, but there were no obvious finger marks. She could make out that she hit it off the kitchen cupboard. She washed and treated it in the kitchen and went back to her seat. She picked up her knitting. Her hands were trembling. Afraid to go upstairs, she sat there quietly till the early hours of the morning, holding in her pee. When she finally went upstairs, she discovered that Frank wasn't there. He had vanished.

* * *

Benny reached out for the lamp, but couldn't find it. She was on the wrong side of the bed—Frank's side: he hadn't come home. She got up and switched on the bedroom light, wrapped her dressing gown around her and teetered downstairs, the doorbell beckoning her. In the half-light through the stained-glass window she made out two padded figures.

"Who's that?" she asked.

"No. 9?" a female voice enquired.

"Yes. 9, the Park. Yes. Who's there?" Benny asked again.

"Mrs. Dunne?"

"Yes, speaking."

"Mrs. Dunne, it's the police. Could you open up, please?"

She shivered. It was the first time an RUC officer had ever asked to come in—they usually barged in. She pulled the cord on her dressing-gown tighter and tied it in a bow.

"Mrs. Dunne," Oyster lips mouthed as Benny drew the door back against her body like a shield, "can we come in a minute?"

She left them to follow her up the hall. Yous'll be a long time waiting on an invitation, she thought. The male officer thumped a light switch, floodlighting the living room cum dining room. Benny winced to show her displeasure.

"Mrs. Dunne, I'm Officer Kilpatrick."

Wrong—Sheer Oyster, thought Benny. She poked at her hairnet and patted her bruised forehead now conscious of her comparatively unflattering demeanour. The officer scrutinised her face for the slightest hint that she had read into her name, as Catholics were wont to do. Benny nodded and, fooled, Officer Kilpatrick continued in her stride, "And this is Officer Montgomery. I'm afraid, Mrs. Dunne, we've some bad news for you. Maybe you should sit down."

"Is it, it's my Nicholas? Oh, my God! Not, not my son. Dear Jesus!"

While Benny's blasphemy grated on Officer Kilpatrick's ears she was glad for Benny's sake that the name was out in the open. Nine times out of ten the first name out of the hat was that of someone other than the deceased. Tonight the name she had was Frank. Why did people—Catholic or Protestant, she had to concede it made no difference—go around imagining the worst, putting themselves through so much unnecessary pain? In her six years in the force she had seen people bury prodigal sons, prized daughters, pampered husbands, much-needed wives in their minds. In one recent case she had even gone to the house of a woman in South Belfast who imagined they had come to tell her of her poodle's final moments when they had in fact found her son dead on the side of the road. Admittedly, it was an unusual example of the phenomenon, but the very same principle was at work—'the worst case scenario'. She could write a book about it: 'The State of Play: the RUC on the Offensive. Chapter One—Hat Tricks; identifying your support lines. The fact was that if you let them speak their minds, the bereaved conveniently named their future line of support. Nicholas was clearly Benny's. Officer Kilpatrick sighed with relief.

"Oh my God, what happened him?" Benny continued her lament for Nicholas.

Officer Kilpatrick resolved to go by her tried and tested strategy which she would detail in Chapter Two. Though she wouldn't say so in the book, it was really the only way to tackle Catholics, who were always on the look out for an opportunity to catch you off-side.

"Is there anyone else with you?" she began. She needed a 'No'.

"No, no," answered Benny.

Officer Kilpatrick hissed imperceptibly, and clenched her knuckles, as if her team had scored. No support meant no complications. She didn't offer family therapy. Her forte was one to one. "Mrs. Dunne, I'm afraid we've found your husband," she pressed ahead.

Benny shrieked. With a flick of her forehead, Officer Kilpatrick all but headed a ball to Officer Montgomery standing in nets at the door, and Benny ducked to give him a clear view. Realising it was now up to him to cover the ground, he puffed out his chest, steadied himself, then gave it his best shot.

"Ma'am, I'm afraid the news is bad. Mr. Dunne's been in an accident. I'm afraid he died."

Benny's shriek became a groan. With his left foot, Officer Montgomery signalled to his team-mate to get into position. She crouched and placed her arm around Benny's shoulder while Officer Montgomery took off to the kitchen. He always pulled back when the going got tough, a habit which never failed to get his colleague's hackles up.

"Is there anyone living close by that you can call on?" Officer Kilpatrick asked as the official minute's silence ended.

"Oh, Jesus, Mary and St. Joseph! Frank! Oh my God!" roared Benny.

She had got the timing wrong. The other side wasn't ready. "Mrs. Dunne," she recommended with one eye now on the clock. (It never paid to hang around too long in Catholic areas. She hated putting the lives of the British soldiers in the jeeps at risk— fourteen of them on the sideline ready to come on at a moment's notice.) "Your husband's body was taken out of the River Lagan last evening. We are working on the assumption that Mr. Dunne fell in and drowned."

She knew she was being a bit rough but their Community Studies' lecturer who doubled as their football coach at the police academy—a Free Presbyterian with a feel for this sort of thing— had always insisted that the sooner people knew what was happening, the sooner they could run with the ball.

"Maybe you'd feel a little better if you had a drink," Officer Montgomery suggested, reappearing with a mug. It would do no harm to slow the tempo down just a tad. "You'll feel much better for it," Officer Kilpatrick reassured her. "Was Mr. Dunne suffering from stress or depression?" Officer Montgomery asked, completing the one-two. "You realise," began Officer Kilpatrick again, "we always have to be open to the possibility that the victim took his or her own life, you must understand."

As Benny shook her head, Officer Montgomery raised his notebook, giving his colleague the yellow card.

"I take it that was a 'no', Mrs. Dunne," Officer Kilpatrick pressed on, ignoring her colleague's warning.

"Yes," Benny squeaked.

"That looks like a rather sore knock you got there," she continued.

"Um, I, I hit it off the kitchen cupboard door yesterday."

Officer Montgomery whistled. Time was up. Thinking that he had noticed the size of her bump, Benny looked over at him, relieved that he had bought her story.

"I see. Em," Officer Kilpatrick hesitated. The future detective in her wanted to pursue the matter of the abrasions but Officer Montgomery's antics had thrown her. "Is there anybody you can call to have come over and stay with you?" she asked instead.

"No, my son is away in Dublin. Em, yes, em, my son, Johnny."

"Do you have a number for him? Would you like me to ring him for you?"

"No, It's okay. I'll manage."

Benny found it funny that the first thought that had popped into her mind was that she didn't want to be giving Johnny's phone number to the police, but she suppressed her laughter.

"Well, we'll just wait in the kitchen maybe, if that's alright," Officer Kilpatrick suggested. Better wind things down. Coach will be proud of me for staying with it all the way, she thought. He'll do the preface for the book yet.

"He'll be over shortly," said Benny as she set the handset back on the kitchen table, interrupting an argument about tactics and team effort.

'Would you like us to wait till he comes?" Officer Montgomery asked.

Benny shook her hand with determination the way she polished the silverware.

"In that case, we'll be on our way then," Officer Kilpatrick announced, embarrassing Officer Montgomery who felt her eagerness to call it a day must have been clear to Benny. "If we can be of any further assistance, please don't hesitate to telephone us," Officer Kilpatrick added, walking off. It's better to say the right thing, she congratulated herself, for while Falls Road types are unlikely to ring to say thank you for calling, they wouldn't think twice about hauling you up before a disciplinary committee.

Benny followed them to the door. She would get a bad name for having them in the house, she thought, and, sure enough, over their shoulders she could see the McElhones already out at their door snooping. To make matters worse, as the officers gently closed the door behind them they wished her "A very goodnight, ma'am!" and their chorus carried on the night breeze. It was a lucky thing that Frank wasn't home, she found herself thinking, for he would have been none too pleased with their visit. She would go up now and warm his side of the bed for him. She wailed, the full force of what had happened hitting her in the chest.

Chapter 8

" That's your phone, Nicholas," Shirley shouted in from the back yard where she was putting out the empty wine bottles from the night before.

"Jesus, they're early!" he replied, choking on his toothpaste with excitement.

"Hello!" he began, retrieving his phone off the top of the microwave.

"Hello! Nicholas?"

"Yes?"

"It's me, Johnny."

"Hi!" said Nicholas, swallowing his disappointment. The new PC was not on its way after all.

Shirley felt her nipples rub off her cotton pyjamas as her chest swelled with pride—it wasn't the deliveryman, and she could tell. They had been together no more than a few months and it already felt like she knew Nicholas better than she knew herself she had grown that close to him.

"What has you up at this hour of the day?" continued Nicholas, trying to put a brave face on things.

"Dad, Nicholas. It's..."

"Dad?" Nicholas queried. He hadn't got him up fencing the garden, had he?

"It's dad. It's dad. I've some bad news. Dad di...dad's dead. He was found dead this morning. I know, it's unbelievable, isn't it?"

"Daaad?" Nicholas whined.

"Nicholas, Nick, can you come home?"

"Oh, my God!" cried Nicholas.

Shirley let the Chianti bottle drop and watched it trickle down the drain, drawing her with it like a river of blood. Shit! That's me stuck out here now with that eyesore, she thought, eying the swing which swayed in the gentle breeze, reminding her of her biological clock. Why the last tenants didn't take it with them when they moved out instead of leaving it here is beyond me!

"Nicholas, dad drowned," explained Johnny.

"Drowned? What do you mean he drowned? Where? How? Whe...? Mummy? How's mummy? Where is she?"

Deciding he needed privacy, Shirley pulled the door over, and reached for the yard brush. She had heard more than enough.

"She's sedated. The doctor put her on something strong."

"Listen, Johnny, I'll get up on the next train."

"Do you want me to pick you up at this end?"

"No, I'll be fine. Honestly! Bye, Johnny! Bye!"

Nicholas waited as long as he could before conceding that the mountain would have to go to Mohammed.

"Is there something wrong?" said Shirley, playing dumb, as the crack in the door dilated revealing a distraught Nicholas.

"It's my...,"

Nicholas stopped, only the left half of his white body visible to Shirley, making her think of a Drumstick bar.

Once a thing's out there, he thought, it's the past, and there's only ever the, the memory, which is always coloured by something else. This is history here, he figured. He placed his hand at his throat like Stalin at Potsdam. It was Stalin, wasn't it, he quizzed himself?

"It's my, it's my da," he announced, squinting as he now took the sun full in his face, regretting the absence of Stalin's military cap. "He's dead."

Jesus, that was cinch, in fact nearly too easy, he thought. *Where's the tears, the lip biting, the hair pulling now when I could do with it? What about all them telephone calls I used to imagine? I couldn't cry now to save my life!*

"Oh, God, that's...! Is there anything I can do?" asked Shirley, brushing the debris into a dustpan. She could run out to the butcher's—a full stomach would keep his tears at bay—or make herself scarce and iron his things for Belfast, or even bring herself to do the Christmas shopping on her own. *Just as long as he doesn't ask me to run him to Belfast*, she thought.

"Maybe you could drop me into Connolly Station, could you?" he finally suggested, interrupting her imaginings, and laying his stage directions to rest. There was no point in asking the impossible, not after her remark the other day about why Fianna Fáil had to go to the North to find a President when there were more than enough people in Ireland who could have filled Mary Robinson's shoes other than that Mary McAleese one. Nothing would get her across that border. "The 10 o'clock would be deadly. It has a buffet service on it," he added to make himself appear grateful.

"What? Yeah, certainly, absolutely, no problem! Do you want to go now?" she asked, looking up the hall to the front door offering light at the end of the tunnel.

"As soon as you can. Just give me a minute to get something on," he replied, hoping that she would restrain him. Wait, here, here's some tears coming now, he thought. Just on time too! Like a toddler working up tears he half spat, half coughed out a sob.

She paced over to him, counting her steps—seven in all, her lucky number. A taxi would be quicker, with the *lána bus* and everything, she thought as she took his hand, but she hadn't the gall to mention it. She plucked him on one cheek and kissed the solitary tear on the other, thinking that she at least had an excuse now to wear the black blouse that she wore to Brid's dad's funeral which more than one person had remarked really made her boobs look small. Nicholas, relieved at the arrival of his tear, rested his head on her crown. *And in Hollywood they just roll down their cheeks like there are no tomorrows*, he thought. *How do they do that?* Shirley buried her eyes in his Adam's Apple and began working her way through the CDs in her head for something to take the edge of things in the car.

* * *

Nicholas strained his ear to catch the announcement on the train's intercom system.

"Your attention, please! Due to a security alert on the line between Dundalk and Newry, all passengers travelling beyond Dundalk are requested to transfer to the bus at Dundalk Station for the onward journey to Newry train station. Passengers for Dundalk, please alight at Dundalk Station."

First up was a man with a book firm against his breast who put Nicholas in mind of a man of the cloth, about to announce *the End is Nigh*, though when he turned, the sight of his open necked shirt and silk cravat suggested otherwise. Behind him a business type took up position, suspending his case at chest height like the Chancellor on budget day. All that was missing was the big Labour smile, he thought. A few paces behind him, a woman gauping at the mobile phone in her hand as if she had found the Pearl of Great Price, and then a disgruntled passenger who might as well have been skating along the way he was swaying to the motion of the train. "Travel by rail, and you'll see Ireland by bus!" he muttered for Nicholas' benefit as he came close. No doubt a Prod getting his dig in, thought Nicholas, as he picked up his Walkman and suitcase and trundled down the aisle behind him, carrying his coat over his shoulder like a hod.

When Nicholas had taken his seat on the bus he realised too late that the man was next to him. "It won't be long now Jeremy, son. That's those bold men in the IRA for you putting bombs on the line!" said the bitch across the aisle of the bus—there was no other way of putting it, he thought—to the wee skitter beside her. He spat out the nail-bitings that had been keeping him company, now sorry that he hadn't taken Bus Éireann which was always full of Catholics because it was cheaper. Jeremy's mother glared over at him at the sound of his raspberry. See, what did I tell you, thought Nicholas? Bat out of hell! Well, you can hump off for all I care! He angled his body in towards the window and his father's voice lapped at his ears, "Blinded Irishmen! That's all they are. They're just too bitter to see. Sure, they'd sell their souls for the punt, if it was the right price." Tears suddenly welled, but holding his breath he fought them back for fear the 'blue nose' beside him, whom he now noticed was reading the previous day's Protestant *Newsletter* just to annoy him, would see.

The bus stopped and an RUC officer climbed on board. We must be at the Border already, thought Nicholas, rubbing the window. She strode up the aisle and halted beside his seat where, slowly swivelling on one heel, she surveyed the passengers. Nicholas removed the gun from her holster, and shot her dead, as he was programmed to do. She saluted the driver and alighted. Nicholas expired through his nostrils with disgust at himself, causing the *Newsletter* to rustle. Is there not enough people dead in this country without you adding to it, he thought, grumbling at his reflection in the window? His father's sandy hair was, he noticed, going grey. Even his blue eyes, also his father's, appeared to have faded against the faint Armagh hills. What did Shirley ever see in me, he wondered? A smile traced itself on Jeremy's shock of black hair as the thought crossed Nicholas' mind that it was his body and not his aging looks that had attracted Shirley the day he ended up going into the wrong changing-room. What a cock-up, he thought, his teeth showing now on Jeremy's mother's neck. And all because of the male painters in the Ladies' changing-room. He saw himself again pirouetting with the grace of a prima ballerina in front of the Gents' changing-room show-ers, then bang straight into Shirley, who grabbed his baton with the dexterity of a relay runner and found her footing and, now, he had to admit, her future. His scrotum stirred and he sat upright in his seat out of deference to his father. And the nerve of her, teasing him in front of the early birds about how come all the other men had made it safely back to base via the Ladies' chang-ing-room, and something about the power of the unconscious! If she only knew! He blushed all over again and closed the curtain to kill stray thoughts of Jack.

A meditation to still the mind? Yes, well, why not? It's worth a try, he thought. He opened the palms of his hands on his lap and rested his gaze on the cup holder in front of him but it immedi-ately reminded him of the rings he had used to hang curtains for Shirley in her bedroom and his mind wandered again. Like, what was the need for curtains? It wasn't like the neighbours could see us at it, was it, now? Sure, you can see nothing with that six-foot wall out the back. His breathing slowed and deepened. The cup-holder mouthed fish-like, mentioning something about its life of service to the Japanese as a resting place for green tea and weary heads. His head dipped then whipped back like a fishing-line, giving him a start. The fish's mouth was now a sun-kissed nip-ple rising from behind a snow-capped Mount Fuji and as the bus rattled on the singed tarmac of South Armagh a pair of cranes spirited him off into a deep sleep from which he emerged at the sound of the bus reversing into Newry train station.

As he travelled into Belfast, the headstones in Milltown Ceme-tery flashed in the city lights, mouthing words in morse about doors daubed for slips of the trigger and the tongue and graffiti plastered up on walls. So many familiar faces brought to their knees, now doing life in perpetuity before their time, he thought. KILLED IN CROSSFIRE, murdered for his faith, killed in action, assas-sinated, died (explosion). Nicholas grunted. And now my father too before his time.

* * *

Mrs. Diamond refused to let go of Benny's hand as the mourners milled around the open coffin. "I'm terrible sorry," she said, by way of condolences. "You never know the moment, do you? And there he was wishing me a very happy Christmas, and as God's my judge he looked the picture of health. It's hard to believe, like. But sure he hasn't a worry now. No, I can see him sitting down at the eternal banquet." At the mention of food, her tummy rumbled on cue. Raising her voice to drown it out she added, "Do you know, my own husband was the same? Did Mrs. Lackey tell you he fell off the....?"

"I just can't understand," interrupted Benny. "I mean, he had walked that stretch a hundred times before." The effect of the sedatives was beginning to wear off, but reality was still some distance away.

"Sure, it only takes a second," Mrs. Diamond began again. "Sure, didn't the very same thing happen last year to wee Bracken from around there by the shops? Do you know the good-looking wee fella that always wore the Parker like it was stuck to him? Made him look like an Eskimo. Maybe it was better for him in the long run though. I mean, I heard them say he had shocking depression. Ach, aye, shocking it was. Shacking! And him only a young fella, like. Sure, my man was the same. Was Mrs. Lackey telling you?"

"Ma, will you have a sandwich? You have to eat something," Nicholas intervened. He had overheard their conversation and figured it was time to put an end to it.

"In a wee minute," Benny snapped at him aware that Mrs. Diamond was trying to tell her something important and that however much she concentrated it wasn't going in.

"I'd love a wee ham sandwich myself, son, if there's one going," said Mrs. Diamond, eager to place her order. She had come hungry. Sure what was a wake for but a good feed? "Do you know something?" she addressed Benny, denying Nicholas time to refuse her request, "my man was gone before he had time to think about it. Aye."

As Benny wrung her hands the undertaker coughed into Nicholas' ear. "We'll be closing the coffin in five minutes, if your family would like to say their farewells," he added.

Perfect, thought Nicholas. He could ferry Benny to safety now.

"Em, Mrs. Diamond, could you move into the hall, please?" he asked. She let herself be herded with the other mourners, then diverted into the kitchen to make up for lost time.

"Ma, where's Kathleen?" Johnny asked Benny who stood in the middle of the room fidgeting with the hem of her skirt.

"Did you try upstairs?" she replied, pulling on some thread.

"Gillian, will you have a wee amharc upstairs and see if she's there?" asked Johnny. Gillian obliged, grateful for the opportunity to escape the inevitable Dunne performance of 'happy families'.

Benny was the first at the coffin. Kneeling at Frank's feet, she held onto its rim with one hand, praying with the rosary in the other. Unsure of protocol, the others watched as she gave lead. When she stood up, Nicholas briskly stepped forward. The first son, he was eager to keep to the pecking order. He kissed Frank's forehead, apparently indifferent to the cold flesh where he rested his lips for some moments. Remaining erect, he prayed intently, fighting back the tears. Johnny panicked—he could never match that. Genuflecting in Nicholas' wake, he knocked against the candelabrum which Nicholas caught. As he stood guard, he shifted his gaze repeatedly from the corpse to his wristwatch. He had to beat Nicholas' three minutes and thirty-five seconds. When Marlene came up beside him, Johnny called it a day. He had set a new record.

Marlene relished the moment—and it was only a moment. She made a sign of the Cross and retreated with her thoughts. Now that Frank was out of the way and Benny was as needy as she had ever seen her, her fingers tingled at the prospect of having her ma under her thumb. Benny licked her tears and reluctantly gave instructions to the undertaker to close the coffin. Kathleen was still nowhere to be found. Up in the attic she wished away her visit to the dentist, her confrontation with her mother and her father's death, and pined for the security of the previous week when things had been so simple.

When Nicholas finally found her, he sat down beside her on the camp-bed and spread his arms around her shoulders like a blanket. "I know how you feel. I'm going to miss him myself," he consoled her. Kathleen cried all the louder.

* * *

An Irish man with Toucan features approached and offered to fill the tank. I'm fine, thanks, Shirley signaled with a wave. How come all the foreigners that end up getting jobs in Ireland are so good-looking, she wondered. 'Can you face this way, please? That's right! Ah-ha! Crown, 102 centimetres around, cheekbones, yes, sufficiently high, nose—cliff-like, but pass—brows, long, slender, plucked. Colour, em, pigmentation, nice tan. Eyes? Pleasing. Posture—excellent! Smile for the camera—we're nearly there. Impeccable arrangement, piano keys, you have there. Side-on, please. Perfect. Welcome to Ireland, sir. Next!' Or maybe the good-looking ones just have more drive, like me, she told herself as she slinked out of her car. The Irish garage hand lifted a watering-can and pursued a car with a trailer. Are you landing a jumbo, or what, Shirley wondered, fixing her eyes on its elderly driver. Do you want me to park it for you, or what? A woman, French—she'd seen her behind the cheese counter at Morton's— negotiated the forecourt with a buggy, directed by her two-year old, whose legs were running away with him. Watch the fucken lorry, Shirley screamed at him without as much as a word. Not another bloody one that needs looking after! She snaked her way through the cars to the garage shop and slid her Visa card on top of some guy with a gun to his head in The Irish Independent. Holy Shit! I hope he's drugged! It'd be nice if they didn't shove it in our faces, under our noses. *Before You Make Up Your Mind, Open It.* Yeah, right! She paid for her petrol and headed in the direction of her apartment.

No place like home thought Shirley as she switched on the television and shed the outside world with her coat. She collapsed on to the sofa. The Teletubbies. That'll do the job nicely, she thought. It would keep her company and help her get rid of the guilt which had clung to her all the way back from Connolly Station like the smell of smoke on her clothes. She could easily have taken Nicholas to Belfast for Frank's funeral—the Christmas holidays stretched before her like a summer's day—but the fear of being killed in an attack had put her off. Approaching the train station, a voice in her head—probably Nicholas'—had reminded her that you could just as easily be killed on the roads in the South as go up in a bomb in the North, but she sent it packing with a *I haven't been killed on the roads yet, and me never off them. And wasn't a little Spanish boy killed in Omagh in that big IRA bomb and him only passing through? Who do you think you're fooling? It'd just be my luck to get blown apart when I shouldn't have been there in the first place. No, why break the habit of a lifetime, I ask you?* The baby face on the television giggled ever so cutely, bright yellow sunrays beaming from his head with approval. *I don't care what the girls from work say! They need to get real! Go to Belfast, my hat!* She thumped a hollow in the scatter cushion and propped it up behind her head for added comfort.

The girls in work had recently been up to Belfast by train. The IRA cease-fire had heralded a new beginning for Southern shoppers who were now flocking in their thousands to the "Black North". They had asked her along, but she had something on, or so she had said. They returned home laden with bargains and tales of wonderful shops that you couldn't find in Dublin. Envious of their rampage, Shirley hadn't been able to hold back. If it was all so wonderful, how come they hadn't stayed the night and gone out on the town? As quick as a flash, Aoife with the eyebrows that stuck together came up with a sorry tale about not being able to leave Brid's bedridden father alone. No harm to her sick father, but it was probably just as well, Shirley had howled, because Southerners weren't exactly welcome in Belfast anyway judging by the fate of the lu-la from Dublin that had wandered into a bar on the wrong side of town—"That's if there is a *right* side of town in Belfast,"—and had to be airlifted to the rehab in Dun Laoghaire, costing the Irish taxpayer a fortune. Surely, they had all heard about him, she had asked Aoife? Aoife's back-up, Sorcha, butted in: he was probably up to no good and, anyway, the News had said he was from Ballyfermot, which said it all really. Shirley had seen white, being from next door in Palmerstown—a distinction she knew half of the country, including Sorcha, failed to make—but Aoife, her eyebrows now bunched together like a caterpillar, beat her to the draw: there was no point in Shirley getting into a snot over Belfast for you could just as easily wander into the wrong area in London or New York and end up in a wheel-chair. And anyway, Sorcha chipped in again, Belfast was Ireland and they had as much right to be there as anyone. They would stay the next time, if Brid could get someone to do the night-shift with her dad. Brid's vigorous nod indicated the queues were already forming. "Count me in for the overnight!" chortled Aoife, if only to annoy the shit out of Shirley who produced a trump card, Frazzell's fish-shop in Belfast where all those people, "though it breaks my heart to say it", got burnt to a frazzle in a bomb, God love them. No, they were out of their minds.

Shirley pulled herself up off the sofa to go hunt for her dressing-gown and slippers. It's bad enough risking your life going to Belfast by train or bus without drawing attention to yourself in a Southern registered car, she told herself. Even Nicholas must realise that. *He'll forgive me. I did the right thing.* She checked down the side of the sofa for her slippers. No sign of them. And then there's my mother to think about, she reflected. She lifted up the drapes. I'm already in deep enough going out with a Northerner, not to mention one with a record, without risking her wrath any further by going up North. *Nothing here. Maybe they're upstairs?* Daddy, of course, would have understood me and Nicholas perfectly—he always had a feel for the nationalist thing: shamrock on St. Patrick's Day, an Easter lily for Easter week—the one with the pin in it—and he could even sing the national anthem in Irish. He took the whole republican thing real seriously, didn't he? She opened the bedroom door. Probably because he was born on the 12th July and couldn't live with the shame of it. Isn't that what you used to say about him, Mummy, when you weren't running to Fr. Semple to give out to him about Daddy buying An Phoblacht every week and putting Northern refugees into the house? *No, can't see my slippers anywhere.* And if Daddy were alive to see me now? Well, for one thing, the bit about me sharing this bed here with my refugee friend would probably make him spin in his grave. "You're ripping the arse out of it!" I can't imagine you using those exact words though, Daddy.

The sudden incongruent image of her as a child on her Daddy's lap, and him telling her not to go to Belfast if it didn't feel right caused her to burst out laughing. However, Philomena caught her eye in the tiny picture-frame by the matching sea-shell jewelry box and quickly dampened her spirits. No, there's no point in opening up all mummy's old wounds, I suppose, she thought. As she pulled out her slipper sticking out from under the bed she spotted the other one by the bath in the en suite. The wrong parent dropped dead at my feet, she thought as she pulled them on, their ears flopping. No, I am dead right to keep Philomena in the dark. I've told her more than enough. An "ex-student". Brownie points there for his being a former seminarian! Music to her ears! "He'll pass the faith on to the grandchildren, if you have any, dear. And at least he left before he had met you because there's nothing worse than when they leave for a woman! And if they leave after ordination, you could never be sure that they wouldn't go back, dear. I always had that fear about your father, pet."

Shirley wrapped herself up in her dressing-gown and sauntered into the living-room where she lifted the tin of chocolate biscuits that she had bought for the Festive Season from under the tree. No, not even Philomena's revelation about her father's time in the priesthood could bring her to tell her about Nicholas' prison history. The Teletubbies were doing their dancing thing. She remembered Nicholas dancing along to them as he sometimes did, bouncing up and down—La-La. She spread herself out on the sofa and half closed her eyes, the biscuit tin falling to the floor. She loved Nicholas. There was something about him. He seemed to understand her like no one else had ever done. Indeed, she was never done telling him that he knew her better than she knew herself. He was also great in bed. He was different from anyone else she had slept with. All candlelight and oils, and, eyes closed, his hands found their way around her with the ease of a blind harpist she had once marvelled at on Channel 4. She recalled her question to him from the previous day. "So, tell me, so, where did you learn such a range, and you locked up in a retreat house all those years? Uh? You'd have been such a waste in the priesthood!"

"To be honest, I know you're going to laugh at this, but sex and prayer aren't a million miles away from each other," he said. "And I had plenty of it in religious life. They're both about finding out what does it for you."

"Plenty of 'it'? Plenty of what? Prayer, I hope!"

He wriggled his left eyebrow and burst into laughter.

"You're such a tease!" she said.

He wriggled his right eyebrow, and she fell back in the bed in a fit of laughter, tucking her knees into her waist for fear he would tickle her. Even now, to hold in her laughter, she crossed her arms on the sofa and pressed her hands against her rib-cage like a straight-jacket. He draped the sheet over his head in the style of the Virgin, covered his genitalia with his joined hands and began reciting the Hail Mary as he knelt at her feet. She brought her hands to her breasts now and heard the stiff sheet crackle again as the Virgin prostrated herself, pulling the sheet down with him, covering them. Irresistible, she thought, opening her eyes wide again. The only thing I don't like is that sometimes you tell me more than I need to hear like the time I was going over the Visa bill trying to figure out what in heavens' name you'd been buying and you launched into the whys and wherefores of why you left religious life. Did I really need to know about that dream with you as a baby at the driving wheel and all the doors flung open and the car "BURNED OUT"?

She had been thinking about Nicholas again she realised as the words spouted out.

"Again! Again!" Po, Tinky-Winky and Dipsy cried out, and a group of toddlers began splashing around in a paddling pool for the second time. If only the nice bits in life could be repeated again and again, she thought as she sat up on the couch. No, she would take a leaf out of Nicholas' book and tell him plain and straight that the whole Northern thing scared the wits out of her. He'd forgive her for not bringing him North. She picked up the biscuit tin and reached into the bottom layer. Her mother had never approved of her habit of leaving all the plain Janes on the top layer, but she just loved the fancy one with the jelly on top. Licking the jelly heart, she studied the television listings. Bus

Stop was showing at five to three, and she adored her namesake, Shirley Temple. If she hurried, she could nip out to the off-licence, buy a bottle of red, and be back in time for the ads. She had a quick check in the mirror and decided that she would probably make it there and back in her dressing gown. She threw on her overcoat. She would buy Nicholas a box of Black Magic in the shop for when he got back. It would relieve her guilt and make it easier for her to tell him the truth about why she hadn't gone North. The black blouse; what about the black blouse, she thought, going out the door? I'll keep it until he gets back. He'd like that.

* * *

Nicholas, Johnny, Brian—Marlene's long overdue boyfriend—and Dan, an old republican comrade of Frank's, carried the coffin as far as the gates of the church where, surrendering to the rain, they thrust it into the hearse with the help of the pall-bearer and ran for cover, but in slow motion out of respect for the deceased. Nicholas took shelter in the limousine which minutes later swung in through the cemetery gates. Good-day he said to their chiselled pillars, then good riddance to the wealthy imprisoned in their vaults, good on you to the headstone of the one-eyed man for keeping an eye out on everyone, and good luck to those who, unable to bear Belfast any longer, had taken their own lives and found rest in the unconsecrated plot. He sat forward and hooked his head around, watching the plot disappear out of sight as he had watched his father for the last time from the Dublin-bound bus in Glengall Street. He had done himself in. Frank had topped himself. He looked over at his mother, caged between Kathleen and Marlene, whose urn-shaped neck, lips of clay, clipped nose and sunken eyes, all enveloped in a black, floral mantilla, now confirmed his intuition and he made up his mind that he had to protect her from the truth.

Nicholas dredged his feet through the torrents of water rushing to their end in the Bog Meadow like biblical pigs. Beside the open grave a mound of bristling canvas, the colour of grass, repelled the rain. Frank had bloated, he thought, before spotting the coffin further along at Johnny's feet. Marlene put up an umbrella to shield Benny and slowly treaded along what she could make out of the path, Kathleen on Benny's other arm. Having fulfilled their public duty, they abandoned her at the graveside. Kathleen moved near the gravediggers on the edge of the crowd while Marlene circled back to the limousine, a few mourners clasping her hand as she drifted past. They presumed it was all too much for her, but what she felt was relief bordering on joy at finally laying Frank to rest for, in her estimation, he had never loved her. Seeing her hunched reflection on the polished car, she was forced to put it down to the pressure of the long face she had felt obliged to pull throughout the wake, though the thought also entered her head that she would miss him because she would have less to moan about now that he was gone, and her heart plummeted like a lift. She pulled her collar up and slipped into the car, thankful for the shaded windows.

Johnny situated himself as close to the graveside as possible with Rosy whom he part covered with the flap of his overcoat. Kathleen had asked him to keep an eye on her. People smiled at him or greeted him with a nod and a wink partly out of deference to his loss and partly in recognition of his concern for his niece. He pursed his lips in gratitude, his eyes seeking their approval.

Nicholas' attention drifted on the familiar sound of the rosary which the priest led from under an umbrella that a young deacon not much older than Jack held over him. Another funeral was going on further down the cemetery and beyond that cars hovered past on the waterlogged motorway. In the sea of umbrellas and hats a face flashed and disappeared like a card in a deck. Jack! Jack! Nicholas' mind was awash with thoughts, none of which he could follow. As the prayers finished a neighbour of Frank's stepped forward to express her condolences and the mourners rushed to form a line behind her as at a newly opened check-in desk. Nicholas looked over their heads for Jack, and spotted him on the path leading to the cemetery gate. His hands manacled by two mourners, he quickly freed himself, and motioned them towards Johnny, who was happy to be centre stage, and pushed his way through the throng.

"Jack! Jack!" he called out but Jack continued on his way. "Jack! Jack!" he called out again. Jack turned around, throwing his head back in a gesture of surprise.

"You made it up," declared Nicholas.

"Yes. I got up today. Are you up long?" asked Jack.

"Eh, I came up on Tues., eh, no, Wednesday."

"Oh, so you are back a few days?"

"Yes, since Wednesday."

"Wednesday?"

"Yep, as soon as I got the news."

"So you're back a while," said Jack.

"Yeh."

"That was quick."

"Yes. I took the train up." Nicholas was on a tread-mill and wanted off, if he could only find the switch.

"On Wednesday morning, like?" asked Jack, repeating his lines.

"Yep. What about yourself?"

That should do it, thought Nicholas. Jack would talk, surely. He felt a surge of hope.

"I got up today," answered Jack, refusing to elaborate.

"Right. Do you…?" Nicholas felt the pull of a hand upon his shoulder and turned.

"Your mother wants you," said Gillian.

"Tell her….," he began.

"I'd better head on. I'm getting drenched," interjected Jack.

"…I'll be there in a minute."

When Nicholas turned back around again, Jack was gone, and he realised then what he had chosen not to believe: Jack had pretended he hadn't heard him when he had called out to him the first time.

* * *

The night after Frank's funeral Benny placed Frank's dentures beside her on the bed and began her official period of mourning.

"God only knows how much I miss you, love. It's nearly a week now and you wouldn't see it go in now, would you? And I always thought I'd be the one to go first. Do you remember you'd say 'Ach, sure, creaking doors always last the longest', and there's you gone now, and me left to pick up the pieces? In the name of God and all that's holy, how am I ever to get over you? You never raised a hand to me, bar that last time, which is more than what I can say for my own father, but sure that was me listening to that wee cat!"

She pulled the eiderdown over her legs.

"I had a great pair of legs. Do you 'member? Sure you were smitten that night at the Trocadero. Strangers in the Night, that's how you put it. And you were better than any of them. You know, our children didn't know how lucky they were to have a father like you. Many's a father would be coming home drunk and not a penny in their pocket but there you were with sweets for the lot of them. Our Kathleen wouldn't think of that now, would she? She'd have known all about it if her father had beaten her around the legs with a belt for going out to the pictures. Aye, and when did you ever pawn her wedding outfit? No, and not a one of them ever had to go begging for the dinner either. They were bloody lucky they had such a father, not like mine!"

She yawned as the heat of the blanket interrupted her stream of thoughts. She tugged it up over her chest, tucked it into her petticoat and rested her head on Frank's pillow.

When she awoke next morning she could hear voices downstairs. Johnny had called to see her, Gillian in tow. Nicholas was delighted. Benny hadn't stirred from her room and he had been too caught up with thoughts of Jack to be looking after her. At Nicholas' suggestion, Johnny and Gillian made their way upstairs. Hearing their footsteps, Benny hid behind the dresser as she had done years before when the greengrocer climbed the stairs in search of her. Not for the first time she had promised him a cup of tea the next time he called in but he had made the mistake of taking her literally. He was a Protestant and, for that reason, she concluded, had failed to understand that she always said one thing but meant another. Another day, she had lain under the bed, and yet on another she had hid in the boiler cupboard, sweating it out till he finished a cup of tea he had brewed for himself in the days before electric kettles. Frank had laughed at her behaviour and suggested that she was afraid of the grocer because of his religion. "Look, you, I'm not defending them, so I'm not," she fought back. "Nobody's saying Prods don't go a wee bit over the top at the Twelfth. Nobody's saying that. Everybody knows Prods wouldn't be seen dead in a Catholic shop during the Two Weeks for their own ones wouldn't allow it. But they make the best of neighbours, Frank. When my da had his first heart attack, they were around to the house the very next day asking could they help us out." "Aye, helping yous out alright! Help you out of the area more likely!" said Frank. She couldn't bring herself to tell him that the grocer gave her the creeps and that she was afraid he would make a pass at her. She held her whisht.

Johnny entered the bedroom and, seeing the empty bed, automatically walked over to the dresser. "Ma, would you come out o' that?" he pleaded with her in an empathetic but firm tone. Gillian couldn't believe her ears or eyes. She had heard of Benny's antics but never seen them.

Benny refused to budge.

"Ma, for God sake, you have to get on with things," urged Johnny, his voice now more forceful. She pulled herself down further behind the dresser wishing he would give her peace, however unlikely. She had never managed to get her way with him, even with father there to yell him into submission. He was born to be a millstone around her neck. He was her last and least wanted pregnancy and she had resented every kick she felt. For almost a year after his birth, he couldn't get his wind up properly, with the result that she barely got a wink of sleep. As a toddler, he had two left feet, and as a child, he wet the bed. Then as a teenager he would never take "No!" for an answer. She constantly went on at him about how he thought too much for his own good, but it went in one ear and out the other. Anybody could tell you that life was meant to go on in the heart, not the head, she would croon. Johnny found that rich, coming from a woman who, as far as he could figure out anything about her, had bolted the barn door in the dark ages.

Johnny caught her hand and pulled her up.

"I don't know why you bother," murmured Gillian under her breath, resenting the fact that if she were to as much as ask Johnny to make her a cup of tea he'd tell her where to get off.

Johnny blew on Benny's shoulders and hair to remove the dust.

"Stop spitting on me! I'll do it myself! At least I'll do it properly," she hollered as she exited her hideaway.

"Listen you! A taste of…" began Gillian.

"Love, would you get Ma a cup of tea? Two sugars, and a wee drop of bainne will do it," said Johnny changing Gillian's prescription. What Benny didn't need was a taste of her own medicine.

"You're the one needs your head examined, not her," Gillian snarled, but for all that did as he bid her.

Johnny put his arm around Benny and guided her back to the edge of the bed. "Ma, will you listen? Da's gone and you're going to have to get on with it."

He could be there for her now, he fancied, but it was himself he was consoling, and Benny's lack of gratitude confirmed this. She prised his hand off her. In her mind, Frank was still far from gone, and that was the way she wanted it. He had been her world. She had placed him on a pedestal. He would always be greater than her, a reality that Frank had come to enjoy. In the early days, he would mock her: the state of her going out the door, the dinners she 'cocked up' (not 'cooked up'); the 'oh, your mother has an idea'. In the later years, however, he needed her blind faith in him, and he pulled back on his criticism, fearing the day she would confront him over Kathleen. As Benny's addiction to 'bingo' intensified, filling the void of child-rearing, he—perhaps irration-ally—dreaded Benny's enlightenment. For her part, Benny sensed his fear but ignored his increasing warmth, preferring to be second fiddle. It was easier that way. And now she missed him at the helm and refused to give him up. Johnny hadn't banked on this. He had thought he could step into his father's shoes with ease.

Marlene pushed the door open with her foot, and as Johnny caught it he realised that Gillian had refused to bring the tea up out of fear she would throw it at Benny. Once, she had flung the vacuum cleaner at her mother in a temper, leaving Johnny in a state of shock. She had also confessed to pushing her niece down three steps at the bank one blustery afternoon at the end of her tether, but worst of all she had flung Johnny across the kitchen floor in the heat of an argument. "If you can't stand the heat, get out of the kitchen," she had railed at him. When Johnny had suggested counselling she threw a tantrum for good measure, slammed the door behind her and ran upstairs to lock herself in her 'huff room'. She came out of it to get the dinner ready, but she huffed for the next four days, blaming him for exaggerating things. When she finally came out of it, she explained to him that it wasn't unusual for people in her parents' home to push each other to get to the stove, and that was all she was doing when she had knocked against him.

Caught in the act, Johnny blushed as he got up from the bed where he had been holding Benny's hand and took the tea from Marlene. His hand trembled and the cup and saucer shook as he turned his back on Marlene without as much as a word. Realising she had come in at an awkward moment, Marlene left as quickly as she had appeared.

"Now, mammy, take a wee sup, and you'll be as right as rain-water," he said.

Benny set the tea on the bed-side table, uninterested.

"Ma, listen, do you want me to stay? Gillian can get a taxi home," Johnny suggested.

"No, sure, Nicholas is here."

You can get your own fucking siúcra, he thought.

Chapter 9

Nicholas checked the time and switched on the car radio. It hadn't taken him long to get used to the buzz of news on the hour every hour once back in Belfast. It drove Benny spare, though it never ceased to intrigue him how she came to life whenever she threw herself into the fray and ridiculed "polyticians" and she was on first name terms with them all—Gerry, David, Big Ian, and John among her favourite objects of scorn. He turned up the volume, delighted that he didn't have to take any lip from Benny for what she termed his "morbid interest".

Police have confirmed that the naked body of a man...

Real news at last, he thought. A naked body—great, that'll give them something other than their loss to talk about back at the house, so it will. The last big thing must have been the Shankill, no, the Rising Sun, no, fuck, the bomb in Omagh! How did I forget that?

...discovered on the side of the road...

The days when you'd be guaranteed some big news every day are well gone.

...on the outskirts of Glenavy at around midday is that of Mr. Jack Lackey, a 17-year-old youth who had been forced to leave the Province earlier this year following a death threat by the IRA. Mr. Lackey had previously been the target of a so-called IRA punishment beating...

Nicholas heard a roar "Ahhhhh! Noooo!" as his voice reverberated off the windscreen. "Jaack! Jaack! Oh God, Jack!" he shouted, his saliva hitting off the dash. The car came to an abrupt stand-still.

The body has been removed to the Royal Victoria Hospital where pathologists will carry out a post-mortem examination later today. Meanwhile, police are carrying out a forensic examination of the site where the body was found by a passer-by walking her dog. It is believed that Mr. Lackey was tortured and that he received a gunshot wound to the head. No organisation has claimed responsibility, but a spokeswoman for the RUC has said that it has all the hallmarks of an IRA killing...

...Workers at Harland and Wolff are today...

"Wolf? Jack. Jack, Jack, Jack, Jack! No, not our Jack! Not Jack! Not my Jack. No, please God, not him! Jaaack! Kathleen! Kathleeen! Who's afraid?"

Nicholas felt his forehead flop against the warm steering-wheel. The sound of car-horns brought him back from reality. He fumbled with the ignition and the car jumped forward.

"Jesus! What the fuck is the rush?" he bellowed as he took off in the direction of Curley's. All he needed was a few small things for sandwiches for the stragglers who were still turning up to express their sympathy with Benny over her loss. He drew up at the lights at Finaghy and a woman pulled up her car alongside him. If she hurries, he thought, she might be lucky and get a few bob back on the booze bottles in the Field where the Orangemen gather. The ground suddenly slipped from under him. Panicking, he made to press his foot on the brake only to find that it was already there. The woman's car had moved, not his, he realised, as she abandoned him, disappearing around the corner. He buried his head in his hands but all he could recall was something on the News about the shipyard.

In Curley's he parked in a mother and child space and alighted, treading carefully on the icy tarmac. The more careful he was, the more he lost his balance, wobbling like a magician's plate until his foot touched down on the gritted, bricked footpath. Once inside the shop, he examined the tomatoes for ripeness and picked up a lettuce before making his way to the delicatessen counter where he asked for a pound of Denny's cooked ham with no streaks, as it said on Benny's note. Next, he got the bread—white for Benny and the "eldery", and brown for Jack and his friends. Two old biddies, from what Nicholas could make out sewn together for protection, nodded to him in unison as he passed them by in the aisle, figuring they knew him from the way he looked at them so intently. He nodded back.

"Nice to see someone's in a Christmasy mood," the cashier remarked to Nicholas who was singing along to 'Santa Claus is coming to town', with the shopping list in his mouth. "Mind you, you do get a bit browned of with it when you have to listen to it morning, noon and night!" she added.

"Ah, sure, it's only once a year," said Nicholas, cursing her under his breath.

The cashier resisted his provocation, smiled to hide her irritation and began scanning his shopping through.

"That's £6.72, please."

"Do you take Laser?" Nicholas asked.

"Perfect!" she chirped.

Nicholas winked at a man at the next till forced to buy a Santa-shaped chocolate lolly-pop for a little boy who tugged at his sleeve.

"Are you collecting the stamps?" she asked, sticking the Laser receipt under his nose.

"No, thank you, Anna," he said as he patted his chest.

She plucked a pen from behind her ear and rolled it towards him just as he took one from his breast pocket.

"Snap!" she said noticing they had identical biros.

Nicholas broke down. Alarmed, Anna followed her nose and rendezvoused with Gloria at the cake counter. "All I did was lend him my pen," she cried. Gloria handed her a tissue and a Snowball.

"Excuse me, sir, are you alright? Is something the matter? Would you care to sit down?" asked the eagle-eyed floor manager who swooped now on Nicholas, clasping him by the arm. "Are you feeling unwell? Can I get you something? Are you on your own? Are you driving? Would you like me to call a taxi? Have you far to go?" He didn't wait for answers, his intention being to dazzle his prey long enough to transport him or her to the seat by the emergency exit to make way for the next shopper. Business was business.

Nicholas sat down, and felt the weight of a bag being tied around his fingers, and with it the weight of his loss.

"Jack!" he cried out.

"Maybe you'd like a glass of water, sir?" the manager asked, awaiting an answer now that the problem at checkout No. 4 was no longer causing an obstruction.

Nicholas was breathing life into Jack whose body lay limp in his arms, his jeans sodden with blood. Sensing eyes on him from the direction of the cake counter where there was now a rush on because of its obvious vantage point he jeered at them, "Here, are yous blind or what?" When Johnny finally hugged him, he knew there was no going back. The manager extracted a signature from Nicholas, who would have willingly signed his life away, and ushered them to the door with a "Happy Christmas!"

"My pen!" Anna shouted after them, brushing the coconut off her chest as if strumming a banjo.

Shit! thought Nicholas, crumpling the shopping list. He had forgotten the Kleenex toilet tissue, 120 SHTS.

* * *

Like dead men walking, Johnny and Nicholas followed MORTUARY as far as a glass partition where Nicholas slumped on the counter and spoke into a microphone to a receptionist who was busy nose-butting a broadsheet.

"Nicholas Lackey's relatives," he said.

"Sorry?"

"Jack Dunne's relatives," he corrected himself.

"Sorry?"

The receptionist stood her newspaper up against her computer screen as if trying to get a fire going, and put on her glasses, presumably, thought Nicholas, to facilitate her escape.

"Sorry about that! The microphone's dead," she said as she came out around to them, playing with the cord of her glasses as if a lock of hair.

"The Lackeys," he said, unwilling to take a chance this time.

"Oh, yes, right you are! Please come this way," she said, pulling on the corners of her starched blouse, causing it, Nicholas took note, to inflate. He fell in behind her, precipitating along the narrow corridor. As the opaque plastic doors at the end swung open into an anti-chamber, Kathleen fixed her sights on her brothers, Benny beside her, clasping Kathleen's hands. Nicholas pressed his palms against her cheeks and a film formed in Kathleen's eyes that said she had done everything to avoid this day. Though it was a defeated look, her parted lips spoke to him of deliverance: she wouldn't have to struggle any more to protect her child. He kissed her on the forehead.

"Will you come in with me?" she asked him.

Benny pushed her at the elbow to ease her up and Nicholas reached for her hand, squeezing it more to comfort himself than to comfort her.

"Would you like to follow me?" asked a nurse, indicating the double doors to their left.

As if we have a choice, thought Nicholas, already keeping to the black squares on the chequered floor. His heart thumped. Sirens in the aftermath of a loud blast, people bandaged in rags, stumbling—must have been that car with a bag on the back seat—

a group making petrol bombs, a girl dealt the card of death by friendly fire, somebody's shoe, a pool of blood into which people spat, the heat of wreckage. Would someone close my eyes for me, asked Nicholas as his past flashed before him. But no one appeared to hear. And then there Jack was, a disembodied face across the room, fluorescent lighting giving his countenance a sheen which was further intensified by the white sheet that hid the rest of him from view. His cheeks were drawn from the side of his nose to his jaw-bone and his lips were pursed as if in pain. Blood dripped into a bucket. Kathleen released Nicholas' hand.

"It's time to bring you home," she sobbed, brushing Jack's hair off his forehead. "I brought you home another day, didn't I? I wrapped you in white then too, love. Seven pounds four ounces. It was a winter's day then too, aye. My Wednesday's child. It's, it's over now, Jack. It's over. I'll take you back home now. Will you come, son, will you? I'll look after you now, I will."

Nicholas closed his eyes, his tears falling to the ground.

* * *

The Church of Ireland chaplain stood at the prison-cell door feeling half sorry that he had dragged himself away from the La Leche mothers. George had waited until the chaplain had done what he was paid to do before telling him that he had already learned of Jack's death on *breaking news*. As was his custom, he had sat through the News to the weather forecast, then dropped into the kitchen for his night-cap. Scraping the last of the hot chocolate from the bottom of his mug he had convinced himself the IRA must have had good reason for 'smacking' his son. He'd take it on the chin. His comrades had always said he was the real McCoy. He wouldn't let them down.

George could tell from the way the chaplain dallied in the doorway that he was looking for an excuse to leave. He knew what he was dealing with. It was well known that the C. O. I. were as a rule always more at home on the loyalist wings, wedded to the loyalists by more than just religious affiliation. Although technically on their books, George had effectively written the Church of Ireland out of his life the day he had heard a Protestant bishop refer to the IRA as gun-toting communicants. The assumption that all IRA members were Catholics had riled him. Besides, it didn't seem right to be having a chaplain officiate at a religious service just for him of a Sunday, though he had no doubt that his fellow Volunteers would have respected his wishes. (He could not attend with the loyalist prisoners for fear of his life.)

"It's getting late. I'm sure you've more important things to get on with," said George, letting him off the hook.

"The Lord giveth and the Lord taketh away," the chaplain responded. Then he was gone.

George returned to his letter that the chaplain—what did he say his name was?—had so rudely interrupted, and cast his eyes over what he had jotted down thus far.

Dear Ginny,

It was grate to hear from you. It's always good to know that we can depend on the support of our people in the US. It's not like you haven't been through it yourselves with the Brits, is it?

It's grate what you done for our kids last summer. Maybe some day I can return the favour, not that this cell is on offer (ha! ha!). And the only pool we have is for the wee bet we have on the horsies. (Ha! Ha! Ha!!) But honestly like, if you do wanna come over you can be sure of a céad míle fáilte because any friend of the Cause is a friend of ours. Just tell Kathleen when you're coming. Jack tells me you're a lawyer. In Dublin they call them LIARS (ha! Ha!) (No offence intended!)

Anyway, on a pint of business, as they say (ha! Ha!), you said you were amazed that I was a Protestant. You see Ginny the first thing you've got to understand like is that the Irish Republican Army is open to everybody. All the greatest Republicans in Irish history were Protestants like Wolfe Tone, Emmet, Pearse, and I think Connolly too. So, I'm not esceptional. I don't go to Church, I mean, or anything like that myself these days cause I've given all that up but I suppose its in my blood and the other Volunteers would have no problem with that.

Anyway, what was I saying? aye, I'm sure Rosy filled you in last year about my case. Whatever way you look at it, this is war, and I am a POW. By right, I shouldn't be in a place like this for fighting against calonal, colonilism. (If the Brits only taught the natives to read and write, they'd be doing well, but, sure, it pays to keep us in the...

George retrieved his pen from under the folds of his blanket.

...dark!!)

He shifted his eyes to his bed, then to Brigitte Bardot, the door, Benny's half-completed windmill, his runners, and finally to the copy of the Irish Constitution as if checking if they wanted to add anything, and then continued.

Whatever way you look at it the Brits are up to no good in Ireland. I mean you've gotta hand it to them. England is at the root of all the evils in Ireland. They've been mistreating the Irish for 800 years!!! They created this war and to date have done nothing to stop it. The Unionists to are just pawns who are bent on robbing the Irish people of their right to freedom.

(There's only so much I can say in a letter because the screws check out our male. (The walls have ears too!) It's just one of those things. They won't break us anyhow.)

But when we get what we need on the table we will call it a day, for the IRA always listens to the people. That's not to say that we'll let the British goverment rail-road us into surrender. At the end of the day, like, we owe it to our fallen comrades to make sure that the Brits don't pull the wool over the eyes of the nationalist people. So if we don't get what we're looking for, then we'll have to defend the Cause, if you know what I mean like. If it wasn't for the Irish Republican Army it'd still be a case of Croppy Lie Down but we're up off our knees now and there's no stopping us now.

He scratched his head. There was something else he had wanted to mention, but it wouldn't come to mind. It would have to wait. It probably wasn't important anyway.

Anyways, thanks very much again for putting the kids up. I hope they were no trouble without their da to keep an eye on them (ha! ha! ha!!) I'll send you a matchstick cottage when I get one ready.
Slán for now.
Seoirseamh

He moved his fingers in and out as if about to pump his blood pressure, placed the letter in an envelope along with the copy of the Irish Constitution and switched off the light.

When he awoke, it was ten o'clock and he realised that his shame at having overslept the morning of the Catholic attack on his neighbourhood in 1969 had finally caught up with him. He'd have to forego a work-out and shower—Kathleen would already be at the gate for him. He was going home.

Freefalling, Kathleen landed on his chest and smelled the man he was before his days at her Majesty's Pleasure, the nostalgic odour of sweat and pee a balm for her wounds. She was safe. George, on the other hand, was disoriented. For the first time in the past fifteen years she had no make-up on. Grief becoming her, he feared that someone might elope with her and he spoke in an effort to elicit something—anything—from her that would convince him that she still had eyes only for him.

"Why didn't you wait in the car?"

"Sure, you wouldn't know the car, George."

She recognises me, he thought. It was her alright, and this was him. He felt lighter. She let go of him and moved along the slush tracks towards the car. George pursued her, do or die.

"God, but you have it spotless," he remarked as he sat into the car. He had to keep talking.

"Belt up!" she said.

Her meaning wasn't lost on him. He sensed her distance. He would shut his trap. She stretched across him to strap him in and he felt uneasy as her fingers brushed against his thigh. He had never seen her drive. It was one of those things she learned to do while he was inside along with holding down a job, looking after the garden, and a long list of activities which, he figured, she never failed to enjoy telling him about over the years, rubbing his nose in it. He had given her a CONGRATULATIONS card the day she passed her driving test. He could see the cartoon car now, the skid marks and the L trailing behind like a kite in the wind. She had bought it and left it into security so that he could collect it and present it to her—one of the little twisted 'delights' of British rule she also loved to moan about. That day he had felt he had lost a little bit more of her. She had got her wings and it had seemed strange to be celebrating her independence. In the old days she had depended on him. He had been the provider, drawing the dole. He had been the one in the driving seat and he liked it. Now, he felt like a minor. He detached the Child of Prague from the dashboard.

"Don't, love. I'm trying to concentrate," she chastised him.

It isn't as if you don't know the road, he thought. Hadn't she made this journey every week for the last seven years thanks to the Dependents' Living Allowance that the Welfare gave Frank for his asthma and which paid for the car? Two could play at that game, he decided. He would stare out the window as if engrossed. Forty shades of green, a young couple passing them out at the speed of light, their music blaring, cars coming straight for him, their drivers on the phone, the mayhem was shocking. If you couldn't bring about order on the roads, how could you ever bring about a United Ireland? Kathleen didn't answer. He hadn't spoken, or else, if he had, he thought, she was still ignoring him.

With one eye on the distant hills in case she caught him staring at her, he took her in.

If he told her he found her attractive—the wart on her neck, the sandy-coloured hair above her upper lip and along the length of her cheek, her nose that twisted to the right, the dark rings around her eyes like old pennies, the corrie in her chin—all the things she tried to cover up—she'd bite off his nose for making fun of her, he realised. She would never believe him. She had never visited him because she had felt loved by him. There was nothing in it for her bar being there for him. He was her third child. Until recently he had always believed that even that fantasy had more to do with appearance than genuine concern for him, but now of late he had come to put her motivation purely and simply down to habit rather than anything else. He was her fix. And what if that habit was broken and he were thrown out on the streets? The traffic, the houses and even the hills were moving too fast for him now to pursue the thought of their future together.

Kathleen broke his train of thought.

"We have to go to Johnny's house first. You have to try the suit on I bought for you. Your dad wants to see you, too. He'll meet you in the Arms after the funeral. Mummy's in two minds about coming. Nicholas tells me she's finding it hard without Frank."

"How is she doing anyhow?" asked George, not expecting a reply.

"And we also have to pick up flowers," she answered.

"What ails my da that he can meet me in the Arms but can't cross over the road to the cemetery?"

"He doesn't want to risk it, George. So Benny said anyway. He was talking to her on the phone. Not after yon loyalist Stone attack that time in the cemetery."

"Jesus! Stone? Stone was one of his own kind. If my da had have been in the cemetery that day, Stone wouldn't have bothered his arse chucking grenades, would he, British undercover back-up or not? What's he on anyway? He's off his rocker."

Kathleen said nothing. As far as she was concerned, Alistair deserved all the criticism he could get. He had never been any help to her.

"What time's the wed...funeral at?" George asked.

"After the 10 o'clock," she said, biting her tongue. Wedding? She bucked. But, she told herself, he wasn't to blame for Jack's death, even if it felt that way. His hands were tied. Stuck in jail, he couldn't help even if he wanted to. No, she would stand by him as she had always done. Other wives had fallen by the wayside at the first hurdle but she had visited a man each week in prison that had never really been there for her from the moment they had left Belfast Central Library together. She had reason to be proud of herself, however much he had failed her. She couldn't imagine a life without him. Hadn't she even gone so far as to say as much to Marlene at Halloween? Marlene had rolled her eyes over at Brian sprawled out on the sofa with a feed of drink in him, and he had winked back. He couldn't have agreed more: George had done so much time inside he may as well never have been in her life. Kathleen had been too drunk to intercept their transmission.

"What's the weather supposed to be like today?" enquired George in a deliberate attempt to avoid any more talk of the funeral.

"I always hate going through this wee black hole!" commented Kathleen to lift her spirits. "It gives me the willies. Look at thon red, white and blue kerbstones, and, like, that's just been freshly painted and it's the middle of winter. Fucking Protestants and their love of the Union Jack!"

"Right enough! Now that you mention it," responded George. Seconds later, his mind was drawn to the funeral again, like a fly to shit; if Frank hadn't died so tragically, Jack would never have been targeted because he would never have been so stupid as to return to Belfast, and he, George Lackey POW, wouldn't be out sightseeing now. The knock-on effect. He would take his medicine even if it did nothing for him to be seen at the funeral of someone who had been executed for bringing a scourge on the community.

Kathleen used her quiet time well, reminding herself of the importance of sticking to what she knew. Whatever about staying with George and making a go of it all these years, there was also the Cause which had provided her with a sense of direction. She couldn't give that up now, especially not in the midst of catastrophe. You know what they say about moving houses, separation and deaths—the three big life changes. She would fall apart. No, she would stick to the familiar.

"It's meant to be wet all day," she now answered George's question, hoping that she wasn't too late.

They pulled into Johnny's street. It was as dirty as George had remembered it. The road sparkled with glass, and a burned out car crowned the green. Moments later, they stepped into Johnny's house.

"Here, try this on," Kathleen said as she lifted the suit from the settee. It was a perfect fit. She was used to shopping for him, right down to his underwear. She had resented shopping for him before he went to prison, but the funny thing was she had found it therapeutic ever since his arrest.

"Will you do the tie for me?" he asked.

She was within reach of his lips as she tied the knot, but neither of them stirred. The task completed, she went into the bathroom to wash her hands.

"We'd better get going. Stick them there shoes on," she said, flattening her hair with the palm of her hand upon her return. "Johnny bought them for Frank's funeral. They'll do you for running around in. I didn't have time to shop for new ones."

There had not seemed much point to her in forking out so much money for one day when things were so tight and George would be back inside within 48 hours.

"Can you manage laces?" she asked, handing him the shoes.

"Let me try," he said, reaching down to untie his runners.

Kathleen felt hurt by his sarcasm. She hadn't meant any harm by her comment.

* * *

"Hello!" said Shirley, picking up the phone in the hallway.

"Shirley?" Nicholas said.

His question filled her with dread. Who else could she be? Something was up. "Love!" she replied, in the vein of 'Love thy neighbour as thyself!' a command for him to go easy on her.

"I hate to…"

"How are you, pet?" she interrupted him to put off the inevitable bad news. She carried the phone into the living-room. The television would take the edge off things.

"I hate to, to ask this of you, Shirley, but could you come up? Could you, please? I just, I don't know, I, I, I just need somebody…I just want you to…It's, it's my. My nephew's been killed out of the blue. My fa…favourite nephew. I mean, I mean, we are close, just…close. I mean, I, we, you…"

"I'm coming, Nicholas. I'm on the way. I'm on my way. I'll do whatever it takes. Just, just, just give me a minute to pack my things. I'm coming up." She would have said anything to make him shut up.

Tears began to flow at the other end of the phone. She had to sort him out quickly.

"Listen, listen, love, I'll drive up this evening. Where'll I meet you?" she asked, taking the control he had lost as she wound the phone cord around her forefinger.

"McDonald's."

"McDonald's?"

"Yeah, McDonald's. It's right where you come off the motorway for Andersonstown. It's, it's well signposted."

"Right, I'll see you there. How long does it take? How far away is Belfast?"

"Maybe three hours maybe."

"Are you sure?"

"What? Yeah, it's about the same as Limerick."

"Limerick? That close?"

Nicholas bristled, realising that Belfast was too close for comfort for her.

"Oh, right," she continued. "I'll meet you in McDonald's at nine so."

"Okay. Bye-bye!"

"Bye, my love!"

Like it or not, she would have to drive. Public transport was out of the question. Buses and trains were a bit like social housing; you just never knew who you could end up next to. Only the thought that it was a '97 car and would create a bit of a dash made the whole idea a little more bearable. Nicholas' family wasn't exactly crawling with money. Maybe she should tell her mother where she was going in case she ran into trouble? No, Philomena would talk her out of it. She couldn't do that on Nicholas.

Inching her way towards the Border, Shirley kept one eye on the road for British soldiers, and one eye on the clouds that got ominously darker. When she noticed that the surface of the hard shoulder had changed colour, her heart skipped a beat: she had been in the North for some time without even realising it. Rounding a corner a British Army watchtower came into view. *Shit! I should have counselled Nicholas at a distance. No, I can do a U-turn over there. No, they're watching me.* The picture of her being delivered to her mother in a body bag—a zip-up hold-all from M&S—finally persuaded her to 'bite the bullet', a phrase that sent a shiver across the lining of her skull. The tingling had barely ceased when she heard what seemed like a shot. "Mummy!" she screamed, cradling her belly-button in her hands. Her eyes still on the road, she extended her arm out straight and felt around on the seat beside her, discovering the core of an apple, an empty bottle of Volvic and a crisps' bag, before laying her hand on her mobile phone. She couldn't get a dialling tone. It was barred: she was in a foreign country. Incommunicado. She stared at it, willing it to work, the way she had willed her dead father to speak. *And all the tight spots I got you out of, like when Sorcha nearly walked off with you the other day at work.* It made no difference—the phone failed to respond to her blackmail. Disgusted, she throttled it then chucked it aside and switched on the CD player for company. Soon afterwards she was relieved to find herself on a bright stretch of road. At least now, she would see her killers, she thought, then kicked herself for her negative thinking, causing the car to swerve. "Shit! Knowing my luck, I'll kill myself," she muttered beneath her breath, hoping that the soldiers wouldn't pick her up on their antennae on the top of the surrounding hills, which Nicholas had told her could pick up conversations as far away as Dundalk, down Mexico way. Mexico. As the first tears salted her lips she could swear she tasted the sea at Cancun. If only.

NEWRY 1 mile. She foundered on a sea of red, white and blue kerbstones, with the odd Union Jack here and there and *your man, what's his name up on that horse?* and felt the surge of hundreds of years of anger grip her chest and then recede almost as quickly again as a sea of green, white and gold washed over her, cooling the sweat on her brow and the back of her neck. Nearing Belfast, however, she was once again thrown into disarray. What if she made the fatal mistake of taking a wrong turn? The rain came on to greet her. It was the last straw.

McDonalds—it all appeared so normal that for a moment she was thrown off-guard but the deception was short-lived, for as soon as she had managed to yank open the door she was immersed in a cacophony of threatening Belfast accents. How do they expect wheelchairs to get in here, she wondered, as the door shut firm behind her? She wanted to run. And now that she was up close, she found the people a touch more common than what she was used to: fake trainers, thick make-up to hide bad skin, too many bobbins. She would risk the toilets nonetheless. Nature had to take its course, never more so than in war.

Nicholas appeared out of the Gents as she exited the Ladies and they hugged each other out of the glare of the customers. It wasn't so much the food that did it for Nicholas at McDonalds as all the separated men with their kids. It made him feel young and attractive. Today, it would help him forget and so he offered to queue. She left him to it, explaining she hadn't had the time to get her money changed. There was no point in bothering him with the truth; nothing would entice her into an exchange bureau north of the border.

Did she want her usual?

"No, a hamburger Happy Meal, and a coffee instead of the kiddies' drink. A large coffee because I could do with a pick-me-up. Do you know what? Someone took a shot at me on the way up."

Nicholas hugged her again, if only to hide his smirk. Someone's car had obviously back-fired.

"Did you get my coffee?" Shirley asked at the sight of the approaching Sprites. A few moments later he returned again with the coffee which he had forgot to order having earlier gotten distracted by a Keanu Reeves look-alike in the next line.

"I, I don't know what end of me is up," he began. Mayonnaise dripped down over his chin and he reached for his wad of napkins. There was no easy way to tell her about Jack, but Shirley was not about to take up the slack as she dug her nails into her burger.

"He was just unlucky," Nicholas tried again.

She knew she would have to grasp the nettle. "He must have been, eh, young," she ventured. "Was he the man killed in the car crash, on the radio on the way up?"

"No, he was, em, he was murdered."

"Murdered?" she crowed.

He could have sworn she had said "burgured" but it was hard to tell, the way she held the burger at her mouth like a harmonica. Either way, the look on her face told him he would have to act quickly to prevent her from choking to death.

"The IRA. They're a law onto themselves. Anti-social behaviour, but it had nothing to do with him," he explained.

"Anti-social behaviour?" she asked, coming down a note.

A hunk of a man at the next table wearing a Giants' baseball cap, a pencil sticking out from under the side of it, looked around at her, then ran his hand the length of a bikini on Page 3 before caressing a rump for the benefit of his mate who quickly undressed her with his eyes. It was long enough for Nicholas to have forgotten Shirley's question.

"Anti-social behaviour?" she asked again, whispering now.

"I don't really want to…It's not the place for it. Not here," he pleaded with her, raising a white napkin to get her to cease fire. McDonalds on the Andytown Road was not the ideal place for discussing the rights and wrongs of the IRA's punishment strategy, especially not with a naïve Southerner.

* * *

George swung into their housing estate and felt his stomach turn. Wheelie bins were strewn like bodies on the roadside, as if the Grim Reaper had just passed through, some with their throats slit, heads hanging off, others face down, some on their backs, still others about to topple over at any moment. While a flock of crows tore frantically at a piece of flesh amid the scattering of bones one of their kin strutted the white line as if cognisant of the Highway Code. What was wrong with the tin bins of old, half-charred, with lids balanced on them like clowns' hats, thought George. Were they not good enough? People had become so complacent, that was the trouble. Nobody banged their bin-lids to signal the arrival of British troops any more and no one gave a damn either. Kathleen braked to avoid a child. A woman raced over in her slippers, scooped the child up by the back of his nappy, and scowled at Kathleen. George barely noticed them, absorbed by the streets which appeared so much smaller than he remembered them. The war he had fought there now suddenly seemed petty too. He blew on the window to cover up his past. Kathleen drew up outside their home.

Rosy jumped the doorstep and rushed over to George, flinging her arms around him. He was an anchor for her on a stormy sea.

"Rosy, my wee love! How are you, mo chroí?" he greeted her.

She had tied a yellow ribbon to the winter cherry, and wore a green ribbon on her dress for the release of prisoners, both gestures which George was glad to see after the dearth of feeling on Kathleen's part.

"Daddy! Will you come up and see my room, will you, later?"

"No probs," he replied.

Slipping past her, George was swallowed up by the mourners in the hall who shook his hand and patted him on the back. In prison, he nursed himself to sleep each night matching up their names and faces. It kept the institutionalisation factor at bay. Now, however, the names that came to his lips seemed not to fit the faces in front of him. It had to be the fault of the lighting. Shading his eyes with his hand, he squinted up at the lily-shaped chandelier, then surveyed the landscape once more. The ceiling and walls needed painting. The carpet was threadbare, the faces foreign. It was a foreign land. His hand still passing from one to the next, he manoeuvred his way into the kitchen. There, the clatter of cutlery and delph overwhelmed him. He had to escape.

"Are you okay?" Kathleen asked as he side-stepped her in the hall.

"That racket's cracking me up. It's all plastic knives and forks in the jail, sure," he explained.

He climbed the carpeted stairs—a double challenge—and slinked into his bedroom. A picture-perfect four-poster with cream see-through drapes glistened in the sunlight, contrasting with the bare hardboard walls that surrounded it. He would have to make love there. He turned on his heels.

"The place could do with a coat alright, couldn't it?" he said to Kathleen who was on the bottom stair awaiting him.

"Yeah, it needs a man about the house." She pointed to the parlour. "Have you been in yet?" He got a jolt. He had forgotten about Jack. As luck would have it, just then the kitchen door opened and Gillian appeared with two pints in her hands. "I'll have a Guinness," he called out to her.

Angered by his indifference, Kathleen took the stairs two at a time.

Pint in hand, George sought refuge in the parlour from the noise, where Jack lay in a closed coffin by the box window. The coffin seemed out of synch with the lively atmosphere in the next room, but the irony wasn't lost on him that it was the very reason that they were all having such a good time. "It took you to get me one day out in fifteen years," he whispered to Jack as he moved closer. He ran his finger over the name inscribed in gold lettering on the coffin lid. It all came flooding back to him. In the event of a boy, their baby could be called anything but William, which he forbade, and Kevin, which, for some unknown reason, Kathleen was dead against. They went through close on a thousand names but failed to agree on anything. On the day of his birth, seven centimetres dilated, the worst behind him, the mention of forceps hit George like a bolt out of the blue and Jack slipped out—in both senses. "I need to go to the Jacks," he muttered as he tipped forward. His sudden urge to vomit had given him a clarity that had hitherto been lacking.

He rubbed his fingers over 'Lackey': In jail, he had once caught the tail-end of a broadcast on BBC Radio Four that claimed that peoples' names were rooted in their occupation or surroundings. In his case, he had reflected, it had not just been a matter of his distant ancestors being lackeys to some lord but he himself had lived the life of a lackey. His name had shaped his destiny. He had started out a working-class Protestant, as badly off as any socially, politically, culturally and economically disadvantaged Catholic, and his marriage to a Catholic, his passage into the Catholic community, and his journey into the IRA had confirmed his status as an underdog. Observing the reflection of his face in the brass plate on the coffin lid, it struck him now that he had also been a lackey to Kathleen. His joining the IRA had more to do with a desire for freedom for himself than a desire for national freedom. She had held all the cards and called all the shots. What could you expect from a 'Dunne'? A 'fort'. She had hemmed him in. He had had to get away from her. The IRA had been his ticket.

No, no, that wasn't it at all. Don't be silly! Jesus, must be the effect of the first Guinness in fifteen years! What do you think, Jack?

In no hurry to go back out and face Kathleen, he lit up a cigarette, directing the smoke away from Jack as if it mattered. Jack, he now realised, had fared no better. A slave to drugs, he had earned a brass plate for all his shenanigans. His killers were probably in the house at this very moment, he surmised. It wasn't quite what he had meant, but, yes, come to think of it now, he and Kathleen had killed him. "No, we did our best," he said, quickly laying his doubts to rest as he blotted out Jack's name with his pint glass. The Brits were to blame. They had robbed Jack of a father. He would have much rather have been at home leading a normal life with his baby son instead of being holed up in some safe house because the Brits couldn't get two simple words into their heads—"Brits Out!"

He exhaled smoke through his nostrils and flicked his ash on the carpet. He would enjoy the quiet while he had it. There was no getting away from it, he thought as he observed the wooden windmills, cottages and harps that he had made from matchsticks over the years in prison—he was of ornamental value. And it must have been obvious to Jack, he now suddenly felt. He placed his hand on his.

* * *

Nicholas knew that his revelation would conflict with Shirley's understanding that the Troubles were essentially a working-class thing that men with nothing better to do had visited upon themselves, but he couldn't hold back. "Coming up on the right, you probably don't remember, see there, the shop with the post-box at the entrance, we have, you have, right next to it, there, see that semi, that's where a university lecturer was tied up and murdered by loyalists," he said, all the while picking burger from his teeth.

"A lecturer?" she asked in a startled voice while pulling at the belt of her coat, which had become jammed in her car door.

"A-ha," he said, making a mental tick in the CORRECT box. "She'd been living here for years doing nobody...."

"A woman?"

"…any harm," he continued, ticking the box below it, "and the loyalists did her in. And you can bet your life the Brits were up to their tonsils in that, uh! She was a……" No, there was no point in mentioning the lecturer's political connections. Shirley didn't need to know that information. And, anyway, it'd do her no harm as Southerners needed a good shock. They had got off lightly for too long. "…a well-respected academic," he added.

"I see, I see," she commented, though she could see nothing bar the road ahead, for her mind had gone completely blank.

"Are you okay?" he asked, resting his hand on her shoulder. "We could always do this some other time. I mean, I could come back this way another day, if you want."

"What? No, no. I mean, it's all the same to me. I mean. I mean, it's important. I, I…" She stopped and tugged on her belt to allow herself time to find words that made sense. And then they popped like corn, "I, I wouldn't miss it for the world!"

Was she being sarcastic or was she being sincere? Probably a bit of both, Nicholas concluded. She probably wanted to see more but was also afraid to look—the way he enjoyed a good horror film through his fingers.

"Well, then, if you're sure, then, the stretch of road in front of you is where the two British corporals were dragged out of their car and done to death. They got it all on TV. Heli-telly, actually! The Brits were watching it all from somewhere up there in a helicopter," he said, pointing to the sky. "Why they didn't intervene to save them is beyond me."

The look of fear on her taut face brought him a certain pleasure, though he assured himself it was nothing personal. "Honestly, we could do this some other time," he suggested, to prove his point to himself.

"No, it's okay." Now wasn't the time for second thoughts, Shirley concluded. Dublin was a long way off. The car went over a bump and her lip quivered. Oh, my God, a corporal, she thought. "Sure, we're nearly there, aren't we?" she asked.

"Yes, a few more minutes basically. This spot, by the way, is where I went down."

"Oh, right," she said as she heard herself wonder what business of his it was to be at the IRA funeral at which the corporal she had just run over was murdered. Maybe he was *involved*.

"And that modern brick building, if you just look left again— we're nearly at Kathleen's now—which is totally out of place, there between the hardware store and the car-park, which is also recent, used to be the Co-op, but it was burned down by vandals. I actually saw it going up in flames, would you believe?" he said, forever the informative guide.

"Ah-ha. I see. I see." She took a deep breath and quietly let it out.

"And coming up on the right soon is the Sinn Féin Headquarters. Do you see it there? It looks a wee bit more fancier than the houses on either side but it's just the effect of the fortified wall. It used to be the doctor's surgery in times gone by. Now, it's Gerry Adams'. The loyalists came up from that street just there, oh, probably only a matter of months ago, no, I'm lying, about a year ago now and shot a man dead right on the doorstep. No, two men, actually. They jumped out of a car with an AK47 and shot them stone dead. The priest from that there chapel seen them, actually."

"Are we nearly there yet?" she blurted out. She regularly took the trip to Limerick on business, but this, she now realised, made Stab City seem like Butlins.

"Aye! Welcome to West Belfast! Sure, I'll take you for a wee dander on the road later. It'll be good to get out of the house."

What did he think she was, like, an eejit? Had he not realised she was only taking the Mickey when she had said she wouldn't miss it for the world? It was almost as if he was enjoying it, though she knew it was silly to think anyone could enjoy all the gore. Come to think of it though, the girls from work had said something about a guy they'd met in Belfast Central Station who was totally into the whole war thing. The IRA had put the nationalist community on the map to such an extent that wherever the Irish went they were respected for the way they wiped the floor with the Brits. Yes, it was as clear as day—Catholics loved 'the Struggle' no matter what the price. But this wasn't the time for tackling Nicholas about the 'tour'. She would go with the flow.

"You've certainly an interesting past!" It was the closest she could get to saying that he loved the whole 'we're up off our knees' thing without giving herself away.

"It's not that it's interesting. Different, maybe," he fobbed off her compliment.

"From?"

"What? You mean, what's it different from, like?"

"Um."

"Well, for one thing, the norm, I suppose. Though, I mean, I have to say though this is kind of the norm for us up here. I mean, it's not just me that has the interesting past—it's everybody. It's a community thing. I mean, you just get on with it, kind of 'hing. Like, what's the point in moaning about it, like? Who would listen to you? I suppose it's been different for yous. I mean, yous wouldn't really understand 'cause you're not from here."

"Yeah, but it's changing in the South."

"About time, too! The war here needs to be internationalised."

"Absolutely!" she said, letting the contradiction go about Southern involvement being a case of 'internationalising' the problem. She pulled at her belt again.

"Here, swing the door open there! I'll hold on to the steering-wheel," he said.

"Will that be alright? Look! Will he do anything?"

"You're fine. You've nothing at all to worry about. They're on cease-fire," said Nicholas now noticing the British soldier propped up against the gable wall of Eastwoods bookmakers.

"But this is an Irish reg."

Nicholas held on to the steering-wheel and Shirley reluctantly and gingerly opened the door.

"Oh, my God, oh, my God! Agghhh! Mummy! Mummy!" she screamed, attaching her fingertips to her head like suction pads.

"You're alright! You're alright!" he shouted, as he threw himself across her and grabbed hold of the door which he slammed closed. "He's not doing anything. He's not going to shoot you. He's just checking you through his telescopic sights."

Shirley continued screaming, unable to hear him. She had seen this scene a thousand times on television—in the Lebanon, Palestine, on the Falls Road, in the Deerhunter movie. And there had been fatalities every time.

Nicholas lost it. "He won't shoot! Calm down! Calm down, will you, or he WILL!"

He dragged her left hand onto the steering-wheel. "Drive, for God's sake!"

"Can we get to your sister's place right now? Can I go home? What am I doing up here anyway? My coat belt! Where's my belt?"

"Listen! That's the least of our worries!" he snapped, thrusting it at her.

Why did I ever say yes? And what if there are television cameras at the funeral? What if mummy sees me? Maybe I could stay back at the house and help with the sandwiches. But would I be safe till they all got back from the funeral? What if the IRA decided to attack Kathleen's while they were all out? Oh, God, am I off my tree or what?

"My belt! Thank God! I'd hate to lose it," she said, tucking it between her legs.

Chapter 10

It was time. Kathleen disappeared upstairs to fetch her rosary beads which she had left on Jack's bed soon after Johnny had told her of his death. She had taken them from around the statue of the Virgin Mary in the hall, and without a word to Johnny, had gone to Jack's bedroom to be close to him. The second she had opened the door she had smelled him and had half expected to find him there. She had thrown herself on his bed which had still felt warm, and had said a decade of the rosary for the repose of his soul surrounded by his things—his poster of British birds, a few tatty school books, a luminous night sky. As her life exploded before her eyes she was convinced that the Blessed Mother still looked after her, though she no longer experienced the apparitions of her youth. Lying there, she had recalled that she hadn't paid him any heed when he had arrived into the kitchen earlier that day to say goodbye, but now she could hear him pour the Coke from the fridge, sucking in the air between his front teeth as he always did when anxious. She had remained with her back to him, mad at him for coming up to the funeral in spite of the death threat that hung over his head, and mad at him for going on so much the night before about how much his grandfather had always loved him. She had stroked her face with his blanket, regretting her anger. "If only I had turned around. If only I had known it was going to be the last time, I would have said something. He would have said something."

Kathleen found the rosary beads and felt at peace as she fingered them. She had brought him home. She had, for once, been faithful to him. Moments later, however, upon pushing open the parlour door, the coffee table, which she had moved to make room for the coffin, caught her eye, and her heart sank. If only he had been brought home to some other house seventeen years earlier, he wouldn't be where the table should be, she thought. Catching sight of her, George nodded to Johnny, and Nicholas and Brian stepped forward. With the help of the undertakers, they heaved the coffin up onto their shoulders. Nicholas shuddered. It was lighter than Frank's. Jack had been so young.

Lost in the crowd that mingled by the doorstep around the hearse, the wisp of the sharp breeze hit Kathleen's lungs and a wave of emotion filled her to bursting, television cameras taking aim on the nearby green. Jack, she realised, was but one more victim of a conflict that wasn't worth a single life, his death the latest one-day wonder. Falling in behind the cortege, she recalled the Disneyland photograph of him in the Irish News the previous morning, squeezed between talk of demilitarisation and a predicted Christmas shopping boom, and lowering her head, parsed her thoughts with her heavy footsteps.

> The vast majority
> of peace-loving people
> eating their Ulster fry
> will have seen your face, Jack.
> "Such, a good-looking man!
> What a beautiful smile!
> Awful waste of a life!
> Will they ever see sense?"
> Smiled back at you no doubt,
> enjoyed a little cry.
> Them'uns killed you, they did,
> with their kind-heartedness,
> their money in the bank.

As another four men came forward to give the coffin a lift, Kathleen stopped and looked around her at the mourners. They hadn't known Jack. They were only there to indulge themselves in the spectacle of her pain, knowing how far she had fallen. Her son, the son of republicans, had betrayed them. She looked them in the eye.

Rosy gripped Gillian's arm, following at a distance along the footpath. George had wanted her to travel with Marlene in the limousine, but she had preferred to see her brother off properly. As she walked along, she noticed a woman and a young man standing in a doorway. It was the house into which her mother had run with Jack and her to take cover from gunfire on their way to school some years earlier during a gun-battle between the IRA and British troops. It was the third time that she had taken refuge that day. Twice Kathleen had sheltered with them in alleyways. Amid the crackle of gunfire she had told the children before leaving for school that they could stay at home if they wanted but that she also wanted the best for them, and she wasn't going to let the Brits stand in the way of their education. Rosy had immediately offered to go and then Kathleen had explained to Jack that he would have to go too because she couldn't very well leave him at home on his own. "C'mere quick, get in before you get your head blown off yous!" the woman had hastened them inside. "Thon's a bloody disgrace! It'd put your head away looking out at that all day! Them yahoos have us crucified. Sit yourself down here, love, beside the fire and get some heat into you. You may as well get some heat into you while you're waiting."

Kathleen had sat down, Rosy and Jack huddling in to her.

"Fighting for Ireland! Uh! Did you ever hear the like of it in all your life?" she continued. "Fighting for Ireland? Damn the bloody bit of it! They've my nerves wrecked this day, so they have, missus! You can't even get across your own door to get in a few wee messages, if you wanted. No, God scurse, it'd be too good for them to go away on round the corner there, wouldn't it, and fight at their own doors? Oh, no! That there'd be asking too much! What sort of parents are they anyway that allows their children run riot, holding us to ransom? Here c'mere, lambs." She sat Jack and Rosy up on a side-board at the side of the fireplace in the shelter of the chimney breast along with her son who squeezed up against Rosy. They would be safe from stray bullets there. Kathleen found a spot on the floor in front of the blazing fire.

They had run into the house of a 'West Brit'. It turned out that she had been a member of 'Women Together' in the mid-seventies, marching along the Shankill Road with other Catholics to call for peace. She wasn't blowing her own trumpet or anything, but she had appeared on the front page of the Belfast Telegraph holding a banner with a nun: 'The people of Andersonstown say sorry'. She still had a copy upstairs, though it was going all orange with time. And she had even met Willie Whitelaw up in Stormont.

Kathleen pulled back from the fire. She had had no time for the likes of Women Together. She had wasted a box of good eggs on them at one of their meetings. They were selling out to the Brits. So, at the first lull in the shooting, she was glad to take her leave. Jack pleaded with her to stay longer, but she dragged him outside, insisting that he had nothing to fear, the worst was over.

Rosy looked ahead now at her mother walking defiantly behind Jack's coffin. She admired her. No matter what the risk, she would never let others get the better of her. Jack, however, had seen it all differently. "What sort of a mother was she that she'd bring you to school through the worst of riots?" he had ridiculed her when out for a drink with Rosy years later. He had never forgiven her, and now it was too late. They entered the church grounds and the procession broke up, the mourners thinning out, cutting Rosy off from him. It was over now. She would let him go.

* * *

"We are blind to grace," Fr. Glover warned his congregation.

Sitting with her eyes closed, Kathleen could hear Brian's keys rattle on his trouser belt, the swish of a dress as Gillian found a seat behind her, the Christmas traffic pick up speed now that the cortege had passed, the Dublin train in the distance, and the drone of the priest's banalities.

"We are blind to grace," he warned them again. It was an oratorical method that he had learned in theologate: repetition was the key to keeping things simple for the faithful who couldn't be expected to understand finer theological concepts, especially not grace. Kathleen wished she were on the Dublin train.

"We are blind to grace, especially when there is pain. The beauty of life stares us in the face but more often than not we fail to see it. We'd rather buy more—more luxuries, more holidays—or do more—more odd jobs, more people to see, more hours at work or in front of the television—and grace passes us by—a smile, a kind word, an act of kindness. The beauty of life stares us in the face, my dear brothers and sisters. And as I observe your faces this morning it stares back at me because in your tears I see the love you had for Jack. And as I look at the sh...shot of him there on his coffin, the beauty of life stares back. We can crib and moan, curse God, ask "Why?" or we can thank Him for the mountains of love that saw the deceased through to the end, and the mountains of love that he shared with us in his lifetime. The choice is yours, but remember we are blind to grace. You have to strain your eye to see the mountains."

Longing to see grace, Kathleen opened her eyes and forced herself to look at the photograph of Jack which Frank had kept by his bedside. George pressed her hand.

"But one thing's for certain. Jack is now safely in the arms of Jesus," Fr. Glover added, cocking his arm for the finale, "for Jesus loves the one whom others hate."

The way he took aim was enough to put the fear of God across Benny and when "Jesus loves the one who mothers hate" rang out her eyelashes fluttered like woodpigeons' wings until her gaze came to settle on George. But she realised at once that he, too, had seen right through her and her eyes sought refuge on the Cross suspended above the altar. She had hated Kathleen, yes, but did her good works count for nothing, dear Jesus? Hadn't she set the altar up on many a bleak, winter's morning when Fr. Glover was still in his bed reading the death notices. Jesus failed to stir. Had He no love for her, she begged Him?

George dropped Kathleen's hand like a hot-coal as Benny's searing gaze momentarily cut him to the core. She had seen through him, like the priest, he thought. He was guilty. He had hated Jack.

Feeling his hand withdraw, Kathleen told herself she didn't have to fear George's judgement. Fr. Glover was right, she had mothered hatred—of George, of Benny, more recently of her father, and even of herself—but the compassion in Fr. Glover's eyes confirmed the love of Jesus for her. Her sins were forgiven her.

"And those who hated Jack enough to kill him will one day have to answer to their God," Fr. Glover concluded before picking off the readers, the altar boys, the choir, the congregation, the flower-arranger, and even the funeral directors, for thanks, leaving only himself unmentioned, and thus their focus on him for the crystal clear sermon that they couldn't have gotten in the neighbouring parish.

Bathed in redemption, Kathleen didn't hear his words of thanks. Nor did Nicholas, for the thought of Jack in Jesus' arms had earlier arrested his attention.

* * *

Many of the mourners had already left the cortege for the comfort of the pub or for a few errands as the family neared Jack's resting place at the bottom of the cemetery. George bristled at the dwindling numbers but felt a surge of pride as the republican plot came into view. He still hoped that one day he would be buried there. He had once held similar hopes for Jack, and felt shame at how things had turned out. He vowed to hold his head high for the duration of the funeral as a soldier might do for fallen foe but his resolve soon petered out with the realisation that his son had paid the ultimate price, not him. Jack had won out. He had paid for his principles—his love of his grandfather—with his life whereas he had to live with the shame of having been captured by the Brits while asleep in his bed because one of his own had informed on him. Jack had beaten him to it. He had robbed him of his destiny and his glory. A single tear formed in his eye. It was for himself.

The gravediggers lowered the coffin after the prayers. Kathleen held her rosary beads tight with both hands and scanned the cemetery for colour as the gravediggers filled the grave with dark clay. The crowd was small now. Jack Lackey was already just another number, she thought. He would be on the year-end list of the 'grim toll' of violence. 'Grim toll' she recited, pausing as she caught sight of a green ribbon here, a golfing umbrella there. The only grim people in Northern Ireland were standing there before her eyes, she thought. The rest would whoop with glee at Jack's death, or congratulate themselves on the fact that, unlike Israel or that other place—Rwanda?—Northern Ireland had not slipped over the edge, that they were a resilient people who knew how to hold back from the brink. They were a people who knew how to make it last, she thought now as she treaded the rival, spangled republican plots. Their division in death was ample proof of this. Jack's body was not yet cold in the ground, and people were already concerned, indeed, she countenanced, in some cases even pleasantly anxious, about who would be killed next. The people of Northern Ireland would settle down to Scene around Six on television tonight and watch close-ups of her and her family and she would have to tell them of her hope that he didn't die in vain, that he would be the last victim, but it would simply whet their appetite for more. She would give them what they wanted—a clear conscience so that they could live with themselves until the next bulletin. What choice did she have? She could hardly wish her suffering on them—going over the brink would hardly sort the North out. She wiped a tear from her eye, the red rose in her hand rubbing against her cheek, and the cameras flashed. She would sell. Her grief would entertain. Her eyes shuttered to hide her thought that it was a conflict that people were too busy enjoying to be bothered to do anything about.

Nicholas caught up with Kathleen and brought her hands to his lips. They were Jack's. He broke down in her arms and wept at the idea that she would never know the cause of his grief.

* * *

Back at the house, Kathleen made a beeline for Nicholas. She was keen to meet the new girlfriend whom she had only briefly sighted prior to the funeral.

"It's?" Kathleen asked, stretching out her hand to Shirley.

"Shirley," intervened Nicholas, eager to show her off.

"I'm very sorry for your trouble," commiserated Shirley.

"I'm glad you could make it. It's good of you to come," Kathleen replied.

The dinner party tone surprised Shirley.

"He could do with a bit of support," Kathleen continued, patting Nicholas on the back. "It wasn't easy on him. He was very good to Jack the last few months when they were together down in his place. He was his only nephew, you know."

"Oh, eh, yeah, I know," Shirley stammered. "But it can't be easy on any of you."

Kathleen batted her eyelids to fend off Shirley's sympathy. She had shunned all condolences to date. "Will you be up for long?" she asked.

"No, not for long. A few days at the most. I have to be back in work the day after Stephenses Day."

Kathleen raised her eyebrows. "Stephenses Day?"

"Boxing Day," explained Nicholas.

"Oh, right. Right enough! Boxing Day! Anyway, I'm sure you'll be glad to see the back of this mad place!"

"No, but, it's...it's...it's a bit like we're in different..." Countries? States? Worlds? The words fell like skittles on the tip of her tongue.

"Jurisdictions," said Kathleen, coming to her rescue,

"No better word," said Nicholas, his eyes shifting back and forth from Kathleen to Shirley like a tennis umpire's, "'Indifferent'! Yep, that's it spot on, Shirley! You got it in one! Indifferent! Southerners are indifferent about the North! I never thought you'd say it though!"

"Ignore him!" Kathleen instructed Shirley. "Will you be up again some time soon? It would be lovely to see you," she continued.

"Eh, what? Eh, yes, yes, I will, now that I've broken the ice," said Shirley, though she had no intention of acting on her word.

"Well, you are welcome anytime, love!" said Kathleen, taking Shirley's hand in hers.

"Thank you!" said Shirley, with a smile that she had perfected in her training in Sales.

"Kathleen, sorry, but do you have a wee second? Fr. Glover's on the road out," interjected Brian.

"Oh, okay. Will you tell him I'll be there in a wee jiffey?" she answered. "I'd better go. You mustn't keep a priest waiting! Sure you can't, Nicholas?" she jested.

"Look after yourself," said Shirley, her smile genuine this time.

Nicholas caught up with Kathleen just as she was on the verge of disappearing out of the room.

"Kate, are you sure you're alright?" he asked, catching her by the sleeve.

"Happy Days!" said Kathleen.

"But..." he began and finished in the same breath. There was no point in his persisting. Nothing he would say would bring her into reality. She was on a high of some sort. She was a woman who carried the weight of the world on her shoulders and was already sizing up the next catastrophe. He released her arm and she slipped away.

He went out to the garden for a breather. It was not just Kathleen that was in denial, he thought, leaning up against the wheelie bin. 'Happy days!" was at best an expression of a community's smug, deluded parochialism. Kathleen and her ilk had drunk too much nationalist elixir for their own good. But it wasn't just Northerners that had their heads in the sand. The waitress in the café the other day around the corner from Shirley's place was another example. All he had wanted was a pot of boiling water with his tea. "No problems!" she had said, stabbing her pad with her pen in anger, but who had said anything about a problem, he had thought? If it was such a pain, why hadn't she just said so straight out? The real problem was people believed all the crap they came out with while their issues floated around them like banshees screaming out for attention but they would sooner drink themselves to death than acknowledge them. Happy Days, my arse!

Resolving to sort out Kathleen's garden at the first opportunity— she had dug it up to sow a lawn but the clumps of clay had once more knitted together where she had left them—he picked up a cup of tea in the kitchen on his way back to Shirley, which burned his tongue, causing his eyes to water. He suddenly felt weighed down: his problem was he cut and pasted reality just like the rest of them.

"Well, where did you go?" Shirley whispered in indirect proportion to her ire but at the sight of his tears her anger suddenly evaporated. "Have you been crying?" she asked, raising her voice.

"No, it's the tea. It's roasting hot."

"Oh!" she exclaimed, her anger once more quickly coming to the boil again. "You never said that Jack had been living with you in Dublin," she whispered again.

"Did I not? Are you sure? Are you sure I didn't? God, I'm nearly sure I did. I suppose there was so much going on with all the changes."

"And didn't you tell me he was your favourite nephew? That sounds a bit strange, doesn't it?" she persisted.

"Did I? I didn't say that."

"You did so. You told me so on the phone."

"What? Why would I say that for, when I have, had, only one nephew? Don't be daft!"

Maybe it had been the shock, she thought, but that still didn't explain why he hadn't mentioned that Jack had been living with him. Had Nicholas been hiding him from the IRA?

"Well, whatever," she said. "But how come he was living with you for a few months? You never mentioned him to me. Was he there when you left?"

"No. He moved on just before me. He found himself somewhere else to live, and a wee job."

"So, did the priests give him a room?"

"No, he had a cottage at the back of the grounds. He used to eat with us though. He had to get out of the North."

"Had to get out? What? God, the poor thing! Why? God, you must have missed him when he left, if he was there a couple of months. How long did you say he was there?"

"Three months almost."

"You must have missed him, the poor, poor thing! Did he keep in touch?"

"Eh, no. I wanted to give him space. He, eh, needed space. He was just getting over a beating. The IRA had beaten him to pulp for stealing cars."

"Stealing cars? Do people around here steal cars?"

Nicholas lowered his bottom lip. It worked.

"Will, will my car be safe?" she asked, the panic now evident in her pitch.

"Do you have an alarm on it?" he asked. Feeding her fears would keep his own at bay and keep her off the subject of Jack.

* * *

"...Cissy. Sure, that Shankill Road bomb thing that killed all them people would sicken you, wudn't it?"

George had been busy imagining how easy it would be to escape out the window of the Gents and leave prison behind for good when the mention of 'Cissy' along the bar gave him a jolt like a bluebottle at his ear. He uncrossed his legs. The lads in school had called him 'sissy' as a boy.

"Aye, it wudn't half, Alma, so it wudn't!" replied Cissy, stopping long enough to take a drink of her pint. "It'd put your head away! Sure, that's just what them Protestants wanted, I'm telling you, Alma! Another bomb to cry their fucking arms off about!"

"Aye, hell slap it into them!" thundered Alma as she slammed her fist down on the bar like a Justice, then fixed her shoulder pads in preparation for sentencing, "for they deserve all they get, the same crowd!"

Cissy held her glass close to her lips and belted out the words in Karaoke style as if reading the lyrics from the screen above her head, "They won't tell you there was a big Ulster Volunteer Force meeting going on upstairs, will they, and those bastards all got out just before the place went up in smoke?"

George looked up at the text winding its way around the bottom of the screen. Sky News.

"Mmmh, aye, and, and, sure, we all know who tol' them like, don't we?" Alma replied, unaware that Cissy's output had been for George's benefit whom Cissy had noticed eavesdropping along the bar.

Cissy didn't lose a second. "Aye, fucking MI5! And see that, that's another thing, that collusion over your man Nelson—that fucking British spy. See his Special Branch minders in the police, like—like will *they* ever do time? No, not a chance. No, Jesus'd get down off the Cross quicker!" she said, now frothing at the mouth.

Cissy waited for Alma to back her up but Alma was too busy trying to get her foot back on the rung of her stool to respond. George eyed the hands on his watch. Alistair had had fifteen years to get to the Gravedigger's Arms and he still couldn't make it on time. And, he thought, as luck would have it, he was probably going to land in right in the middle of Cissy and Alma's diabolical diatribe.

Afraid of losing George's attention altogether while Alma delayed with whatever she was doing, Cissy took to the floor again even as she twisted her lipstick.

"No, it's always the Protestants, what happened to the Protestant side. Sure, they're never happy, for fucksake. No, they wudn't be happy if you strung diamonds around their arse!"

She slapped some colour on her lips and pressed them together vice-like.

"You never hear them going on about McGurk's bar, now, do you?" she added, forming a red question mark with her lips for her secret admirer.

As George read her lips, the Gents' window came to him in minute detail—the floral pane, the wooden, navy frame, the polished, brass handle. Talk about a three-minute warning—he could be out in a matter of seconds.

"It's never what happens to the Catholic side. No, not a chance! No, Protestants always sensationalise their own," Cissy continued, drooling as she climaxed, "Nobody sensationalises us!"

George cringed and raised his hand to his head to take off his hat which was beside him on the counter. He ruffled his hair instead.

"That'sss what I'm tellinn' you! It wazz the ssame 'hinng with that Ennisskillennn lark," Alma slurred her penny's worth, now having found her balance on her stool.

Marlene Dietrich, eat your heart out, thought George.

At least now, thought Cissy, your man with the fine head of hair along the bar would know that she wasn't paranoid: Alma shared her theories.

"Oh, the IRA deliberately sss…set out to plant a bomb to kill people at a mem..me.. memorial ssservice. Like ffffuck they did!" Alma continued. "You know what happened there?"

It was an accident, George thought. The IRA had planned to drop the bomb in Omagh but had run out of time and had no other option but to drop it off in Enniskillen. And as if that wasn't unfortunate enough, any other year the Cenotaph in Enniskillen would have been coming down with British soldiers, but that morning it just so happened soldiers were sparse on the ground and it was packed with civilians. It was a run of bad luck.

Cissy pursed her lips, her cheeks puffing up to enable her eyes to disappear in the affirmative, leaving George to wonder why Alma would bother to impart her wisdom to a woman who so patently knew what was coming. It didn't stop her.

"The Uls-ter De-fence ReRegiment…" The title had proved a mouthful for Alma and she now drew her breath as if about to fart, before expelling the remaining words, "were sssent in the night before to check that monument out and they didn't bother their arses, the lazy bbbbunch of bastards! 'Right, we dddone it', put in for their overtime, when they done nathing."

Cissy cracked up, blowing her beer over her trousers and the gold-plated trinkets on her bracelet.

"Or I'll tell you better," Alma began again, cheered by Cissy's reaction, "They probably found it and didn't let on, 'cause there was no soldiers killed, just all them civilians with their poppies, and who had to be protected, like, but there was no military casualties, you know what I mean."

Cissy stood up to wipe her trouser-leg and pulled her blouse down to hide her bum. George wouldn't have noticed how big her hips were if she hadn't tried to hide them and now that she had drawn his attention to them he agreed that they were better covered and he shuddered at the thought that he would have to make love the next day before he returned to prison.

"Aye, you're right there, Alma,—they make it up as they go along, those fucking Protestants!" said Cissy, wriggling her bottom back into the groove of her stool.

"What'll it be?" the barman asked George.

"I'm waiting on someone," he replied, moving to a stool at the end of the bar to be out of earshot of his companions. Cissy hissed as he departed. The vain thing, thought Alma, presuming she was blowing on her lipstick.

The door opened and a cropped, grey-haired man walked in behind one of the gravediggers. George didn't recognise Alistair at first—he was thinner and smaller, but his gait gave him away. His shoulders and head bent forward, his arms tight at his side, he scuttled like a blackbird towards the other end of the bar.

"D..," George stopped. 'Da' was too intimate. "Alistair!" he shouted without stirring from his stool but his voice refused to carry. Cissy and Alma looked up to case the Protestant, and George regretted his mistake. "Da!" he called out. This time it lifted on the smoky air and his chest felt decidedly lighter. Determined that George should shake his hand and bridge the abyss that separated them, Alistair stuck his hand out like a divining rod as he rounded the bar. "Ach, what about you, son?" he asked, testing the ground. George took his hand. "I'm awful sorry," said Alistair.

"What can I get you?" the barman butted in.

"We're fine," George snapped. What can I get you? What can I get you? The only thing that interests you is what you can get out of us, he thought.

Sensing the tension, Alistair intervened, "What would you like, son?"

"Eh, well, whatever you're having."

"Two pints of Guinness, please!" said Alistair, happy to be in command.

The sounds 'Guin-ness' caused George's shoulders to relax, and only then he became aware of how irritated he had been by the conversation further along the bar. The action in Enniskillen *had* been a mistake. People make mistakes.

"Here, gimme your coat, Da, and I'll put it on the back of my stool!" said George surprised by his eagerness to be nice to a man who had abandoned him for half a lifetime. Old habits die hard, he thought. It had always paid to look after da.

"Nah, sure, it'll be okay here," said Alistair.

"No, here, show me!" George insisted.

"Honestly, it's no bother, honestly," said Alistair, unconvincingly raising his hand like the Red Hand of Ulster. George ignored his hand and lifted his coat. "Now, that's better, isn't it?" he said, hanging it on his stool.

"Thanks, son!" said Alistair, delighted with the fuss George was making of him.

"It pays to be kind!" said George.

"So, how are you?" asked Alistair.

"I'm getting there. This old eye is bothering me a bit though. Probably only a sty," said George.

"Ach, you wanna see the eye I had on me last summer!" Alistair moaned, pulling on his lower eyelid. "I got a terrible infection altogether. Can you see the scar? It was a bloody awful nuisance. The doctor put me on antibiotics for a week, and I was going around the house half-blind like Warrior."

If I caught cold, you would have to be dying with the flu, wouldn't you? George's cynicism disappointed him. He could do better. "And how are you now, Da?" he asked. *There, see, that wasn't so bad.*

"I'm okay. But the old back has been giving me a lot of trouble lately. You 'member the time I slipped carrying in the coal from the back yard when your mother was alive and I had to have time off work?"

George had forgotten the incident, but nodded just the same.

"Well, it's come back to haunt me."

"Have you been to the doctor about it?"

"No, sure, I haven't had a minute with all the meetings about the, the eh...do you know your granddad had the very same complaint?"

"Jesus, Da, maybe you should get that checked out. You're a terrible man!" Alistair flinched and George quickly clarified what he had meant, "The way you're always looking after everybody else!"

Alistair picked up his glass, obliging George to continue.

"Maybe you'd have been better staying at home but and resting that back of yours. Is it any wonder you're in pain? And running across the town to me!" he said, still endeavouring to bring his father back on side.

He doesn't want me here, thought Alistair. "Look," he began in anger. No, there was too much at stake. He would let it go. "Maybe I'll get the big doctor at the Mater to have a look at it when things settle down. Things aren't the best at the minute, son. They're putting their people out of their homes right, left and centre, and the aul' fellas like me are trying to meditate, mediate. The only thing that's driving it is drugs. They're an awful bloody scourge."

"Sure, they're everywhere," commented George, saying the right thing now that his father was back on track. Alistair smiled and George tapped his fingers on the counter to quell his sudden fear that he had given away too much ground. He had to be careful not to let his side down. Drugs weren't as big an issue for Catholics as for Protestants.

"How is Kay doing?" Alistair enquired, appreciative of the ground George had given.

"It's hard on her," George began. "It must be, though Jack was away for a while before he was...before the.. before he died." His eye caught his beer-mat—some guy surfing the waves.

"Still and all, it can't be easy," said Alistair. "God, but I remember when your mother died. It wasn't easy, no, no, it wasn't. You think it's behind you and then it comes up from behind and floors you again. It's different now, of course." He sighed. "You get used to it, but it'll be a while till she gets over it, I'm sure, not that you ever really get over it."

Though George had told himself in the cemetery that he would ask Alistair for nothing, he now instinctively mirrored his father's need for sympathy, "No, you're right. I'll never get over it but to be honest Jack was down in Dublin up until near the end, so...eh, I'm not saying it's not hard on her, like, no, I'm not saying that at all. Your heart would break for her like, but in a way it makes it easier for her too. At least she won't be sitting waiting for him to come through the door, never knowing what's going to happen to him."

"Well, aye, I suppose there's that like. But it can't be easy. Sure, God knows, I've been there myself." Alistair was back on his favourite subject but George hadn't heard him.

"But, you know," George began again, addressing his glass, "nothing would do but that he would come back for his grandad's funeral. He was like a fath…er to him, to, to Jack, I mean." By the time George had felt the word 'father' on his tongue, it was too late to do anything about it.

"Speaking of which, do you know who I met the other day?" Alistair asked in an attempt to brush over George's painful revelation.

"No kidding!" answered George, the horse bolting.

"Iain Donard."

"No kidding! Iain Donard? God, it's been yunks since I heard of him! What's he up to these days?"

"He's married now and has two kids like, eh, yourself."

George recoiled, his buttocks tightening.

"And do you know what? He did time."

"What? You're having me on! Are you serious? For what, like?"

"Dabbling."

"Fuck! Iain? No way?"

"Yeah, as God's my judge! They caught him in Glasgow, red-handed, drugs in the boot."

"Jesus Christ! Iain Donard. Seems like only last week he was in the cubs!"

George shook his head in disbelief and smiled at the memory.

"Did you know that I was doing a bit of voluntary work with young addicts?" Alistair vouchsafed, lulled into a false sense of security by George's smile.

"What? Eh, no, away on o' that! You're having me on! Addicts?"

"Stranger things have happened, so they have!" said Alistair, looking straight past him.

George found the words harmless but the gaze hit where it hurt. Alistair had never forgiven him for his defection to the Catholic community. George invited further rejection to confirm his instinct, "Did I ever think Jack would end up the way he is today? Did you ever think I'd turn out the way I did, did you?" The alcohol was beginning to take effect. "You must look at me sometimes and wonder where you went wrong."

"Ah, sure, nothing could be done," Alistair commented.

George could have taken confirmation, maybe an admonishment, even hatred, but his father's refusal to engage set his belly on fire. He ground his teeth to contain his anger at himself for expecting anything—even the consolation of rejection—from Alistair, then turned on him for release. "Nothing could be done? It's not like you couldn't have stopped them with all your connections! If they hadn't have put me and Kay out of our home, none of this would have happened. None of it!"

"Here, hol' on a minute, you!" said Alistair, wagging his finger, "Don't you go blaming me for the past, sonny! You made your own bed! What were we supposed to do? You should have gone somewhere else when yous got married instead of putting people in a predicament. You didn't think of us, did you?" He struggled all the while to calm his voice out of deference to Cissy and Alma who were now looking their way.

"Predicament? C'mere here till I tell you something! Predicament? What fucking predicament? What, like? We were the ones in a fucking predicament, not yous! I married a fucking Taig and yous couldn't hack it. You couldn't get us out of the area quick enough! And do you know what? If it wasn't for Kathleen's family we'd still be on the side of the road for fucksake."

"Listen here, you!" Alistair let loose in hushed tones without much sense of where he was going. "No son of mine is going to talk to his father like that! Do you hear me? Kathleen's family? Kathleen's family are the whole fucking problem here! Where do you think she gets it from? She didn't lick it off the stones! Nobody put you out George. Yous put yourselves out! You're eluding yourself, George. The whole road knew her da was a republican, aye and you were happy to rub our noses in it! Oh, aye, they all knew, except you! Explain that one to me!"

"What the fuck are you on about?" George shouted, wiping the beer from his upper lip. "We put ourselves out? Like fuck, we did! Your heads are up your fucking arses, but, sure, what else is new? Siege mentality? Yous are the ones doing the fucking sieging. You got us out because Kathleen was a Catholic, and there's no getting away from it no matter what way you package it. Yous are all the fucking same—innocent as the day yous were born!"

Alistair shook his head from side to side, his delay speaking volumes. "The trouble with you is you've been living with them for too long! They leave us streets behind!"

"Oh, aye! Pan-nationalist front!" George boomed sarcastically.

"Well, you're the one who said it!" Alistair shot back, flipping at the sight of the imaginary Union Jack that George waved in his face. "Catholics have got the best jobs, the media wrapped up wee buns, and the social services tripping over them like there's no fucking tomorrow. They could teach us Prods a thing or two! You better believe it!"

"Ah, fuck away off out of that! The Catholics never had it so good? Oh, well, how come yous slit so many of their throats?" asked George.

Alistair clasped his glass, harnessing his indignation, but George wasn't about to let him have the last word. "Listen you to me!" he began again. "The Catholic people has always got the crumbs off our, your table, and even that annoys the shit out of you. I'm telling you it's as clear as day. Yous'uns are never happier than when you're whinging! The fact is yous wouldn't trust a Catholic as far as you could throw them, and you, for one, couldn't see the back of Kathleen quick enough! So don't come crying to me about how easy Catholics get it!"

"That's, that's not one bit true, and you know it! No matter what you think, I didn't bring you up to marr..eh, hate Catholics, and you know that full well! I'm, I'm not that type of person," hollered Alistair.

"No, you're not, sure you're not! I brought myself up!"

Alistair made believe he hadn't heard the personal accusation. The question of religion was easier to handle. "Look, your mother and I never said a word about Catholics, and you know that. In fact, if anything, we were more the other way. And, for the record, I'm not bigoted. No way! I'll speak to any Catholic or anything, within reason."

"Oh, right, you're not bigoted! Here, pull the other one, it has bells on it! If you were so fucking trusting of Catholics, then why were you so keen to boycott my wedding to one?"

"Look, listen till I tell you for once and for all. Your mother and I weren't against you marrying Kay. We just weren't happy with the way it was sprung on us. That's all."

"Sprung on you?"

"We, we wouldn't have cared who you married, George, Protestant or Catholic, but it all happened so fast. You didn't even know the girl. We were only concerned for you."

"Oh, right. Concerned parents! 'Concerned Parents Against Catholics' would be more in your line!"

"Look here a wee minute, George! That was the first time we ever met Catholicism face to face. And we were more than understanding. Anyway, I didn't come here today for my good name to be trailed through the muck. I came here today to offer my condolences. My grandson was murdered by the IRA."

"Your grandson? Don't you come salving your conscience to me! You never seen him when he was alive, so don't go breaking your heart for him now that he's dead! And by the way in case you think your point's lost on me, well it isn't! If we had a fucking police force that we could turn to, the IRA wouldn't have to step in!"

"Look, George! Look, nobod..., look, can we drop it?" Alistair wanted out but he revved up again. "Nobody's, nobody's saying the police aren't angels. But that doesn't mean that we have to go around shooting them but. Anyway, you know as well as I do, when Catholics are in trouble, their first port of call is always the RUC."

"Oh, aye, Catholics are going to get on the phone to the IRA, like? Oh, aye! 'Em, tell me!" The voice was male. "Do you have the number for the quartermaster?'" "'Aye, just a wee minute.' The voice was female now. "I think I have it stuck behind the Sacred Heart picture on the wall along with the credit union book. Cud you hang on there till I run and get it for you?'"

"Well, seems like it worked that way for Jack!"

Alistair had gone for the kill.

"Listen, you! Leave Jack out of it. Jack was a different story. I don't agree with shooting, but Jack should have known better than to be doing what he was doing. You can't have a community living in fear of their own. It breaks my heart to have to say it, but that's the way it is."

Alistair dug in. "Oh, so it's okay when the IRA shoots him, but if the RUC shot him, we'd never hear the end of it. Shoot to kill? Do you know, this here must be the only fucking country in the world where the police are done for doing their job, which isn't to go out to shoot to kill. And don't you think that's what I'm trying to say! It's not. The RUC's hands are tied, and that's because yous have them that way."

"Yeah, I've heard it all now!" said George. Tapping one finger on the counter twice, he signalled two more pints to the barman, but Alistair shook his head from behind him, counting himself out. He had had enough, in every sense.

"Listen, it's not working out. I think I'd better be going. I was wrong to expect things to be otherwise," said Alistair now running his fingertips along the inside of his shirt collar as if searching for the tag.

He made to get up but George grabbed him by the arm. Alistair looked into his by now well-oiled eyes.

"Da," he croaked, "Sit down there a wee second till I tell you something. Do you know something? Wait till I tell you! I'm not joking you. When I stood at that grave today, I was only, only sorry it was fucking him, and not me. To tell you the God's honest truth, I mean, I've, I've done a thing or two in my life, and I'm not one bit proud. Do you know? Not one bit pr.... Do you know what I'm getting at, do you? Da, do you get my drift? I can't say in here, like. All picture, no sound," he said, now nodding in the direction of Cissy and Alma. "Da, you know what I mean, like. Do I have to spell it out for you?"

"Look, son, we've all done…"

"Da, the God's honest truth is if I had to do it all over again, I wouldn't. Now, will you keep that to yourself, will you, Da, like a good man?"

"I, I, I…you, you know, George, would you not be better running away on home out o' that instead of talking a load of aul' shite?"

George had opened the door that Alistair had longed to pass through, but in the event Alistair was stuck. He had heard more than he had bargained for.

George felt a pain shoot across his temples that he had experienced years before after he had come in second in a cross-country marathon and had felt the deceptive warmth of his father's arms around his shoulders. "You should have come first!" he had scolded him.

Alistair pulled his coat from behind George. Cuddling his pint glasses George heard his mother joke as an empty bottle landed in a barrel behind the bar, "If you shook Granny Lackey, she would rattle, she has that many Mogadon in her."

"Will you have anoth..?" George began. He looked up. Alistair was gone. Was it something he had said? The look of daggers that Alma and Cissy gave him told him that he had said too much: George was the enemy in their midst.

Chapter 11

"Sure, people are that busy these days they hardly get time to draw their breath."

"Tell me about it!" replied Kathleen's first cousin twice removed unaware that Kathleen's little moan had been at her expense.

Kathleen was keen to see the back of her, having had her fill of mourners and their incessant whining about the woes of the world under the pretext of offering their sympathies. It seemed like everyone had the words "I can tell you a better one" on their lips, tragedies of one kind or another, more often than not someone else's, that were always the saddest thing. Her cousin had told her of a young man in Glenavy who had been beaten to death, oh, maybe eight or nine years before, by Loyalists, and his mother had dropped dead, as true as God, when she got the news. It was meant to cheer Kathleen up, and she had nodded appreciatively, biting her upper lip to prevent her from saying anything she shouldn't.

"Oh, the *Telegraph*'s here," her cousin announced picking the newspaper up off the floor as they reached the front door.

"Six Tele, Sex Tele, Sex Tele!" Kathleen crooned, mimicking the newspaper boy selling the six o'clock edition of the Belfast Telegraph in Royal Avenue. Her country cousin delayed further as she laughed politely at the mock, broad Belfast accent while Kathleen's mind drifted to the one task left for her to do before George returned to prison in an hour—love-making.

When Kathleen entered the bedroom, George was already undressing and she fled the scene, a bundle of nerves, later emerging from the bathroom in her black underwear. She pulled the blinds shut, lit some incense to settle herself, then pressed her boobs down into her new bra before the mirror. All the while, George lay silent, incapable of taking take his eyes off her out of fear. She got into bed. The first move had to be his, she decided. She had waited fifteen years, she thought, and could wait some more if need be.

"Well, what kept you?" she complained when George found the courage to put his leg over hers.

"What kept me? I was the one who was waiting! What kept you?"

"What do you mean, what kept me? I was hardly going to force myself on you, now, was I?" It had always been her standard reply but it had been so long since he had last heard it that it shocked him. Women don't force themselves on you, he remembered, flicking through the sex manual in his head. And then there was the rule about mouth to mouth only. "If God had have made *that* for that purpose, he would have flavoured it," she used to say.

"I thought maybe you'd jump on me just for once!" he sulked.

Piqued, Kathleen offered him the bare minimum, kissing his lips—stuff they were both familiar with from their encounters in the prison visiting area.

"Tell me—why did you undress in the bathroom?" he asked, far from satisfied.

"Why are you picking on me again?" she asked.

"I'm not picking on you!"

"Then why are you asking?"

"I just wondered. I'd like to have seen you undress," he said. He had watched her undress in his cell night after night but he wasn't about to tell her that.

"That makes two of us," she fired back, still stung by his criticism.

It was like old times—foreplay had always been a matter of marking territory. He lifted himself into position.

"Think you might need some help," she derided him as she moved her hands downwards to facilitate him. It was small.

Desperate, he let her jibe go. She caressed him as best she could remember but it wouldn't respond.

"Here, I'll go solo," he proposed.

"That's disgusting!"

"Well, it hasn't let me down yet these past fifteen years!"

He massaged it, patted it, stretched it, coaxed and cajoled it, but it played dead. "Look, we can give it another shot later. We still have time," he said, talking to her back as he pulled the duvet up around him to hide his shame.

"That's the one thing we don't have!" she said, glancing at the alarm clock by the bed. They had thirty-five minutes until Johnny arrived back with Rosy. He had taken her out to her grandmother's over two hours earlier to leave them time "to do the business", but Kathleen's first cousin had put paid to Johnny's plans.

"Look, I don't know what's wrong," George moaned. "It won't work. It just won't work. It's the cold in this bloody place. Can we put on the heat? I'm foundered."

He had to get it on for the lads on C wing. Otherwise they would give him a drubbing, funeral or no funeral.

"Maybe we should just leave it," she suggested, shutting down. If he couldn't get a hard, it had to be her fault—she couldn't do it for him.

"No! Look, I'll put on the heat myself!" he said, getting out of bed.

"No, I'll do it. I'll do it, for God's sake. You wouldn't know where it is, never mind how to put it on."

Men and their dicks, she thought, as she flung back the sheet. Why does it always have to be a case of all or nothing, when less is more?

When she returned, George was dressed. He had decided it was easier to pretend to the lads he had had his batteries recharged than go at it again.

"My nuts were frozen off me," he said in the face of the flash of hatred that lit up her eyes.

"What's the point in me putting the heating on and you going and getting dressed? Is that it after fifteen years? If you can't get it on, then that's it, it's all over, is it, uh? Well, I'm about sick of it, so I am! I run after you for fifteen years and this is it," she bawled.

She had just wanted to feel his flesh against hers. That would be more than enough for now. The night the soldiers had dragged him away she couldn't help thinking that she wouldn't have to do it any more, and then when the gates closed behind him for good, her legs had drawn closed like a canal lock. It would take her time to get used to the whole sex thing again. She wanted to go at it slowly.

"Why, why the hell do you have to humiliate me? What have I done wrong?" George yelled.

"I am sick, sore and tired of running after you, George!" she screamed.

"Oh, aye, that's lovely! That's fucking choice, that is! Wait till I tell you, Kathleen, you're not the one that's doing time, are you? You're not the one has to sit and look at four walls all day!" he howled.

"I am, George Lackey! I'm doing my time too and don't you tell me otherwise! I'm putting in the hours just as well as you are! Saving myself for you into the bargain, and all you do is lie back and think of Spain. I must be off my bap! Well, fuck away off to the sun for all I care! Away back to your cronies and your three meals a day, and your wanking!" She flung herself into bed.

George off-loaded, "Don't bother your arse saving yourself for me! If I'm such a burden, why don't you get on with your life? But, no, you have to…, look, you're not saving me, you're not saving me! No one's asking you to be there for me. I can eat my own Mars bar of a Wednesday! You can go ply your wares elsewhere, Kathleen! And if I wanna wank, well, what the fuck has that got to do with you anyway? What am I supposed to do? Uh? Save myself for you? That's a joke! My time's hard enough!"

He stomped off, leaving the bedroom door open in the hope that she would call him back, but she held her tongue.

"I'm taking a taxi back," he called up to her moments later.

"No, George, don't! I'm sorry!" she cried out.

He breathed a sigh of relief because he lived for Wednesday afternoons and the only person in the world that cared about him, but her change of tune only encouraged him to keep the pressure on. "Look, what's this about?" he cried out, peering up at Juliet now leaning over the bannister. "What the fuck has got into you?" he added, thinking Romeo never said that. Kathleen burst into tears.

"I don't, I just don't know what's going on, George. Everything! The whole shebang. It's, one minute it's my da, the next it's Jack, and, and now you're, it, I, I, I knew, I knew where I was two weeks ago, but now the ground's shifting under my feet, George. Don't, don't walk out, George! Not like this!"

He bounded up the stairs, and fought back a smile as he took his damsel in his arms, conjuring up a kerchief from his breast pocket.

Kathleen took the hankie and cleared her nose, and with it, her head, and rounded on him again.

"Jack's dead, George. Do you understand that? He's dead! And your cronies saw to that!"

"Don't you go blaming me!" said George in a voice tempered by guilt.

"Well, if it weren't for you we wouldn't be in this mess, would we?" she harangued him, tucking his hankie into her bra.

"Me?" he asked, poking his chest. "If it weren't for me? It isn't like you were a fucking saint yourself, was it? Where were you when the child needed his mother's love?"

"I didn't drive him to drugs, did I? If you'd have been here to look out for him, he wouldn't be, wouldn't be where he is now, would he?"

"You aren't telling me anything I didn't already know, Kathleen. The world and his mother knew he was dealing!" said George, taking the wind out of her sails.

"Aye, and no doubt your cronies told you! Oh aye, why wouldn't they? They'd be in a position to know—before the facts! No doubt they were the ones issued the death threat, too, the same hard men."

"Look, leave the 'RA out of it!"

"Fat use you were to him!" she bellowed.

"Anybody'd tell you children need their mother, Kathleen. Whatever way you look at it, I was out of the picture all along!"

At the sound of a bell the fight stopped and they looked each other in the eye. George rushed downstairs.

"Well, well, well, and how are the lovebirds?" asked Johnny before he'd even crossed the door, Rosy blushing at his side.

"Come ahead on in!" said George with a smile on his face like the proverbial cat.

Johnny threw George a right hook and then a left within an inch of his tummy, the way lads do when the deed is done. "So, is that yous, then?" he asked.

"Yep, that's us sorted, thanks. Kate, are you near ready, hun?" George called up to her.

"Yes, love!" she said for Johnny's benefit, the term of endearment taking it out of her.

Johnny winked, and George patted him on the stomach to seal the deal.

"All's well that ends well!" said Johnny.

How apt, thought George, grinning. He grabbed his coat and bag. Rosy pounced on him as Kathleen shuffled by them on her way to the car. He followed her out reluctantly.

"Dad, you forgot your card. I forgot to give you your card!" Rosy shouted after him as he swung into the car, one hand on the roof.

"Thanks, Rosy! I can always depend on you!" he remarked. Kathleen took the bait and growled, and Rosy glowed as he gave her one more kiss for the road. You can sort your own seat belt out this time, thought Kathleen.

They fell silent in the car. A set of skid marks got her thinking of how she had come to lose the plot. The Brits had arrested her with the colour party's gear after the funeral of an IRA Volunteer. She had made out that the hats were her own, and that she wore dark glasses for medical reasons. They released her without charge. The IRA was impressed, and she soon progressed to better things, including doing back-up for George on the streets. Then, after George was imprisoned, a judge whose house she cleaned two mornings a week on the Lisburn Road was shot dead while leaving his son to school. The RUC lifted her for questioning. She took Jack with her into custody in Castlereagh Holding Centre hoping that the authorities would release her once they saw the child, what with her man in prison and all. "No one's taking my fucking child from me!" she squealed as they dragged her across the yard of the barracks, trailing Jack behind her. A policewoman warned her that the child would have to be put into care. She realised then that she couldn't use Jack as a shield any longer. She had been clutching at straws in an effort to put off the inevitable. Some of her comrades had already been through the whole inter-rogation thing and she knew how hard they had found it. Benny collected him. She was released without charge on the third day of her detention. She had managed to hold her tongue as she had been trained. Anyway, she firmly believed that she had had no idea that the information she had given Big Mick would be used for the killing. In fact, maybe it hadn't. And, anyway, while the judge was kind to her—he had told his wife to pay her double on a Saturday morning—he was part of a system that put national-ists away for next to nothing. But she had quietly scaled things down after that for the sake of the kids. Jack had taken to wetting the bed after her arrest. Then, three blokes came to the door one night and told her they needed her house for a "wee job".

"We'll be out of here in no time," Tony promised as they tum-bled in past her. Boxes in hand, they opened the first bedroom door they came to only to discover Rosy and Jack asleep in their beds. They made their way to the next room and laid their gear out on the floor.

Kathleen sat in the kitchen mulling over her options. If she phoned the police, the IRA would kill her, and the kids would be taken into care. On the other hand, if she let them get on with it, they would be out soon and she could pretend it never happened. She went into the living room and switched on TV, turning up the sound to drown out the noise from upstairs. If you couldn't hear them, it wasn't happening, she figured. She sat tight and was get-ting her time in nicely when one of the men came downstairs and went into the kitchen. "Missus!" he shouted. Kathleen opened the kitchen door. "Have you any more of these? The others could do with something," he asked, licking a spoon as he held up a can of beans.

Kathleen mumbled something incomprehensible and then found her flow. "Yous march in here and you help yourselves to beans from my cupboard without fucking take nor leave! Like, what the fuck do you think this is, like? Fucking Butlins?"

"Jesus Christ, missus, it's only a tin of fucking baked beans! It's not like I'm fucking stuffing your turkey here!" he shouted, chucking the spoon in the sink.

"Well, you aren't the one has to put food in their mouths, are you?" she screeched, pointing to the ceiling.

"Ah, for fucksake, here, you can ram your fucking beans up your hole, for all I care," he cried out, banging the empty can on the counter.

Neighbours was well over on the television when the rumbling upstairs stopped. She listened for the sound of the front door closing and then tore up to the back bedroom. The floor was covered with scrap wire. She fetched a brush and shovel, water and a bucket. She would have to clean the evidence herself. She scrubbed throughout the night till she was satisfied there wasn't a trace left. In the morning when she switched on the radio the newsreader said that British soldiers had stopped a car in Slemish Way during the night and three men had been arrested transporting a bomb to the city centre.

George was right, she acknowledged, the kids needed a mother. She had put their lives at risk. The IRA had knocked on her door because they knew she would keep her mouth shut.

George broke her silence. He wanted things sorted before the prison turnstile went clackety-clack. He would swallow his pride.

"Did I tell you Alistair's starting to believe?"

Kathleen awoke as if from a dream, not knowing where she was.

"Aye, he's starting to come round," he continued. "He's starting to see the truth. He said he has fuck all time for the police, and Catholics have taught Protestants all they know. He went on about the old days too, like, that we sprung the wedding on them, but I just told him that was a load of crap. We've no regrets, you and me."

"No regrets?" asked Kathleen. "I neglected Jack, George. He deserved a good mother. Maybe it'd have been better had they taken him into care that time they took over the house. Maybe none of this would have happened. It could have been so different."

"That time what? What time?" he asked.

She suddenly felt snowed under. She hadn't told him the half of it. How could she ever tell him everything?

George stiffened. The prison had just come into view. He had his time to do. "Listen, love, we can't change the past now. We can't change any of that. You have to get on with it," he said, still in a fog about what she had been alluding to.

He stepped out of the car and, realising that she wasn't going to get out, blew her a kiss before pushing the door closed.

Frank—she would have to talk to him about Frank, she thought, as she watched him battle with the turnstile, loneliness enveloping her like the mist that covered the watchtower. That's what had been bugging her all day—Frank. She turned her car around, wishing she could turn her life around with the same ease.

Chapter 12

Opening the front door Nicholas let slip a smile which he immediately regretted. The novice master beamed back at him.

"May I come in for a second? I shan't delay you," said Fr. Tim, toeing the saddle-board.

Hard pushed to hide his shock, Nicholas caught his breath. "Eh, yep, sure, em..." he muttered, seeing stars. This can't be happening, he thought; he had moved on, begun a new chapter, found himself, but now his knees were knocking.

"I was here yesterday, but there wasn't a soul to be seen," said Fr. Tim, his voice echoing in the narrow hall, increasing its authority which Nicholas had hoped he had heard the last of the day he had left the novitiate.

"Yes, I just got back from Belfast last night," Nicholas volunteered against his will.

"Oh, I see," said Fr. Tim curtly, clearly conveying his annoyance at the fact that Nicholas hadn't sought permission to travel.

Nicholas held on to the knob—hard, smooth, cool, made for moments such as these he thought—until his guilt passed through him, leaving a tingling sensation of old in his feet.

"It was nothing terribly urgent. I just wanted to drop you off your post," Fr. Tim said, now applying the carrot in place of the stick. "You are a popular chap, you know! A lot of fan mail here!"

Nicholas cringed at the false familiarity of Fr. Tim who now led the way into the bed-sit, dangling the mail at his side like a bone for the mutt behind. He stepped over Nicholas' underpants as if avoiding a puddle and reconnoitred the garden from the window, allowing Nicholas time to do the necessary. Nicholas took the hint and stuffed his pants under his pillow then premeditatedly ushered Fr. Tim to the chair furthest from his bedraggled love-bunk, all the while scouring the room for tell-tale signs of Shirley.

"So how's it cutting?" asked Fr. Tim.

"I'm getting there," Nicholas answered, visualising a chain-saw boring its way through a Christmas tree. English through and through Fr. Tim loved his Irish sayings and Nicholas thanked his lucky stars he hadn't subjected him to his usual "Top of the morning to you!" routine which was on a par with the "please God!" that Southerners like Shirley indulged in after every second sentence, both of which put him in mind of the Quiet Man and what's her name with the red hair.

"All these things take time," said Fr. Tim, steering Nicholas away from thoughts of Maureen O Hara. "You know, if you ever need to speak to someone, I'm sure Fr. Doherty would be happy to offer you spiritual direction."

Nicholas heard a television, and a charcoal artist's impression of the auld' one next door formed in his head, stockings down around her knees, her apron that always smelled of cat pee crumpled in at the waist, face featureless, head on her shoulder, out for the count in front of her widescreen. He wanted to join her. When he had confided in Fr. Doherty about his difficulties with celibacy the latter had scoffed, "Sure, don't we all?" then swung round to catch the end of the Embassy World Snooker Championships on TV. Nicholas suddenly stood up, alarming Fr. Tim but his feet lost their nerve and refused to frogmarch his guest to the door. His mouth kicked in instead, "Would you care for some tea?" The sound of his plum English accent scared him. Had Fr. Tim got in on him that much that he had even taken on his accent? He pulled on his earlobe, as if disapprovingly.

"Go raibh maith agat," replied Fr. Tim, the meaning only clear to Nicholas from his papal wave. Phew, thought Nicholas, sitting back down on the bed. "You know, you aren't technically out yet," Fr. Tim continued. "We haven't sent your documentation to Rome, you know. Therefore, maybe it would be beneficial for you to engage with Fr. Doherty presently. Even if you were only to meet with him once a week, at least that would help you maintain contact with your superiors. Then you could use the next six months or thereabouts to discern where the Lord is leading you, please God. And if the Lord is leading you elsewhere, we could arrive at some financial arrangement for your future. We wouldn't want to see one of our men stuck."

'One of our men'? 'Stuck'? Apart from the tar on the novitiate wall, the break was clean, thought Nicholas. 'Money'? He said 'money', didn't he, he thought next. Look, better not bite the hand that feeds you! He'll be outta here in a few minutes. A fee can be negotiated over the phone. Shirley's knickers, he wondered next, are they behind me? "Is Fr. Doherty still living in front of the Provincial House?" he enquired, spreading his hands out behind him like a tent.

"Oh, yes, indeed, still in the parlour counting out his money!"

Easy to see why that particular anti-Christ talks, thought Fr. Tim, casting a beady eye on the spiders promenading on the grubby carpet between them oblivious to the battle of the Two Standards being waged in their midst.

"Well, sure, I know where he is then," added Nicholas in an effort to prompt his departure.

A smile graced Fr. Tim's face for the second time in almost three years, forcing Nicholas to think on his feet. "Well, I'm, I'm going out now to catch the ten o'clock," he lied.

"Oh, yes, indeed! How awfully thoughtless of me! It wouldn't do to detain you from the Blessed Sacrament."

Fearing his silence would betray his lust for money, Nicholas thanked Fr. Tim for the mail as he escorted him out. "A pleasure!" said Fr. Tim. "And how is Jack doing these days?" he asked, struggling with the Yale lock on the door.

"Here, let me do that for you. It gets a bit rusty, like myself," replied Nicholas. "Em, he's dead." There, that should get rid of him, he thought. Fr. Tim's jaw dropped. "He was murdered by the IRA," Nicholas continued, now noticing Fr. Tim's heels which were covered in a fine film of snow. How, he wondered, would he make it over to Shirley's as promised, if the snow didn't let up?

"Oh, goodness! Oh, I am so sorry! How wretched!" said Fr. Tim.

"Pardon?" said Nicholas, at a loss as to why Fr. Tim felt wretched about him not being able to make it to Shirley's.

"Ar dheis Dé ar an anam!" said Fr. Tim.

Oh, yes, Jack, thought Nicholas. The more sincere people try to be, the less convincing they are.

"It's just one of those things. Life goes on," he said, brushing off Fr. Tim's concern as the latter moved to embrace him as a brother in Christ. Nicholas wrenched open the door in the nick of time—he had for some unknown reason double locked it after Fr. Tim had come in—and smiled, and Fr. Tim had no alternative but to embrace himself, pretending to beat off the winter chill.

"Well, Nicholas, thank you ever so much for the welcome and the offer of tea. You know where I am. I do hope everything goes well for you. I shall inform Fr. Doherty that you will be in touch."

He knew when he wasn't wanted. Nicholas hastily offered him a handshake as was the custom in the novitiate, thinking that it could only work in his favour in the long run.

After Fr. Tim had left and Nicholas had stamped away all snowy traces of him from the carpet, he checked the bed for Shirley's knickers, finding a pair the same colour as the duvet—probably inconspicuous to the naked eye, he told himself. But he would think that, wouldn't he, he thought, with all the money at stake? Snow caught his attention through the patio doors and he stood catching single snowflakes in his gaze until the cold crept in around his ankles and the hairs in his nostrils twitched. He took his mail, climbed into bed and pulled the duvet up to his waist, resting his back against the wallpaper smoothed and dirtied by the heads of previous tenants, then sifted through his letters. S.A.G.—no doubt a letter from Benny with news of her aches and pains and a commentary on who had or hadn't died, all of three months ago, he thought. Saint Anthony could do worse than Guide her through the days ahead. He set it aside. He had enough woes of his own. A letter with a Dublin stamp mark: who could be writing from Dublin? He peeled it open and unfolded a page of A4 paper.

Salvation Army Forecourts
Bachelor's Walk
Dublin 1
Republic of Ireland

Dear Nick,
I don't know what to say. I'm sorry for blaming you for every-thing. I'm really sorry. I wish I could take it all back. If you never wanted to speak to me again, that's fine but I want you to know you mean a lot to me.

My head must have been up my arse. How could I have walked out on you without as much as a whisper, never mind a thank you?

Remember that first day when you massaged my wounds, well, my life changed that day. You taught me how to love myself. My body was always a foreign body to me. When the 'RA beat me, I hoped they'd kill me. I wanted to die.

Do you remember mummy used to call me Johnboy when I was a child? Well, Johnboy died a long time ago. Johnboy wasn't a boy that mummy or daddy could ever accept. They wanted a boy that would fight a war, a boy to fight their cause.

Johnboy loved to dance around the living room when no one else was looking. He marvelled at the sky at night. When the wind blew the towel against his body on the beach at Ballyholme he laughed like mad. You'd find him up the fields looking for birds eggs. He was the boy whose first crush was on a fella in the year ahead. They could never have understood that.

Nicholas, God knows I tried to live the life that they wanted, but I wasn't meant for war. I longed for peace. I longed for a life where I could go to school without dodging bullets, and where I would no longer live in fear of being stopped by the Brits who harassed me because of daddy. But I wanted more than that. I wanted to be at peace with me but my ma and da's fight for freedom didn't include the freedom for me to be me. I went underground.

And then you came along and taught me to believe in myself. Someone who appreciated me and wanted the best for me. You respected me. You cared for me. You let me be me. In your lingo, you were the face of God for me.

And then I ran. I thought I was in the way of your vocation. But the truth is I now know I was ascared. I was afeared you would come to hate me if you really knew what I was about. There are parts of me I was so ashamed of. Do you know what that is like? Do you know how that destroys people? Dara was a convenient bridge for me to flee myself.

I MISS your TOUCH, Nick. Please meet me just once. I am not asking you to be there for me. I just want you to forgive me and tell me that you are fine. I would hate anything to happen, to happen to you and all the hurt I caused you on my conscience. From the moment I stepped off that bus that day and you were there to meet me, my life changed for the better. Thank you for that.

Please, please, please get in touch.

Love from the heart.

PS Don't worry about me. It's not that bad here.

Nicholas' tears of consolation—for he now knew how much he had meant to Jack—and regret—Jack had died believing that he had read his letter and couldn't forgive him for walking out—spilled onto his letter.

"If only, if only I'd told you I missed you, I'd always be there for you, that, that I held nothing against you. If, if…" Frank's funeral came to mind. He had blown it. "Why didn't I speak to you, Jack? Why didn't I….? I, I let you down! Can you forgive me? I let you down in the end! I loved you so much, Jack. God knows, I loved you."

He rocked himself back and forth, hugging his pillow. He yearned to hold Jack, to smother him with kisses, to nurse him, and be nursed by the only man that had ever been willing to be close. When he got up to close the curtains, it was already pitch dark outside. Seeing himself in the bathroom mirror, he began sobbing again. Jack would never see this face speckled with splashes from his flossing—speckles which, he had to admit, seemed to add to his look of misery, and which he would have to take Windolene to one of these days if only to keep on the right side of Shirley who had given him grief on the state of the place when she was last over. This face of his, too, was bruised from a lack of love. And the one person who had really loved him was gone. Emotionally drained, he flopped onto the bed where, soon, newly weds posed for photographs. He pushed forward through the wedding guests to take their picture. They had identical faces.

When he awoke, his dreams evaporated like rain off a summer pavement and the light around the edge of the Velux blind gently coaxed him into getting up. Shaving, he recalled a billboard he had seen on the way to Central Station after Jack's funeral: *God saw all that he had made, and indeed it was very good* (Genesis 1:31). It had stood out because it lacked the usual hellfire and brimstone that he associated with Protestant billboards. He looked at his drawn face. God had made something good in him. Jack's letter was proof of that. He had to believe it. The phone rang. Shirley wanted to know if he was back safe, and if he'd like to call over. It was music to his ears.

Shirley greeted him on the doorstep with a perfunctory 'moi-moi'. Her hug in McDonald's had given him cause for hope and now he realised that that had taken Jack's death and he cursed himself for expecting anything more in public.

"You look rested. Did you go for a swim or what this morning?" she enquired, seeing the bright side where there was none.

"No, I slept in, actually."

They moved inside. He would draw her out of her shell now that she was out of view. "Thanks for coming up North, love. I know it can't have been easy, with all the strange people and everything."

"No, no problem," she began, rubbing snow off his duffle, already more at ease, "though I have to say I was glad when I got back over the border again. Home Sweet Home! You just feel on edge up North after a while, don't you? And guess what? You wouldn't believe it, but on the one day in the year when mummy decides to watch the news, she sees you on it!"

"Oh, shit! What did you tell her? Is that you in the bad books now?"

"I told her the IRA shot your nephew for no good reason, and that she had nothing to worry about. There's hardly a person up there hasn't buried somebody."

"I bet she thinks we're Provies!"

"Well, actually, I also told her that Jack had been training for the priesthood and was living with you in Dublin."

"Jesus, you did not! Fuck! What am I supposed to tell her when I see her?"

"Don't worry! You'll be grand. Just tell her that he was living with you in the retreat house," she said, throwing her arms around him to shut him up. He melted. He loved it indoors where she was less prone to the need to perform.

"I could have done with this yesterday," he said.

"What? Look, listen, love, before we get into anything deep, what about something to eat?" She ran her knuckles over his right cheek in a razor motion, tenderly.

"Sounds great! I haven't had a chance to shop since I got back."

He sat down at her computer. The very thought of food had lifted his spirits. He would write a letter to Fr. Doherty, requesting some money.

"What disk did you say I could save on the other day?" he called out to her in the kitchen.

"I'll show you in a minute."

"Can I use this zip dick, eh, zip disk?"

"What?"

"This zip disk. Isn't that what they call them?"

"A zip dick? Nice one! Are you sure there isn't something you want to tell me?" she joked, appearing at the kitchen door, smelling of feta.

He laughed until it was clear that she wasn't going anywhere. "Like what?" he asked.

"Like who you were sleeping with last night?" she continued unsure of the source of her enquiry for which, to her surprise, she soon found grounds in his defensiveness.

"What? Are you off your head? I told you I slept like a log, not like I'd sleep if somebody was in bed beside me."

"Oh, somebody was in bed beside you?" she persisted.

"What are you on about? Did I say that?" he asked, swatting at some dust glistening in the sunlight.

"Yeah, straight from the horse's mouth!"

"No I didn't. I said 'if'"

"There you go! Now, you're telling me you did say it. Getting all up tight, are we?"

"Nope!" said Nicholas.

The toast popped and Shirley took her leave. "Nick, tell me. Have you ever had sex with a man before?" she asked moments later, taking up where she had left off.

A cigarette with a red line across it, double yellow lines, a can with an X through it—the images offered him the answer he needed but the word just wouldn't come. He crossed his legs and arms, knowing full well the signal he was sending out, but what was he supposed to do?

"There's no need to be shy! Lots of priests are gay," she said as she sat down across the room from him, deliberately giving him the illusion of space.

"I told you I wasn't a priest," he said, then licked his lips to reward them for getting him out of a tight corner. "Who are you fooling?" her eyebrows read, causing sweat to drip from his armpit onto his elbow. "Have you ever slept with a woman?" he quizzed her, determined to shake her off his tail.

"Yes. It was no big deal, I might add. But, yes."

"Right!" he said, but "Shit!" is what he heard in his head as he tucked his feet up on the chair in an attempt to look calm. He needed time to digest the information.

"What about you?" she asked, refusing to let up.

"What do you mean, what about me? I've slept with you, haven't I?"

"Have you slept with a man, is what I'm asking?"

Nicholas felt fear in the pit of his stomach. If he delayed, she would know, but if he told her, she would run. A fucking catch-22's what we have here, he thought. Jack's letter suddenly came to mind: he was loveable, and he had to start believing it.

"I, I have, but only once. I mean, only one."

"Well, did you enjoy it?"

"I, I, I, I suppose I did. Yeah."

"Do you still have contact with him?"

"No, no, it was, it was Jack. I, I slept with Jack." He looked down at the floor, playing 'Xy Osy' with the tiles, and missed the affection in the crinkles around her eyes. "Yesterday I got a letter from him that he wrote before he died. He thanked me for all the ways I loved him and helped him to believe in himself."

"You loved him?"

"I did." In his mind's eye he drew three Xs across on the tiles.

"And was he there for you?"

"Yes, he was," he said, now raising his head, astounded that he was talking about his sexuality with a woman who until now had seemed as light as a feather and the perfect distraction from his pain.

"That's brilliant! He must have died happy in one way," she commented, quietly pleased that the man that he had loved was dead. At least she didn't have a rival. "Do you want some tea, Nicholas?" she asked, now ready to move on.

"No, I'm fine. I'm alright. Actually, I have to go to the loo." He needed time out to take in what had happened.

"Does Kathleen know?" Shirley called after him.

"Know what?" he asked, resisting her obvious question.

"About you and Jack."

"Eh, no. That's the difficult part. Does anyone know about you?"

"No, you're the first person I've told. Oh, except, you know, her-self!" She laughed.

He felt a surge of admiration for her and, finally relaxing, tore off some toilet roll to chew as he dribbled. "Maybe Kathleen doesn't need to know," he said, half hoping that she would agree. "Can you, can you just imagine what she'd say, Shirley, if I told her that Jack and I were having sex for the last three months of his life?"

He flushed the toilet, drowning out her response.

"Do you want some coffee instead?" she asked him as he entered the kitchen.

"No thanks, I told you I hate the stuff. I'm just going to have another bash on the computer, if that's okay?"

"Fine! Fire ahead! You can use the zip dick!" She giggled and Nicholas smiled at his own expense.

* * *

"That must be my phone, Johnny! Wait a minute! No, that's yours, is it, Johnny?" said Kathleen lifting her hand-bag to her ear. "No, it's mine. Fuck, it'll cut out by the time I get to it."

"Here, show me!"

Johnny wrested her bag from her and dug out the phone from under a pile of Mass cards for Jack, then slapped it into her hand while she continued driving.

"What do you do?" she asked, flustered, as if cradling a new-born child.

"Here, gimme it! I'll do it for you!" he said.

"I'll never figure the damned thing out! It's a waste of Nicholas' good money!"

Nicholas had bought it for her so she could keep in touch with Jack when he came to live with him in Dublin but she had never got the hang of it.

Johnny held it to her ear like a sea-shell.

"Can you, can you just imagine what she'd say, Shirley, if I told her..."

"Hello, Nicholas?"

"...that Jack and I were having sex for the last three months of his life."

"Nicholas? Hello, Nicholas?" At what sounded like the roar of the sea, but was actually the toilet flushing, she thrust the phone into Johnny's face. "Shit!" she exclaimed.

"Did he get cut off? Those fucking cross-border calls are a disaster!"

"Shit! Shit! Shit!" she said to the rhythm of the cha-cha.

"What is it? Could he not hear you? He'll probably call you back."

"Will you send him one of those message things for me?" she asked, pulling on to the hard shoulder.

"Who? Nicholas?"

"Yeah! The, the..."

"No probs!"

"Tell him, tell him it was well for them having sex the past three months."

"Having sex?" he asked, confounded.

"Yes. Will you write it for me?"

"What? Yeah, whatever!"

They were just about to move off again when the phone beeped. Johnny held Nicholas' reply up to her, averting his gaze.

"Would you type, *'No, you have'*?" she asked.

Johnny did as requested then went back to erase Nicholas' message, which he felt, to be fair, or so he told himself, he couldn't not read in the process: *Who told u? Has Shirley been talking?*

The phone beeped again. Kathleen asked Johnny to type 'A little birdie' in response to the latest message and once again he couldn't but look at the text from Nicholas before deleting it: *I don't understand. How? When?*

Moments later, the phone rang and Kathleen snatched it from Johnny. "Hello!"

"Press the middle one!" Johnny exhorted as the phone rang at her ear.

"Hello!"

"Hello, Kathleen. It's me, Nicholas. I, I had wanted to tell you myself."

"You did."

"No, you know what I mean."

Kathleen fell silent.

"Hello? Kathleen? Hello? Are you there still?"

"I have to go."

She downed the phone.

"What was all that about?" Johnny asked.

"Can I take two on this, can I? I'll fill you in later," she replied, aware that she would have to put him in the picture sooner rather than later because he would hound her until she told him.

"Sure!" said Johnny, sitting on his hands, doing the utmost to suppress his curiosity.

* * *

"Ah, Jesus, I've fucking gone and blown it now!"

"What? What happened? Who was that? What is it?" asked Shirley.

"Agghhh!" Nicholas' fingers masked his face like streaks of war-paint. "I've gone and fucked up big time!"

"What in God's name's the matter? Has it hung again?"

"Shit! I, I must have hit the speed dial and, and,—how the fuck did that happen?—and I got through to Kathleen. Shit! That's you telling me to sit down on the toilet. It must have hit off the floor."

"What?"

"When I was in the toilet! Shit! Shit! Fuck!"

"You mean she, you mean, she, she didn't hear, oh my God! She heard us!"

"Yes, the heap! Oh, Jesus! I'm fucked!" he said, wondering how he could tell her that he had thought at first that she had been on to Kathleen behind his back.

"Oh, my God! What did she say?"

"She…"

"Have you it switched off now?" Shirley asked.

"Yes!" he answered, then checked once more to be sure, to be sure.

"Oh my God! You poor thing!" she said on the verge of laughing from nerves.

"I'm going to have to speak to her," Nicholas explained.

"Oh, you poor, poor thing!"

Nicholas threw himself down on the couch and buried his face in Shirley's favourite cushion—a touch of the Arabian nights about it. "Fucking mobile phones!" he screamed, now throwing punches at the diamond-shaped mirror in its centre. "And all *you* can do is laugh!" he castigated Shirley, but she only giggled all the more.

* * *

"Kate, go you away on in to the prison yourself. I'll quake with the Quakers," said Johnny. She had barely spoken two words in the care since Nicholas had phoned and he reckoned she could probably do with time alone with George.

"Okay. Well, then you take these fags in with you. I'll tap George for some," she said, grateful for his proposal to check out the Quaker canteen. She needed time to clear her head before meeting George. She couldn't speak to him about Nicholas' call. He would never understand. That kind of thing just didn't happen in the IRA. It might go on in British jails, but it didn't happen in Ireland.

Johnny took the cigarettes and sauntered over to the canteen, telling himself in an effort to settle his anxiety about being out of the loop that her gift was a token of her appreciation.

"Could you empty your pockets, please?" a dyed blonde prison warden asked Kathleen from behind a desk which never failed to remind Kathleen of her time in school. All that was missing was the inkwell, but she imagined it now without difficulty, and could even smell the blotting paper, a musty smell mixed with toxic ink. She wriggled her nose and emptied her pockets, placing her things on the desk.

"Is that the lot?" the warden droned. It was the same routine as usual and the same monotone voice.

Kathleen nodded.

"Could you lift your arms, please?"

Pretending she was having a fitting—it always made the ordeal easier—Kathleen extended her arms and parted her legs, but still coughed and jiggled her feet, conscious that it was the closest anyone ever got to her.

The warden frisked her as if dusting a chair—arms, back, seat, and, finally, sturdy legs. Kathleen pictured a knee-length sheepskin coat, tucked in at her waist, and matching beige slacks.

"There's some nip in that wind today, isn't there, love, just?" the warden commented, retreating behind her desk.

Kathleen said nothing not wanting to encourage small talk.

"Can I just check your mouth, love?"

Kathleen covered the cellophane-wrapped 'comm' from the local Sinn Féin office with her tongue and opened her mouth, blasting the warden with her nicotine breath.

"Lovely!" said the warden.

'Are you a fucking dentist to be commenting?' Kathleen heard herself think. She had tried hard to repress the question since her trip to the dentist's, but to no avail. Now, she felt a failure—not, she accepted, that it made one blind bit of difference to the warden who busied herself with Kathleen's keys and ten pound note which she stuck in an envelope and licked.

"You can take your loose change with you, love," the warden explained unnecessarily.

Kathleen slid the coins off the desk one by one. They had been giving her the same instructions for the past fifteen years and she resented them now as much as ever.

"I just need your wee signature here, love," said the warden, spinning the receipt book around to Kathleen.

Love 15, love 30, love 40, thought Kathleen. That was all the sense love made. She signed for the envelope, which she would collect on the way out.

To the sound of the door being bolted behind her, Kathleen took three steps—the Lion, the Witch and the Wardrobe—down into the immense kindergarten that was the visitors' waiting-room and surveyed the scene. It never ceased to amaze her that the British government did all in its power to keep Protestants and Catholics apart—peace walls, security gates, fences—but flung them together in the visitors' waiting-room in Long Kesh, the one place where they needed to be separated. Today the loyalists huddled by the window. She found a safe spot opposite the mural of Donald Duck twirling a yellow, frilly brolly above his head, picnic basket at the ready. She had spent many an afternoon rehearsing conversations with him or with Pluto strolling behind him in his stars and stripes. Her rehearsals were a trapdoor that helped her make things disappear before she met George in the visitors' room but now she couldn't focus sufficiently to get her troubles off her chest for the simple reason that although the Australian Open appeared to have everyone's rapt attention, she knew the others were actually reading her mind. They were a dab hand at sussing people out from a crossed leg, too much make-up, or even the manner in which you flicked ash on the floor. And the women were better at it than the men, which only made her more uncomfortable because the room was a veritable harem this morning. She developed a sudden interest in golf and let her ash linger, only relaxing her guard when she reached the decidedly male visiting room where George was already waiting. As she sat down opposite him, he stretched his hand out to her, but she held her hands firm beneath the table.

"Is it that bad?" he asked.

"It hasn't been easy. Let's put it that way," she said, studying the troughs in her palms.

"Where's Johnny?"

"He decided to leave us to our own devices. He thought we could do with the time after all we've been through."

"Oh, right," he mumbled.

"Yep!" she said, playing with her wedding ring now.

"Has Nicholas gone back?" he asked, taking up the slack.

"Yep!"

"So, things are getting back to normal then?"

"What's normal when your son's been taken from you, and you're stuck in here?" She looked up and he reached across to her again. She slipped off her ring then put it back on again and rested her hand on the table for him to hold.

"George," she began as if to continue but stopped, having suddenly lost her thought.

"What?"

She scrutinised his face as if looking around a room, trying to remember what she had gone in to get—glasses, scarf, hat, earring.

"Nicholas gave me a ring. He texted me."

"He what?"

"He texted me. You know, he sent me a message on the phone. You know the way. Not that I understand it myself, but you type things in on the 'hing. You press the numbers and words come out."

"Aye. Go on!" He was fed up—texting, something else on the outside he knew nothing about.

"He..." She had lost her way again.

Losing patience, George prompted her. "Well, what had he to say that has you in this state?"

"He told me something. He told me something about Jack."

"What now?" he asked, flipping his lighter over and over on the table. From her sullen expression, he expected the worst.

"Jack went to bed with Nicholas."

"He, he, he what? Nicholas fucking did what?"

"I, he slept with him."

"Slept with him?"

"Yes, George. He, they had s..sex together in bed."

"Our Jack had sex with who, Kathleen?"

"Look, do I have to fucking spell it out for you? It's nothing to do with me. They had it together. Sex!"

"Jesus fucking Christ! They what? You're fucking kidding me. You're having me on! You better be having me on here!"

Kathleen saw Donald Duck as clear as day, now pointing the umbrella accusingly at her. "Look, it's in the past now," she said, trying to put a lid on her fear.

"Wait till I get my hands on that fucker!" he shouted. Heads turned. Kathleen realised they had an audience and George was using it against her. She fought back. "Look, Jack's de..dead now and there's nothing can be done about it. When you get up in the morning and you realise he's not coming back—he's not coming back, George—then you know there's no point in going on about the past. Anyway, he was old enough to do what he wanted." Her sudden defence of Jack surprised herself.

"Yeah, and look what doing what he wanted got him into! If I get my hands on him, I'll...!" He looked up at the ceiling to stem his tears. It was too late for beating the shite out of Jack.

"Listen, you! Nicholas was all he had. Maybe, just maybe, he was good for him," she persisted.

"Good for him? Christ almighty! And does *she* know? What's she—a fucking front? Does she know?"

"Yes, Shirley knows, aye."

George thumped the table repeatedly with his fist and Kathleen blinked to its beat.

"George, does anyone really give a fuck about what men do with their dicks?" she said, when he had finished.

"Listen, you, I told you my nuts were frozen off me!"

"I'm not talking about that."

His thoughts had been on their aborted attempt at sex.

"Do you know?" he began, suddenly more mellow, his eyes studying the summersaults of his lighter which he flipped over again and again on the table. "I wrote to him the day before yesterday. I had written the letter and all when I realised that...It's still sitting there in my cell still."

Kathleen stretched out her hand to him and he took it.

"I told him I was sorry for letting him down, for putting him through so much. Sure where the fuck was I? These'uns have me locked up like an ODC. I'm no fucking Ordinary Decent Criminal! I told him, I told him that if I could I'd rather have had all his pressures. I let him down."

"It's too late, George! It's too late for regrets. We have to face reality! We have to!" His belated regrets had fanned her anger once more. She withdrew her hand and bit on her lip to fight back tears. The last thing she wanted was his pity.

"Have you a fag there?" she asked him, attempting to regain her self-control.

"Did you not bring me any in?"

"I gave them to Johnny. He had none of his own for the canteen."

"Is he in on all of this?"

"No, he's not. I didn't tell him nothing."

A voice inside wondered how much longer she would have to keep on telling people things she herself would rather not know.

George pushed her a cigarette across the table and rolled one for himself. As he put it to his lips, it hit him: his son was a fag.

* * *

"Ma, did you get my message?"

"What message, love?"

"The message I left on your mobile."

"That thing takes messages?"

"Ma, it's technology, that's all it is."

"It's an awful bloody curse, that's what it is, Rosy, love."

"Ma, soon you'll be thinking there was never life before it!"

"I wish! Believe you me! I wish!" Kathleen murmured.

"What?"

"Nothing!"

"All I wanted to know was what you wanted for dinner."

"You're gonna cook dinner for me? You will and your hat!"

"Maaa!" she bleated, "somebody has to look after you some time!"

"Listen, love, till I tell you. Do you not think your poor mother could do with a wee rest? There's been enough change in my life without that. Anyway, you're time enough to be running after me! You'll be running after someone with the dinner soon enough yourself, if God spares you!"

"No, I won't! Are you daft? I won't be running after no man. Are you mad? Here, will you show me that mobile phone of yours till I erase my message."

"Erase your message?"

"Aye, have you the phone there?"

"It's in my bag, love. What do you want it for?"

"I told you—to erase the message. Otherwise you'll have hundreds of them. Do you know your code?" asked Rosy, taking the phone from Kathleen's handbag.

"It's five hundred and sixty, five hundred and sixty-four. Jesus, what is it now? 5, 5, 563. No, no, hold on a wee sec till I get my glasses on. I writ it down on a bit of paper somewhere. My mind's not my own these days."

Kathleen lifted her reading glasses from her coat-pocket and rooted in her bag.

"Five thousand, three hundred and sixty-two," she called out, holding her glasses to her eyes.

"5, 3, 6, 2," said Rosy entering the code. "Ma, you have a ton of messages here!"

"A ton of messages? What? Who'd be ring…?

"Ssssh! You've eleven new messages"

"Eleven new messages?"

"Ach, Rosy, is them there your keys over there on the floor?"

"Shussh a wee minute, mummy! Auntie Maura says to say she's asking for you. She'll call back."

"Aunt Maura?" Kathleen exclaimed. "Jesus bless us, but I'm falling to pieces here!" she added, the gold cross slipping from the chain around her neck as she stooped to pick up Rosy's keys.

"It's Aunt Maura again. She wants you to ring her when you get a chance. The dog had to be…."

"…put down," interrupted Kathleen, fixing the clasp on her chain. "Sure, I know that. That was away the Monday before last, or even longer. I've heard more about that blooming dog! Do you want a cup of tea, pet?" she asked, dropping the keys on Rosy's lap.

"Marlene says she won't be over tonight."

"Tonight? Here, that was last week sometime too."

"Ma, ma, it's, it's…Here, take it! It's granddad. He's, he's…"

"Granddad? I, I don't, I don't wanna…Jesus Christ!" She swiped at the phone as Rosy foisted it on her.

"Ma, he's cry…..ma, hurry up, take it, here, will you, quick? Wait! Hang on! Hang on! I'll save it. There! Here!" Rosy saved the message and shoved the phone into her hand. "Press 8!"

Manoeuvring the phone like a magnifying glass, Kathleen brought the number into focus and pressed eight.

Hello, Kay? Kay, is that you, love? Kay? Oh, Kay, hello, hello, it's me.

K, Special K, OK, Oh Kay, KO, que sera sera—the sounds rattled through her head and she collapsed on the sofa as if in a hail of bullets.

I just wanna say, too, I just want you to know that, I've always loved you, Kay. I have. I've always loved you. I didn't do you any harm. I only, I had your good at heart. I do. Won't you believe me, will you? I love you, Kay. I love you, princess. I loved you more than any of them. Never let them tell you anything different! They can all go to hell! There's not one understood you the way I do, my Special K.

It wasn't your fault, love. You didn't do any wrong. You didn't. We loved each other, whatever about whatever way they seen it. Please don't hate me. I'm, I'm your father, Kathleen. I'm s...s.....sorry about Kevin. It was my fault. Forgive me, won't you? I wanted...

Em, Kathleen, I hope you're doing okay. It was nothing important. I just wanted you to know that I got back safely to Dublin, in case you were worried. I'll give you a buzz later. Oh, this is Nicholas, by the way.

The phone slipped from her hand and Rosy shook her looking for signs of life. "Ma! Ma! Ma, are you alright? Ma, are you alive, for Chrissake?"

Kathleen gagged.

* * *

Nicholas was glad of the momentary reprieve as Kathleen's door jammed on her carpet. Through the mosaic glass, he could see her change colours in the television light. She set her tumbler on the floor and put one foot to the ground.

"Oh, you!" she said, drawing back.

"I, I'm really sorry about, eh, what happened the, the other day," he began.

"Oh, so it's the other day you're sorry for, is it?" she shot back, picking up her glass of vodka. "It's not the other day you should be sorry for, Nicholas. Jack—I sent my wee boy down to you to look after, but, you know, all you done was use him to feather your nest. Your love nest!"

A piece of fluff the size and colour of a wren's egg on his duffle caught his eye. He plucked at it.

"Did you hear me?" Kathleen boomed sergeant-major like. Nicholas stood to attention and dropped his hands by his side. "Love bloody nest!"

"Please, Kathleen, don't, please don't do this to me!" he begged.

"Don't do this to me? What about me? What about my Jack? What about us?" Kathleen stopped long enough for another gulp of vodka, which was long enough for Nicholas to gird himself against the onslaught. He crossed his arms.

"Take yourself off, Nicholas, for I don't give a fuck any more! I've been fucked around enough!" she continued, cheered by the alcohol slipping down her throat.

"I'm sorry," Nicholas apologised to her glass, unable to look her in the eye.

"Sorry? Do you think that makes one blind bit of difference? Do you? Do you think that'll bring me, him back, do you? Well, it won't! Do you know what? I don't give a fuck if you're sorry!

It's too little too late! I don't give a fiddler's fuck about anything anymore!"

Nicholas saw Jack in her fierce countenance—his chin had jutted out and his magical eyes had flared in her sunken sockets as her nostrils constricted—and felt a sudden surge of determination to stand his ground.

"Kathleen, I did all I could for Ja..."

"You helped yourself to a defenceless youngster," she cut him off. "Do you not think he'd been through enough without you feeding off him too? Do you not?" She tucked her feet up under her and pulled the flap of the dressing-gown over her knees to hide her thighs. "Can you imagine what it was like for him? Can you? He trusted you, and you abused him!"

"I abused him? I, I, I loved him!" he shouted, his face sizzling. "I loved him more than you'll ever know! I gave him more love and affection than he'd ever knew. The 'hing, the thing is yous had no time for him, no, so don't...! The struggle came before Jack in your book, and that's the God's honest truth! Tigers don't change their spots, Kathleen. You gave up on Jack a long time ago, and he knew it!"

Kathleen gripped the arms of her chair to contain her rage then leaped up and rushed in his direction. He jumped aside, and she flung open the door of the drinks' cabinet behind him.

"I have a letter here from him. I want you to have it. He wrote it just before..." he began again. He shook the letter open like a napkin and stretched it out to her but she proceeded past him into the kitchen, a bottle of Vodka in her hand.

Nicholas called after her, "He would have wanted you to read it, Kathleen. Look, this isn't about me any more. This is about Jack."

She was beating a tray of ice-cubes off the sink when he placed the letter beside her. She reached for her reading glasses on the shelf above her head, blew the cigarette ash off them and holding the letter up to the light of the window began to read. Nicholas heard whimpering and hoped it was a puppy at the door. She removed her glasses, dried them with the belt of her dressing-gown and put them back on.

"Kath..." he began. She put her hand out in an effort to stop him approaching, patting the air as if a child's head, and the smell of Domestos caught his throat and nose. "John...John...Johnboy," she groaned.

"There, there, there!" he soothed her, each word a stepping-stone towards her. He buoyed her up and with a deep breath guided her out of range of the odour.

"He had so much wanted to live," she said, slabbering on his coat. We killed him. We as good as killed him—his da and me! I knew the past would catch up with me some day, Nicholas. It was only a matter of time. Johnboy! Do you know something, I never knew him, sure I didn't? It's funny how you can, how you can carry someone but never know them. Do you know, I would give anything to have one more day with him now? To see him walk through that door again!" She wiped her nose on her sleeve as his tears fell on her thick, greasy hair. "And find me drunk!" she added, laughing. "I cared more about this frigging house, the colour of that pelmet in there, that wallpaper border, them pictures. For what, like? So that George would come out one day to a home? I've spent the last I don't know how many bloody years putting my house in order! Uh, putting my house in order? That's a geg! Putting my house in order? Just look at the state of me!"

"Ssshh!" said Nicholas. "You, I mean...," His tears forced him to stop. Kathleen squeezed his forearm. He took a deep breath. "You, you did your best," he said.

"No, Nicholas. You were the only person that really loved him. You knew him. You knew him better than any of us because you took the time to know him."

His chest chugged as her words pounded him and his eyes spurted tears.

"Do you know something? You loved him with these hands, Nicholas. You healed him with these hands, and I'm so glad, so glad he got the chance to know you. God, I'm such a bitch for saying all those things to you!"

He shook his head from side to side. Kathleen tore some Tesco kitchen roll and ripped it in two.

"Do you 'member how you'd hold him in your arms and dance when he was a baby? Do you 'member?" Nicholas asked as she dried his tears. "Well, one night I seen him through the windie of his wee cottage dancing around the place. He was so happy, and, and so beautiful. You couldn't live his life for him, Kathleen. He had to do that for himself. When you danced with him, he knew that you loved him. And he knew how to love too. You taught him that. And when his time came to die, I don't know what he thought, Kathleen, but I know he had knew joy. He had discovered in seventeen years what manys a person'd find difficult to find in seventy. He was at peace with himself. And do you know, Kathleen, I don't know, but I think, I think he was ready. I think maybe, maybe he was ready to, you know, die. Maybe, maybe he wanted to."

"I wanted him to go straight across the Border right after daddy's funeral," Kathleen began, "but nothing would do but he'd stay behind for his granny. Nicholas, can I, can, em, Kevin, Kevin was da's son, eh, can I, do you want a drink, Nicholas, do you?"

"Kevin?"

"Kevin?" she echoed him.

"Da?"

"Da? Eh, yeh, the baby," she replied, realising what she must have told him.

Kathleen had replayed Kevin' short history in her mind again and again since Frank's phone message. She hadn't realised she was pregnant until she was well into her second trimester. Benny had taken her to Doctor McCord's, concerned that she hadn't the energy in the evening to do her school homework. "Could it be a virus?" Benny had enquired of the doctor. "It must be, for there's a shocking bad one doing the rounds," she had answered before the doctor had time to respond. She was forever answering her own questions. It was a habit that normally annoyed Kathleen but that day she had felt indifferent and had peered through the skylight window at the Big Bear which winked down at her. The doctor had bristled at the cheek of her mother's attempt at diagnosis, "If only it were so simple," he happily contradicted her. At the mention of pregnancy, Benny passed out, leaving the doctor to break the news to Kathleen.

"I'm afraid you're pregnant," he explained. "I wouldn't, if I were you," he added, waving his index finger at Kathleen as she strained over her bump to pull her mother up off the floor.

Pregnant? What's that, she had thought, letting go of Benny's arm which fell to the floor like the arm of the rag doll Kathleen kept in her bed. It had to be fatal, she surmised, observing her mother out cold on the floor, one high heel lying under the doctor's desk. Typical of you to disappear just when I needed you, she had thought.

The doctor could see from the blank look on the fourteen year-old's face that he would have to spell it out for her.

"You're going to have a baby," he prophesied, blowing smoke into her face from his potent cigar.

An endless Havana beach like the one on the ad on television flashed before her eyes; tanned bodies, smiling couples, parasols, smoke, but in a brave effort Kathleen rejected the offer of an escape route and forced herself to speak, "But how's this possible?"

"You, you tell me!" the doctor commanded, resenting the young hussy's games.

Kathleen could tell him nothing.

"Has your mother not told you about the birds and the bees?" he confronted her.

The birds and the bees? Her head began to spin. Storks! Bloody storks! Just then her mother had come to her senses and insisted that no daughter of hers would bear a child before her time, and to that hooligan from the 'lower' estate whose people were jailed in the 50s IRA Border campaign. Kathleen would be shipped off to England for the operation. The doctor nodded his consent, careful not to put anything into words, while Benny struggled to fit into her shoe.

Once home, her father had urged that the baby be kept. Benny finally relented on condition that her mother, Marion, rear the child down the country, then wept and scolded herself for her oversight. How could she have let it happen? She had rarely let Kathleen across the door. Benny then cleared her throat to have a go at Kathleen, but Frank stopped her with a clenched fist, and a stamp of his boot that left a black mark on the linoleum that would always remind Kathleen of that night. "Drop it! What's done is done. There's no use raking up the past! She's our daughter and she's carrying our child. Let's just...the least said, the better!"

"You know, and I thought he had stood by me that time," Kathleen explained to Nicholas who was clearly in shock. "I was just so naïve. I knew nothing about anything. Men had 'outside plumbing and women had 'inside plumbing', so mummy said to shut me up one day in the Ulster Museum and stop me pointing at the nude statues. There was no mention of anything like that again until I bled at a school concert, certain that I was bleeding to death. She said it was a 'woman's thing' and gave me a sanitary towel. And do you know what she told me when I tackled her a few years back, she said that at least she had shown me how to put it on, for Lisa Donohue—do you mind the wee girl from down the Loney that knocked about with Marlene—had put it on her forehead and tied it at either side around her ears. So, you know, I was supposed to consider myself lucky after that. And what, and what Padraig Corr from the lower estate had got to do with anything had always boggled me."

"Dad, dad.... he..." began Nicholas.

"I know, Nicholas. I didn't want to say. You know, you think you know someone. Eh, you, you...I didn't mean...I don't mean... I'm not talking about you."

"Can I have a vodka?" he asked. "No ice" he added.

* * *

"Can I, eh, I kiss you goodnight, love?" Benny asked as Kathleen disappeared down the path, leaving her to stew in her own juices.

Benny had pleaded her case with her: nobody knew anything about those sorts of things in them days. None of those things were ever talked about. Besides, times were hard then and she didn't have the luxury to stop and think. She had to sell Kathleen's pram to get the dinner, and had begged from Frank's aunts for the money for coal of a winter's day. Kathleen stood her ground: claims of poverty and ignorance were no excuse— she had connived. Benny defended herself tooth and nail: if the Catholic Church with all its might couldn't get it right on abuse, then what chance did she have all on her own? None! Evasion, cried Kathleen. Benny raised the bar: her father had beaten her and left her on the kitchen floor for three whole days. It was only when Oprah spoke of rape that she had put two and two together and realised what had happened to her, so how could she possibly have understood what was happening to Kathleen? Kathleen berated her for visiting a rapist till his dying day, but Benny rushed to his defence: hadn't he sat them all down to tea, pulled fresh lettuce from the garden, and regaled them with tennis balls found in the cemetery where he cut the grass as a favour to the parish priest? It was hard to hate someone like that. He didn't mean it. He knew no better. Knew no better, roared Kathleen? Benny was in denial, and Kathleen should know for she had been there long enough herself to bottle it and sell it. With that, Kathleen had turned to leave and Benny had gone all soft.

Benny switched off the lights and listened to hear if Kathleen would close the gate tight behind her, not wanting all the dogs of the street doing their stuff in her garden. Once assured, she made her way upstairs to her bedroom where from under the dresser she pulled out an old pair of Frank's shoes, set them on the floor by her bed and let it all out.

"I was an eejit to have listened to you. How could you do this to me? How could you have put us through this? Look at the fine mess you've gone and got me into. There's no doubt about it! You strung me along! It's alright for you running off and leaving me to pick up the bloody pieces, and me not able. If I'd have seen it coming, I'd…

"Why didn't you talk to me? I deserved better, Frank. I lifted and laid you for long enough, didn't I? Never had to lift a frigging finger! God forgive me for cursing this day but you're the cause of this. I didn't stand a chance, did I? Jesus, how stupid can you get? You'd have thought I'd have seen you coming a mile away after what I'd been through! Uh! And I thought the world of you because you never raised a hand to me. No greater fool! I should have known by your bark what your bite was like. Loved her? You loved her? You call fornicating with your daughter loving her? What about me? Where was I to go? Could you see the state of me knocking on doors and not a penny to my name?

She picked up a shoe and pulled the laces taut to either side.

"Oh my God! You...You...you jumped out of bed like a man on a mission. Sick? There was damn all wrong with her! Damn the bit of sickness! But how was I to know? 'I'd just climbed up on the bed to change the bulb!' and forgot to put your boots back on! I couldn't, I couldn't take it in! You'd have had to have eyes in the back of your head for you! You made me do it! You did it, Frank! You cruised and coasted like my da! What chance did I have? What would I have done without all my bits and pieces, had I left you?"

Benny flung his shoes into a corner and screamed. She undressed, climbed into bed, took her rosary beads from under her pillow and prayed for forgiveness. Over the coming days she pulled on her hair until a bald patch formed there for all to see. She would do her penance.

Chapter 13

"Happy Days!" said George as Geordie, just back from the toilet, slotted another pint of stout into his grip. The beer was flowing to welcome George home from prison. For over a year it had looked probable that his release under the terms of the Good Friday Agreement wouldn't go ahead because Families of the Bereaved had been complaining to the Secretary of State that their deceased loved ones would never walk through the door again, whereas their killers would walk scot-free. In the end, it all happened so rapidly that it took the feet from under George, literally. His letter of freedom still in his hands, he fell back and knocked his head off the Birdman of Alcatraz. He had five hours to get ready for life on the outside—nowhere near enough time to finish the matchstick cottage he was making for Shirley. Would he be the laughing stock if he asked the governor to stall his departure by a day? Misunderstanding the spirit of the question, the governor told him he would have plenty of time for making cottages when he set up his gift-shop for tourists in west Belfast in the wake of the IRA surrender and that he would even plough in some of his own hard-earned money. George noted that his offer came with a twinkle in his false eye that he had had implanted after an IRA attack on his car. That very same evening he had marched through the prison gate, his head full of business dreams, none of them involving that bastard that they should have finished off when they had the chance.

As he and Geordie split their sides at the joke about Bono suffering from stage fright in the toilets, out of the corner of his eye George caught Kathleen mingling among the guests, a tray of drinks in one hand, two bowls of cocktail sausages in the other. Unflappable, there was no other word for it, he thought, as she pulled a nest of tables out with her foot, though he hated the quintessentially British nature of the word which reminded him of the only British institution he was mad about—the flap-jack. What he couldn't see was that Kathleen was falling apart. Only that morning, faced with the carnage of her life, she had cried out in an unforgivable moment of weakness, "Why me?" and the Man Above had quickly poured concrete over the cracks: it was what He had wanted. It never entered her head that she might have wanted it herself. Thus it was because God loves little angels that He had taken her week-old baby; her seventeen year period as a grass-widow had been His way of bringing her closer to the celibate Christ and Jack's death had been the Lord inviting her to stand at the foot of the Cross like Our Lady. Even her father's transgressions were put through the sieve of faith. For George, what was unforgivable was that Kathleen hadn't made any flap-jacks though she had promised to bake him some. But, then, that spoke volumes about her, didn't it, he thought. The party was for her, not for him. He hadn't wanted any "do" but she had argued that Jack would have wanted a celebration, though how she came to that conclusion was beyond him. The fact that she wanted the world to know she had stood by the man in her life was more to the truth, he reckoned. As she placed the sausages on the table she smiled at him and he bared his teeth back at her, his buttocks tightening with resentment. Granny Lackey was right to have drowned the female kittens, he thought. Whatever desire he had to start up a wee business to make the past up to her crumbled.

Geordie farted, rescuing George from his depression.

"You'll never guess what happened to me this morning up at the top of the Shaws Road there when I was heading down the road to get some messages for tonight," said George.

"What's the scéal?" Geordie asked. He was pleased that their conversation was on the move again. His farting had had the desired effect, although he doubted anything interesting could have happened on the Shaws Road now that peace was on everyone's lips.

"I'm a car, right, and this motorbike just comes shooting out straight at me and I swerve one way and the fucking bike's gone the other and the next thing I know is I'm in the bushes there beside St. Paul's and my fucking 7-Up's piddling all over the show."

Geordie first checked his trouser zip and then gave a loud laugh that outdid George's. Kathleen interrupted their hilarity. They hadn't noticed her sidle up to them.

"And have you been like this for long?" she asked, knitting her brows together as she examined George's face.

"What?"

"Does this type of thing happen to you often like? Have you spoken to anyone about it?"

"What? Sorry, what, what, what are you on about?"

"The car thing!"

"What, what are you talking about now, Kathleen? What, what car thing?"

"'I'm a car'," said Kathleen.

George and Geordie convulsed again, while Kathleen's drinks came close to toppling off the tray. When they had all recovered, she offered them some sausages. Geordie joked about how they could have done with the silver service waitress in Long Kesh and Kathleen feigned a compliant smile in the way women do when they mean to mock male egos, but it was lost on them, though this came as no surprise to her given that they oozed virility from their years of press-ups at Her Majesty's pleasure, having replaced the war effort with a fascination for their bodies—and not a woman in sight! Not that they would ever see it like that, she thought—except Jack. She chuckled, but George and Geordie noticed nothing, now on to the one about how Liam Averill had escaped from the prison dressed up as a woman.

Zig-zagging back to the kitchen for more cocktail sausages, the bare flag-poles jutting out from buildings on her way up to bring George home came to Kathleen's mind. They had made her think of 'knobs' and the futility, even sterility, of a conflict in which men had tried in vain to prove themselves. The thoughts had embarrassed her but they had probably been a case of nerves, she now told herself, what with George coming home and everything and the whole sex thing to face into again. She heard a further roar of laughter from George's corner. There was no end to his joking these days, she mused. How would she ever get through to him? It had been so much easier in jail. Not only had her words flowed, but his lines had been predictable as well. And a love that she could swear by had nested in her heart then—a yearning for the day he would be free. Tiocfaidh ár lá? Our day has come, alright, but this is not the way it was meant to be, she thought.

She could never have guessed that for all his laughter George was just as thrown by the new dispensation as she was. As he went to the toilet for the umpteenth time that night, cursing his fourteen pints, the realisation rained down on him that he had married her out of spite against his family: the fact that they would never accept a Catholic had been his signal to marry one.

Not that he had consciously gone out of his way to spite them or anything. Indeed, he never would have done it had he had the slightest inkling he was playing into their hands. The very thought churned his stomach. He kneaded his bowel now with his cold fingers. Like, why give them the pleasure of seeing him turn out the failure that they had always predicted? And he had more than come up to their expectations in that respect: jail, Jack stiffed for drugs, boats burned with the Protestant community, alienated from his family. He had married for the wrong reasons, but, still, she was all he had.

He climbed back into bed beside her. He had done seventeen years inside and would do his time with her now, no matter how much she whined. There was too much to lose. The mid-Ulster Unionist supporter on Talkback on the radio earlier was wrong about how the "killers" from the "Maze Prison" would go back to the gun because they couldn't live without it. No way, José! What he couldn't live without was knowing where you stood—the loyalist prisoners housed on the other side of the prison had provided him with that security. He sniggered through the stench of beer. Kathleen grunted. Maybe the more she whined, the easier things would be, he thought. She could provide the comfort of the enemy.

"Move over, will you?" he scowled, prodding her hips with his foot.

* * *

It didn't take George long to get into his old habits, making love in the mirror. There he saw a couple coupling, and was overcome by the belief that he adored the woman in his arms. He would whisper sweet nothings for the sensation in his number one and invoke God Almighty as he came. Once, he called out Kathleen's name and her ears pricked up, but the lyrics of "Oh, take me home, Kathleen!" had been going through his head.

Kathleen would stand there attempting to forget her disgust at his preoccupation with the mirror, and the fact that she may as well not have been there, and imagined all the things she could be doing—smoothing, putting in a last wash, wiping the cupboards—things she had less and less time for since George's release from prison. Occasionally, particularly on longer stints, she would sneak a glance in the mirror, though she convinced herself that it was only to satisfy herself that she was indeed the one attached to him. Ultimately, her pleasure was to be found in bed where, buoyed up by the rancid smell of his fluids, she mulled over his sweet nothings and entertained the notion that he loved her. They did it for her every time, bar one. On that particular evening, having performed his duties and signed off with the usual accolades, George was exasperated to see her take off downstairs.

"What do you want? Do you want toast done on both sides?" she called up to him.

"What, what are you at?" he replied, vexed by her impromptu absence. He liked their little routine and the fact that she rocked herself to sleep after sex, suggesting he had satisfied her.

"What do you mean, what am I at? Do you want toast done on both sides or don't you? It's a simple question."

"You know I hate it done on one side!"

When she reappeared, George went on the offensive.

"What are you on about now?" he shouted. "You and your 'what do you want'?" His drone was a take on her voice.

"Well, so long as *you*'re happy!" she replied.

"Happy? What's that got to do with it? Did I ask you to make me…"

"It's never about what I want, is it?" she cut across him.

"…toast?" he said.

George felt vindicated. He was right to have gone on the attack. She had been getting at him. Toast wasn't the issue.

"Look, I've asked you millions of times to say what it is you want," George continued, "but you just stand there shrugging your shoulders. You wouldn't stoop to asking! That'd be too much like having your cake and eating it!"

"Asking? What's the point? I wouldn't get a look in with you and that bloody mirror! You and your muscles!"

"Say whatever you like, but you know fine rightly I'd do whatever you want! What is it you want, Kathleen? Kinky sex?"

"Whatever I want? That's a joke and you know it!"

"Ach, you were always the same. Never happy! Give you a mile, and you'd want an inch! When things were tough, you were happy. Now that I'm home, all you do is moan. If it's as bad as you make out, why don't you take yourself off?"

"Leave? Me? What would I be leaving for? This is my home! You go! Off you go and see how long you'd survive in the big world without me propping you up. Uh! You wouldn't last the course!"

"Kathleen, have you forgotten something? I did seventeen years without you."

Her head would burst. She wanted to tell him everything—now. Only that would stop the pain.

"If, if I have to chain myself to this bed to talk to you, to tell you what's…, I will—even if it kills me."

George slid his head down along the headboard on to the pillow and pulled the blankets up to his chin. He was right. She had come to him in the garden shed a few weeks earlier when she was in the throes of cleaning out the dining room for the welcome home party and had said, "I'm thinking of moving…the dresser. What about it?" His heart had skipped a beat before she had even mentioned the dresser. *I'M THINKING OF MOVING.* He was right. She had it in for him.

"I don't know where to…"

"Is this about me?" he piped up.

"No, it isn't. Well, it, no, yes, it is in a way."

"Shoot!" he said. Execution by firing squad seemed the quickest way to get it over with, but he was simply putting on a brave face. He was terrified.

Kathleen shivered at the thought of Jack's bullet but forced herself to get on with it. "When I was 4 or 5 maybe, he held me, eh, Granny was…in the bed, uh, dead. I loved her so much. She loved…me."

George read her lips as if to better comprehend her babble but it was to no avail.

"Look, what has this got to do with me?" he harangued her.

"Dad loved her. He would lift her up the stairs to bed. She was wheelchair bound. He did everything for her. She was my granny. She loved…"

A tear rose to her eye, and he watched it gather speed as it slipped onto her lip and rested there. He wanted to curl up inside it.

"She loved…" She began again, trawling for words that lay entwined below the surface. "She loved me so much." The words swept up and out as the tears streamed down her cheeks. "She, she, she understood me. I could have told her anything. I could lie."

"Lie?"

"Yes, mummy would stand me in front of the crucifix and warn me to tell the truth or face burning in hell because God was watching and could see everything."

"But what had you done?"

"I hadn't done anything. I'd come home late from Colette's' house sometimes, or I'd be playing in Laura's garden, and…"

"So, you, she put you through this for playing with your friends?"

His fear was gone, dissolved in Kathleen's tale of her mother and grandmother. He was off the hook now.

"I wouldn't tell her the truth sometimes." Her words were barely audible. "I couldn't tell her about him, I think. That's why I forgot."

"Who? About what?"

"About dad."

"What about your dad?"

"I'm your dad," she murmured to herself, twisting the string in her knickers around her index finger. "Damn black knickers!"

George recoiled. She had always donned black knickers for him. His mother had had a thing about formal dress, and, consequently, removing Kathleen's black knickers was, for him, like breaking all the rules. Not that he had confessed this to Kathleen who had taken him at his word: he liked black against her white skin.

"There's nothing wrong with them there knickers. What do you mean, I'm your dad?" asked George, eager to move her on.

"'I'm your dad. Would I hurt you?'" She hated those words but had made them her own, pronouncing them even now in a childish voice.

"Hurt you?"

"He'd take me everywhere. They all said I was the lucky one, his blue-eyed. I was his shadow. He hid the bread behind a loose brick in the wall so that we could come back to feed the ducks. We went back, but, but, I wasn't the lucky one. I was the blue-eyed one, yes, but I wasn't lucky. We went back."

Her destination seemed a long way off, and George drifted momentarily.

"He took me everywhere, and everywhere he'd go he'd whistle all those old songs. I'd look up at him. He was my world. I was his shadow. But I hate him. I do. I hate every fucking bone in his body. I, I, needed him. Would you credit that? He fucked me up and over, but I needed him."

George heard "Over and out!" in a distinct English accent but had no idea where it had come from. He wanted out.

Kathleen reached for her watch and knocked over a glass of water on the bedside table.

"I am here for you, Kathleen", George blurted, meaning the opposite. Kathleen momentarily basked in his affection.

"I wish I could hate him more! I wish, I wish I had killed him myself. I wish...I wish the fuck you were here! You bastard!"

Sensing he was the bastard, George shuddered.

"He a...abused me. He used me, the sick fuck! He did what he wanted with me. Who am I, George? What am I? For the bin? He, he came inside me, George. And she must have known. And I needed him. He was all I'd got."

George heard voices from the bedroom in the house next door, a wasp dying on the window-sill, Kathleen's watch tick on the bedside table. "The bastard!" he said under his breath, his hands searching for comfort under the blankets.

"I went to the dentist a few years back," she said as she left the bedroom to get some toilet tissue. "He took away my innocence." It was a phrase she had stored up from Emmerdale Farm. It served now to deaden the pain for her somewhat. George visualised the arrows on a remote control and searched for 'mute' as she approached the bedroom and the sound of her voice grew. "You know, Jack asked me out of the blue one day if I was sad when I was a child. I told him that I had a really happy childhood. Could you credit that?" she said, still feeling inspired by her favourite soap.

"One day, eh, he took me with him to the swimming-pool in the Falls Park. He took me by the hand the whole way down the road. He was whistling away to himself as per usual. He bought me a poke, a 99, at the gate and stopped to talk to Sady whatdoyoumacallit, em, Sady, who worked at the bowling green. It melted all over my dress, and Sady took me into the clubhouse to get cleaned up. She gave me this box of tiny Easter eggs, shaped like a wheel, because, she said, I was my daddy's little princess." Her lost innocence suddenly stopped her in her tracks. "Em, what was I saying?"

George refused to help her out.

"Oh, aye, the pool was packed. You know yourself, the half of them came only to get a wash. I was bursting to get into the water. You could hardly see the bottom of it for the dirt. He got in the water with me. And then, that's that's when...I don't know, it just, I just felt this thing betw...I felt this pain. I think I thought I'd done something. I wanted him to help me. That's where, that's when my life stopped. It stopped right there, George. People say that's where they grew up, but my life just stopped, do you know what I mean? I never once thought of it again until the thingy... the dentist brought it all back. There's never a day goes by where I don't think about it, isn't that what people say? Huh! I forgot it. Could you credit that, George? What sort of an eejit am I? How can you just forget something like that?"

"Like what?" he asked, refusing to take it in.

She put her arms around him. "I just need someone to hold on to."

"I'm not a life-raft," he barked, and pushed her away.

George's feet were cold throughout the night, and no matter what he did he couldn't get them warm. This was not the woman he had married, he thought, tossing and turning. And, if she had taken all these years to tell him all that had come out, then there was probably more stuff inside. Maybe it made more sense for them to be apart? Maybe he could do something with the shed in the back garden? Maybe make that his living quarters for a while? Maybe even build some matchstick cottages while he was out there, that way it wouldn't look so bad to the neighbours. He wouldn't want them to be gabbing about Kathleen and him.

Shirley was in her early morning rage, and Chloe was screaming and kicking on the toilet door in the hope that Nicholas
would let her in to escape her wrath. Determined not to let his
daughter disturb his prayer time, he closed his eyes and breathed
from his navel in Yoga style, but even this proved insufficient to
quell his mounting anxiety. His vocation to marriage was evapo-
rating as quickly as the beads of sweat on his forehead. He peered
down at his feet tucked in at his thighs and, remembering the
climbing skills that had brought his religious calling to a speedy
end, begged them not to walk at the first opportunity.

The urge to walk had first presented at the long-term car-park
in Dublin Airport some three years, two months and four days
earlier on return from his honeymoon when, struggling with
Shirley's laden luggage-trolley, which seemed to have a life all
of its own, Benny and Philomena's cacophony had arrested him
in his tracks. It was meant as a surprise, but to Nicholas it would
forever have the hallmarks of an ambush. They had pounced on
him, got him in a head-lock, then sucked on his face like leeches
as they pressed him to their bosoms until he practically lost consciousness. Suffocating in middle-aged flab, all he could make
out from the corner of his eye was PAY HER—Shirley's fancy,
Majorcan hair-do had blocked out the last letter on the parking
ticket machine—and it was then that the enormity of his mistake
struck him like a ship in the night: he didn't have what it would
take to keep Shirley and him afloat. As the three of them pecked
at the pesetas in the palm of his hand for money for the ticket
machine, he was swept away on a stream of semi-consciousness.
He who had done everything by the book—hung around with the
boys on the street, attended a single sex school, spent four years
pent up with the lads in prison (albeit unplanned), and done a

stint in the priesthood where he had even bedded a man out of love for the Father—had managed to fall prey to someone from the other camp who had played hopscotch and swung on lampposts and now linked arms with his assailants to go "powder my nose." *I do*! *I do*? *No, I don't! I don't take you as my wife! I can't!* The words pounded him like shells. He couldn't take any more. Adrift amid the departing Gorgons, he latched on to the idea of a burger and chips that floated before him now like driftwood, and bravely considered the situation. The problem had to be that he had broken ranks and defected, a thought that suddenly dragged him down beneath the surface once again. When relief came, it did so in the shape of a burning conviction that flared only a matter of seconds, but still long enough to provide him with the hope he was so desperately in need of: he was back between the sheets with Shirley in Palma where defection to the opposite sex was the furthest thing from his mind as they laughed at Frank's antics in Angela's Ashes and he only turned the pages upon receipt of a kiss from his beautiful bride. He was in love. Finally on terra firma, Nicholas coolly reviewed the grounds for his bout of nerves. Was it the unsettling effect of being set upon by two matriarchs, not knowing to whom to swear allegiance? Possibly—the very idea of split loyalties had always filled him with confusion. Maybe it was a lack of oxygen to the brain brought on by their attempt to smother him? But a pocket of air had ventilated through the V-shaped gaps. Could it have been the way they had confabbed to rob him of his cash, when he was feeling particularly vulnerable of being financially dependent upon Shirley? Unlikely, because everything was split down the middle now that he had signed the dotted line. So, was it the PAY HER sign that had thrown him? That seemed ridiculous, but he couldn't rule it out. Whatever the reason, he would never know for certain because the three now heavily made up maikos pattered back towards him and, festooning him with caresses, whisked him off to Philomena's car where he finally worked up the courage to ask them to stop at the first M that came into view. It was only when he had felt the weight of a Big Mac in his gut that he was in any sense his old self again. It must be something to do with burying my teeth in meat, he thought—a male thing. When all was said and done, he told himself, he was a man's man, and with that, his nerves had settled.

During the intervening years the question of how he had ended up sharing a bed full-time with a member of the fairer sex had continued to plague him intermittently. During one such bout, after an argument with Shirley who had promptly decamped to Philomena's, he explained to Chloe that his marriage to her mama was like being relocated across the 'Water' with a new identity under an RUC supergrass programme. Chloe's response, like her mother's that day, was predictable. "Grass! Grass!" she called out, licking the pane of the patio door in the hope that he would open it to let her out. Deflated by her lack of interest, he abandoned his plan to tell her the whole story, which was that for him relocation had been especially harrowing since, unlike the case with paid police informants, there had been nothing by way of compensation to soften the landing on the other side. There had only been Shirley, and she was a handful—particularly when she was late for work, as she was now.

Even as he tried to rein in his loathing for the woman he now heard tearing around the kitchen, from the safety of the toilet, Nicholas wished her gone, a desire that became more compelling the more Chloe pummelled the toilet door. Shirley screamed. Chloe had spilled porridge on the floor. Stay-at-home dad extraordinaire, he hadn't had time to clean it up because she had had an emergency pooh—the effect of the porridge—and he had completely forgotten about it. He roared at Shirley now to leave it to him and reminded her to get a move on as she was already late for work. Chloe wailed at the sound of his fearsome voice. Feeling pangs of guilt, he wondered what he would tell her in her tender teenage years when she popped the million-dollar question about how they'd met. If her current spate of tantrums was anything to go by, the truth of the matter, namely that he had run into her mother having gone through the wrong door at the pool, would hardly placate her in her pubescent hormonal state. He would have to make something up. He would ask her to sit down and listen, and to his astonishment, she would do as he bid, lighting up a cigarette as she made herself comfortable in his rocking chair. He would put it to her that romance had brought her mother and him together and that their love for one another had subsequently cemented their relationship, (which was what Shirley was fond of telling him, though he would omit to reveal this to Chloe). In his mind's eye, true to her nature, Shirley would be reclining on the chaise-longue, which meant that it would be a Bank Holiday, for otherwise she would have been at the office. And guess what? Shirley wouldn't even have heard Chloe's question, let alone considered a response to it. However, he would keep his cool and take a deep breath: there was no point in getting upset about the fact that she liked him to deal with all the serious issues which more often than not she failed to notice until he had brought them to her attention. Chloe was just on the point of rubbishing his explanation—at least this is what he had deduced from the look of disbelief in her imaginary eyes—when a thump on the toilet door and a shout that was altogether incomprehensible brought him back to himself.

He sprang off the toilet seat and threw the full weight of his body against the door as Chloe pushed it open. As it slammed shut, thought of his defection to the other side overpowered him and he slid to the floor, with his back to the door. The penny dropped. It all boiled down to Ladies and Gents. It was nothing less than separation of the sexes that had brought him and the raving lunatic in the kitchen together. Separation of the sexes guaranteed ignorance about the other, and ignorance was bliss, and bliss was the essential ingredient that gave people enough Dutch courage to make it up the aisle. That's what had happened to him. How many of his mates would have tied the knot had they known their wives the way they knew them the day they walked out? None. Love was blind for a reason. Some day soon he would let Chloe in on the fact that he had married her mother because he didn't know her. He would also warn her to take a long forenoon before committing because, as in his own case, the afternoon might be wet.

"What are you doing, daddy?" Chloe now chirped. She had switched her modus operandi, banking on her sweet little girl act.

"I'm praying, love," he explained. It was as much an appeal to her reason, which he now desperately wished to foster, as an explanation of his actions, but his underlying motivation was lost on her.

"Can I see?"

"No, chicken. You can blow the candle out for me later. Okay?"

He expected the worst—a roar, or at the very least another kick on the door, but he was pleasantly surprised.

"Okay, daddy!" she replied, seeing her mother galloping up the hall.

"Okay, my arse, Nick!" Shirley boomed. "Get your butt out of there and get this child a drink! I'm away! I've a timetable to keep to, unlike some people around here."

Nicholas' schedule, particularly his prayer slot, was a frequent subject of debate between Shirley and him, but he stuck to his guns—prayer before breakfast was an absolute must—because once he exited the toilet, or his prayer-room, as he called it much to Shirley's disdain, the battle was lost. He would typically be carried away on a tide of minor indulgences reminiscent of his pre-prison days: 'cas' look, shoes always matching the colour of his sandy hair, the blasé jeans look to accentuate his blue eyes, or the more serious sunglasses-cum-something-continental look which constituted an attempt to hide himself in order to, paradoxically, attract more attention. His choice of outfit was more often than not dependent upon Chloe whose patience inevitably ran out on his second or third fitting. Then it was off to playschool, wondering if the other parents would take note of Shirley's BMW which he had the use of except when she had to go to the Galway Office and needed to make an impression. By lunch-time his main concern was whether anyone noticed him sipping cappuccinos over a panini in La Banca with his reading material—a Penguin classic on Mondays and Tuesdays, the Irish Times Property section on Wednesdays, the entertainment section for 'achingly funny' new plays on Thursdays, and Business section on Friday. No passing bill-board escaped his notice, and no offer on the radio missed his attention. In the afternoons, Chloe in tow, he could find himself heading to the city centre to buy an overcoat in the middle of summer, or a third pair of sunglasses in the middle of winter. By tea-time the Internet was the Lord of his desire. His fall from grace had been as swift as Lucifer's. The rot had set in at Dublin Airport with the realisation that Shirley had snared him.

Nicholas turned his check at Shirley's broadside about him sitting on his butt all day, and asked St. Jude, the Patron saint of Hopeless Cases, to intercede for her. Could he put a word in the Big Man's ear for her audit at work so that they could sort out what really mattered—the state of their marriage? Once assured that St. Jude was on the job, he readied himself for battle. Failing an immediate miraculous intervention, he had no alternative but to defend his patch when he opened the toilet door. He winked at himself in the mirror to psyche himself up, then ran his hand down over his face like a knight closing his protective mask. Once you went soft, fraternised with the enemy, tried to make her happy or keep her on side, it was over. A man's gotta do what a man's gotta do, he thought. When all was said and done, he would have to inform Chloe some day that he stayed with her mother because he loved the thrill of a good scrap. There was nothing more to it.

Fired up by his confusion, he pushed open the door and charged forth bearing his toothbrush.

"If you got out of bed earlier, you wouldn't be late! You've a timetable to keep to?" he shouted at Shirley.

Shirley had actually forgotten her broadside but the mention of 'timetable' triggered her memory. She clashed once more in daily joust. "Don't you be getting on your high horse with me! You really don't have a notion about life in the real world, do you? Hardly surprising, though, after a spell in the clink and three years wasted locked up in a retreat house! Some CV! Is it any wonder you can't find work?"

"The real world? Oh, yeah! I just lounge around the house all day? Isn't that it? Who gets her to playschool?" Nicholas growled, pointing his toothbrush at Chloe who cowered behind the clothes' horse. Shirley placed her hands on her hips in defiance but he held his nerve. "Do you put the dinner on the table, and arrange our nights out?" he continued, "Do you? Aye, and who brings up all the important issues before the house and this marriage falls down around us? I'm doing the work of two here!"

Shirley felt the lance go in. "The work of two?" "Are you the one out earning the money? Oh, no! The work of two? I'm the breadwinner in this relationship, Nick, and don't you forget it! I put dinner on the table. Oh, but that doesn't count for anything with you, of course!"

"Yeah, well, you're either too busy at work, or too tired from work, or too busy planning work to get anything done! As long as you have a man on your arm for your business dinners, you're happy. I didn't marry you to be put on a shelf! I should have known better, shouldn't I? As long as you had your white dress and your wedding, you were happy."

He flung Chloe's bowl into the sink and set about wiping the porridge off the floor. It seemed like an age to him since he and Shirley had woken up and kissed in bed earlier. He sighed but was still not about to go soft in spite of his sudden desire to make up now. He had just enough time for a quick pee at her expense. It would annoy her if he wasn't available for the standard kiss goodbye at the door, in the vein of the 1950's wife seeing the breadwinner off.

Chloe barged into the toilet and grabbed his penis just as he was taking up position.

"Does uncle Johnny have one of these?"

"Let go! Let go!" Nicholas pleaded.

"Is uncle Johnny's bigger?"

"Let go! I'll get you a lolly later! Let go!"

Chloe settled for the promise of a lollipop, and released her grip.

"Good enough for you!" Shirley scoffed. "You'd never think of sitting down instead of peeing all over the pot, would you? No, I forgot, that would demand too much effort from Mr. 'I have it all under control!"

Chloe pulled the bobbin from her hair and dispensed it down the toilet as he stood washing his hands with his back to her.

"Look, Nick! Look at me!" Like an adult leading a child by the hand, she directed him to the toilet bowl.

"What the hell, what the hell are you playing at now?" he roared.

Chloe burst into tears, crying as loud as she could to attract the attention of his opponent, but it was no use. Shirley was taking a break from arguing.

Nicholas took the elastic band from his wrist, which he kept there for emergencies, and set about fixing her hair again. The more it hurt, the better, he thought. The band caught her hair and she slapped him on the arm.

"Ouch! Stop it or I'll kill you!" he cried out, pulling on her hair.

The first time he had hit her he was wrecked with guilt but he gradually bought in to the belief that a clatter now and then never did anyone a bit of harm. Later still, he progressed to shaking her—it left no marks and, unlike clattering, was unlikely to kill her. Now he suddenly was ridden with regret for having tried to scalp her for the simple reason that she was sure to make him pay for it by playing up on him the rest of the day. Shirley's criticism proved a welcome distraction from his anxiety, "If only you didn't waste half the morning sitting in there praying and making her late for playschool!"

"But.." began Nicholas, only to be drowned out by her.

"You're as lazy as bloody sin! I could see through it if you were doing Tai Chi, or Zen, or Yoga, but that praying nonsense! What has Jesus ever done for you, sitting on your arse? If you'd get up off your backside and earn a bit of money instead of wasting mine on your mobile phone!"

She hit where it hurt: he was never off the phone to his mother. Nothing would stop Shirley now that she had gathered momentum. She was a juggernaut going through.

"You're your mother's son alright. 'A couple of Hail Marys and everything will be fine!'" she said, mimicking Benny's Belfast accent. "In the real world, people work their butts off! But you just sit tight. Your mother sitting up there holding court, and you all under her thumb! Drug our child? Over my dead body! Oh, yeah, the loving mother! Loving mother? Like shit!"

He had phoned Benny the previous week to ask her what he should do with Chloe who was waking up in the middle of the night with nightmares. She had suggested giving her enough Calpol to knock her out for the night. In the old days, she explained, they used brandy.

Shirley refused to let up, "She put ye all to sleep. Ye are still asleep, if you ask me! But, of course, you won't ask me, for what would I know? I'm only the child's mother! But I tell you what, I'm well able to look after Chloe and myself into the bargain. I don't need a manager! I'm not Rangers!"

"Yeah, you bring a horse to a trough..." shouted Nicholas. "Is it not time you were leaving?" He had heard enough for one morning.

"I'm not the one who needs to leave!" Shirley shot back at him, but he gave her a look that suggested she had lost the plot.

"Come on, love. I'll look after you, because your mother won't. She has too much to do!"

Nicholas stuck out his hand to Chloe. He needed her on his side, but she ignored him, sensing that her mother was the better bet. Taking her by the hand against her will, he made his way into the kitchen. He hoped his guilt-trip would get Shirley off his scent but she was having none of it. She followed him into the kitchen where he was trying desperately to focus on getting Chloe a drink. In his heart of hearts he knew that his determination to hide his face behind the fridge door was a sure sign that she was right—Benny had put them all to sleep. She had copyright on the quiet life. She had tiptoed around her father, then around Frank, and she had even managed to get the children on side, blinding them to the truth about his abuse. She had taken over the controls to get her way, and he too was a chip off the old block.

Shirley bided her time, knowing that sooner or later he would have to show his face. "Don't you go guilt-tripping me!" she fired at him as he closed the fridge door. "You're every inch your mother's son! You're a bloody vacuum sucking the life out of me! Well, I'm not going to take the knocks just because you have to shine!"

She pulled on her coat and kissed Chloe goodbye while Nicholas cast his eyes over the room looking for something—anything—to tidy up in order to pretend to her that he was in control. He had dug himself into a hole. She was right—he had to shine at her expense, and it was due to something more than simply the separation of the sexes. He wanted to bring her to heel now for all the pain he was feeling, but he was drained. He would come clean. He moved towards her to speak.

"I'll be off so! Someone has got to bring in the beef!" she said as she dumped an Actimel bottle in the bin, then stomped past him. He heard the door bang with a vengeance.

Sensing Nicholas' vulnerability, Chloe swooped on him.

"I want Barney."

"Yes."

"Barney, daddy!" she now shouted, his answer having lacked the requisite degree of conviction.

"Yes, okay."

"I want Barney, daddy!" she whined, tugging at his pyjama leg.

"Yes."

"Now, daddy! I want to see Barney now!" she screamed, moving into position to bite.

"Yes" he snapped.

"Daa-daaa!"

Nicholas prised her off his leg. He would make her work for being such a pain. "Right, you have to clean up the den first! One, two, three. I'm counting to five. One, two, three. Two, three," he began again. He couldn't face another argument.

Chloe got down to work in the den while he placed Jack's worn letter under the clock in the living-room. It was his prayer-book. If he couldn't believe that Jack loved him, how could he ever believe that God loved him? As he made his way to the den on his fourth count of five, he made up his mind to ask Shirley to write him a love letter when she got home that evening. He needed to accept that she loved him. Besides, he needed her, and he would tell her so tonight.

Chloe had managed to put the dolls in the doll-house. That was all. She had basically been playing, but he wasn't about to make a scene. He set up the video and settled her down on the settee. If he was lucky, she might keep quiet for the next half an hour in and he could enjoy the luxury of getting dressed on his own.

As he searched for his vest in his bedroom he came across Shirley's frilly Belgian underwear that she wore at conferences. He was suddenly overwhelmed by a wave of self-pity and a desire to be nice to himself—to paint his toenails, apply a facial maybe. When did he ever have a massage? When did any man ever peck him on the cheek, link his arm, or call him up to ask him to a 'boys' night out? He needed pampering. He slipped into his yellow Sudden Storm Y-fronts that Shirley had bought him on a business trip to Amsterdam, curled up under the duvet and cuddled himself. He dozed. When he awoke a few minutes later he felt like he had slept the sleep of the dead. Pulling some trousers out of a drawer, he remembered that he had dreamt of wearing Shirley's satin pantaloons, but he hadn't the nerve to do it. Besides, Chloe was sure to mess them up. "Chloe? Oh, shit, Chloe!" he shouted. He had forgotten all about her. For a brief few minutes—thirteen in all, he checked,—she had ceased to exist.

"Chloe, what are you doing?" he called out to her. He raced downstairs, now expecting the worst—a few weeks earlier she had pasted the kitchen wall with Vaseline—but found her rolled up like a hamster on the couch. Time off. He would finish getting dressed and have some lemon tea in the conservatory before she awoke.

Observing crows and starlings rivalling over some bread on the lawn he hummed *What's love got to do with it?* He hated so much about Shirley—her values, her behaviour, and even her personality. Though he complained about her arriving home late from work, the truth was her delays were a blessing because lately everything about her grated on him. On Sundays, when he had maximum exposure, he typically found himself drained by the end of the day. She would insist on family time, usually some sort of outing in the morning, then tart baked with her own fair hands at four o'clock, like at Head Office in Germany, and a 'sex slot' last thing at night after she had caught up on her emails. Of late, it was obvious that she enjoyed the baking more than the sex—kneading the dough, brushing the pastry, filling the sink up with messy utensils (which she would leave for him to wash the following morning), and gouging out the leftover orange with her front teeth. It was all about the foreplay. Once the tart was in the oven, it was a case of out of mind, out of sight. Nine times out of ten he would be called upon to salvage the offerings. Her baking was indicative of her attitude to her marriage, or so he had contended in the heat of an argument one day: the build-up had been everything—their romantic weekends away, the wedding preparations. The moment she put her wedding ring on, it was done and dusted.

While he eventually had a fire-extinguisher installed by the cooker, he could find no means for putting out their blazing rows. Forever the optimist, Shirley maintained that as opposites attract they would hold together naturally. He argued that it would be the end of them because she had always longed for someone to take control of her life, and he had always yearned for someone to control. She was horrified, but not surprised by his negativity, and managed to burn three cakes that afternoon, one after the other.

Even if his thoughts were negative, he thought, he would enjoy the quiet while he had it. He poured more lemon tea then pressed 'release' on his chair which jerked backwards into a horizontal position, frightening the starlings away. He sipped his tea. This in itself was a prime example of how they pulled against each other, he thought. Shirley only ever drank coffee, which he detested. The many other significant differences which separated them suddenly cast their shadow over him like a dark cloud. He was always cold, and she was always warm, with the result that at night he wanted the bedroom door closed and she wanted it left open. In the end, they had compromised, leaving it slightly ajar, but he moaned about the draft so much that she did what she should have done at the outset and let him have his way. The conservatory too was another source of conflict. It was a luxury he could have done without but she had gone ahead with it against his will. A conservatory was a necessity, not a luxury, she claimed. Oh, yeah, for the middle-classes, he said, reminding her that deprivation for her as a child was having no BBC. If having no RTÉ had been the only problem in Belfast, he would have been on the pig's back. Shirley dismissed his "smug, false class consciousness" with her best assumed Dublin 4 accent, and remarked that his working-class credentials never seemed to stop him from buying the best of everything with her salary. He derided her for being a snob, of which the very term 'class consciousness' was "a good example."

Then there was the fact that Shirley was so sure of everything, whereas he was always doubt ridden. She bet her life that they would always be together, whereas he was certain they wouldn't last the course. She was also forever the optimist. For her, the glass was always half full, whereas for him, it was always half empty. It was crystal clear to him that their relationship was a nightmare that needed a complete overhaul. For her, the relationship was a dream come true that needed a bit of 'lightening up' now and then—especially him.

He got up and closed the conservatory window and the starlings once more fell on the lawn like raindrops. Stirred by the din, Chloe radioed for help, "Pee-pee!" Her voice was angelic now and he was happy to tend to her needs and escape his own.

"Come upstairs and we'll get you dressed. You can do your pee in the bathroom."

Chloe smiled up at him as she sat on the loo. He swooned.

"Do you know, pet, I'm going to try really hard not to hit you for the rest of the day?"

She touched for kick. "The Little Mermaid! The Little Mermaid!"

He found the videotape in a jigsaw puzzle box just as she was contemplating tipping over a box of crayons on the floor in protest at his tardiness. "Oh, fuck! The candle!" he yelled.

"Oh fuck! Oh fuck!" she parroted him.

He had forgotten to blow out the candle in the toilet after he had finished praying. He extinguished it and rushed back into the living-room to check the time. He was late for playschool. His forgetfulness had been getting much worse recently. He was fraying at the edges. He put his hand in his pockets for the car keys and pulled out leaves, chocolate wrappers, two stones, hair-clips and loose crisps—all from the previous day. He gritted his teeth.

By the time he walked Chloe up the path of the playschool his annoyance was gone and, much to her embarrassment, he broke into hopping. The hand that held hers had been held once too. The sense that God was close when people touched had stayed with him since his time with Jack. He would take the bull by the horns and talk to Shirley when she got home. He had to turn the ship around. He was getting tired of being responsible for everything, excluding the pay-check, while it was clear that all the tea in China could not persuade Shirley to do the painful work of relating. He would sit her down opposite him and have a heart to heart—it was the one 'opposite thing' he enjoyed whenever he could pin her down.
  * * *

"Here, pussy, pussy, pussy!" Nicholas said, calling Susy over. The cat began rubbing up against his leg then jumped on his lap to lick his face. He beamed. He always felt loved when she got affectionate. He would use that image of her as a springboard for prayer. Even now, as he monitored the Thai stir-fry, he could already see Jesus shooing Suzy away to kiss him the way he kissed the little children in Mark 10.

The phone rang. It was Shirley calling to say that she had a lot on at the office and wouldn't make it home for dinner before 7:30.

"The traffic's shit!" she announced as she later set her briefcase down by the stairs. It was 8:30. "And the frigging men drivers! They're only dying to get killed!"

"Like, you couldn't put your case somewhere else, could you, before Chloe gets at it instead of leaving me to clean up all the mess?" he greeted her.

Probably this morning's unfinished business, she thought, moving her briefcase. He felt lighter now that she had done as she was told.

"And what about a kiss hello?" he asked as she squeezed past him. She gave him a peck.

"Mummy, mummy!" cried Chloe as she hurtled down the hall.

"Are you not in bed yet? Just let me get my coat off first, pet. I'm dying for a pee, my little lovebird! Nick, would you keep an eye on her till I go to the toilet?"

He needed her to take over at the helm but he held his tongue. He had a lot of things to get off his chest later, and there was no point in blowing it now. He marched Chloe back into the kitchen where he began to reheat dinner. Joining them later, Shirley launched in to talk of work.

"Will you hurry up and sit down and eat while it's hot?" Nicholas moaned.

She was so engrossed in her monologue that she hadn't noticed him set dinner on the table. She sat down, took Chloe up on her lap, and squinted her eyes at him affectionately.

"I love you this much!" she said, spreading her arms out like wings.

It always did it for Nicholas. He raised his arms and squinted back at her.

"Dinner!" Chloe crowed in an effort to divert the attention of the lovebirds in her direction.

Shirley picked up her knife and fork to buy time from her. "Do you know something? I'm so glad you're at home with Chloe. You're just so good at the parenting thing!"

He raised his hands to stop her, the way he did when she was reversing in the car and he was afraid she was going to hit the driveway wall.

If he couldn't take a compliment, that was his problem, she thought.

"Don't allow me to eat any more of these!" she begged him, tucking in to the crisps and salsa dip.

I do enough for you without looking after your diet, too, he heard himself say, but he kept his counsel. "Have you been doing some thinking about things? Or is it guilt that has you saying nice things about me?" he quizzed her.

"Why is it compliments are so hard for you to take?" she asked.

"Well, would you write it down for me?"

"Write what down? That you are a good parent?"

"Yeah! It'll be an alternative to the Good News according to Jack!"

She smiled at his attempt to meet her half way. It was an offer she couldn't refuse. She had long wanted him to get rid of Jack's letter as she had had enough of him going on about how much Jack had loved him.

"I'll do whatever it takes, love."

"Whatever it takes? Well, there is one more thing. What about a weekend in the Galway Great Southern?"

"Can I come?" Chloe chipped in.

"No, you're doing a Home Alone on it!" said Shirley. Chloe frowned. "And what would we be doing without our wee Chlo?" Shirley continued, tickling her under the chin.

Nicholas interrupted their mutual rapture. "Is this another one of your pigeons that you throw up in the air," he cupped his hands and gently released a bird into the air, "and then shoot down..." he lifted a shot-gun, "in the next breath? Pugggh!"

Shirley laughed to make things easier for herself.

"I've been thinking," said Nicholas.

"What else is new?" she commented. She wished she had held her tongue and so was relieved when he gently responded, "No, listen, I just wanted to say I'm sorry for the things I said this morning."

"Oh, so you take back what you said about me neglecting Chloe?" she said, still sparking almost in spite of herself.

"No, I'm just sorry that I said it the way I said it," he replied, disappointing himself with his unwillingness to cede ground.

"See, what did I tell you? You can never win with you! A spade is never a spade, is it?"

Sensing the tension, Chloe struck up a tune, "Darling, it's better down under where it's wetter, take it from me."

"Look," he continued, over Chloe, "I just wanted to say that I too have work to do. You were right about my mother. She controlled us. And I'm doing the exact same thing to you."

Shirley eyeballed Chloe who was still singing loudly, but it had no effect. "Do you want to see the Little Mermaid video?" she asked, trying instead to buy her off.

"Darling, it's better down under where it's wetter," Chloe repeated the refrain, now doing Aeriel's Hawaiian hand movements.

"Sorry, Nick, just give me a minute." Shirley got up to go put on the video. He feared the worst—she would probably end up watching the video with her. She was on the run again.

"Now, that's that sorted. Will we watch Frazier tonight?" she asked on her return.

He frowned because once she was on the subject of television, she was a lost cause.

"Anyway, what were you saying?" she asked.

He disguised his shock by looking her in the eye as if he hadn't doubted her for a second.

"I was saying..."

"...that you were trying to get me to keep my mouth shut," she completed his sentence.

"Well, yes, maybe, I suppose so, but, but not in so many words." He resented her judgement, but held back.

"Oh, so there are different degrees of silencing people, are there?" she asked.

"Look, this is really hard for me. Could you just hold it a second till I get this out, and then you are free to say whatever you like?"

She acknowledged his plea with a shrug of her shoulders, which said at one and the same time that he could have as much time as he wanted and that he had better be quick.

"I control you, Shirley. That's what I'm meant to do. Men have been doing it for centuries. I take away your power as much as I can."

"Jesus, but you can be so fucking serious, Nick! Is that it, or are there more pearls where that came from? You know, we have a word for people like you down here. 'Gobshite!' At times, you're an awful gobshite, like!"

He bristled but folded his arms to aid his concentration. Her reaction was a sure sign that his points were getting home. He would not allow her to distract him.

"Gobshite? Actually, a dry alcoholic might be a better description," he continued.

"And what, might I ask, does a dry alcoholic binge on?" she asked.

He ignored her sarcasm. He had baited her again.

"On blood."

"Bl...blood?"

"Yes, they suck the life blood out of people to feed themselves. This country is full of them, North and South. People who take other people down to survive themselves. They manipulate, guilt-trip, abuse, dominate, put down..."

"Alright, alright, so you suck the life-blood out of me! You're no different from your da then!" she barked, annoyed that he was getting too deep again.

He was glad she had cut him short because the only reason he had kept on at examples of what people do was to get a reaction. He would go for broke now. "No, Shirley, there's a pair of us in it. We're both at it. You and me. And if we don't do something about it soon, there won't be. We're driving each other apart."

Her lower lip suddenly dropped. "If only I could put the clock back," she muttered.

"Put the clock back?"

"If, if only I hadn't said all I said this morning, we wouldn't be in this mess."

"Listen, Shirley, we'd want to be putting it back four years, if it's clocks you're worried about!"

"But how did I not see it coming to this? How did I not see the signs?" she asked of herself.

"Because you've been schooled in the quiet life too. You could fucking run the country with your eyes closed, but the moment you cross this door, you fall to pieces. What was it Shirley? What happened to you?"

He bided his time, awaiting some explanation for her behaviour.

The numbers for her Visa PIN, house alarm, mobile phone code, message minder, photocopier, ATM, and Lotto formed a human train in her mind—7682, 0135 hache, 0hache3, 6213, 171-4824*11, 1100, 2601, 29-12-6-34-31-15—that danced its way in and out of function rooms, the toilets, her wedding suite, then exited the hotel under an archway of hands, wrapping themselves around a tree in the courtyard as the guests sang Congratulations and Celebrations. She wanted to speak but was afraid in case only numbers came out and she wouldn't be able to stop. After mumbling one, two into a microphone a couple of times she took a deep breath and began, "I'll do whatever you want." She began to sob.

"There you go again! It's not about what I want. There's two of us in this relationship, whether I like it or not! What did they do on you, Shirley, to screw you up so much?"

Her sobbing became a flood of tears and he felt guilty in spite of the fact that he knew that that was what she wanted because he always gave in when she cried. All he could manage was to repeat himself.

"What did they do on you, Shirley?"

"Mummy, why are you crying, mummy?" Chloe called out from the doorway.

"It's, it's okay, petal, I burned my finger on the, on the oven."

"There you go again! See! Keeping it sweet! Is it ever going to change?" he asked.

"I want some crisps," Chloe demanded.

"Crisps?" howled Nicholas. "No way! You can't be hungry! You're only after your dinner, you. Listen, it's time for bed for you! The whole street's in bed, and Wee Willie Winkie's on his way."

"I'll put her to bed," said Shirley. "Can we talk about this other thing later?"

"No, I'll put her to bed. You stay put and have your dinner!" He wasn't willing to run the risk of her falling asleep with Chloe.

"What did you enjoy today?" he asked Chloe, snuggling up beside her in her bed.

"The park, and pooh-pooh!" she said, teasing him.

"But we weren't in the park today!" he confronted her.

"Barney, swimming, granny's, the shopping," she rattled off the venues as if spinning a tombola. She hated his questions. He had hounded her once for over ten minutes to get her to tell him how she had felt when her teacher had put her in the corner for calling another child names. She had finally spat out the truth—"sad".

"And I enjoyed the shopping too!" he began. "I was so proud of you pushing the trolley for me, my little lamb! We'll go shopping another day, won't we?"

"The next day."

"Yes, another day, chicken. Now, night-night, God Bless, see you at seven!"

"Da da, are you cross with mama?" she asked.

"Yes, but it's okay to be cross sometimes. Now, night-night, God Bless, see you at seven!"

"Will you lie down for five seconds?"

He lay down, resting his face against her tummy, and yawned with exhaustion. He had been longing for this moment from the second she had woken up. He was glad to see her wake up in the morning and glad to see her go to bed. Each day was a graft. There had to be something more, he reflected, yawning again. Happiness—the banal fulfilment of social duties—could never sufficiently reward him for his efforts with Shirley and Chloe. He wanted joy—the joy of knowing Shirley deeply and of being intimately known by her. It was the joy he had tasted with Jack. But he would have to shoot her to slow her down enough for them to enjoy each other. The problem was she feared that whatever she enjoyed would be taken from her by her big bad God in the sky.

The untimely death of her father who had dropped dead beside her in church hadn't helped any. Her venial sins had killed him— that was what she believed, though she knew it was stupid. He would share his thoughts on joy with Shirley when he went back downstairs, he thought. He would tell her that happiness was a quick fix, the McDonalds of the spiritual world, but that it was so convenient that he found himself settling for it time and again. They had to dig deeper. For love. Joy.

Shirley found him curled up asleep on the bed with her panta- loons on. She put her hand over her mouth to stifle her laughter. She hadn't noticed them earlier. She would allot him five minutes in the morning to say whatever he had to say, but she had essen- tially covered all she needed. There was only so much analysis a relationship could bear. Life was short and you had to keep going.

Chapter 15

It was July, and North and East Belfast were warming up for the Twelfth of July Orangemen's march. Violence was expected on a large scale and Nicholas had persuaded Shirley to agree to his having the Dunnes down for the weekend. Secretly Shirley hoped the Dunnes would be a distraction from her woes, though she didn't tell Nicholas that, and regretted the fact that George, the most interesting of the whole Northern contingent, had opted to go to a Rangers' friendly. He had finally come out in support of his team, deciding his republican friends could like it or lump it. Her agreement came, nonetheless, with two conditions; one, that it didn't become an annual event because she wasn't running a refugee service, especially when she had just been made redundant, and, two, that they kept off the subject of Northern politics. Her last trip to Belfast had done her head in. All she had said—in the privacy of Kathleen's kitchen—was that it was gas the way Northern Catholics were forever giving out about the Crown but accepted the 'half-crown', and Kathleen and Mrs. Diamond had given each other a look that said they expected no less tactlessness from a Southerner. What Shirley had failed to grasp was that Mrs. Diamond had finally understood what had happened that day she had found her neighbour at the oven: Mrs. Lackey had been trying to kill herself.

When the Northerners arrived, Nicholas suggested a walk on Dun Laoghaire's West pier. He had been fearful of the prospect of an evening of small-talk, and had figured that people could break up into small groups out on the walk. Shirley let him get on with the organising; his controlling side sometimes had its advantages. As it transpired, they gravitated towards one another on the pier according to who they wanted to avoid.

Johnny walked alongside Benny who complained that he was more a hindrance than a help as he attempted to support her on the uneven surface. Nicholas looked on with envy, only half listening to Kathleen by his side. Johnny's ability to settle for the smallest of gratifications in life—a rebuke from his mother itself gratefully accepted as an acknowledgement—never ceased to amaze him. His jealousy, however, was tempered by the knowledge that the fact that Johnny had got it hard had meant that he had always got the lion's share of whatever love was doing the rounds.

Marlene sauntered hand in hand with Brian. She walked close to the pier wall, keeping away from Kathleen who moved along the seaboard with Nicholas. She was unable to forgive Kathleen for bringing up the whole affair about Frank's abuse, which threatened her belief that Frank had loved Kathleen and not her. She had even gone so far as to blame her for his death, conveniently forgetting that she had often wished him dead herself. Her belief had served her well, enabling her to become an expert at the art of the poor mouth, with the result that she had had everyone eating out of her hands, including Brian. Now her fear of losing Brian was such that she was even afraid to put her hand in her pocket for a handkerchief for her nose which dripped in the cutting sea breeze.

The picture of young love, Rosy strolled along with her arm wrapped around Steve's waist. They had met at the Prisoners' Defence club. As they lagged behind the others, they appeared engrossed in each other, but the reality was that Rosy was doing everything in her power to keep her distance from the others. She wanted to avoid all talk of Jack. She had known for a year now that Steve, the son of the Peace woman in whose home she and Jack had taken refuge with their mother as children, had lured Jack to his death. He had set him up for the IRA, unaware, he told Rosy, of what the consequences would be. She loved him and valued his honesty as a sign of how much she meant to him but she feared the others would never be able to accept him. Besides, how was she to tell her mother that she was three months pregnant?

Gillian carried Chloe on her back. Shirley assured her that she was used to the pier and wouldn't stray, but Gillian held on to her. That way she was assured of Shirley's company—the perfect anti-dote to the Dunnes, a woman with a life, a career. For her part, Shirley was in no hurry to put her in the picture about her redundancy which had shaken her to her core and brought on a renewed attack of grief for her late father that she just couldn't shake off no matter how much she tried to chill out in front of the television.

Nicholas and Kathleen were lost in conversation.

"You must miss George being away all the same," Nicholas probed.

"Well, there's not much I can do about it. He's his own boss. He has his own money from the Social Welfare. We kept our monies separate, so we did."

"Separate?"

"Aye, I told Welfare he hadn't come home when he got out of the Kesh, sure it wouldn't be worth it otherwise."

Nicholas stared at her. Surely, she couldn't mean that it wouldn't be worth sticking together if their incomes weren't separate. Could things really be that bad? Sure, hadn't she run up and down to prison once a week for seventeen years out of love for him? She worshipped the ground he walked on, surely?

Seeing his frown, Kathleen rushed to clarify her position. "I mean, like, it wouldn't be worth it money wise. You know, they'll open that prison as a museum some day yet and some poor wee guide'll be down in the cells shining a torch and they'll find George Lackey there. 'Ho, ho! Who's this then?'"

Nicholas laughed to let her off the hook. Kathleen felt uncomfortable. It was time to talk about what she had really wanted to say in George's absence.

"There's something. Eh, I squealed on, on George. I, I saw him run after he had fired the shot at the Brit. I, I, there was one of those leaflets from the Brits that they put through the letter-box, about explosives found up on the Glen Road, I think it was, and I phoned the number on it. I don't know what came over me. I squealed. I just went and blew it."

Nicholas stopped dead and she tugged at his sleeve in an effort to shunt him on before the others noticed something was wrong. He moved at her insistence. She continued speaking. She had to get it all off her chest.

"How do you live with that, like? How do I tell him that? I mean, how he never seen it, and it staring him in the face, is beyond me." She started to laugh nervously. "And do you know what the worst is? It's the thought that if I hadn't have squealed on him, Jack wouldn't be dead today because his father would have been at home for him."

Nicholas' chest heaved with regret. He knew he had to hold it in.

Kathleen already felt lighter. "Jesus, I'm so glad to be able to say this, Nicholas. It's been a long haul!"

"Sit over there till I get your picture!"

Johnny shooed them back towards where the others were already getting into position for a photograph. Brian made space on the bench for Kathleen, and Nicholas made his way behind them.

"Move in just a wee bit at the sides there."

Johnny herded them with a wave of his hand. They huddled together. To the untrained eyes of the passers-by their closeness suggested an ease and warmth that didn't, in fact, exist. They smiled on request.

Kathleen was the first to break loose. She moved towards the edge of the pier.

"Who's game?" she asked as she peered down at the sea.

"Ma, have you lost the run of yourself or what?" asked a bewildered Rosy.

"Ach, come on! You only die once! Come on, Nick, what about it? Are you on?"

"What? Jump?"

"Go on, Nick, you could do with a wash!" Shirley teased him.

Kathleen took him by the hand. "Come on! We'll jump together!" She led him back to the pier wall to get a run at the jump.

"Come on, ye wild things!" exclaimed Johnny while the others whistled and catcalled. In a matter of seconds they were at the edge. She let go of his hand and glided over the edge like a seagull. Fear gripped Nicholas in his abdomen but he couldn't stop himself. The weight of his body had already taken over and his legs left the ground. They found each other under the water and pulled each other up. Laughing raucously, they made their way up the steps to the others who roared and clapped.

The next morning, when he prayed on the toilet, Nicholas felt elated. Jumping off the pier had been a joyful experience, an experience of being out of control. It was the joy he sometimes felt when he collected Chloe at playschool. The children would taxi into position at the door in single file like airplanes ready for take-off. The teacher would gently push Chloe over the threshold into his hands, and as he reached out for her he felt part of a bigger picture over which he had no control. All the Dunnes and Lackeys were awaiting permission to take off. Sometimes there had been changes in the schedule, and people had taken off in an unexpected order, like Kevin or Jack, or even his father. Like the candle flickering in front of him, his light would burn out, a thought which now brought a smile to his lips. He had to go before Chloe, but not, of course, before Shirley. And if God screwed up, there would be a scrap. He blessed himself and went to get breakfast ready for the visitors.

He would tell Kathleen he was okay about what she had revealed to him the day before. It was not as if he wanted to blame her for Jack's death anyhow. He could maybe count on a love letter from Shirley today too. She had been talking about writing it before she got the news of her redundancy. If she didn't get around to it, he would buy her a card for her to write it on. At least, he told himself, he would do it right, for she had bought him a card on his last birthday with the words 'To My Darling Wife' printed on it.

A father to three daughters, **Adrian Millar** is a stay-at-home dad.

Formerly, a columnist with *Dad's World* in *The Irish Examiner*, Adrian is the author of two novels, *Tomayto Tomahto* and *The Quiet Life*, both of which are available on Amazon. He is also the author of *Sociological Fantasy and the Northern Ireland Conflict: New Approaches to Conflict Analysis*, (Manchester University Press, 2007). In 2014, Adrian compiled and edited *The Beauty of Everyday Life*, a book of 35 stories on the beauty of everyday life by some of Ireland's best-loved personalities. *The Beauty of Everyday Life* is available on Amazon. All royalties from the book go to Teen-Line Ireland, a charity that provides a free-phone helpline to teenagers who might be feeling distressed or alone.

Adrian lives in Co. Kildare, Ireland, and can be found on Twitter @AdrianMillar, on Facebook at Mindful Dad, and at www.adrianmillar.ie.

Printed in Great Britain
by Amazon

84382581R00139